IDO

Carrie Duffy grew up in North Yorkshire before moving to Paris at the age of eighteen. After studying PPE at Trinity College, Oxford, she trained as an actress. She has worked professionally as both an actor and dancer, and she currently lives in west London. *Idol* is her first novel.

CARRIE DUFFY

Idol

HARPER

This novel is entirely a work of fiction.
The names, characters and incidents portrayed in it are
the work of the author's imagination. Any resemblance to
actual persons, living or dead, events or localities is
entirely coincidental.

Harper
An imprint of HarperCollins*Publishers*
77–85 Fulham Palace Road,
Hammersmith, London W6 8JB

www.harpercollins.co.uk

A Paperback Original 2011
1

A catalogue record for this book is
available from the British Library

ISBN: 978 0 00 742150 3

Set in Melior by Palimpsest Book Production Limited,
Falkirk, Stirlingshire

Printed and bound in Great Britain by
Clays Ltd, St Ives plc

Mixed Sources
Product group from well-managed
forests and other controlled sources
FSC www.fsc.org Cert no. SW-COC-001806
© 1996 Forest Stewardship Council

FSC is a non-profit international organization established
to promote the responsible management of the world's forests.
Products carrying the FSC label are independently certified
to assure consumers that they come from forests that are managed
to meet the social, economic and ecological needs
of present and future generations.

Find out more about HarperCollins and the environment at
www.harpercollins.co.uk/green

To my Mum and Dad.
Although you probably shouldn't read this.

PART ONE

1

The bulletproof limo sped down London's Park Lane, making a left as it swept up to the entrance of the Dorchester Hotel.

Jenna Jonsson peered out through the tinted windows in disbelief. Everywhere she looked she saw crowds of people – hysterical fans pressed tightly against the metal crash barriers screaming her name, the waiting paparazzi poised for the killer shot.

Jenna inhaled sharply, her dazzling green eyes widening in astonishment. She was 23 years old and breathtakingly beautiful, the hottest property in the music world right now.

'My God, it's crazy,' she murmured to herself.

Gerry King, her manager, looked over. 'Are you okay?' he asked, concerned.

'I'm fine,' Jenna insisted, trying to fight the feelings of insecurity rising in her chest. It was her first major event following a well-publicized break, and being back on the scene was overwhelming.

'Don't worry. You look sensational,' Gerry reassured her.

He wasn't lying. Her skin was tanned and flawless,

her incredible body encased in shimmering Roberto Cavalli, cut high on the thigh and slashed heart-stoppingly low at the front to reveal her magnificent cleavage. Diamonds glittered at her ears and throat, and a mass of glossy, blonde curls tumbled down her back. She was the epitome of raw sex appeal.

'Thanks,' Jenna smiled gratefully.

The car pulled to a halt and the silent, dark-suited security guard seated opposite her jumped out. Jenna watched as he spoke to the security team, his eyes scanning the tightly packed crowd, constantly alert for any possible threat. The fans were working themselves into a frenzy; in spite of the freezing winter weather they'd turned out in force, waving banners with her name and singing the chorus of 'Sexual Rush', her latest hit.

'See you on the other side,' winked Gerry, as the guard headed back across to the sleek limousine. At a signal from inside he opened the door. Then Jenna stepped out and the place erupted.

Flashbulbs exploded like firecrackers in the night sky, the noise from the crowd reaching a deafening roar as Jenna hit the red carpet on spike-heeled Jimmy Choos. It was as though someone had flicked a switch – the adrenaline kicked in and Jenna felt her nerves instantly vanish, shining like the superstar she was.

She placed a hand on her hip as she turned to face the cameras, catching her breath as she took in the sheer number. She could hardly believe that they were all there for her.

'Jenna – over here!' came a yell from the press pit where the world's media, banked steeply on their stepladders, waited eagerly for their piece of her.

Instinctively Jenna broke into an irresistible smile,

her lips full and glossy, her eyes sparkling with excitement. This was the shot that would grace every tabloid front cover the following morning – Jenna Jonsson, the newly crowned princess of pop, fresh from her unprecedented victory at the MTV Europe Awards where she'd just won an incredible six gongs.

'Jenna, what can you tell us about the rumours you've split with Will?'

Jenna froze. Her smile died on her lips, the pain in her eyes impossible to hide.

'I . . . I really don't want to talk about that . . .' Jenna began hesitantly, the memories of Will's infidelity still fresh in her mind. Horrified, she felt tears prick at her eyelids and she bit down hard on her lip. '. . . But what I will say is that I have no ties, no commitments, and I intend to enjoy myself tonight. Bring on the champagne!'

Jenna's pulse was racing, her breath coming fast, as she heard the reporters rush to share the news with fans watching all over the globe.

'You heard it here first, folks. Jenna Jonsson exclusively confirmed to us that she *has* split with Will Rothwell, son of multi-millionaire property developer Charles Rothwell. That's right guys, Jenna's back on the market . . .'

Pull it together, Jenna admonished herself, all too aware that every emotion would be magnified by the cameras. The question about Will had upset her more than she'd expected. She'd been counting on him to accompany her to the awards tonight; she needed that emotional support of having him on her arm. And then she'd found out he was cheating on her. The girl was just 17 years old, at boarding school with his younger sister. How fucking humiliating. Apparently he was finding it 'difficult' dating someone so successful, so he'd needed to screw some barely legal bimbo without an original thought in her head.

Jenna had told him to grow a pair of balls and walked out, shaking with anger. She was hurting badly, but she didn't intend to give him the satisfaction of seeing her like that.

Will Rothwell was history, Jenna vowed. Tonight she had her mind on something – and *someone* – far bigger.

The rumour was that Phoenix were going to be attending the after-show party. A world-famous American rock band, with looks to die for and an insane amount of talent, Phoenix had exploded onto the scene five years ago and their reputation was wild. Jenna was beyond excited.

Get a grip, she told herself firmly.

With a final wave at the crowd and the drooling paps, Jenna let herself be guided into the hotel. It was a jaw-dropping sight and she stared round in awe, noting the way the marble floor shone like glass, the whole ballroom bathed in a soft, pink light. Huge vases of white lilies had been mounted on podiums and looked spectacular against the black and gold classical backdrop.

Jenna scanned the room, smiling in thanks as she accepted a glass of champagne from a passing waiter. Then she raised it to her lips and almost dropped it.

Christ, it was him. It was Nick Taylor.

Jenna's pulse went into overdrive, her heart beating out of control. Nick Taylor was the drummer with Phoenix and the hottest guy on the planet – five feet eleven inches of strapping, blond good looks with piercing blue eyes and a killer smile to boot. To a London girl like Jenna, he looked like the ultimate American cowboy, with his powerful, muscular body and sexy, Southern accent. But Nick was more interested in riding women than horses. He exuded sexuality, smouldering with an animal magnetism that women seemed powerless to resist. And he did little to discourage them. Jenna wasn't stupid – she'd heard the stories and knew that his womanizing was notorious. He was legendary for never being pictured with the same girl twice, yet the ladies still flocked to him, and Jenna was as smitten as any of them.

She was vaguely aware that someone was trying to speak to her, but she wasn't paying attention. She couldn't take her eyes off Nick as she watched him make his way across the room, radiating confidence and charisma. The crowd pressed against him, the women vying for his attention. Jenna wasn't surprised – he looked utterly gorgeous, devastatingly handsome in the Armani tux he was wearing. His bow tie was undone and thrown around his neck with an almost arrogant indifference; his shirt unbuttoned just enough to show the smooth, tanned flesh beneath.

Then, almost as if he'd known exactly where she would be, Nick raised his head and looked straight into Jenna's eyes. Her stomach went into freefall, a bolt of electricity surging through her as she heard herself gasp in shock. Nick's face creased into a smile of recognition and he began slowly walking towards her. The sea of people parted to let him through – he didn't even have to push, just walked with that easy swagger, the crowd moving naturally out of his way. And then suddenly he was standing right in front of her, so close that she could see every lash framing those amazing blue eyes, each curve of that luscious mouth . . .

'Congratulations,' Nick murmured. His voice was rich and gravelly, deliciously sexy.

'Thanks,' Jenna squeaked, horrified to discover her voice seemed to have gone up two octaves. Her heart was pounding and she knew her cheeks must be flushed. She lowered her head in embarrassment, not realizing how impossibly cute it made her look.

'Good to finally meet you,' Nick said smoothly, in that low, Southern drawl. He leaned in to kiss her on the cheek, his fingers resting lightly on her waist. Jenna was sure she would melt right there and then, dissolve into a puddle at his feet.

'You too,' she faltered. 'I can't believe you're here. I mean, I heard you were coming and I hoped it was true but I didn't know for sure . . .' she raced on, mentally cursing herself for saying something so stupid.

'Well I definitely noticed *you* were here.' He looked her up and down with a slow, assessing and decidedly sexual gaze. Jenna felt the heat rising in her face as waves of lust flicked through her belly.

'I . . .' Jenna began, but she had no idea what she was trying to say. He was mesmerizing. If he'd taken her hand right there and then she would have followed him without hesitation.

'Aren't you going to introduce us?'

Someone beside them spoke and Jenna tore her gaze away to see Zac Knight, lead guitarist with Phoenix, standing with his arm around his supermodel girl-friend, Amber. Zac was almost as gorgeous as Nick, but in a very different way. Where Nick had classic boy-band good looks, Zac was the archetypal rock star, with his dark, wavy hair and razor-sharp cheekbones. His chocolate-brown eyes swept quickly over Jenna as he told her, 'Amber's been dying to meet you.'

Jenna thought she might hyperventilate. *This* was unprecedented!

Zac was legendary for avoiding industry events like this. He'd married young, before the band took off, and he'd been through a messy break-up with his wife,

Jessica. He'd fallen head over heels for Amber when they met backstage at New York Fashion Week, wrestling with his conscience as he agonized over whether or not to leave his wife. Amber had finally solved the problem for him by breaking the story to Page Six of the *New York Times* and ensuring that a first-edition copy was hand-delivered to Jessica Knight. It was a hell of a way to learn that your marriage was over.

Jenna could still remember the vitriolic headlines and stared curiously at Amber, the woman who'd been labelled a home-wrecker for luring Zac away from his childhood sweetheart.

'We met once before,' Jenna told her breathlessly. 'At a party in Marrakech.'

'I don't remember,' Amber told her blankly, looking at her with an expression of disdain.

What a bitch! thought Jenna, returning the haughty stare.

Okay, so Amber was undoubtedly stunning, Jenna conceded grudgingly, as she took in the silver column dress that emphasized Amber's slimness and poise. The sleek curtain of copper hair and flawless pale skin demonstrated why she had become the darling of the fashion pack – and why she had become Zac Knight's girlfriend. But her attitude certainly left a lot to be desired, thought Jenna, bristling with indignation at the put-down.

'Well, it's great to meet you,' Zac said lightly. His laid-back accent and relaxed manner quickly melted Jenna's rigid expression. It was impossible to stay mad on a night like tonight, when she was standing between Zac Knight and Nick Taylor!

Very gently, almost possessively, Nick put a hand on her arm. It was a gesture of complete confidence, and Jenna caught her breath at the skin-on-skin contact.

'I don't wanna be greedy, but I think I'd like to monopolize you this evening,' he said silkily, his gaze never leaving her face. Jenna felt her stomach flip-flop at the way he looked her over.

'I guess we'll catch up with you guys later,' smiled Zac, as Amber slipped a wafer-thin arm around his waist.

'Over here, baby, there's some people I want to introduce you to. It was nice to meet you, Jenna' Amber lied, steering Zac through the crowd as she led a chorus of exclamations and air kisses.

As Nick bent his head low to speak to her, Jenna thought she might pass out. She could feel the warmth of his breath against her ear, the intense contact making her skin tingle. And that accent! Phoenix were named after the band's home city in Arizona, and all the guys spoke with a slow, sexy drawl. It was so fucking delicious, Jenna didn't think she could ever get tired of it.

Amazingly, the crowd seemed to leave them alone. It was as though Nick Taylor's presence acted as a barrier that no one dared penetrate. He was sending out a clear message that Jenna was his and no one else should touch her. She could barely believe that he knew who she was, let alone that he wanted to spend the evening *monopolizing* her, Jenna thought, a thrill of excitement shooting through her as she recalled his words.

'So,' Nick began, breaking into an easy smile that lit up his face and made his blue eyes sparkle. 'Enjoyin' the party?'

Life had always come easy to Nick. Since his schooldays back in Arizona he'd had no trouble attracting the ladies, keeping the prettiest girls in class on a constant rotation. More interested in music than schoolwork, he found that being in a band sent his pulling power off the scale and he exploited it to the full. He'd even managed to juggle two girls on the night of his high-school prom, making Kacey Ann Kruger wait in line for fruit punch and hotdogs while he deflowered Tiffany Wilkinson in a dark corner of the parking lot.

'Yeah – I mean, it looks amazing,' Jenna gushed, 'but I don't seem to have had a minute to myself.'

'Everyone's trying to grab a piece of you, huh? I'm not surprised,' Nick grinned, pointedly looking her over as he allowed his gaze to linger on that hand-span waist and those incredible breasts. Man, he certainly wouldn't mind grabbing a piece of Jenna Jonsson.

'So what are you up to at the moment?' Nick asked casually. 'Only me and the guys – well, you prob'ly heard what went down with Josh . . .'

Josh Starr was the lead singer with Phoenix and three days ago he'd quit the band. Rumours had been bubbling away in the press for months, with leaked reports that it had turned pretty nasty towards the end. Jenna was devastated.

'You're not splitting up, are you?' she asked in alarm.

'Hell, I don't know. I don't think so. I hope not anyway,' finished Nick, his tone suddenly despondent. He had to raise his voice to make himself heard above the flurry of conversations around them. 'We've talked about carrying on for a while – at least for another album – but with guest artists. A kinda collaborations project, I guess. But nothing's official yet – it's just an idea we've been throwing around.'

A thought suddenly occurred to Nick, and he began to speak before he could stop himself. 'Why don't you work with us on a track? It'd be awesome.'

'Work with Phoenix?' Jenna exclaimed, hardly able to believe what he was saying. It was her childhood dream come true! The opportunity to record with her heroes, to see the masters at work – and, of course, to spend an insane amount of time with Nick Taylor . . .

'Are you sure? I mean, would the other guys want me?'

A sly grin spread across Nick's face. 'Yeah,' he drawled. 'We all want you.' She looked so cute standing there, those huge, green, baby-doll eyes full of insecurity. On the one hand, she was a ball of energy, bristling with confidence and a mesmerizing sexuality, yet there was an air of vulnerability that couldn't be hidden. He felt a strong urge to take her in his arms and protect her, and an equally strong urge to take her in his arms and fuck her brains out. *Don't think about that now*, he warned himself, feeling himself start to get hard. He would come back to that later, when he was banging some groupie.

Jenna blushed, glancing away in embarrassment. He was ridiculously handsome, able to make her dizzy with a single look. 'I'm such a huge fan,' she rambled. 'I've always loved your music, right since the beginning. This would just be a dream. I mean, I'd cancel everything to work with Phoenix.'

'So is that a yes?' Nick laughed.

'Yes!' Jenna exclaimed, her excitement impossible to hide as they clinked their champagne glasses to symbolically seal the deal. 'Yes, yes, yes!'

2

Sadie Laine was curled up on her sagging single bed, in the boxroom of the East London house share she rented for an extortionate fee. The walls were damp, the paint was flaking, and the mattress she was sitting on smelt faintly of mould. It was not, Sadie thought with a growing sense of frustration, the kind of place she had dreamed of living when she was a child.

The old-fashioned TV blared in the corner. No swanky flat-screen for her, just an enormous monster of a thing that was a hand-me-down from her parents and took up all the room on her tiny dressing table. Sadie squinted at the screen as she wrapped her duvet tightly around her and snuggled into it. Her long, slim legs poked out of the end, and her feet were swathed in thick, pink socks. The radiator was on the blink again, and the landlord hadn't yet made good on his promise to fix it.

Sadie let out a sigh as she pushed a few stray tendrils of hair away from her beautiful face. Her dark, glossy hair was roughly pulled back in a messy ponytail, perfectly framing her fine, angular features, but the crease between her eyebrows gave away her anxiety.

It's not fair, she thought miserably, as she watched the glamorous scene play out on the TV screen in front of her. Breaking off another piece of chocolate from the slab beside her, she popped it into her mouth, not caring that she'd already tripled her daily calorie allowance.

Sadie was watching the highlights of the MTV Europe Awards, where at this moment Jenna Jonsson was speaking into the camera. She looked incredible as she chattered excitedly to the interviewer about how thrilled she was to have won. She threw out some inane cliché about how all of her dreams were coming true. Sadie pursed her lips and pressed mute on the remote.

All of Jenna's dreams might have been coming true – life wasn't working out quite so well for Sadie.

For as long as she could remember, all Sadie had ever wanted to do with her life was dance. From the moment she had slipped on the obligatory pink leotard for her first lesson in the local church hall, she knew she had found her passion. Growing up in the London suburb of Streatham with her younger brother and sister, there wasn't a lot of money to spare, but her parents scrimped and saved, working extra shifts to ensure their beautiful, gifted daughter could pursue her dream.

It soon became clear that she was seriously talented, and by the time she hit her teens she was already competing on the national circuit, winning prizes in every category. Jazz, Latin, hip-hop – Sadie was a natural at every style she tried. She loved the way she could get lost in the music, relishing the grind of learning the routine and putting her own interpretation on it to make it truly individual – a hair flick here, a sashay of the hips there. Most of all, she adored the

14

adulation of being up on stage, addicted to the adrenaline rush that came with performing. It was the ultimate buzz.

Then came the big one – the National Championships, held in Manchester. The prize was life-changing: an all-expenses-paid trip to LA, to spend four weeks working with street-dance stars Ghetto Angels. Rumour had it that, if your work was good enough, you'd be invited to perform with them at their next gig.

It was an amazing opportunity. Sadie didn't think she'd ever wanted anything so badly in all her life. Ghetto Angels were incredible, the hippest things in the dance world right now, and she knew that this could catapult her into the big league. She worked on her routine day and night, rehearsing the steps obsessively until she could do them in her sleep. She was the one to beat, the dead cert to take the prize. That was, until Jenna Jonsson and her pushy mother had shown up . . .

'Knock knock,' came a voice at the door.

'Yeah,' Sadie responded lazily, recognizing it as her housemate Carla.

Carla poked her head round the bedroom door. She was a petite brunette with an English rose complexion and a body she could contort into positions that made men salivate. A fellow dancer, the pair had worked together one summer at a holiday camp. The show had been terrible – they'd got through it with good humour and a lot of alcohol – but by the end of the season each knew they'd made a friend for life.

'How're you doing?' Carla crossed the room and plonked herself down, cross-legged, on the corner of Sadie's bed.

'Shit,' Sadie replied succinctly.

'Well I brought something to cheer you up,' said Carla, brandishing a bottle of Smirnoff and two glasses filled with ice. Sadie's eyes lit up. 'But you have to *share* it with me,' Carla warned her.

Sadie poured them each a generous amount and mixed it with Diet Coke. 'One Skinny Bitch, on the rocks,' she grinned, passing it to Carla. She settled back against the flattened pillows and the two of them turned their attention to the television, where the EMAs were in full swing.

'Makes you sick, doesn't it,' Carla observed, as they watched yet another superstar receive a gong from a fawning presenter.

'Uh huh. All those happy, smiling, Botoxed-to-the-hilt, nauseatingly rich people,' ranted Sadie, warming to her theme. 'They're just hypocritical, self-congratulatory, sycophantic wankers,' she finished triumphantly.

'Wish you were there?'

'Absolutely,' Sadie agreed instantly, as the two of them burst into laughter.

'You probably shouldn't be watching this,' Carla told her, as they re-ran footage of Phoenix receiving their Ultimate Legend award. 'It's going to make you feel even worse.'

'Not at all,' Sadie shook her head, making no attempt to change the channel. 'Looking at Nick Taylor always cheers me up.'

'He *is* amazingly hot,' agreed Carla. 'Especially in that suit. I bet he's a total bastard though.'

'Just my type,' grinned Sadie, as she raised her glass at the TV screen. 'I wouldn't mind trying to tame him.'

Carla smiled indulgently. Then the image changed again, and the tiny screen was filled with a full-length shot of Jenna Jonsson making her way into The Dorchester.

'God, that dress is gorgeous,' Carla enthused.

Sadie snorted. 'She's overdone it with the Fake Bake, though. I mean, *no one* can actually be that colour,' she sniped, as she took another slug of vodka. She was 23, the same age as Jenna, and yet the differences between their lifestyles couldn't have been more stark.

'Hon, you've got to get over it,' Carla pushed gently.

'I can't!' Sadie protested. 'You know that. However hard I try, I feel like that was my big chance and I missed it. I'll just be stuck here forever. Ninety years old and still in this shitty little boxroom.'

Her dance career had hit a lean patch that seemed never-ending. A few months ago she'd landed an ensemble role in a West End revival of *42nd Street*; it promised a one-year contract, a prestigious venue and fantastic exposure. Sadie was ecstatic. Then, two weeks into rehearsals, the company had gone bust and the producer had disappeared off the face of the earth. Since then she could barely get an audition, let alone a job. She'd been trying to cover her rent by doing promo work, which was badly paid and soul-destroying. You name it, she'd promote it, usually while trussed up in some ridiculous tiny outfit or freezing her ass off on a street corner handing out leaflets. It was hardly the glamour she was longing for.

'Well, I'll be stuck here with you,' Carla tried to cheer her up. 'Look at me – scraping by on the occasional bit of cruise-ship work, spending the rest of my time teaching yoga to a bunch of stuck-up, ungrateful bankers. *And* I've got a crap boyfriend,' she admitted, in a rare moment of frankness.

'At least you've got a boyfriend,' Sadie muttered. Her love life was about as successful as her career – going nowhere fast. She seemed to attract a succession of bastards and losers and she was sick of it. She knew it was un-PC to admit it, but she wanted a real man – someone confident and successful who could take care of her. Gorgeously fuckable was always a bonus, too.

'Oh cheer up,' Carla teased her good-naturedly, as she poured them both another drink.

'Make mine a triple,' Sadie said morosely. Despite what Carla had said, Sadie couldn't snap out of her dark mood. The image on the screen seemed to taunt her. Jenna Jonsson – young and beautiful, with the world at her feet. It reminded Sadie of just how far their lives had diverged.

They'd known each other vaguely for years from the dance circuit. They'd never been close – mainly because Jenna's domineering mother, Georgia, kept her well away from everyone else, worried that befriending the others would dull her competitive instincts.

Then five years ago came the Nationals. They were both eighteen, both in their final year of eligibility for the competition. It was the break Sadie so badly needed, and she was prepared to do anything to win.

So, apparently, was Georgia Jonsson. Sadie had seen her prowling backstage, her stick-thin figure poured into a low-cut dress, her ash-blonde hair teased up into a voluminous chignon. In her day, she must have been stunning. Now she was mutton dressed as lamb.

Jenna took to the stage before Sadie, giving a competent performance that was nothing to write home about. Nerves had obviously got the better of her, as she made the occasional, well-covered mistake. But she looked fantastic, naturally, her blonde hair curled into ringlets and tumbling down her back, her revealing costume clinging to her newly acquired curves like a second skin.

Sadie had been so nervous she thought she might be sick. The venue was enormous, bigger than anywhere she'd ever performed. But once she hit the stage, the tension evaporated. It was as though her body knew exactly what to do and she let the sensations take over, a joyous feeling of freedom that she surrendered to completely.

Sadie had given the performance of her life. Technically she was perfect, but it was so much more than that. She danced with spirit and soul, her body moving like a dream. She blew the competition out of the water and she knew it. She could still picture it now – if she shut her eyes in the cramped bedroom she was transported back to that day, moving as though she was flying, her feet barely seeming to touch the ground. She'd been aware that no one in the room could take their eyes off her, the straight-laced judges in the front row captivated by her ability.

'And the winner is . . .'

Sadie recalled lining up on stage with the rest of the girls, looking out at row upon row of expectant audience members. Her heart was racing, but she was confident. She wanted this so badly, she could almost feel the hot Los Angeles sun beating down on her body . . .

'. . . Jenna Jonsson!'

Sadie gasped in astonishment. She remembered looking across at Dickie Masters, the head judge, with his shiny bald head and ginger moustache. He looked ridiculous – short and fat in a tweed blazer and

19

crumpled trousers – as he beamed at Jenna, his jowly face so red it looked as if it was going to burst.

Jenna seemed to be the only person more surprised than Sadie. Her mouth fell open; her face was a picture of confusion as she stared across at her. Sadie found that she couldn't meet Jenna's eyes. She looked away, found a knot in the wooden floor and concentrated her energy on that. That way, she could pretend it wasn't happening.

Jenna soon got over her reticence. She shrieked with delight, then burst into tears as they handed over the plane tickets. The next moment her mother was up on stage and they were posing for press shots with an enormous silver trophy. Jenna's tears had been dried and she looked her usual radiant self, sandwiched between her mother and Dickie Masters. That was the last Sadie had seen of her – she and the other girls had been quickly shepherded off stage, expected to pick up their belongings and get out. Nobody loves a loser.

Back in the changing rooms, the others had commiserated with her, said they couldn't understand what had happened. A few of them went further – thanks to her mother, Jenna wasn't popular on the circuit and the bitchy comments flew. Then one by one they'd left, leaving Sadie sitting alone in the changing rooms. She felt dazed as she went over and over her performance in her mind. Was it possible she'd been wrong – that what she'd felt inside was so different to what the judges saw? But then why had everyone told her she deserved to win? It didn't make any sense.

Gradually the numbness faded, replaced by a cold, hard ball of fury that began deep in her stomach and spread throughout her body. She *should* have won.

She *deserved* it. No one had worked harder than she had and no one had given a better performance. So what the hell was going on?

Suddenly she jumped up, changing out of her costume in record time and snatching up her bag. She didn't even bother to take off the heavy stage make-up, her face a riot of colour and sparkle as she raced out of the changing rooms and back through the main hall. It was empty now; the audience had left and the seats were being cleared away as the cleaners moved in. It seemed sad somehow; nothing like the glamorous, noisy spectacle it had been earlier. Sadie didn't stop to reflect. She wanted answers.

As she reached the judges' room, she got them. The door was ajar and at first Sadie thought everyone had left. Then she caught a glimpse of Dickie Masters. He wasn't alone. Pressed up against him, her hair flying wild and her skirt hitched up, was Georgia Jonsson.

They looked so bizarre together that Sadie almost laughed out loud. Georgia towered above the diminutive Dickie – his nose barely reached her breasts; but that seemed to be just the way he liked it. His head was redder than ever, his face buried in Georgia's cleavage as he made a noise that could only be described as snuffling. Georgia was stroking his smooth, bald head.

'Oh yes, Dickie, that's the way Mummy likes it,' she purred.

Dickie's hands seemed to be everywhere, fighting to pull Georgia's dress even higher. He squealed in delight as he encountered the top of her stockings, his chubby fingers running feverishly over the garter straps. Then his hands moved to his trousers, struggling to pull off his belt and unzip his fly as he released his white, flaccid cock. It hung, small and limp, from his Y-fronts. Georgia took it in her hand and squeezed. It instantly responded and Dickie shuddered.

'That's right,' whispered Georgia, 'Mummy will make it better.'

Some instinct made her look up – right over Dickie's head and straight at Sadie. Sadie expected her to cry out, to jump away in embarrassment. Instead Georgia had merely smiled, her expression triumphant. Then she had raised one stiletto heel and kicked the door shut in Sadie's face.

'Sadie, are you okay?'

Sadie started, aware that Carla was looking at her worriedly. Even now, the memory of the anger and injustice she'd felt was overwhelming.

'It's just so unfair,' Sadie burst out, startling Carla with her ferocity. 'Life, I mean.'

'I know, hon,' Carla sympathized. But Sadie was on a roll.

'Aren't you sick of all this?' She waved her hand around, indicating the messy room with the holes in the carpet and the furniture that was falling apart. 'This is not the life I'm supposed to be living. Do you know what I mean?' she asked desperately. 'I don't want the nine-to-five grind, watching every penny with never enough to spare. I want excitement and glamour and hot sex with a gorgeous man who showers me with diamonds . . .'

'You're drunk,' Carla told her gently.

'What if I am?' Sadie shot back, all her pent-up frustration spilling out. 'I'm sick of living like this.'

'So change it,' Carla said simply. 'You're the only one who can.'

Sadie fell silent, thoughtful for a moment. On TV the cameras had gone to a wide shot, showing Jenna

Jonsson in all her glory as she waved at the crowd, signing autographs and blowing kisses.

'You know what? You're right.' Sadie sat bolt upright, her eyes fiery. 'I'll show Jenna bloody Jonsson. Anything she can do, I can do better. I'm going to make it, Carla – all the way to the fucking top. And I'm not going to stop till I do!'

3

'Absolutely no way.'

Gerry King stood frowning before Jenna, an imposing figure with his arms crossed firmly over his chest. In his dark Savile Row suit, his sandy-coloured hair flopping boyishly across his brow to disguise the fact that it was thinning at the front, Jenna's manager looked younger than his 44 years, and the expression on his face implied he was not to be argued with.

Jenna, however, felt that this did not apply to her. They had worked together for so many years now that they both felt they could be disarmingly frank with each other, without the risk of upsetting or offending. Jenna knew just how far she could push her luck and still get away with it – it was a skill she had down to a fine art.

'*What?*' Jenna let out of a squeal of indignation. 'Gerry, you have to be joking! Can't you see what a fantastic opportunity this is?'

Gerry sighed, knowing she wasn't going to let this one drop.

'Phoenix?' he repeated doubtfully. 'They're a rock band, Jenna. You're a pop star. It's not going to work.'

'But it *will*,' Jenna insisted, unable to hide her enthusiasm. 'Everyone's doing it these days – collaborations with unexpected people. It's the latest thing, and it'll be totally hot.'

'Speaking of *hot*,' Gerry pronounced the word distastefully. 'Would this sudden desperation to work with Phoenix have anything to do with Nick Taylor?'

Jenna flushed bright red, annoyed with herself that she was so easy to read. 'I really admire him as an artist,' she stated earnestly, as Gerry roared with laughter.

'Yeah, and I love Pam Anderson for her acting ability,' he chuckled. 'Seriously Jenna, Nick Taylor eats girls like you for breakfast. I'm not letting him anywhere near you.'

'What the hell's that supposed to mean?' snapped Jenna. She hated being treated like a child, and was blissfully unaware that the more petulantly she behaved, the more she sounded like one. 'I can handle myself, Gerry, and I want to do this. Anyway, I've already said yes so I can't back out now,' she finished triumphantly.

'Jenna,' Gerry began tiredly, wishing she could be just a little less argumentative sometimes and save them all some trouble. He looked at her with affection as she stood there, bubbling over with excitement and energy, just as she had been the first day she'd walked into his office.

He could still remember the first time they'd met. She'd been totally overshadowed by her dominating mother, Georgia, who was fiercely ambitious and determined to live out her failed dreams through her daughter. She and Jenna's father, Mikael, had divorced when Jenna was tiny. By anyone's standards they were a pretty unlikely pairing – Mikael was a Swedish academic who had little in common with glamorous, party-girl Georgia, and the novelty of their odd-couple relationship had soon worn off. Georgia had never remarried – she devoted all her energies to pursuing her daughter's career, and found being single worked to her advantage.

Yet despite Georgia's overbearing behaviour, Gerry couldn't fail to notice Jenna's amazing presence in the room. The story was that she'd been out in LA, working with some dance group, when an A&R guy had spotted her. Ultimate Management had taken one look at her and signed her on the spot. They didn't care whether or not she could sing – Auto-Tune could take care of that. But boy, could she sing.

Gerry, based in London, had been assigned to work with her on the European side. He'd known straight away she was going to be huge. And he was right – in less than two years Jenna was tottering on the brink of superstardom, her level of fame surpassing even her mother's wildest expectations. She was in demand on every major continent, her life one exciting, hectic tread-mill of recording, gigs, interviews and appearances. Until the accident in Munich.

It had been during Jenna's first major European tour. She and Georgia had argued – nothing serious, just the usual mother-and-daughter spats. But Jenna had announced she would be taking the tour bus with the rest of the crew, while Georgia boarded the VIP helicopter. It came down shortly after take-off, crash-landing in the Englischer Garten. Georgia and the pilot were killed instantly. The autopsy showed traces of cocaine in the pilot's bloodstream and witnesses remembered seeing him indulge at the after-show party the night before.

Jenna had been destroyed. She'd tried to contact her

father – he'd moved back to Sweden and she hadn't heard from him in years – but when she told him what had happened he showed little interest, and made it clear he had no intention of flying over for the funeral. It was left to Gerry to step into the breach, and he'd stayed by Jenna's side 24/7 during the darkest times, knowing she had no one else. By his own admission he'd neglected his other artists, and at times he worried he'd totally overstepped his professional boundaries.

But they'd got through it. The tour had been cancelled and Jenna dropped out of the public eye for a while – some days she couldn't even get it together enough to climb out of bed. But slowly, gradually, the old fire returned. When Jenna finally made her much-heralded comeback almost a year later, she was bigger and better than ever before. She'd cleaned up at the MTV Europe Awards, and now she wanted to record with Phoenix . . .

'Look, there simply isn't time,' Gerry explained, his tone matter-of-fact. 'Your entire schedule is manic for at least the next twelve months. We have magazine and TV interviews, promo appearances, photo shoots and live radio shows all booked. Then there's the next tour to think about, a new album to record, maybe even a possible movie deal or fashion line to put your name to . . .' Gerry looked at her pleadingly. 'Can't you see it's just not possible for you to go swanning off to LA, not even for a few days? The schedule would kill you.'

Jenna smiled innocently, curling up in her chair like a cat. 'What if it wasn't in LA? What if I could get them to record in London? That way I could still—'

'You won't,' Gerry cut her off.

'But if—'

'*No*, Jenna.'

Jenna simply nodded her head, keeping her gaze downcast as she distractedly pushed back her cuticles. 'Okay,' she shrugged easily. 'Whatever you say.'

Gerry eyed her suspiciously, wondering where the temper tantrum was. The Jenna Jonsson he knew didn't just back down like that – she would fight him every inch of the way. He narrowed his eyes, scrutinizing her face, but Jenna just smiled sweetly back at him. Gerry scowled. He had a bad feeling about this.

On the other side of the Atlantic, in downtown Los Angeles, a similar argument was raging in Clive Goldman's state-of-the-art office. Clive was the manager of Phoenix and, like Gerry King's, his day wasn't exactly going the way he'd planned it.

'You told her *what?*' he exploded, causing his already ruddy face to turn a veritable shade of purple. Nick ran his hands through his hair, messing up the artfully dishevelled look it had taken him forever to perfect that morning, and raised his hands in defence.

'I just thought it could be good,' he offered languidly, as he leaned back in his chair and propped his feet up on Clive's $10,000 desk. 'We were talking and the idea kind of . . . came up, y'know?'

'No, Nick, I don't know. And get your fucking dirty feet off my fucking Parnian desk!' Clive's voice got louder with every word.

'Keep the noise down, would ya?' Nick winced behind his sunglasses. 'It was kind of a late one last night.' His voice was rough, and he had the hangover from hell. He'd been welcomed back to LA by Courtney, some pretty little actress-model wannabe with a great rack and a very willing disposition.

'Christ Nick, don't you ever take anything seriously?'

'You should chill out, Clive; everything's good – you know what I'm saying? The sun is shining and the women are sweet . . .'

Clive inhaled sharply, trying to control his temper as he turned away from the band and crossed the sumptuous deep-pile carpet to the window. From the cluster of skyscrapers in Century City, the sprawling mass of LA spread out far below and the view extended as far as the mountains to the east. The sun was blazing, but it was early still and the smog hadn't yet lifted, wreathing the city in its choking grasp. Clive saw none of this. Letting out a deep breath, he turned back to where the hottest band on the planet were lounging on his office sofas as if they didn't have a care in the world.

'Guys, I'm running a business here, not a fucking crèche,' Clive pleaded. 'Everything here is carefully planned – that is why it works. Phoenix are a business, a brand. Do you understand that?'

'I guess,' Nick shrugged, unconcerned.

'What do you guys think?' Clive turned to the rest of the band. He was well aware that Nick saw himself as God's gift, and seemed to have got his dick in a twist about this hot little British chick, but he was pretty sure the others would see sense.

Zac and Ryan remained silent. Clive clenched his fists in triumph. Divide and conquer.

'Come on guys, this could be amazing,' Nick implored. 'Jenna Jonsson is so hot right now, and we've gotta keep things fresh. Imagine, our first comeback song after Josh with Jenna on lead. No one would be expecting it.'

'I guess it could be pretty awesome,' Ryan suggested hesitantly. The bass player of the group, he was easily the quietest and enjoyed a much lower public profile than the rest of the band – which was exactly the way he wanted it. Fiercely private when it came to his home life, he'd married his childhood sweetheart three years ago, and already they'd produced two children. With his cropped brown hair, cute face and casual dress sense, he looked like the ultimate boy next door.

'Zac? What about you?' Clive asked in exasperation.

Zac said nothing, pressing his lips together in stony silence. It seemed clear he wasn't in favour.

Clive looked smugly at Nick. 'I can tell you one thing for nothing: this will never happen. I know Gerry King, and I know how he works. He's setting up this girl as a serious solo artist – a major player, in it for the long haul. He doesn't have time for her to be dabbling in some side project, and there's *no way in hell* he'll agree to this.'

Jenna's gaze flicked quickly round the room as she peeped out from under her perfectly mascara-ed, impossibly long lashes. Her smile was unfaltering and effortlessly dazzling, expertly hiding her nerves as she took in the swathe of journalists packed into a function room at the Sanderson Hotel in central London. There must have been about 200 easily, Jenna thought with a pang of trepidation, taking a sip of water to clear her throat as Clive Goldman expertly fielded questions from the assembled press pack.

Performing for the cameras was Jenna's natural arena, and she loved it, but she had to admit to feeling an uncomfortable squirming in her stomach. She was anxious for this collaboration to get off to the best possible start and knew that positive press coverage was vital. She just hoped she didn't do anything to mess it up before they'd even got started.

Intent on charming the reporters, Jenna shifted slightly in her seat to what she felt must be a more flattering angle. She looked immaculate as always; her white Dolce & Gabbana jeans clung to the curved lines of her perfect rear, her long legs tapering down into dazzling jade-green heels. A brightly coloured Marc Jacobs halterneck completed the look, and showed off her toned, tanned arms and back. It was a young, fresh and funky image. Large gold hoops jangled at her ears as she shook her head slightly, throwing out her hair behind her and relaxing into the seat she had chosen between Nick Taylor and Zac Knight at the press conference table.

'Philip White, BBC. Are there any plans for you all to tour together?'

'They might be sick of the sight of me by the time we've finished recording,' Jenna quipped. There was raucous laughter from the male journos in the room, who couldn't see how anyone could get tired of looking at Jenna. Most of them had enjoyed a private moment with Jenna's image locked in their head.

Zac smiled politely, and added, 'Seriously, though, it's a long way off and none of us can say what we'll be doing after this. We've all got crazy schedules. And, of course, it depends on the reaction to the music . . .'

'But we'd love to do it, though,' cut in Nick eagerly. His shirt was unbuttoned, showing a smattering of dark blond hair, and he was wearing his trademark sunglasses. 'It's just a question – like Zac says – a question of time. But Phoenix are definitely impatient to get out there and tour again, and Jenna'd certainly be a welcome addition.'

'Katia Giacomo, E! News. Why have you made the decision to record in London?'

'What can I say? We'd go anywhere to work with Jenna,' Nick grinned, as he threw his arm around her, his hand squeezing her shoulder. Jenna's stomach flip-flopped with excitement. She tried to play it cool, hoping the cameras wouldn't pick up on it.

'It's a great city,' Ryan added. 'We're looking forward to spending time here.'

'So you're planning to relocate?'

Ryan nodded. 'I'm renting a house so my family can come over. The kids are young, so I don't want to be away from them for too long – you miss so many important moments . . .' He trailed off, sounding almost wistful. 'But I don't want to speak for the other guys.' He looked over to Zac and Nick, but it was Clive that intercepted.

'I'd prefer not to go into details of where the band are staying – we don't want to cause a riot,' he grinned sourly, taking a sip of his water. The heat in the room was getting to him. He was sweating lightly, and he loosened his collar.

A young guy in a cheap suit held up his hand. 'Zac, I understand Amber's working in London at the moment. Will this give you a chance to see each other more?'

Zac looked at the guy as if he was a moron. His hatred of the press was legendary. 'Yes,' he replied shortly.

There were discreet chuckles from the other reporters. Jenna tried to keep her face neutral at the mention of Amber. She'd met her twice and she didn't like her.

Clive quickly interrupted. 'Come on guys, let's move

it along here. Yes?' He pointed to a woman in the second row.

'Julia Page, Sky News. How do you think Josh Starr will react to the news that you're to work with Jenna?'

Zac glanced nervously at his manager, who nodded almost imperceptibly.

'I don't really know what Josh would think,' he began slowly. 'He's made his decision, and we wish him all the best.'

'But is there any bitterness there?' the reporter pressed. 'Or has it turned out to be a blessing in disguise as you now have the chance to work with Jenna?'

A flicker of worry crossed Zac's brow.

Clive leant forward towards his microphone. 'Sorry, we're running really short of time. We'll just take one last question. Bob, yes?'

The CNN reporter jumped to his feet as Julia Page sat back in disappointment.

'This is a question for Jenna,' Bob Williams drawled, a sly grin flashing across his features. 'You've long expressed your admiration for Phoenix – Nick Taylor in particular,' he added, as the other reporters sniggered.

Jenna could feel her cheeks burning, remembering how she'd cited Nick as her ideal man in countless interviews.

'I was wondering if you're still of that opinion, now that you've met him?'

Jenna laughed brightly to hide her embarrassment, her smile lighting up her face. The press were gunning for a sniff of romance between Jenna and Nick – and Jenna was pretty keen on the idea herself.

'I've found all the members of Phoenix to be extremely generous, welcoming and phenomenally talented,' she began carefully. 'I'm looking forward to forming an exciting and stimulating relationship with them – strictly professional of course,' she added quickly, looking up coyly from underneath her lashes at a grinning Nick Taylor.

4

It was a glorious spring afternoon in the City. Shafts of sunlight filtered between the tall, grey office blocks and reflected off the stark, glass, ultra-modern buildings that had sprung up all over the City in recent years. The harassed-looking workers had shed their jackets and were striding through the streets in shirt-sleeves, their eyes hidden by black Ray-Bans. Parks, squares and even churchyards had been colonized by staff on their lunch break, looking to make the most of the unseasonably good weather. The hot sun was making everyone feel sexy, and Sadie was loving the vibe.

She was strolling along Bishopsgate with Carla and pretending not to notice the appreciative looks she was getting. Every man that passed checked her out, and Sadie was revelling in the attention. She'd just been to the lunchtime Pilates class that Carla ran at the City Works gym, and was bathed in a post-workout glow. Although she wasn't wearing a scrap of make-up, her skin was flawless and her cheeks were flushed and healthy. Her supple, toned limbs were evident through the fitted sweat pants and T-shirt she was wearing.

She had put on a few pounds over the past couple of weeks and her usually skinny dancer's figure had rounded out into sexy thighs, her small breasts had swollen a little fuller. The City high-fliers, surrounded by over-groomed women in their staid suits with immaculate hair and make-up, couldn't keep their eyes off her.

'Here?' asked Carla, as they scanned the menu outside a smart-looking Italian bistro.

'Good for me,' Sadie grinned.

They sat down at an outside table beside a large group of business people. Sadie turned her face up to the sky, feeling the sun beat down on her skin as she loosened her hair band and shook out her dark, glossy hair.

'I'd love a glass of white wine,' Sadie smiled, as the waiter approached. 'And a risotto verde.'

'I'll just have a mineral water and a goat's-cheese salad . . . without the goat's cheese.' Carla winced in apology at the confused waiter. 'And with the dressing on the side.'

Sadie looked at her carefully. 'You do know you've just ordered a glass of water and a plate of lettuce?'

'Yeah . . .'

'Mmmmmm,' Sadie smacked her lips together sarcastically. 'Sounds delicious.'

'I'm having a fat day,' Carla retorted crossly.

Sadie stared at her friend – she was a size four and there wasn't a trace of fat anywhere on her body. Her hip bones jutted out and you could count her ribs when she inhaled. 'A *fat* day?' she repeated.

'You know what Tom's like,' Carla shrugged as though that explained everything. Tom was Carla's boyfriend. He worked in IT, which as far as Sadie could tell meant he spent his time surfing the Internet and downloading porn. 'He's really into Asian women – Japanese, Filipino – and you know how skinny they are,' Carla explained.

'So are fourteen-year-old boys,' Sadie lectured. She had never liked Tom. He and Carla had been together for years, and as far as Sadie could tell they only stayed together out of habit. Carla couldn't seem to see how much better off she would be without him; as far as she was concerned, any guy was better than being alone. 'Look, just because Tom has weird fetishes doesn't mean you have to starve yourself.'

'I just want him to love me,' Carla whispered, her doe eyes filling with tears.

'Hon, he's a bastard,' Sadie told her frankly.

'Your area of expertise,' shot back Carla, turning her anger on Sadie.

'Touché.' Sadie raised an eyebrow. She could tell Carla was upset, so she let the matter drop. 'Anyway, *I'm* the one who needs to go on a diet,' she continued, as she sipped the deliciously chilled Pinot Grigio. 'I've barely worked out at all since *42nd Street* was cancelled. Laziness and comfort eating are not a good combination.'

'Don't be ridiculous, you look fantastic,' Carla reassured her. 'Every man in here is practically drooling into his lunch.'

'Well it's nice to have *these*,' Sadie smirked, indicating her breasts, 'but I really need to get back down to my performance weight. I haven't done anything for weeks. Thanks for dragging me out,' she smiled gratefully. Despite her protests when Carla first invited her, Sadie felt a lot better after the Pilates class. She enjoyed the familiar buzz as her body was kick-started back to life. She knew that she needed to get back into some sort of routine – and soon. She planned to start auditioning again next week and she needed to be on top of her game. It would be steamed veg and dance classes all the way from now on, she vowed, wincing as the waitress brought a delicious-looking panna cotta over to the table next to them.

'No, thanks for doing *me* the favour. It's nice to see a friendly face among all those tight-arsed Botox freaks,' Carla grinned, as she fished out the slice of lemon from her glass.

'Too many calories?' teased Sadie.

'Fuck off,' retorted Carla, good-naturedly. 'You might be able to look amazing 24/7, but not all of us have that luxury. Speaking of which, I'm off to the Ladies to tidy myself up a little. All these rich bitches are giving me a complex,' she asserted, grabbing her bag as she pushed her chair back and went inside.

Idly, Sadie glanced over at the surrounding tables, settling back to watch the hustle and bustle as people hurried past on their way to Liverpool Street. Everyone seemed to be wearing freshly buffed shoes and expensive suits, their braying voices loudly discussing incomprehensible terms like derivative clearing and projected EPS. But she couldn't deny that everyone looked fantastic. The women were impeccably dressed in chic designer outfits and sky-high heels, their hair professionally styled and their make-up immaculate. And the men . . .! Sadie allowed herself a small smile, and resolved to discuss the topic with Carla as soon as she got back. They'd have no problem finding Carla someone hotter than freaky Tom. The men here all looked sexy as hell, with their crisp, white shirts and light tans, no doubt cultivated at Christmas in St Barts and topped up on the ski slopes at Klosters.

Her gaze landed on a guy a couple of tables away,

and Sadie almost knocked over her wine glass. Christ, he was gorgeous! She felt as if she'd just received an electric shock, one thousand volts straight through her body. Thank God she was wearing dark glasses so he couldn't see her staring. He looked directly at her and his gaze was so disconcerting that she dropped her eyes, feeling her cheeks flame.

Cautiously, she glanced up from underneath her long, dark lashes. He was no longer looking at her, but some instinct told Sadie that he was still highly aware of her presence. He was chatting and joking with his colleagues; the women burst out laughing at something he'd said and Sadie felt an inexplicable pang of jealousy.

Then he glanced over at her again, as if to check that she was watching. This time Sadie didn't look away. Damn, he was attractive. He must have been almost twice her age – early forties, she would have guessed – but he had that complete confidence and authority that comes with maturity. Maturity, and a shit-load of cash, Sadie smiled to herself, as she noticed the Rolex on his wrist. His hair was dark, flecked with grey, and his features were exquisite – strong jaw line and a heavy, Roman nose which gave his face a distinction and gravity, offset by the way he was grinning now. He looked fun, she thought, feeling a delicious flutter in her stomach. He looked *sexy*.

Sadie glanced up as Carla slid back into her seat, now perfectly made up with her glossy brown hair freshly brushed. 'I feel better for that,' she exclaimed. 'It's like I'm naked without lip gloss.' She noticed Sadie's agitated state, the spots of colour high on her cheeks. 'What's wrong with you?'

'Hot man alert,' Sadie hissed through pursed lips.

'I know, they're everywhere.' Carla sat back languidly as the waiter placed their food in front of them.

'Not like this one.'

'So who's your intended victim?'

Sadie nodded discreetly to where the man was once again talking with his friends.

Carla wrinkled her nose. 'Not bad. Not really my taste, though. He's been checking you out since we arrived so he's definitely interested.'

Sadie was pleased by the confirmation.

'What about your vow to make it to the top?' Carla asked, a teasing glint in her eye. 'Won't he be a distraction?'

'A girl's got to have some fun,' Sadie pouted. 'Let off a little steam, if you know what I'm saying.'

'I know what you're saying,' Carla grinned. 'So are you going over?'

Sadie shook her head. 'No way. He can come to me.'

'Well he'd better be quick . . .'

'Fuck,' swore Sadie, as there was a clattering of chairs and the women gathered their handbags. The group stood up and the man walked off without so much as a backwards glance. 'Bastard,' she hissed, as she watched his retreating form. His shoulders were broad, his back toned and defined through the white cotton shirt. She imagined his strong, muscular chest pressed against her, his breath hot on her neck. She wanted him badly.

'There'll be another one along in a minute,' Carla reassured her. 'What about that guy over there?' she suggested, indicating a young City slicker with over-styled blond hair who was talking loudly into his BlackBerry.

Sadie merely raised an eyebrow. She pushed her food aside; suddenly she had no appetite. She took a large gulp of wine, hoping it would dull the nagging sensation of humiliation. She felt like a loser and she didn't like it. 'Shall we get the bill?'

'Sure,' agreed Carla, who was toying with a leaf of rocket.

Sadie signalled for the waiter, who came rushing over. 'No, there is no charge, madam. The gentleman who was sitting over there paid for your meal.'

It took Sadie a moment to comprehend what he was saying, but then a satisfied smile slowly spread across her face. 'Did he now?' she purred, feeling the familiar rush of excitement in her stomach.

'Yes madam. And he asked me to give you this.' The waiter handed over a neat, elegantly printed business card. Sadie took it, brushing her fingers thoughtfully over the raised print. *Paul Austin. Senior Investment Manager. Willis & Bourne.* It was thick, creamy card, expertly embossed. Very expensive. Very tasteful.

'He's bound to be a bastard,' Carla warned her.

Sadie smiled triumphantly. 'Let the game commence.'

Jenna's emotive voice rang out powerfully in the cramped recording booth. Lost in the sound of the music, she swayed her hips slightly, causing Nick to miss a beat as his concentration was broken by the sight of her gyrating crotch.

'Okay, let's do that line again,' sighed Don from behind the glass wall of the production box. It was the second day of recording for the Jenna/Phoenix collaboration, and only four weeks since the press conference, but already the optimism and excitement of that day felt like months ago. Don had a sneaking suspicion that this wasn't going to be the easiest job of his career.

At 55 years old, Lancashire-born Don had been in

the business a long time. Physically, he was a huge, hairy guy with a ZZ Top beard and a cut-the-crap attitude that endeared him to the artists he worked with. Don had collaborated with some of the biggest names in the music industry, and partied with some of the world's most stunning women, but had stayed resolutely faithful to Patty, his wife of twenty-eight years. All the same, he was a guy and couldn't fail to admire that high, round butt and those pert tits.

Yet, whilst his was what he liked to describe as a healthy appreciation, he felt Nick's appreciation was a little too healthy. Hell, it was so healthy it was practically doing cartwheels round the room. His timing on the drums was awful, and it wouldn't have surprised Don to find him dribbling on his snare.

'Excellent, we're getting there,' Don yelled, as Jenna belted out the line and Nick managed to complete the riff.

Zac looked up and adjusted his headphones. 'I think we should do it again,' he suggested quietly.

'What's the problem, Zac?'

They were working on a track called 'Without You'. Penned by Zac, it had been intended for Phoenix before Josh quit, but Jenna had insisted on having creative input and a writing credit.

'I don't think the vocal was quite right,' Zac replied firmly, not meeting Jenna's gaze.

'I thought Jenna got it down just fine. Take a break and we can always run through it again later,' Don suggested.

'Since when have we settled for *just fine*?' Zac pressed, his voice taking on a harder edge. 'It wasn't right, so we should do it again. I don't know how other artists work, but we've always had our success through hard work. Our music speaks for itself, and we don't rely on any other . . . assets . . . to sell records.'

Don was taken aback. Where the hell had that come from? Zac had always seemed like such an easy-going guy, yet he seemed to have taken a strong dislike to this cute chick and Don felt clueless as to why that should be. Sure, she could overdo it with the pampered princess act, but that was something they could easily get past if they were going to get this music out.

'How about we take a break and go back to it in a while. Everyone's starting to flag.'

But it was Jenna's voice that replied. 'No Don, it's fine,' she said curtly, stunned by what Zac had said. She'd always been a huge fan of his, but maybe it was true when they said you shouldn't meet your idols. 'I'll do it again. I haven't come this far by taking it easy on myself,' she added pointedly, glaring defiantly at Zac. She didn't know what his problem was, but if he thought she was going to roll over and die, he had another thing coming.

They reset the backing and Jenna launched into the song, feeling the power of the music build up through her body as Nick thrashed on the drums and Ryan hammered out the bass line. Unconsciously she began to move to the rhythm, feeling the relentless beat of the drums pulse through her, the squealing of the guitar electrify her veins. Many of her rivals wrote her off as simply another identikit pop act, but anyone who underestimated her was making a big mistake. She'd worked her arse off over the years to get where she was now, and she knew she was damn talented.

Screw him and his criticism, thought Jenna, fixing her gaze on Zac, who remained hunched over his guitar like an animal with its prey. His well-defined muscles rippled under his grey T-shirt, and Jenna felt a burst of injured pride followed by the shot of adrenaline she needed as she ripped into the song.

When the track finished, a deafening silence rang out in the studio. A single word came from the production box. 'Perfection.'

Slowly, Jenna brought her focus back to the room. The rest of the band was gazing at her, awestruck.

'You were fantastic, you totally nailed it,' gushed Nick.

'That was pretty amazing,' admitted Ryan. 'The feeling you put in there – it was so connected.'

Jenna grinned with pleasure as she realized the effect she'd had on them. Unable to help herself, she sneaked a glance at Zac.

This time, he met her gaze. 'That was good,' he agreed grudgingly. 'I guess that wraps us up for the night. See you guys tomorrow.' He grabbed his battered old jacket and walked out of the studio before anyone had a chance to reply.

'Zac, wait,' Jenna called out impulsively. She was sick of the way he was acting towards her, and wanted to find out exactly what his problem was. His attitude was making the situation awkward for everyone, and after her success in the studio she was on a high, geared up for an argument.

Slamming through the door after him, she ran out into the corridor to find Zac being embraced by Amber, immaculate in a simple black dress and sky-high ankle boots.

'Oh, I didn't realize . . .' Jenna faltered, trailing off.

'Hi Jenna.' Amber greeted her coldly, her eyes not matching the friendliness of her words. She kept her arms firmly around Zac, a possessive gesture deliberately designed to exclude.

'Hi Amber,' Jenna replied smoothly, trying to sound composed even though her mind was racing. 'I just . . . wanted a quick word with Zac. But it's not important. It'll wait until tomorrow.'

'It must have been pretty important if you ran out here to tell me,' Zac challenged her. There was an amused glint in his dark eyes. 'What did you want to say?'

You bastard, Jenna swore to herself. It was all she could do not to spit the remark out at him. 'I said it could wait until tomorrow,' she told him coldly, turning on her heel and walking back into the studio.

'Fine.' Zac gave a small shrug and threw his arm across Amber's shoulders, steering her towards the exit.

Jenna stood alone in the corridor, her breath coming fast. She'd show that arrogant prick. Jenna Jonsson was not to be underestimated – and Zac was going to find out he'd made a big mistake.

5

Despite her protestations to the contrary, Jenna *did* care what Zac thought. She couldn't help it. In spite of his arrogance and his dismissive attitude towards her, she wanted his approval. More than that, she was determined that this collaboration with Phoenix would blow everyone away, and she knew that for that to happen she needed to start working hard and get the band on side.

Ryan was a lovely, sweet guy – quiet, but from a natural shyness, not hostility. Nick was eating out of her hand, she thought with a grin. Now *he* was a lot of fun. There had been a lot of flirting, a lot of teasing and giggling, but nothing more. *Yet.* Don was a sweetie, and the best in the business – he worked them mercilessly, but got fantastic results, and Jenna had the utmost respect for him. But Zac . . . Jenna couldn't work him out. He was behaving like a total bastard towards her, but that wasn't what she'd heard about him from everyone else. They all seemed to think he was a great guy. Yeah, so he could be a little absorbed in his work at times, but that was something you accepted when you were working with a genius. So what was his problem with her?

Jenna was mulling the situation over as she lay alone in her super-king-size bed, unable to sleep. Zac's criticism had hit her harder than she had expected. All of his comments seemed to centre on her work and her attitude. She knew that he could only respect anyone who took their work as seriously as he did, and when she turned up day after day in her little outfits, looking to flirt with Nick and have a laugh with the production staff . . .

Jenna cringed as she thought of it. Okay, so maybe she could be a little childish at times.

Right, Jenna resolved firmly, *tomorrow sees the start of the new, mature me.*

And the first thing to change would be her clothes, she decided, jumping out of bed and heading over to her walk-in wardrobe with a growing sense of excitement at the thought of a reinvention. Other artists did it all the time, thought Jenna, picturing herself at highbrow events wearing Audrey Hepburn-style shift dresses, or fitted shirts and tailored trousers. Elegant – but still sexy, of course. Or maybe she could go for grown-up rock chick – thick black opaques and biker boots, teamed with a low-cut vest and fierce blazer.

As Jenna pulled aside the rows of skimpy, bare-all tops, the micro-miniskirts and the tiny hot pants, she felt she could perhaps see the problem. Resolving to throw away all items of clothing she owned in baby pink, Jenna rummaged through rail upon rail of designer labels and located a pair of white, flared Ralph Lauren trousers, a demure, high-necked shift dress from last season's Victoria Beckham collection, and the bold floral print skirt she'd finally decided on. *Just because I want to be refined doesn't mean I have to look like a Tory wife*, she concluded, finding a pair of ultra-feminine Chanel ballet pumps, which lacked the spiked heel and fetishistic appeal of most of her other footwear.

Just you wait Zac Knight, thought Jenna fiercely, climbing back between the luxurious Egyptian cotton sheets and flicking off the light.

Sadie emerged from the grimy Tube, breathing in the fresh air of Green Park. She looked sensational in a deep red wrap dress that fitted perfectly, emphasizing the slim contours of her body, and she'd teamed it with a sleek pair of knee-high boots. Men were checking her out as she walked along, a spring in her step and a swing to her hips.

As she reached the May Fair Hotel a few minutes later, the uniformed porter in his long coat and top hat opened the door, smiling at her as she stepped through. Sadie made a left and headed towards the bar. Her stomach was churning with excitement and nerves, but she knew she looked good.

Paul Austin was already there, seated at the counter. Her heart skipped a beat when she saw him. He looked unbelievably handsome, just as she'd remembered him, and in the stylish bar he seemed completely at home, radiating power and confidence. His suit was expensive and well fitted, his face serious as he swirled his whisky on the rocks. Then he glanced up, his face creasing into a smile as he saw her. He stood up to meet her and his eyes slowly ran over every inch of her body, watching the way her hips rolled, the way her small breasts rose and fell as she walked towards him. Sadie felt a thrill of anticipation run down her spine.

Paul leaned over to kiss her cheek. 'You smell delicious,' he murmured, lingering for just a second too long.

Sadie felt her stomach contract, a rush of heat low in her belly. The air was thick with tension.

'I've ordered for you,' Paul told her, indicating the glass of white wine on the counter beside him.

'You remembered,' Sadie said delightedly. She'd been drinking wine in the restaurant where she'd first seen him.

'I remember everything. I haven't been able to stop thinking about you since that afternoon.'

His eyes were trained on her unwaveringly. Sadie felt as though he was mentally undressing her, picturing her in the tiniest scrap of Victoria's Secret. She took a sip of wine to calm her nerves, but her hands were shaking. A drop spilled over the edge and trickled down the outside of the glass, leaving a trail through the condensation. Instinctively Sadie caught it with her finger, then placed the tip in her mouth and sucked gently.

She heard Paul's breath catch in his throat and she looked up, her eyes betraying a mix of fear, confusion and pure, undisguised lust.

'Sadie.' Just one word. The way he said her name, she felt herself melt. Instantly she knew why she was there. She wanted him badly, and there was no way of hiding it.

'Let's go.' Paul's voice was low and husky as he threw a note on the counter, grabbed Sadie by the hand and pulled her towards the exit.

'You know . . . I don't usually do this kind of thing . . .' Sadie gasped, her breath coming fast as she felt heat flood her body.

'Well I'm glad to be the exception,' Paul smirked, pushing his tongue deep into her mouth as his hands roamed frenziedly beneath her clothes.

Sadie moaned in pleasure and staggered backwards, feeling as though her legs wouldn't hold her up. Her back hit the wall and Paul fell against her, his firm body crushed against hers. She could feel his swollen cock through his trousers and she fumbled with his belt buckle, eager to free him.

'I should let *you* know . . . that *I* don't usually do this kind of thing . . .' Paul mimicked her words, his mouth hot against her ear so that the skin on the nape of her neck prickled deliciously.

Her hand slid inside his pants and she felt him, hard and thick as she grasped his shaft. Paul closed his eyes and groaned in delight as her fingers slipped down to his balls, stroking and squeezing with just the right amount of pressure.

'Then *I'm* glad to be the exception,' Sadie managed to stammer, biting down on her lip to stop herself from crying out as he roughly pushed up her top and greedily bent his head to her breasts. Her nipples were tight and his tongue flickered expertly over them, circling and sucking.

They were acting on instinct now, slaves to what their bodies were telling them. Sliding a hand down to her pussy, Paul couldn't believe how wet she was. The thought of her creaming herself for him turned him on even more and he knew he couldn't wait any longer.

Pulling a condom from his wallet he slipped it on and picked her up, his muscular arms flexing as Sadie wrapped her legs around his waist and he lowered her onto his throbbing cock.

Her back pressed into the wall as she clung to him, her nails digging into his shoulders as he began to move inside her, groaning with every thrust. She could feel him deep inside, his groin rubbing relentlessly against her clit as the pressure began to build.

'Paul, I'm close,' she cried. 'So fucking close . . .'

Without missing a beat he carried her over to the bed and they crashed down onto the pristine hotel sheets, Paul above her as he began to thrust faster. Sadie heard herself moan and for a moment her world was reduced to nothing except Paul and how good he felt, how amazing he felt inside her. She cried out, unable to help herself as waves of pleasure rocked through her body, and somewhere she heard Paul groan before he finally grew still.

He rolled off her, snapping off the condom before propping himself up on the pillows. Lazily, Sadie admired his body. He was definitely in amazing shape for a guy of his age. He was well built and muscular, his skin tanned and his abs defined. His hair was greying a little around the temples but Sadie liked that. It gave him a gravity, and showed that he wasn't vain enough to dye it.

'I meant what I said, you know,' Sadie told him, as she languidly stretched her exquisite body, totally unselfconscious about being naked. 'I don't usually do this kind of thing.'

'Have sex?' Paul teased her, resting one arm behind his head to show off his impressive biceps. 'Because you certainly didn't seem like a beginner to me.'

'Have sex with total strangers in hotel rooms,' Sadie clarified, watching Paul's face for his reaction. He leaned over and very slowly traced a finger between her breasts, down over her stomach to her navel. Sadie shivered in delight.

'And *I* meant what *I* said. I don't usually pick up random women in restaurants.' He paused. 'But you were so beautiful I simply couldn't help myself.'

In spite of herself, Sadie smiled. It was a corny line, but what the hell, it made her feel good. She could tell he was into her, and the sex had been amazing. She hadn't been wrong about the chemistry between them. Even while Carla insisted she was crazy, Sadie had dialled the number on the business card he'd left her and had arranged to meet in the bar of the hotel. It was immediately obvious that they were there for more than a polite drink; the sexual tension between them was off the scale.

'Every man in there wanted you, and that's why I couldn't let you get away. And do you know how I could tell you wanted me?' Paul asked as Sadie shook her head. 'When you looked at me your nipples went hard,' he grinned. 'Like tight little bullets through that sexy top of yours. Just like they're doing now,' he added, brushing his fingers lightly over her breasts.

Sadie squirmed under his touch, desire filling her face as she looked up at him with flushed cheeks and wide pupils. Damn, this guy could get her so hot. He was clearly an arrogant bastard, but in her experience men like that could be a lot of fun. Just as long as you didn't expect too much from them – romance, commitment, consideration; these were all things that a guy like this was never going to provide.

'Are you married?' she asked suddenly.

Paul hesitated for a moment. 'Yes. Does it bother you?'

'Shouldn't it bother *you*?' Sadie shot back.

Paul sighed, pulling his hand away from her. 'I'm not going to bullshit you, Sadie. Yes, I'm married. We've got three kids – all boys. The eldest is eleven.'

'Right.' Sadie swallowed hard.

'We haven't had sex in months. It's a marriage of convenience now – she's got her shopping and her gym classes, I've got my work. But she throws great dinner parties and charms all of my colleagues. She's given me three adorable boys and I want to be there for them. There's no way I'm going to leave her.'

'I wasn't asking you to,' Sadie said irritably. 'This is just a fuck for me too, you know.'

Paul laughed. 'So I'm just a fuck to you, am I?' he asked, his hands sliding over her buttocks and drifting tantalizingly along the inside of her thighs.

'Yes,' Sadie replied, fighting to keep control even though she knew her body was betraying her.

'That's a shame because I'd like to see you again. I think you and I could have a lot of fun together.'

'If by fun you mean no-strings sex, then I'm all for it,' Sadie retorted, determined to beat this bastard at his own game.

Paul was impressed. 'My kind of woman,' he remarked, and she could see the desire written on his face. He'd lied when he said he and his wife no longer slept together, but after fifteen years of marriage and three children, it paled in comparison to the thrill of an illicit liaison with a woman half his age. Everyone he knew was at it – the stay-at-home wife to provide the kids and the beautiful home, then a hot, young thing on the side for a little light relief. Along with cars, boats and exotic holidays, a mistress was just another necessary accessory for rich and powerful men.

Paul leaned towards her, his fingers tracing a line across her perfectly flat stomach. His touch was light, and Sadie shivered involuntarily. 'Ah, sexy Sadie,' he grinned. 'You intrigue me. There aren't many women who are so honest about what they want.'

'What can I say?' she said with a flirtatious shrug. 'I'm just not like other women.'

'Too true,' Paul agreed. 'So tell me about yourself. I want to get to know you – in more than just the biblical sense.'

'What do you want to know?' Sadie asked easily.

'What do you do? Model?' he guessed. 'Personal trainer?'

'I'm a dancer.'

His eyes lit up immediately – the classic reaction. Men loved it when Sadie told them what she did for a living. They immediately pictured her contorted into some graphic sexual pose, imagining she could put her legs behind her head while they rammed into her, or envisaging sleek, toned thighs clasped tightly around them.

'I love what I do and I'm very ambitious,' she warned him, her face becoming steely as it always did when she talked about her career. 'I'm going places. I'm just waiting for the right break, but I know I'll make it.'

'I'm sure you will,' Paul agreed. 'You've got the right attitude, a beautiful face, and' – here he looked her up and down with barely concealed lust – 'the hottest body I've seen in a very long time.'

'Thanks,' Sadie said coolly. She didn't feel he was flattering her; his comments were pretty accurate as far as she was concerned. 'What about you? How do you earn your millions?'

'Oh please,' Paul shook his head in mock deprecation. 'I only make millions if it's a particularly good year.'

'Yes, I can see you're practically on the breadline,' Sadie teased, stretching luxuriously in the enormous bed.

'I'm in finance,' Paul explained. Sadie looked at him quizzically and he continued, 'I work for a private equity firm in the City. I deal with clients who have more money than they know what to do with – and I make them even more. It's about turning millionaires into billionaires,' he boasted. 'Increasingly I'm handling single clients, rather than corporations – high net-worth individuals who've made their money in business or in the entertainment world. We invest their money and take a percentage of the profits.'

'Do you enjoy it?' Sadie asked curiously.

'I love it,' Paul replied without hesitation. 'It affords me a fantastic lifestyle, and I work damn hard for it. I play hard too,' he added, with a wink.

'I can tell. This room's gorgeous,' Sadie commented, looking around properly at her surroundings for the first time. They'd been in such a hurry to tear each other's clothes off that she'd hardly even noticed where she was. Hell, she couldn't even remember if they'd locked the door.

'Oh, this is nothing,' Paul said dismissively. 'Rooms in Europe are tiny compared to those in the States. And I always say that a room's not a room unless it comes with a hot tub,' he grinned.

Sadie smiled back, saying nothing. Her eyes flicked over the enormous armchairs, the deep pile carpets and the heavy wooden writing desk. Discreet Bang & Olufsen speakers were mounted on either side of the bed, and the whole place was decorated in a classic colour scheme of chocolate and cream. Sadie thought that if this was what Paul casually dismissed as 'nothing', she'd love to see his idea of luxury.

'But it *is* very discreet,' he explained as he moved towards her. His eyes were dancing, and Sadie knew exactly what was on his mind. Undoubtedly he was hot, and the things he did to her drove her wild. But there could be other advantages to this situation, she realized. *This* was the lifestyle she wanted – the expensive clothes, the hotels, the hot tubs. Yeah, she could definitely get used to this. Not that she wanted to become anyone's wife – hell, no, she was still totally focused on her career, dead set on becoming a success. But maybe Paul could help her with that. Having a gorgeous, loaded man who adored her might turn out to be very helpful indeed. He'd mentioned clients in the entertainment industry – she wondered if he had any good contacts.

Sadie leaned forward so that her breasts pressed against his chest and gazed up at him with wide, innocent eyes. 'I just realized I never thanked you for the meal . . .' she murmured.

'You can thank me now,' Paul said, twisting her long, dark hair around his fingers and gently pushing her downwards to where his erection was growing once again. He sighed with pleasure as he felt her warm lips slide over his cock, her tongue gently flickering over the head. Then he settled back against the pillows, and smiled in satisfaction.

6

Despite Jenna's change of clothing, the following day's recording was the usual tense affair. She bounced into Sarm Studios looking radiant, with her long blonde hair freshly washed. For once she hadn't blow-dried it, letting the natural wave take over and tumble softly down her back. Her make-up was subtle, and she had added just a touch of lip gloss. Tod's loafers and a delicate pair of pearl earrings completed the image.

'Wow Jenna, you look . . . real classy . . .' Nick finished before he could stop himself.

Jenna laughed a little too loudly, hoping her cover hadn't been blown. 'What's the matter, can't I dress like a lady once in a while?' she joked, looking away nervously as Zac sauntered into the studio.

'All right?' he enquired gruffly, barely looking at her.

'Not bad,' she replied civilly. 'You?'

Zac picked up his guitar, throwing the shoulder strap across his slim, muscular back. He began to strum absentmindedly.

'Yeah,' he replied, meeting her gaze for once. 'I'm good.'

'Excellent,' replied Jenna irritably, wondering why

his flippant remark annoyed her so much. Why did he always have to seem so in control of every situation, making her feel as though everything she said was juvenile and ridiculous?

'Going somewhere special?' he asked easily.

'I just felt like a change, all right?' Jenna snapped back, as Zac smiled benignly.

The day went downhill from there.

Although Zac rarely openly criticized Jenna, there was a distinctly uncomfortable atmosphere that never seemed to lift. Something, somewhere, wasn't quite gelling, and the music so far was worryingly second-rate. Despite rarely voicing his opinions, it seemed obvious what Zac thought of her – that she was lazy and uncommitted – and Jenna was worried that the production staff privately agreed with him. Stories had already begun to circulate in the media about how the Jenna/Phoenix collaboration might be over before it had even begun, and Jenna had been leaning hard on Gerry to stop these stories and get some positive stuff out there.

Suddenly she caught sight of her reflection in the glass wall of the production box and twisted slowly from side to side, wondering if this change of image really suited her. The knee-length skirt was unflattering, and from the side her calves looked enormous . . .

'Damn – sorry,' she apologized, as she missed her intro. 'I was miles away.'

'Try to concentrate, sweetheart,' Don pleaded wearily, sinking his head into his hands.

'Sorry guys. I'm ready now.'

'That's good of you,' muttered Zac under his breath.

He glanced across at Jenna with a lingering trace of exasperation. She looked so vulnerable standing alone in the vocal booth, her eyes large and downcast, twirling her hair round her fingers with embarrassed discomfort. Okay, so he couldn't deny that she was sexy. But she was also infuriating as hell, Zac insisted to himself. It was her whole damn attitude – the way she just swanned around in cute little outfits, flirting with the crew and thinking that she could charm Don and get away with second-rate work. Even the more demure clothes she was wearing today couldn't hide that magnificent figure. Zac had been as surprised as anyone when she'd turned up looking like a society deb who'd been dressed by her mother, but Jenna Jonsson could probably still look hot in a garbage bag, he realized, his eyes skimming involuntarily over her rounded thighs, curving in to an impossibly slender waist. The neutral make-up served to highlight her mesmerizing eyes and plump, inviting lips . . .

'Zac?' Don's voice came angry and questioning from behind the mixing desk.

'Sorry, what?' Zac looked around, confused.

'Your solo?'

Zac glanced down stupidly at his guitar, which was hanging uselessly at his waist. 'Now?' he asked, stalling for time.

'Well, preferably thirty seconds ago, but yeah, it tends to follow the bridge.'

'Sorry, I was miles away,' he replied, mimicking Jenna. 'Can we go again?'

'Looks like I'm not the only one who can fuck up,' Jenna couldn't resist commenting. She aimed the remark at Nick, but it was easily loud enough for Zac to hear, which was her intention.

He turned on her angrily, enraged by her arrogance and maddened that she was the reason for his lack of focus. 'Yeah, I fuck up occasionally because I'm human,' he shouted. 'What I don't do is fuck up every other take, because I'm too busy checking out my own goddamn reflection!'

There was a deathly silence in the studio.

'Screw you,' Jenna spat, her eyes gleaming angrily and her breath coming fast.

The tension was palpable. No one spoke, but all eyes were on the pair.

'Grow up, Jenna,' Zac said quietly. 'Think of somebody else for once.' He looked down at the floor, not trusting himself to meet her eyes.

For Jenna, the remark hurt all the more because she knew it was true. She'd been behaving like a spoiled brat and she hated herself for it, but she would rather have died than admit it to that condescending arsehole. She glanced across at him through narrowed eyes. His chest rose and fell quickly under his T-shirt, indicating his fury. His dark hair had fallen across his forehead and stubbornly stayed there.

'For fuck's sake,' roared Don exasperatedly. 'Are we finished now, children? Can we get on with it?'

Zac lifted his gaze and glared at Jenna, his dark brown eyes boring into her own. 'I'm outta here,' he announced, swinging his guitar strap over his head as Jenna threw up her hands in exasperation.

'Zac?' Don yelled pleadingly. He wondered what the hell had got into the guy. He was usually so pleasant and laid back, but since Little Miss Pop Sensation had turned up, he'd been foul-tempered and snappy, constantly catting with Jenna. What was it with those two, he wondered?

Don sighed to himself. One thing he was sure of was that this track would bomb if the group couldn't get on. If it could be done well, the music would be dynamite, no doubt about it. It was just a question of getting these kids to bond, and work together.

'Zac, wait a second,' he shouted, a note of appease-
ment in his voice. 'What do you say we take a break
for a while – order some food, then work through the
night to get this thing nailed?'

Zac hesitated for a moment.

'Okay,' he replied casually, pulling out his iPhone.
'I'll just call Amber, tell her I'm going to be late.'

Don looked at Zac with relief, and a grudging respect.
'Thanks,' he commented.

'No problem,' said Zac with a shrug.

An hour later, the group sat flaked out on the vast,
welcoming sofas in the chill-out room adjoining the
studio. The pungent smell of Nick's spliff hung heavily
in the air, and the table was littered with discarded
takeaway boxes, crushed beer cans and empty bottles
of champagne. The alcohol was flowing freely, but had
only heightened the emotions that existed previously;
Jenna and Nick were flirting like crazy, and Zac had
sunk deeper into his dark mood. He sat on the floor
with his back against the sofa, his taut, denim-clad
legs stretched out across the carpet as he drank in
silence.

Don shot a quick glance at Jenna and Nick. Noting
that they were both laughing loudly, engrossed in each
other, he leaned forward to talk to Zac.

'Work with me here, man,' pleaded Don. 'There's a
really strange vibe, and I can't work out what's going
on with you guys. We need it all to come right,' he
continued, as Zac remained unresponsive, looking
blankly ahead. 'Is this going to work or not? Because
I'll tell you something for nothing – at the moment,
this is looking like an extremely expensive disaster.'

Zac didn't say anything, but took a long drink of his
beer.

'I can't work with her Don,' he said finally.

'I know she can be a little difficult,' Don sympathized, 'but surely you can cut her some slack?'

'A *little* difficult?' exploded Zac, struggling to keep his voice low. 'She's lazy, stubborn; she treats this whole thing as a game. She just won't take anything seriously.'

'Hey, she's not that bad,' Don laughed, surprised at the vehemence of Zac's outburst.

Zac raised an eyebrow.

'There's nothing wrong with having a good time,' Don said gently. 'This whole process is supposed to be enjoyable, you know, not some kind of endurance test.'

'Don't blame me,' retorted Zac. 'What are you saying? That if I'd lighten up a little then everything would be okay? That I'm the one causing the problem?'

'Hey, calm down,' said Ryan lightly. He moved across to sit closer to them. 'That's not what Don was saying. Yeah, we're having a few problems, and we gotta work through them. But you can't blame Jenna for not being Josh.'

'I know that. It's just . . .' Zac paused, and his brow creased as he struggled to find the right way to explain himself. 'I accept that Josh's gone, and it's not going to be the same. But it shouldn't be this difficult to work with someone new. I get the feeling that with anyone else it would have been easier, whereas with her . . .' Zac trailed off, and they all glanced across to see Jenna – whether by accident or design – rearrange her endless, tanned legs so that her deliberately demure knee-length skirt rode a little higher up her thighs, the clinging fabric wrapping tightly around her shapely butt.

'I know what you mean,' Ryan conceded, dragging

his eyes away. 'She's probably not the easiest person to work with – and Nick doesn't always help the situation. But sometimes I think you don't give Jenna enough credit. She really wants this to work.'

Zac made a noncommittal noise.

'It's got to be intimidating for her too,' continued Ryan. 'We've been with Josh for so long, then suddenly she has to step into his shoes and there's no guarantee it'll work. There's no guarantee everyone will like her – us *or* the fans.'

'She doesn't look like the type of girl to be intimidated by anything,' Zac muttered, darting a look across the room to where Jenna was giggling as she gulped down another mouthful of champagne.

'Oh come on, Zac. She might act confident, but you can tell a lot of it's just a front. I'm sure she's nervous as hell really, so try and go easy on her, yeah?'

'She just . . . gets under my skin,' finished Zac lamely.

'Yeah . . .' nodded Don, looking thoughtfully at Zac.

'Oh, that feels good!' squealed Jenna from the other side of the room.

They all looked across to see Jenna's shoes discarded on the floor, her right foot in Nick's lap where he was drunkenly attempting to massage it.

'Ohhhhhh, right there,' Jenna groaned, flexing her foot in pleasure and squeezing it against Nick's thigh.

Nick felt himself grow instantly hard and pressed his fingertips into the delicate skin of her foot, mesmerized at the way she was writhing around on the carpet, arching her back and moaning. Yeah, she'd look pretty damn good rolling around on a rug in front of a roaring fireplace, Nick thought to himself. Maybe he should buy a place in Aspen and fly her out there. He moved her foot to one side, gently opening her legs a little. If he could just get her legs a little wider, he'd be able to see right up her skirt, Nick realized. His cock was chafing against his pants so hard it hurt. Man, imagine if she wasn't wearing panties – he'd be able to see her, ready and waiting for him. Imagine that – Jenna Jonsson lying in front of him wearing nothing but a thin scrap of fabric. He wondered if she was a natural blonde. Or maybe she was waxed, with just a little landing strip to guide him in. If they were alone, all he would have to do would be to walk over and yank up her skirt – take her right there over the sofa.

Nick knew she wanted him, and the thought made him feel uncontrollably aroused. Maybe if the other guys were engrossed in their own conversation, no one would notice if he just moved a little closer and ran his hand along those soft, yielding thighs before slipping a finger inside of her. He'd stroke her ever so gently, and feel her get wetter and wetter, until she was begging him to give it to her. Or maybe she would touch herself and he would just watch . . .

'What are you boys talking about?' Jenna demanded to know, realizing that the others were heavily involved in conversation. She jumped up, pulling her foot from Nick's hand and leaving him flushed and alone on the floor.

'We were, er, discussing how the record's coming,' replied Don uncertainly.

'Oh fantastic,' gushed Jenna, as she picked her way across the room, stepping delicately over the discarded pizza boxes and making no attempt to pull down her skirt which had ridden up to show acres of toned, tanned thigh, kept a beautiful shade of honey brown thanks to her regular St Tropez treatments.

'So how do you think it's all coming along? I'm thrilled with the way it's turning out – I'm having an amazing time working with you all,' Jenna told them earnestly. The champagne had gone to her head, but she meant every word she said. Squeezing herself onto the sofa in between Zac and Don, she purred, 'You're all so incredibly talented.'

Zac bit down hard on his lip. He'd told Ryan he'd try and go a little easier on her, but he wasn't sure it was a promise he could keep. He swallowed, trying to prevent himself from saying something he'd regret. He could feel the warmth of her body next to his, could smell the Chanel No. 5 that she had optimistically spritzed on that morning as part of her new image.

Zac stood up suddenly, causing Jenna to lose her balance on the sofa. She burst into giggles as Don helped her upright.

'I should get going,' Zac announced, struggling to keep his temper. Everything Jenna did drove him crazy. 'I told Amber I'd be back as soon as I could, and we're obviously not going to get any more done here tonight.'

'Maybe we could work on the track some more now?' Jenna asked hopefully.

'I don't think that's a good idea.'

'Why not?' shot back Jenna, her eyes flashing danger-ously as she began to get defensive.

Zac paused and took a deep breath, remembering his vow not to get mad with her. 'Well, look at Nick,' he tried to joke. 'He's hardly in any fit state to play, is he?'

Nick was laid out on the floor, his blue eyes staring blankly at the ceiling. 'Are we done here?' he asked, struggling to sit up. 'You want a ride home, Jenna?' He tried to focus on her face, but he could see two of her. He liked the idea of two of her.

Jenna smiled. 'Thanks for the offer, but I'll just call my driver.'

'It's no trouble, really, it's on my way,' slurred Nick.

A natural-born charmer, Nick was used to getting what he wanted. From girls to money to a place in one of the world's biggest bands, life came easy to Nick.

Zac forced a laugh, trying to make light of the situation. 'You're wasted, Nick – there's no way you can drive, not even the few blocks over to Jenna's. You'd be DUI'd the second you get behind the wheel.'

'You live close by?' asked Ryan, turning to Jenna. Jenna nodded, wondering how Zac knew. She was pretty sure she hadn't mentioned it. 'I can give you a ride if you want,' Ryan continued.

'Hey, I'm a proper Southern gent. I've gotta make sure the lady gets home safely,' roared Nick.

'She'll be fine, Nick. Which is more than can be said for you,' muttered Zac.

'Would that be okay?' Jenna asked Ryan uncertainly. 'I hate to bother my driver so late, and if you're sure it's not out of your way . . .?'

'Not a problem,' Ryan replied generously. 'I haven't been drinking anyway, 'cos Kelly hates it when I come home trashed.'

'Thanks,' replied Jenna, giving him a broad smile that lit up her face.

'Jenna, *I* will give you a ride home,' declared Nick, attempting to get to his feet as he waved his arms expansively. 'It is absolutely no problem for me – don't listen to what these bastards are saying. Or we can just share a cab to my hotel,' he added, with a wink.

'It's fine, it really is,' Jenna insisted, tempted though she was to take up Nick's offer and spend the night in some decadent suite where they could fuck so hard she wouldn't be able to walk tomorrow. But she didn't think that would go down too well with the others – Zac would probably fire her for lack of professionalism. 'I'll get a lift with Ryan.'

'Ryan,' Nick whined, his forehead creased in an expression of bitter disappointment. 'But that's not fair. You're married!'

'Which is why she'll be safer with him than with you,' explained Don firmly. 'Now let's call you a car.'

'This is totally unfair,' complained Nick.

'Quit acting like a jerk,' snapped Zac, tiring of Nick's behaviour. 'I'll see you guys tomorrow,' he added shortly, as he headed for the door.

'Do you want a ride too?' asked Ryan. 'I don't mind the drive.'

'No, thanks. I'll make my own way back.'

Zac glared at Jenna and walked out of the door.

7

'Ryan?' asked Jenna.

She settled back comfortably into the vast seats of his Range Rover, watching the bright lights of London flash by. It was drizzling lightly outside, and Jenna's breath on the window caused it to steam up, obstructing her view. She shivered slightly, realizing with a stab of annoyance that she'd left her jacket in the studio.

'Yeah?' asked Ryan. Following his GPS he signalled right, turning from the main street with its parade of shops into a wealthy-looking residential area, lined with beautiful white stucco-fronted houses.

Jenna hesitated. 'Why does Zac dislike me so much?' she finally asked.

Ryan's hands tightened slightly on the steering wheel, and he kept his eyes firmly fixed on the road ahead. 'He does like you Jenna,' he began uncertainly, his words lacking sincerity. 'It's just that . . . oh, I don't know. He does like you Jenna, don't worry about it,' he reiterated.

'Oh come on, Ryan,' shot back Jenna, her voice rising slightly as she felt herself beginning to get upset.

'You've seen what he's like with me – he can't stand me. He won't talk to me, he barely looks at me . . .'

'Hey, it's not that bad,' Ryan insisted, worriedly glancing across at her. 'He's having a little trouble adjusting after working with Josh, but he doesn't hate you Jenna.'

'I don't know what else I can do,' she continued desperately, as though he hadn't spoken. 'I've tried to make him like me, I really have. I *so* want this to work. And now it's causing a problem with the band, and Don's getting pissed off with me . . .' Jenna trailed off, her breath coming fast.

'Don's not pissed off with you,' reassured Ryan, sounding surprised. 'Why do you think that?'

'Next street on the left,' snuffled Jenna, trying to keep her voice steady as she felt the tears gathering in her eyes. She almost wished she hadn't started the conversation, knowing that if she began to cry she wouldn't stop. But she *had* to know. The situation was depressing her, stifling her enjoyment of what should have been one of the most exciting and creative periods of her career.

'Look, don't take any notice of Zac,' said Ryan dismissively, trying to keep his tone light. 'That's just what he's like.'

'No, he's not,' Jenna protested. 'Everyone who's worked with him says he's the sweetest guy, and I've seen what he's like with everyone else. He gets on fine with them, and they all love him. It's just me he's got a problem with.'

'Jenna, sweetheart, please don't beat yourself up about this,' Ryan implored, wishing there was something he could say to make her feel better. It was heartbreaking listening to how upset and vulnerable she sounded. 'Zac's obviously got some problems at the moment – he is being a little different, yeah. But we're all feeling the brunt of it too.'

Jenna bit her lip, looking unconvinced.

Ryan sighed. 'I promise you, Jenna, it's got nothing to do with you,' he insisted, not knowing if it was true or not, but feeling that it was the right thing to say.

'There's parking just here on the right,' Jenna told him with a sniff. 'He's said he thinks I'm lazy, but I swear I'm not, Ryan,' she insisted, her eyes shining wet with tears.

'Jenna, don't get upset,' pleaded Ryan, his brow creasing in worry as he swung into the parking spot and turned off the ignition.

'I'm working so hard to please everyone, and he just doesn't care!' The tears began to flow and Jenna let them run freely.

'Jenna . . .' began Ryan, reaching across the seat towards her. He held her awkwardly and she clung to him, her body wracked with sobs. Ryan took a deep breath, trying to gather his thoughts. He wished he knew what to say to her; he felt so useless and awkward, unaccustomed to dealing with such emotional outbursts. His hands felt large and protective as he held her tiny frame, breathing in the faint smell of her perfume.

'Jenna,' Ryan began, as he sat up and disentangled himself from her. Gently, he brushed her hair away from her face. 'I think you should head on in and get yourself a good night's sleep. It's been a stressful night, and I'm sure you'll feel better tomorrow. Get a big glass of juice or something, help you sober up.' The words came out clumsily, reflecting Ryan's discomfort. He was tired and he wanted to get home to his wife and kids – Kelly would probably be waiting up for him, he realized.

'Oh shit, I'm so sorry Ryan,' Jenna apologized, embarrassed as she wiped her eyes. 'I'm just being silly – you've been so good to put up with me.'

'No problem,' Ryan mumbled.

Neither of them spoke for a few moments as Jenna rubbed her eyes tiredly, running a finger underneath her eyelashes to try and wipe off the smudged mascara. Finally, she spoke. 'I hate to ask after all this, but could you do me one favour?'

'I guess,' Ryan shrugged.

'I really don't like getting in by myself – the house is so big and quiet. It was stupid of me to buy it really,' she smiled. 'It's far too big for one person, and I sometimes get a little freaked out. Tonight especially, I'm feeling so on edge. Would you come in with me, just for a few minutes until I'm settled?' Ryan paused and Jenna forced a smile. 'You'll get a free cup of coffee out of it.'

'I don't know . . .' he began slowly. 'I should be heading back. Kelly's expecting me, and I don't want to be too late.'

'But it would only be for a few minutes . . .' Jenna saw Ryan hesitate and felt her cheeks grow hot as the anger rose in her chest. Deep down, she knew it wasn't his fault, but she desperately needed someone to lash out at. 'Okay, fine. Forget it,' she snapped furiously, her eyes blazing. 'None of you like me, do you? We should just call this whole thing off right now because it's obviously not going to work. Apologize to the rest of the guys for me, would you – that's if they even care!'

Jenna jumped down from the car and slammed the door.

'Shit,' swore Ryan, leaping out of the Range Rover. 'Jenna! Jenna, wait,' he yelled, running after her across the street. 'Jenna,' he shouted, grabbing her by the shoulder.

She had reached the doorstep of her house and swung round to face him. It was raining harder now, and her hair streamed out wildly behind her, her face accusing and streaked with mascara.

'Jenna, I'm so sorry,' Ryan apologized. He looked at her worriedly, aware of the commotion they were making in the quiet street. There didn't seem to be anyone around, but the last thing he wanted was to draw attention to the pair of them. 'Look, I'll come in with you and we'll get you a drink, get you sorted out, and it'll all be okay. Come on,' he added, resting a hand on her back as he led her into the house.

'I'm just going to go and freshen up a little,' said Jenna as they stepped into the entrance hall, feeling embarrassed about the way she must look.

'Okay.' Ryan stood awkwardly in the corridor, not sure where to go as she disappeared upstairs. 'Can I make you a drink?' he yelled after her.

'Sure, coffee would be great,' Jenna shouted back.

Ryan looked around him, trying to work out which direction the kitchen was in. The Holland Park house was undeniably gorgeous. Designed by the Candy brothers, the interior was modern and dramatic, all sleek furniture and a neutral colour scheme broken up by stunning statement pieces. The contemporary style belied the 'Old England' appearance of the exterior, with its white stone walls, wrought-iron balconies and potted bay trees either side of the heavy black door.

Inside it was very tidy and somewhat devoid of personal items – Ryan got the impression that Jenna probably didn't spend a lot of time there. *I can sympathize with that*, he thought, remembering how in the early days when the band were trying to break through, they'd toured incessantly, spending months on end away from home. He'd married young and started a family almost immediately but, despite the pressure, he and Kelly had got through it. Not everyone had been quite so lucky, he realized, thinking of Zac and his ex-wife Jessica.

Having located the kitchen, the kettle had just boiled when Jenna walked in. Her face was clean of make-up, but her eyes were still puffy and her cheeks were more flushed than normal, betraying her earlier outburst.

'You shouldn't drink coffee at this time of night. I made you some tea instead,' Ryan said, pouring out the water. 'I've been in England for a few days now so I think I've got the hang of it,' he grinned.

'Thanks,' smiled Jenna. Their fingers brushed as she took the mug from him.

'Careful. It's hot,' warned Ryan.

'I'll be careful,' Jenna teased, blowing gently across the top of the mug. She realized Ryan was watching her and wiped her eyes self-consciously.

'I hate the way I look when I cry,' Jenna explained shyly. 'My eyes swell up and I look like a pig.'

Ryan laughed. 'Well, you'd have to be the cutest pig I've ever seen,' he answered clumsily.

'Gee, thanks,' Jenna replied, but she was laughing as she led the way through to the magnificent living room. It was located at the back of the house, a huge, high-ceilinged room with long, full-length windows looking out onto an impressive expanse of garden. The lounge was largely minimalist, with buttercream walls and pale furniture; only the ostentatious gold and crystal chandelier, and the gilt candlesticks over the fireplace, added a touch of drama to the otherwise muted room. Jenna plopped down on one of the squashy cream sofas, and Ryan joined her.

'God, I'm so tired,' Jenna yawned, resting her head against the soft fabric.

'It must be the stress,' commented Ryan, taking a sip of his tea. 'You've had a hard day.'

'Yeah, I'll say,' agreed Jenna. She paused, listening to the rain falling against the windows. 'Am I just being stupid, Ryan? I mean, am I completely overreacting to everything, and just annoying the hell out of the rest of you?'

She looked so earnest, her beautiful green eyes open wide in anguish, that Ryan smiled.

'Of course not,' he reassured her. 'We'll get there. It's new to us all, and it's just going to take time. Zac's having a harder time adjusting than we are, that's all. It's nothing personal.'

Jenna smiled gratefully. 'Thanks.'

'And I'd think the attention Nick gives you more than makes up for it.'

Jenna grinned, squirming with embarrassment. 'He's terrible, isn't he? I bet he's like that with everyone,' she commented carefully, feeling her heart begin to race a little.

'Hell, I don't know really,' Ryan lied, trying to avoid the subject. 'He's always had quite an eye for the ladies. But I'd say he really likes you,' he added quickly, as Jenna's face fell.

'It's okay, I know what he's like,' she admitted. 'I know it's just fun, and I enjoy it. It's such a dream even working with you guys.'

'We're not that special,' Ryan shook his head.

'Millions of fans can't be wrong,' Jenna grinned, as

she lay down on the couch and closed her eyes. Neither of them spoke as Ryan drained his tea.

'You really like him, don't you?' he asked Jenna gently. 'Nick, I mean.'

'I don't know. Well . . . yeah,' she admitted drowsily. 'Don't tell him though, will you? He's big-headed enough already.'

'I won't,' Ryan promised.

There was a long pause as Jenna snuggled down on the sofa. Eventually, she spoke, her voice sounding slow and distant. 'Yeah, I do like him,' she confessed sleepily.

'Just be careful, yeah?' Ryan urged. But Jenna didn't respond. Her breathing was regular and slow, and Ryan realized she was asleep. He checked his watch – just after midnight. Carefully, so as not to wake her, Ryan climbed off the sofa. When he reached the door he paused for a few moments, thinking how beautiful she looked – so innocent and vulnerable, almost childlike, with her long, blonde hair tumbling over her face, and her skin cleansed of make-up. Then he turned and hurried back down the corridor, noiselessly opening the front door and letting himself out. The silent street appeared deserted as he climbed back into the Range Rover and drove off.

Jenna woke groggily from a deep sleep, wondering why her limbs ached so badly. Sunlight streamed in through the high arched windows and, as Jenna slowly opened her eyes, she was shocked to realize she'd slept all night on the sofa.

Blearily, she glanced up at the wall clock: 9.50 a.m.

'Shit,' she swore, wondering what time she was due in the studio that day. Oh well, she shrugged, deciding she didn't care. They could damn well wait for her.

Let Ryan explain why she might be a little late, Jenna thought drowsily, as the events of last night began to come back to her.

Last night. What had happened exactly? Oh God, groaned Jenna, as she rolled over and buried her head in the cushions. Had she made a complete fool of herself? She remembered flirting outrageously with Nick, and then Ryan had brought her home . . . Oh no, she'd been really upset – she remembered yelling at him in the street. Shit, how embarrassing.

Ryan had been sweet though. He was such a nice guy, and hopefully he wouldn't hold her behaviour against her. She just hoped it didn't get back to Zac – he already thought she was acting like a diva, and she didn't want him to know that he had upset her so badly.

I'll show him, Jenna insisted, pushing last night's feelings of insecurity out of her mind. Letting her emotions run out of control was not the way she had got to the top, Jenna reminded herself. Today, she would be completely in command.

She stretched luxuriously in an effort to shake some of the heaviness from her limbs. She needed to start getting a handle on her life. She had been so stressed and tired last night that she hadn't even made it to bed – hell, her standards were really slipping. Thank God she'd taken off her make-up when she got in, Jenna thought, reaching up to touch her face. It felt soft and smooth, and Jenna sighed with relief; the last thing she needed was a break-out on top of everything else.

Sitting up carefully, Jenna swung her long legs over the end of the sofa and paused. She needed a glass of water – or maybe some coffee; rocket fuel would certainly get her going. Picking up the empty tea mugs,

Jenna padded through to the kitchen. While she was waiting for the kettle to boil, she flicked on her laptop.

'Oh fuck, no. Oh Jesus!' swore Jenna as she logged on to TMZ and saw the lead story.

8

The offices of Willis & Bourne were located on the twenty-fourth floor of the Broadgate Tower, in the heart of London's Square Mile. Paul Austin, as a senior executive, had a private office at the far end of the corridor, guarded by his PA. As the early morning sun filtered through the tinted windows, Paul sat behind his kidney-shaped desk, leafing through a copy of the *Financial Times*. There was an unfavourable report on a Japanese telecoms firm in which he'd just invested a large portion of his clients' money. It did not make for happy reading. Irritably, he tossed the paper aside and turned his attention to the Internet, flicking through share prices, business headlines and breaking news.

One headline caught his attention – it involved Jenna Jonsson. Paul read swiftly through the article and found himself even more interested. So, Miss Jonsson wasn't as squeaky clean as she made out, it seemed, and some lucky guy was getting to bang her. Paul's cock leapt in his pants at the very thought of it. Jenna was one hot piece of ass – he'd have sold his own grandmother for a fuck with Jenna. Then again, Paul Austin would willingly have sold out his grandmother for a lot of things in life – loyalty was not one of his defining traits.

Paul's interest in Jenna went beyond that of the casual voyeur or horny teenager. As of last month, she was one of his newest clients. It was still fresh in his mind, the way she'd strutted into his office dressed like Business Barbie, in a tight pencil skirt that showed off her high, round butt, and a low-cut white blouse that strained against her tits every time she leaned forward. Of course, she'd brought her manager with her, some jumped-up flunky in a suit who'd watched Paul's every move like a hawk, so he'd had to keep things professional. He'd talked at length about dry stuff – real estate in Bulgaria, mineral mining in South Africa, investment yields, long-term trends and so on. She'd nodded that pretty little head and all he'd been thinking about was how much he'd like to put his dick between those luscious, glossy lips and force it deep into the back of her throat until she gagged.

It was highly unusual for a client of that calibre to visit him in his office – usually it was a question of their accountant contacting him directly and all communication went through them. But he gathered she'd been on some kind of independence kick since her mother died. Wanting to take over her own affairs, manage her own money or some such bullshit. *Stick to singing, sweetheart*, thought Paul with a sneer.

But hell, as long as it had led Jenna Jonsson straight to his office, who was he to complain? Maybe next time he could get her to come over without that ape of a manager. He could ring her up with some spurious excuse; pretend to be consulting her because he really valued her opinion on whether they should invest in American pharmaceuticals or ethical fashion in India. They could conduct business over dinner. Or in a hotel

79

room. Yeah, that's the kind of business he'd like to conduct with her . . .

Which reminded him . . .

'Come through please, Angela,' he requested, pressing a button on his phone. Angela Lee was his PA. She was in her mid-thirties, short and a little on the chunky side, with mousy hair cut into a bob and black-rimmed glasses. It was better that way. In the past Paul had hired a succession of attractive and willing temps, but numerous affairs and one narrowly avoided harassment claim later, he'd plumped for the plain yet capable Angela.

She arrived in his office with her notebook and pen at the ready. Her clothes were smart, and she'd made an effort with her make-up, Paul noticed, wondering whether to point it out. He decided not to. 'I'd like you to order something for me.'

'Yes?' Angela gazed up at him, her expression eager to please.

'Well, when I say for me, I really mean for a friend of mine,' he smirked, as Angela pressed her lips into a disapproving line. She knew what was coming – it wasn't the first time he'd made this request.

'I'd like you to order some lingerie. The recipient's name is Sadie Laine and I'll email you the address. Get something from Agent Provocateur. Something red and trashy.' If Sadie was going to behave like a whore, he'd treat her like one.

'What size?' Angela's pen hovered above her notepad.

Paul sat back in his ergonomic chair, brushed a piece of lint from his Gieves & Hawkes bespoke suit and looked her over appraisingly. Behind him the wide glass windows offered a stunning panoramic view over the City, the world's financial hub where billions of dollars were traded every day by the rich and powerful.

They were the Masters of the Universe. Men like Paul Austin were untouchable and they made their own rules.

'I'm not sure exactly.' He pretended to consider the issue. 'She's considerably thinner than you are – she works out, you see. You don't go to the gym, do you Angela?'

Cheeks flaming, Angela shook her head. She made a mental note to join tomorrow.

'I didn't think so. She has a flat stomach, slim hips.' His eyes trailed over Angela's body, coming to rest on her chest. 'And her breasts are larger than yours. Do you think you can work out the sizing from that, hmm? Just do your best, sweetheart.'

'I will,' Angela assured him. Her face was still flushed from the way his gaze had lingered on her breasts. She found herself wondering who his latest floozy was – where she lived, what she looked like. What she had that Angela didn't . . .

Over the months that she had worked for him, Angela had seen a string of mistresses come and go, one after the next, all at the beck and call of Paul Austin. He didn't seem to realize that Angela was waiting for him, ready to fulfil his every desire. No matter how hard she tried with her appearance – skirts getting shorter, outfits tighter and more revealing – he rarely paid her a second glance.

She knew she was a walking cliché, the wistful secretary in love with her boss, but she couldn't help herself. She regularly found herself wondering what it would be like to be the wife of a man like Mr Austin. Angela had never been the pretty girl, the popular girl that all the boys wanted. When the women in the office went on a night out, Angela was never invited. She would see them in the toilets on Friday evenings, applying lip gloss and styling their hair, all chattering and laughing, and she longed to be part of that group. She knew that dating someone like Paul Austin would bring her instant status. If she was with him, they would have to be nice to her. They would have to treat her with respect.

Instead, Angela spent her Friday nights at home in her dingy studio flat, dreaming of the day when Mr Austin would finally notice her as something more than his über-efficient secretary. She would curl up in her lonely bed and let her hands slip down between her legs, wrapped up in the fantasy, imagining him striding masterfully across the office towards her and . . .

She realized she'd been staring at him. He was looking at her, an amused expression on his handsome face. 'Is everything okay, Angela?'

'Fine.' She recovered herself. 'Fine. Will there be anything else?' she asked, trying to keep the hopeful note out of her voice.

'I think that's everything.' Angela turned to go but Paul stopped her. 'Oh, have there been any messages for me?'

'Yes.' Angela checked her notepad and made a face. 'Your wife called. She said not to forget that you're having dinner with John and Melissa Van Nordstrom, and if you could try to get home early because the boys have been asking to see you.'

'Thank you,' Paul said smoothly, not displaying the slightest trace of conscience over having his PA juggle his wife and mistress.

If she was being honest with herself, Angela knew her boss could be a complete and utter shit. But that didn't stop him being the most attractive man she'd ever laid eyes on. There was something magnetic about him, a confidence and charisma that drew women in. She knew he wasn't happy with his wife – that was obviously the reason he had so many affairs. Angela could make him happy, she felt sure of it. All she needed was an opportunity.

'One two three four, cross turn slam change. Good. And again . . .'

Sadie was sweating hard. She felt it trickle down her back, beading between her breasts as the dance teacher issued rapid staccato instructions, rattling them off like a machine gun. Behind his voice was the hard pounding of some underground R'n'B track, a relentless beat as the singer rapped over the top. It was turned up so loud that the windows vibrated.

She was at a hip-hop class at Danceworks, the dance studio just off Bond Street. Around her the young and gorgeous gyrated and grooved, all united in one purpose: to dance. Beside her was a sexy mixed-race guy with a shaved head and a tight white vest. His body was ripped, his muscles bulging; it was incredible to Sadie how such a big guy could move with such precision and swiftness. To her right, a girl with backcombed, dirty-blonde hair and grey jogging bottoms rolled up to her knees ran through the steps as if she'd been born doing them. Their moves were fast and sharp, their attitudes fierce. They revelled in the physicality, the sheer joy of movement.

Sadie was locked in concentration, trying to master the complicated routine. She knew she needed to just let loose and feel the moves, but she couldn't seem to relax. It was over a month since she'd attended a dance class and her body was letting her down. In frustration, she swiped a hand across her forehead. Despite the chilly day outside, the studio was baking and the large standing fans did little to cool it. Sadie had pulled her dark hair back into a tight ponytail, but strands were working loose as she danced, plastering themselves to her damp cheeks. She was wearing an ancient pair of baggy black drawstring pants and a loose white vest top. The laid-back clothes emphasized her long, lean limbs with their sinewy muscles. Her breasts were small and sharp through the thin cotton top, her stomach flat and toned. She looked like a dancer. She looked fantastic.

'One and two and three and yeah, punch, punch, stop, roll . . .'

Jeez, this guy was relentless! But Sadie was determined to get it. She realized how long it was since she'd properly worked out. Moves that used to be easy, automatic, now took effort. And she tired quickly – her stamina was shot, and she was sweating like a man. But she couldn't deny that the buzz was there. The adrenaline was pumping, the endorphins rushing through her body, giving her that sweet natural high that she craved. This was what she loved and she was excited to be back out there. She was up for the challenge, willing to do whatever it took to fulfil her ambitions.

To raise the stakes, Sadie imagined this wasn't a class but a real performance. Gone were the grimy mirrored walls, the dusty floor and the pile of abandoned exercise mats in the corner. In her mind she was out there, live on stage in front of thousands of people with all eyes focused on her so she couldn't mess up. She saw herself standing alone in the darkness with a single spotlight picking her out as she wowed the crowd. The thought unconsciously made her up her game – her movements became sharper, her head snapped up and her eyes came alive with that joyous sparkle that couldn't be faked. Was this what Jenna Jonsson felt like, she wondered suddenly? Was this what she experienced every day, this rush from being watched, adored and idolized?

'Okay, one final time, make it good people, give it everything . . .'

Sadie barely heard the teacher as he restarted the music. Her body was racing through the steps instinctively, her mind not stopping to think. This was blissful – she felt like she was flying. She was strong, sexy and powerful. She felt her body move, her hips grinding, pelvis rolling, ribs slinking from side to side. For a second she closed her eyes, imagining the adoring crowd below her, wowed by her every movement and in awe of her talent.

Then the fantasy changed and she imagined she was dancing for Paul. She visualized his face in the crowd as she put on the performance, his pale blue eyes trained on her intensely, that handsome face unable to tear his gaze away from her. He'd probably come in his pants right there, she thought with a grin. He'd love the way she was moving, all that rolling and grinding. She couldn't wait to see him again. She'd barely stopped smiling since that afternoon in the May Fair. Maybe she'd do a private show for him next time. Yeah, persuade him to book a suite somewhere with its own pole . . .

'And pow! Hold the final position . . . and finish! Okay, great class people.'

The group collapsed, exhausted but elated. Some clapped – a few even whooped. Then they quickly dispersed.

Sadie headed downstairs to the changing rooms. Her limbs were aching but she felt amazing. She showered quickly, dressing casually in skinny jeans, vest top and a cropped jacket with an oversized scarf from H&M wound several times round her neck. She pinned her damp hair up and applied a little Maybelline mascara. She didn't bother with any other make-up. She didn't need to – her skin was flawless and glowing, flushed pink from the exercise and the hot shower. Swinging her bag over her shoulder, she headed back upstairs.

'Bye Faye,' she called out to the glamorous bleached blonde on reception.

'Great to see you back again,' Faye grinned, giving her a little wave.

Stepping outside, Sadie turned up towards Selfridges, wondering if she could afford to treat herself to a little something. Maybe a new lip gloss, or even a pair of shoes for her next date with Paul . . .

She felt her mobile vibrate in her bag, and her heart leapt. She hated to admit it, but her very first thought was that she hoped it was him. As she pulled it out, Sadie saw her agent's name flashing on the caller display.

'Hi Gill.'

'Hi Sadie.' Gill got straight down to business. 'I've got you an audition for this afternoon. Three p.m. in Soho, can you make it?'

Sadie felt a jolt of excitement shoot through her stomach. Every audition was a chance to progress her career. Even if you didn't get the job, there was always the opportunity to meet people and make new contacts. Who knew where it might lead?

'Sure,' she replied. 'No problem. I'm in town at the moment and I've got my dance gear with me. What is it for?'

'It's a commercial,' Gill explained. 'For some new shampoo. You're looking all down and miserable, then you use the shampoo and suddenly you're up and dancing. The brief says elegant – you're floating and twirling like a ballet dancer, not raving at the disco.'

'Okay Gill, no problem.'

'Excellent, I'll text you the address. Have you picked up a copy of *The Stage* this week?'

'Not yet . . .'

'Get one. I'm not your skivvy, y'know – you've got to put some effort in too.'

'Okay Gill, will do,' Sadie smiled.

Gillian was always on the go, gabbling at a hundred miles an hour in that south London accent. She was a hustler, an ex-dancer who'd turned forty, divorced her husband and started her own agency. She tended to bark out details and Sadie kept her answers as short as possible.

'Great. Speak to you later, hon.' Gill hung up.

Swiftly, Sadie turned around, heading into the maze-like backstreets of Mayfair to find a newsagent. She had a spring in her step as she walked. Not only did she have a hot, sexy, loaded new guy, but her career was getting back on track as well. The hip-hop class had left her full of energy and boosted her confidence. She looked good and she knew it. She felt the familiar tingle of excitement and nerves at the prospect of an audition, but she was up for it, eager for the chance to get out there and prove herself. Yeah, Sadie Laine was back in the game and she was going to be more than just a contender – she wanted to be a serious player. With self-belief, hard work and a shed-load of talent, how could she possibly fail?

She found a newsagent and headed inside to pick up a copy of *The Stage*, but something else caught her attention. It was the headline on the front of every tabloid, and the accompanying photos of Jenna Jonsson and Ryan Jackson.

Well, well, well, thought Sadie, her mood brightening even more as she saw the battering her old rival was getting from the papers. *Looks like both of us got laid last night.*

9

'Jenna, what the fuck is going on?' Gerry King screamed down the phone.

'I don't know, Gerry, I don't know. Oh God, I'm so sorry. I swear nothing happened – it's all lies, I promise,' Jenna apologized hysterically.

'I've been trying to get through all fucking morning – where the hell have you been?'

'I'm sorry, Gerry, I've only just woken up. I guess my mobile was off and—'

'Jesus, it's all right for some,' interrupted Gerry, under his breath.

'. . . And then this morning when I saw the news I turned it back on, but it wouldn't stop ringing, Gerry, the phone just wouldn't stop!'

'Do you know what a mess this is Jenna? I've spent all fucking night trying to sort this out, while you were blissfully unconscious.'

'I'm so sorry, Gerry.' Jenna was crying now, struggling to get the words out. 'It wasn't my fault, I don't know what . . .' She trailed off, not even knowing what she was trying to say.

'Look, get yourself over here and we'll take care of it. Figure out some way to get out of this hole.'

'Just tell them it's all lies – sue their fucking arses.'

'It might not be that simple,' Gerry warned ominously. 'I didn't want to do anything before I spoke to you, but we need to put out a statement – my people can't hold them off for much longer.'

'You want me to come over? You think I'm in any state to go out?' Jenna exploded. 'I look like shit and there are a pack of photographers out there. Do you know how many people are out there, Gerry?' she demanded. 'The street's packed and it's absolute mayhem. My neighbours are going to be so pissed off,' she added irrationally.

'Okay, fair point,' admitted Gerry, forcing himself to stay calm as he realized how upset Jenna was. 'But I need to talk to you. I'll come over, okay? Stay put until I get there.'

'I'm hardly gonna go fucking shopping!' screamed Jenna, but Gerry had hung up. She stared at the phone in her hand and it immediately began ringing again. Withheld number.

Out of some morbid curiosity she couldn't quite explain, Jenna answered it. 'Hello?' she asked cautiously. An unfamiliar male voice began yelling at her. 'Jenna, what can you tell us about this morning's reports that—'

Jenna hung up and quickly turned off the phone. Feeling nauseous, she collapsed onto a chair, looking around her in despair. By now the papers had been delivered and Jenna had spread them out on the kitchen table where the damning images stared back at her.

Both *The Mirror* and *The Sun* carried the same photo on their front page – it was dark and grainy, yet undeniably showed Ryan embracing her in the car.

It's Always the Quiet Ones! screamed *The Mirror*, noting Ryan's reputation as the quiet one from the band. With shaking fingers she turned to the fourth and fifth pages, which contained more lurid headlines and further inflammatory photos – Ryan and Jenna embracing in the car; Ryan and Jenna arguing in the street; Ryan leading Jenna into the house, one arm resting on her back; and finally, Ryan leaving her house, appearing to glance guiltily down the street. He wasn't, of course, but that was the clear inference, and Ryan's expression unfortunately tied in with that. The final picture was timed 12.06 a.m., almost an hour after the first.

Jenna felt sick. Her coffee sat untouched on the table beside the two empty mugs from the tea that she and Ryan had drunk the night before.

Randy Jen Does It Again! proclaimed *The Sun*, before going on to a double-page feature detailing all the guys she'd dated over the past few years, including her split with Will Rothwell.

After working her way through some of the world's most eligible bachelors, Jenna Jonsson, 23, has now turned her attention to eligible married men, commented the accompanying text.

Oh, and, surprise surprise, thought Jenna, as she skimmed one of the articles and noticed they'd dredged up the old and untrue rumour that she'd secretly dated Prince Harry for a while. Well, who cared about the truth if it made a good story, thought Jenna angrily, throwing down the paper in disgust. Large, wet tears streamed down her face and dripped onto the newspapers, blurring the words as the ink began to run. Jenna wished they could wash the words from the paper and erase everything that was written there. It was just too horrible to think about.

A wave of unbearable loneliness engulfed her as she realized just how desperately she missed her mother. Since her death, Jenna had had no one to turn to. Her father was in another country and clearly didn't give a damn about her. She didn't have any close female friends – her mother had always warned her not to get too close to her rivals as it might dull her competitive edge, telling her that no matter how sincere people might seem, they wouldn't hesitate to sell a story on her for the right figure. Georgia had drilled it into her only daughter that everyone could be bought and no one could be trusted. It was a miserable way to live, but Georgia was convinced the rewards were worth it.

At the moment, Jenna wasn't so sure.

Scanning over the list of guys she'd dated, she realized with horror that the newspapers were right. She couldn't even remember the last time she'd been single for any length of time. She'd bounced from one relationship to the next, looking for the love and security she craved. It didn't matter how unsuitable the guy, as long as they could temporarily fill the void. She pursued the richest, the best looking, the most powerful – anything to quell her own feelings of insecurity. And now she had no one.

Maybe she could ring Susie, the girl who always did her make-up for major events? They'd worked together since Jenna first started out so she was able to treat Jenna as a human being rather than reverentially, as a living icon, the way everyone else seemed to. *But I don't want to pour my heart out to some make-up girl I last saw three weeks ago . . .*

Infuriatingly, the name that kept popping into her head was Ryan's.

She wanted to call Ryan.

Jenna found a tissue and wiped her eyes as she mulled over the situation. Maybe it was a bad idea. But, on the other hand, it wasn't as if any of this was true – surely his wife would realize that? Ryan would understand what she was going through and could give her the comfort she craved. He was a nice guy. He might even come over, Jenna thought hopefully, before the baying of the press pack outside reminded her that would be impossible.

But he had been so good to her last night, and she desperately needed someone to talk to . . .

Finding her Birkin bag dumped on a chair in the lounge, she rifled through it until she located her second mobile. The private one. The one that no one but Gerry and her father had the number for. Without giving herself time to hesitate, she rang Ryan's mobile number.

'Please hold the line. Your call is being transferred,' the monotonous voice at the other end repeated for what seemed like an eternity. Jenna's heart began to thump as she paced the floor impatiently.

'Clive Goldman's office,' said an exhausted-sounding voice with an LA accent.

Ryan must have had his calls transferred to his manager's office, Jenna realized. He was probably being besieged by the press, too, with his family having to take the same shit she was dealing with.

'I'd like to speak to Clive Goldman.'

'Mr Goldman's not available right now,' the secretary said shortly. 'Can I take a message?'

'It's about Ryan Jackson—' she began hesitantly, before the woman cut her off.

'We're not making any further comment at this time. A statement was released a couple of hours ago which I can fax or email if you give me your details. At this time, there's nothing more to add to the story regarding Ryan Jackson and Jenna Jonsson.'

'This *is* Jenna Jonsson,' stated Jenna arrogantly, her patience finally snapping. 'Mr Goldman might want to speak to me.'

There was a brief pause. 'Certainly, Miss Jonsson,' came the polite but frosty reply. 'If you could hold for one moment, I'll just check he's available.'

Jenna held. A few moments later she recognized the gruff tones of Clive Goldman.

'Ms Jonsson, what can I do for you this fine morning?' he began sarcastically. 'Or should I say, the middle of the night, because that's what time it is here and I haven't been to fucking bed yet.'

'I, er . . .' Jenna trailed off, not sure what she wanted now that she had him on the line.

'Yes Ms Jonsson? I'm a busy man.'

'I wanted to speak to Ryan,' Jenna stammered finally. She gripped the phone tightly, her heart pounding in her chest. 'I tried to call him, but it was diverted to you.'

Clive Goldman let out a guffaw of incredulity. 'I'm sorry, Ms Jonsson,' he chuckled when he'd recovered. 'I don't think that's going to be possible today.'

Jenna swallowed hard. 'I just want to talk to him,' she said, trying to keep her voice steady. 'I didn't do anything.'

Clive's voice took on a hard edge. 'Look, I don't know what your game is, but you've caused enough trouble.'

'But nothing happened,' Jenna protested desperately. 'Surely you've spoken to Ryan? He must have told you that.'

'Quite frankly, Ms Jonsson, that has very little to do

with it. The accusation has been made, and what we're engaging in now is a little exercise called damage limitation. I've been in touch with your manager and I understand he'll be coming to see you shortly. If you want to contact me again, I suggest you do so through him, because I'd really like to get home to my wife sometime before sunrise. I would also suggest that, for the time being, you don't try to contact Ryan Jackson. Have a nice day, Ms Jonsson,' he finished, his voice laden with sarcasm.

'I didn't do anything,' Jenna repeated, her voice barely a whisper. But Clive had hung up.

The phone sat uselessly in Jenna's hand and she simply stared at it, not knowing what else to do. Why was everyone treating her like this? Nothing had happened! Her eyes felt hot as a new wave of tears pricked at the corners, and Jenna bit her lip, determined not to break down again.

The doorbell rang and Jenna started. She hurried to the front of the house, wondering if Gerry had arrived or if the press had simply recommenced their hounding. Discreetly, she attempted to pull aside the curtain to see who was at the door. But the waiting paparazzi were alert to every movement and, as soon as the curtains twitched, a barrage of flashbulbs lit up the street.

'Shit,' she swore, hoping she hadn't just given them tomorrow's front page – Jenna Jonsson, trapped in her own home like a guilty prisoner. She touched her hair; it felt flat and greasy. She knew her face must be flushed and puffy.

Jenna's mobile began to ring. Glancing down, she realized she was still clutching it in her hand.

It was Gerry.

'I'm outside,' he yelled, struggling to make himself heard above the pandemonium in the usually tranquil street. 'Can you hear me?' he bellowed. 'Let me in!'

'I'm coming now, Gerry,' Jenna shouted, turning off her phone as she hurried through to the front hall.

She stayed hidden behind the door as she opened it and, after a slight scuffle with an over-eager photographer, Gerry squeezed his way in. His suit was crumpled, his face bright red and sweating. Jenna thought she had never seen him look so angry.

'What a fucking mess,' he roared at her. 'What the hell's going on, Jenna?'

'Please don't shout,' Jenna pleaded. 'I feel like shit.'

'*You* feel like shit?' exploded Gerry. 'I'm the one who hasn't slept all night 'cos I was trying to clear up your mess – fielding calls from the press, trying to kill the story. You're the one who's had the easy ride, gallivanting around doing what you damn well please as usual.'

'I haven't *done* anything!' yelled Jenna. 'Jesus, why is everyone treating me like I've committed the crime of the century? *Nothing happened,* Gerry,' she stated, slowly and deliberately. 'I was upset, Ryan was nice to me, he brought me in, we drank tea. How is that a story that requires half the world's press on my doorstep?'

'Come on, Jenna, you've been playing this game for long enough now. Didn't you think about what it would look like? Christ, if only you'd given it another half an hour before bursting into tears, it might have been too late to make the morning editions.'

'Fuck you!' retorted Jenna, feeling adrenaline surge through her. 'Don't you dare speak to me like that. You think you're having a hard time? All you have to do is sit in an office playing games with the press. I'm the one who has to go out there and get labelled a slut and a home-wrecker. I don't know what my mother would think,' she added.

'She'd probably think it was good publicity.'

There was a loud crack as Jenna slapped him.

Gerry held his stinging cheek, his breath coming fast as Jenna glared at him, her eye contact unflinching.

'I'm sorry,' Gerry said finally. 'That was out of order.'

'Damn right it was,' shot back Jenna, her green eyes blazing.

There was silence as they stood glaring at each other, the tension heavy in the air.

'This is really not what I need right now,' Jenna said quietly, her voice threatening to break.

Gerry sighed. 'Okay sweetheart, I'm sorry,' he apologized. 'This is getting us nowhere. I came over here to sort out how to get us out of this mess, not to have a slanging match.'

'I know,' Jenna agreed grudgingly.

'What were you upset about?' asked Gerry, and Jenna knew he was asking less out of concern for her and more from a managerial point of view. If something was affecting his client, he needed to know.

Jenna paused, wondering how to answer. She didn't want him to pull the whole Phoenix venture after she had worked so hard to get him to agree in the first place.

'Zac . . .' she began hesitantly. 'We're having a few teething problems – a sort of . . . clash of personalities. It's not my fault, Gerry,' she protested, seeing the look on his face. 'I'm working really hard, but he doesn't appreciate it. He doesn't seem to like having me around. The rest of the guys say it's because he's used to working with Josh, but I don't know. Anyway, Ryan gave me a lift home, we talked about it, and I got upset,' she shrugged. 'He was great. And now this . . .' Jenna finished, indicating the salacious headlines.

Gerry was silent, digesting this revelation as he followed Jenna's gaze to the papers on the table. 'I hate to ask you this,' he began finally, 'but I have to know, Jenna. You have to be entirely honest with me – did anything happen with Ryan?'

'Gerry! How can you even ask me that?'

'Okay, okay,' he backtracked quickly, holding up his hands. 'I just needed to know.'

'Well now you know,' Jenna snapped back petulantly.

'I heard you spoke to Clive Goldman earlier,' Gerry continued, acting as though she hadn't spoken.

'That's right,' Jenna said breezily. 'You've got your finger on the pulse as usual. Can I even go to the toilet without you knowing about it?'

'That wasn't a clever thing to do, Jenna,' Gerry reproached her, ignoring the outburst.

'Well, I guess I've done a lot of things that aren't so clever this past twenty-four hours,' she snapped.

'He said you wanted to speak to Ryan?' Gerry pressed.

'So?'

'Jenna,' began Gerry, rubbing his forehead with exasperation. 'What the hell are you playing at?'

'I was lonely, Gerry,' Jenna yelled back. 'There was no one here for me and I was going through hell. Ryan had been so great last night and I thought he was the only one who would understand. I wanted to make sure he was okay – that it was all okay with Kelly and everything . . .' she trailed off lamely.

Gerry looked back at her wearily. Her eyes were red from crying, and she looked as though she might burst into tears again at any moment. There were times when he forgot how young she was and how much she'd been through.

'I'd leave it for a while,' he said lightly.

Jenna swallowed. 'What's going to happen?' she asked after a pause.

'I think you need to get away – leave the country for a week or two until it all blows over.'

'But what about Phoenix?' Jenna asked, panicked. She'd worked so hard to get Gerry to agree to the collaboration in the first place, she couldn't have it snatched away from her now.

'Do you want to carry on working with them? You think you can sort out these problems?'

Jenna nodded vigorously.

'Are you sure? Because I'm not willing to put both our reputations on the line for something that could be a total fucking disaster.'

'I'll sort it, Gerry,' she insisted.

'Right.' Gerry looked at her closely. 'I'll contact Clive while you're away, speak to the band and see what they're saying.'

'Why can't I speak to them?' Jenna asked, suddenly suspicious.

Gerry sighed. 'Look Jenna, I don't know exactly what's gone on here, but it's clear there've been some problems. I just think it's better, for the time being, if you give the guys some space, let the dust settle. Then everyone can decide what they really want to do. Okay?'

'But—'

'Just trust me on this one,' Gerry said firmly.

Jenna took a deep breath, but kept her mouth shut.

'How about if you borrow my villa?' Gerry suggested. 'Hide out there for a few days?'

'Thanks, Gerry. That'd be fantastic.'

'Get out there, get your head straight, then come back and make me a hit record. Okay, kiddo?'

Jenna started to smile.

'That's my girl,' Gerry winked. 'You, sweetheart, are going to be fabulous. Trust me.'

10

Sadie was completely naked beneath her short, beige trench coat. As she keyed in the entrance code to the exclusive, gated apartment block in London's Docklands, she felt sure that everyone must be able to tell, from the porter who gave her a lascivious wink, to the overly Botoxed woman who eyed her with suspicion as she passed her in the lobby.

Self-consciously, Sadie waited for the lift to the penthouse. She pulled her collar more tightly around her, hoping she hadn't just given the concierge a glimpse of her breasts. Her long, bare legs tapered down into sky-high Louboutins, the latest present from Paul.

He'd sent her numerous little gifts over the past couple of weeks, each with detailed instructions on what she should do with them. First there had been the set from Agent Provocateur – French knickers, peephole bra and garter belt, all in red, which she had been told to wear with black stockings and a dress that was 'easy to remove'. Paul sent a taxi to pick her up and she had spent the journey across London feeling horny as hell, squirming into the back seat. Paul evidently felt the same – he was pacing the room as she arrived, his erection clearly visible through his trousers. He'd taken her as soon as she entered the room and she'd been ready for him, her body on fire, slick between the legs. She'd come within seconds.

Two days later, a courier delivered the most beautiful silk dress by Issa. Full length and midnight blue, it poured over Sadie's stunning figure like water. She stood in front of the cracked, three-quarter-length mirror in her untidy bedroom, a world away from the sumptuous room at the May Fair, and gazed at her reflection. She wanted to cry. She didn't think she'd ever looked so elegant in her life. She looked like a movie star.

The note simply said *Look beautiful* – and Sadie didn't disappoint. She swept her dark hair up to show off her superb bone structure, and added drop earrings with a turquoise stone. She kept her make-up light and fresh; she knew that her youth was her asset and didn't want to smother it beneath layers of foundation and powder.

As she was dressed for dinner, she assumed they would be going out for a meal. She was excited, wondering how it would feel to be seen in public with this handsome, powerful man. Would he flaunt her brazenly, or would they go somewhere discreet and secluded? But Paul's appetite wasn't for food – it was for Sadie.

This time she entered the hotel room to find him sitting casually on the bed, as though waiting for something. He was still wearing his work suit but had removed the jacket and tie. His white shirt was unbuttoned, offering a tantalizing glimpse of that strong, tanned chest with its smattering of dark hair. He was the kind of guy that Sadie couldn't imagine ever slobbing out in jogging bottoms or jeans. He radiated authority and control, and the well-groomed image was an integral part of that.

Paul commanded Sadie to stand in the middle of the room, where he could see her. Sadie did as she was told, as Paul went on to give her step-by-step instructions of exactly what he wanted her to do. On his order she unzipped the dress and let it fall, slithering down her body to land in an expensive heap on the floor, and revealing the strapless bra and delicate lace thong beneath. Paul did nothing. He merely watched, yet his eyes were eating her alive and his cock was straining against his trousers. Slowly, he ordered Sadie to fully undress, and then to turn around so he could view her from every angle. The exposure was torture, yet the anticipation of what was to come was exquisite. Finally he told her to touch herself.

Sadie moaned as she gently slid her fingers inside the damp triangle and began to slowly stroke herself. She knew exactly where to touch, able to do the things that turned her on the most. Sighing, she closed her eyes.

'Open them,' Paul snapped.

Her face was flushed with desire as she looked at him. She could make out the lines of his firm, hard body where his shirt was pulled taut against the strong muscles. With longing, she gazed at the bulge in his trousers and slipped a finger inside herself. Her knees began to give way but Paul wouldn't let her fall, commanding her to stay upright. He was mesmerized, loving the power he had over her. She would do anything he said at this moment, and he knew it.

'Now come for me, Sadie,' he whispered hoarsely. And she did. It was blessed, sweet relief as she felt her body tighten and explode into black. Paul watched as her stomach muscles convulsed and then relaxed. He finally allowed her to drop to her knees before he strode over and found his own release, his warm, clear juices flowing over her neck and breasts. The dress on the floor had been stained worse than Monica Lewinsky's.

After that, he'd sent Sadie an oversize Prada bag containing a spanking paddle and a pair of handcuffs. They'd certainly put those to good use. There had been bondage clothing, and a variety of oils and lotions. And now Sadie had received his most extreme request yet – the sexy-as-hell Louboutins, with their fuck-me heels and a note saying: *Wear these. Nothing else.*

It was as though he'd been building up to this. Testing her boundaries and seeing how far he could push her. Yeah, having a secret lover who was filthy rich was certainly a way to get some excitement into your life, Sadie reflected. It was thrilling. Addictive. She was seeing him every other day during the week – the weekends were for the kids, he'd reminded her, always making sure that she didn't get too attached, that she knew what the score was.

Sadie was fine with that – it suited her perfectly. It meant she still had time to herself, time to pursue her other great passion: her career. She firmly believed that her relationship – whatever it was – with Paul had made her dancing even better. It had revealed a sexual, provocative edge that came out of knowing her own body and being confident in her sexuality. That, and walking around like a bitch on heat the whole time.

'Wow, Sadie, that was *hot!*' commented Carla, after they took a class together.

'Yeah, you were on fire,' agreed their friend, Leonie.

Besides, Paul had hinted that he might introduce her to some of his clients. He was always bragging about his contacts – that he knew this television executive or that record producer. His social and business circle was wide. He had friends in the entertainment industry, in the arts, journalism, law and banking. And he'd told her with pride that even when his clients lost out on the deals he made, he *always* made money.

'It's a win-win situation for me,' he'd boasted.

Vaguely, Sadie wondered when he found the time to work. They seemed to lose whole afternoons in one hotel or another, never tiring, never satiated. The sex was undoubtedly incredible. They delighted in discovering each other's bodies, pushing the boundaries and exploring their limits. Paul was so masterful, so assured, that Sadie, at 23, felt like a novice beside him, yet she was loving being taught by this handsome, older guy. Paul, in return, found himself unbelievably turned on by how responsive she was, by how absolutely he could dominate her.

And now she was walking down the long corridor on the top floor of the apartment block, her new heels sinking into the plush carpet. Standing outside the door, Sadie brushed down her coat, checking her appearance one last time before she raised her hand and pressed the buzzer. She felt excited and strangely nervous as she wondered what Paul had in store for her today. Her heart began to beat a little faster, the familiar anticipatory heat flooding her belly.

Then Paul opened the door and all her nerves evaporated. He looked delicious, in a charcoal grey suit and his usual crisp, white shirt. He pulled her to him, kissing her deeply before showing her into the apartment.

'Paul, it's beautiful,' Sadie breathed, as she stared round, open-mouthed.

It was a split-level duplex, 2,000 square feet with huge windows that flooded the room with light and overlooked the Thames below. The living area boasted an enormous L-shaped sofa that could easily have seated twenty, and the whitewashed walls were hung with large pieces of abstract art.

'My bachelor pad,' Paul grinned, as he strode over to the glass coffee table where a bottle of Krug and two glasses nestled inside a silver ice bucket. 'My wife doesn't even know this place exists. It's for very close friends only.'

The bottle opened with a pop, the liquid foaming up as Paul poured them each a glass.

'To us,' he toasted.

'To us,' Sadie agreed, unable to keep the smile from her face. As she drank the champagne, feeling the tiny bubbles tingle in her mouth, she couldn't remember a time when she'd ever felt so happy. Sadie had sworn to herself that she wasn't going to fall for this guy – that it was purely about the sex, and she wasn't going to get involved – but it was pretty hard to keep that promise when Paul was behaving like this. She didn't think any man had ever made her feel so special, so loved. He treated her like a goddess.

Sadie drained her glass, licking her lips. Paul watched her and smiled. He poured her another, then led her out onto the terrace. It was small but perfect, with just a few potted plants to break it up, and a round table with two chairs. Paul's building was a little higher than those around it, so the balcony

106

wasn't overlooked. Trellises had been placed at either end, ensuring complete privacy. Sadie put down her champagne, and gazed out over the view, the low, grey skies seeming to stretch forever over London and east to the suburbs beyond. Below them, the muddy brown waters of the Thames flowed past, the imposing structure of Canary Wharf looming up just round the river bend, with the City skyscrapers in the distance.

Sadie gasped as she felt Paul come up behind her, running his hands slowly along the inside of her legs underneath the trench coat. His thumbs pressed into her inner thigh, his strong hands sliding firmly upwards, caressing her butt cheeks. Then his hands slid round to the front, his palms gently parting her legs as he began to stroke the slick nub.

She pressed her body back against him and Paul held her close, his mouth next to her ear as he growled, 'Do you want me to fuck you here, hmm? Is that what you want, sexy Sadie?'

Sadie couldn't answer. She was crushed against the railings, with Paul behind her and the deep, flowing water far below. 'Paul . . .' she breathed.

Gently, he turned her round so she was facing him. In the six-inch heels, Sadie was the same height, and they stood eye to eye. He could see the way her cheeks were flushed, her lips parted.

'No,' he said finally. 'Not out here. I have a surprise for you.'

'A surprise?' Sadie's eyes lit up. 'What is it?'

'You might find out if you're lucky. Now be a good girl and drink your champagne.'

Sadie giggled and did as she was told, following Paul back inside where he promptly poured her another glass, draining the bottle. At the back of her mind,

Sadie had the thought that she should probably slow down. It was just after lunch and she'd barely eaten; already she was beginning to feel light-headed.

Paul took her by the hand, leading her up the spiral staircase to the mezzanine level. Idly, Sadie wondered what the surprise was. Perhaps he had scattered the bed with rose petals, and was planning a romantic afternoon. Or maybe the bathroom contained a fabulous Jacuzzi, surrounded by candles and filled with scented bubbles.

Paul opened the door and indicated Sadie should go through. She smiled up at him, her eyes sparkling happily. As she walked into the bedroom, it took a moment for her eyes to adjust to the darkness; the blind was pulled down, and the lights were dimmed. Then she saw. Sitting on the bed was another woman.

'Paul . . .?' Sadie began uncertainly, turning to him. The woman was of Oriental appearance – Malaysian, Sadie would have guessed – and she was in her late twenties. She was wearing a black latex basque, with thigh-high boots that made her legs go on forever, and she had very long, very black hair slicked back into an excessively tight ponytail.

'Do you like your surprise?' Paul smiled.

'I'm not . . . What's going on?'

'This is Leilani,' Paul began easily. 'I thought it might be fun if you two got together.'

'I . . .' Sadie faltered. The woman was watching her, an amused look on her face.

'I thought you might enjoy it. I know I would,' Paul murmured softly. His breath was warm against her neck, his tone persuasive.

'Who is she?' Sadie demanded, trying to put the pieces together. Her words were a little slurred, and she took a slug of champagne to steady herself. Was this his wife? It certainly didn't seem like it, unless his wife had a thing for fetish clothing and slutty underwear. It was pure hooker chic.

And then the penny dropped.

'She's a prostitute!' Sadie burst out.

'That's not very polite,' Paul admonished her with a smirk. 'I prefer the term escort. You should be flattered; she's one of the best in the business. I didn't just pick her up off the pavement outside King's Cross, you know.'

Sadie swallowed, feeling uneasy.

'Not getting frigid on me are you? I've got a wife for that.' Paul laughed at his own joke. 'Perhaps another drink might chill you out. I have your favourite.'

He moved across to the dresser, and Sadie noticed a tray set up with a bottle of Grey Goose vodka, three glasses and an ice container. Paul fixed her one, adding a block of ice with a generous measure of alcohol.

Sadie took it. She hesitated for a brief moment, then knocked the drink back in one, the clear liquid burning her throat. It was instantly soothing, numbing her thoughts and making her delightfully fuzzy-headed. She glanced up at Paul standing in front of her and saw the familiar flames of desire blaze in those pale, blue eyes. He was looking at her in *that* way. The way that said he wanted to fuck her right now, that he would explode if he couldn't get his cock inside her.

Involuntarily, she felt a rush of heat between her legs. What the hell, Sadie thought hazily, her inhibitions rapidly disappearing. Maybe it would be fun. Wasn't that what this fling with Paul was all about? Trying new things, learning about herself sexually. She'd never considered herself a prude, and she badly wanted to please him.

Maybe Paul was right. This could be one hell of an experience. It could be wild.

She stepped towards him and Paul was instantly upon her, holding her head tightly between his palms as he kissed her deeply, his tongue roaming inside her mouth. She didn't hear Leilani get up from the bed but suddenly Sadie was aware that she was behind her, sliding her hands round to the front to undo the belt on Sadie's trench. One by one, she undid the buttons until the coat was hanging open. Sadie pressed herself against Paul as Leilani slipped the coat from Sadie's shoulders, leaving her naked apart from the black Louboutins.

Paul began to unbutton his shirt as Sadie stood awkwardly. He pushed her gently towards Leilani and Sadie acquiesced. She closed her eyes as Leilani drew closer, feeling the other woman's mouth on hers. It was soft and warm, more gentle than kissing Paul had been. Feeling brave, she caressed Leilani's shoulders as Leilani began to kiss her neck, her hands on her breasts, her mouth moving down to her nipples. Sadie lazily opened her eyes, wondering where Paul was. He was completely naked now, smiling as he watched the pair of them.

He indicated they should move to the bed. Sadie slipped out of her shoes and climbed on, sinking into the soft sheets. The bed was enormous and she lay back, drunk and horny. She felt hands on her – she didn't know whose – but they seemed to be everywhere, doing everything she wanted. She felt a warm breath between her legs, a tongue flicking at her breasts, and then Paul's cock was at her mouth and she opened her lips and took him.

Sadie felt like she was floating, as though all of her feelings were crystallizing into the one point of heat between her legs, so intense it was almost unbearable. She could feel the first delicious waves of orgasm building, pulling her in, until that was all she could think about. Closing her eyes, she lay back and surrendered to it.

11

The day after the scandal broke, Jenna found herself in glorious seclusion, holed up in Gerry's luxury villa on the Cap d'Antibes. Stretching lazily on a sun lounger, Jenna extended one toned, slim arm and carefully applied lotion, admiring the way her skin had already begun to darken to a rich, golden colour. Her pale blonde hair had turned almost platinum following its exposure to the hot Côte d'Azur sun, and she looked stunning.

Jenna readjusted the thin scrap of fabric that was her Melissa Odabash bikini top and settled back comfortably, allowing the humid air to wrap itself around her in a reassuring embrace. The villa was equipped with a top-of-the-range security system and surrounded by high, spike-topped walls, meaning total freedom from the dreaded paparazzi. Jenna hadn't seen the papers since she'd left England and she didn't intend to. She had faith in Gerry to handle it, and for the moment she didn't want to consider anything more taxing than chilling out and de-stressing. Jenna took a deep breath as she tried to encourage her body to relax completely, inhaling the faint scent of the clematis plants that sprawled freely over the white stone walls.

Gerry's villa was beautiful, but somewhat eclectic in its design. The interior walls were all exposed stone with a few brightly coloured paintings by Picasso and Gauguin to break the monotony of the ashen backdrop. A huge stone fireplace, piled high with logs, dominated the main sitting room and was surrounded by an enormous semi-circle of white sofas.

The kitchen, with its tiled floor and solid oak table, looked more suited to a traditional Provençal farmhouse than a luxury villa on the French Riviera. Jenna had checked the fridge and found it stuffed full of glorious-looking cuisine, including a vast dish of Mediterranean-style couscous, fresh pasta sauce laden with roast vegetables, and masses of fresh fruit and salad. In the bread bin were fresh baguettes as well as a loaf of American-style sliced bread and a tempting range of pastries. Fortunately, the villa also contained a small annexe that Gerry had had converted into a gym, so Jenna decided that she could indulge in the delicious-looking pâtisserie; as long as she resolved to work it off later on the treadmill.

The master bedroom was amazing, and completely over the top. It was surprisingly feminine – an explosion of frills, nets and voiles – leading Jenna to think that Gerry's wife had been the one working closely with the designer. In the centre of the room stood an enormous, heavy, wooden four-poster bed, a stunningly romantic creation draped in white muslin. Sleeping there made Jenna feel like the heroine from some children's fairytale. The floor-to-ceiling windows faced due south, filling the room with beautiful pools of sunlight, and they led out onto a pillared balcony, which overlooked the infinity pool and immaculately kept gardens below.

It might not be the Hotel du Cap, but I could definitely enjoy this for a few days, thought Jenna, as she pushed her Gucci sunglasses further up her nose and relaxed into the soft fabric of the sun lounger, confident that the press would be unable to find her in the secluded hideaway.

Jenna's refusal to read the British papers or even check her email while she was in France meant that she remained ignorant of Clive Goldman's latest PR masterstroke. The day after she flew out to Nice, Clive released a picture that made the front pages of all the papers. It showed a beaming Ryan standing with his arms round a radiant Kelly. The accompanying text informed the reader that Kelly was three months pregnant with their third child.

Back in the UK, Gerry was making good on his promise to resolve the situation with Phoenix. He and the band were at the Fulham offices of Ultimate Management, on a video call to Clive in LA. Wrangling had been going on for over an hour, and everyone was flagging.

'Okay guys, it's your call,' Clive explained to a lethargic Phoenix. 'Naturally, we'd prefer it if the single went ahead – successfully. As callous as it sounds, this *has* been excellent publicity. I've spoken to Don and he mentioned that although you're having a few problems, there's some good material coming out.

'But if you guys really can't work with Jenna and the record's going to be . . .' he hesitated, selecting the right word, '. . . compromised, because of that, I don't want to put your reputation on the line. This is the first track you're putting out there without Josh and it has to be incredible or else the press will be writing Phoenix's obituary.'

There was a pause while the band collected their thoughts. Unusually, it was Ryan who spoke first. He blamed himself for the current situation, mad at himself for not scoping out the street that night. He'd been so preoccupied with Jenna that he hadn't even thought to check for paparazzi. It was a schoolboy error. Now his band faced being written off before they'd even made their comeback, and his newly pregnant wife was pissed at him.

'I think . . .' he began, then trailed off as he thought about how to phrase the ideas in his head. 'I mean . . . Is it really worth it? Carrying on like this?' Zac's head snapped up, and Ryan found he had the rapt attention of the others. 'Maybe we should call it a day?'

He let the thought hang, waiting to see the reaction. Clive didn't speak and Ryan was grateful for that; he knew it was something the band had to work out for themselves.

'I mean, it feels to me as if nothing's changed since Josh left. We're still going round in circles, having the same old arguments, and it's not getting us anywhere,' Ryan explained tentatively. 'I just thought I'd put the idea out there. I thought it needed voicing.'

The room fell silent. Gerry cleared his throat awkwardly, knowing that this discussion was something he wasn't part of. He was here to fight Jenna's corner, but this decision was ultimately down to Phoenix.

'I don't wanna do that. I want to carry on,' stated Nick mutinously. 'Phoenix means everything to me. Come on guys,' he appealed to them. 'So many bands break up for stupid reasons, and never achieve half the things they could have if they'd just tried a little harder. I *know* we can work through this,' he urged them. 'Think of all the things we've done, all the dreams we fulfilled – impossible things that no one else ever has. Remember when we were just four kids starting off and we wanted to conquer the world? We fucking did it, guys. We dreamed it, and we lived it, and I don't want to throw all that away.'

Nick sat back in his chair. He'd said his piece and it was out of his hands now.

Finally, Zac spoke.

'I don't know what . . . I don't know,' he finished, his brow furrowed with confusion. 'I need to think about this properly, but my instinct is that no, I don't think we should split. We went over all this when Josh left, and I guess my position now is the same as it was then – that we're not over yet, and there's still a lot we can do. Ryan?'

'I don't want to split either,' Ryan began slowly. 'I guess . . . I just thought I'd throw it out there and see what happened.' He smiled, relieved, at his band mates. The feeling of tension lifting was palpable across the room.

'Well, I'm happy I still have a band,' Clive commented. He tried to keep his tone light but his relief was obvious, even from five thousand miles away. 'So where do we go from here?'

'I kind of had an idea,' began Nick hesitantly. 'Half an idea really,' he grinned, looking round the room. 'It's just . . . well, you know I've got my place in Ibiza?'

Zac and Ryan smiled in recognition. Nick's holiday retreat in the mountains had been the scene of some wild partying when the group wanted to escape.

'It's all fitted out with recording equipment now, kind of like a small studio. I had an old farm building converted a few months back, so I can play around, test out some ideas while I'm out there.'

'I think I get where this is heading, but spell it out for me,' said Clive, looking amused.

'Well,' Nick grinned, 'Why don't we all head out there for a few days? Or however long it takes? It's such a beautiful spot, and it might be just what we need. It'd be so relaxing – the sun, the sea . . .'

'And the rest.' Clive raised an eyebrow.

Nick flushed and ran a hand through his hair. 'What do you think guys? It'd be awesome. A sort of working vacation, but we could all just chill and run through some ideas. It might give the single a really interesting vibe.'

For the first time since the meeting had begun, Zac smiled genuinely. 'Yeah, I guess it could be fun,' he replied, breaking into a grin that made his dark eyes crinkle at the corners.

'And Don can do some polishing up back in London,' Nick rushed on. 'We can just lay down the basics and he can do all his mixing and work his magic later.' He looked eagerly round the room, his eyes betraying his excitement at the thought of decamping to the Balearics with his band mates for a few leisurely, hedonistic days of music and partying.

That, and the thought of Jenna Jonsson in a bikini.

'What do you think Ryan?' asked Clive, noticing that he hadn't spoken.

'Yeah, totally. I think it's a great idea,' he enthused. 'I mean, I'll have to check with Kelly and all. I don't really want to leave her for too long now that she's pregnant, so we'd probably all fly out – the kids as well – but maybe a few days away would be good,' he rambled, wondering how Kelly would react. Although he was fairly sure she believed him that nothing had happened between him and Jenna, her pregnancy hormones were making her pretty insecure. He wasn't sure she'd thank him for agreeing to this.

'Sure,' laughed Nick good-naturedly, punching him on the shoulder. 'Bring your whole brood – it'll be fuckin' awesome!'

'And Jenna?' Clive asked. 'Gerry, do you think she'll go for it?'

Gerry's mouth twitched at the corners. A working vacation in Ibiza, with her favourite band on the planet? 'Yeah, I reckon she will,' he said casually.

Nick whooped, throwing his arms above his head in triumph.

Clive nodded slowly, spreading his hands as though to acknowledge defeat. 'Then I guess I have to give it my blessing. Go ahead. Just don't fuck it up,' he added warningly.

Tom Anderson was not a religious man, but every day he thanked God that he'd been born in the age of the Internet. For in Tom's life there was only one thing he really cared about. Something he loved more than his girlfriend, Carla, or even his mother. Pornography.

A self-confessed geek, he'd already been interested in computers when the Internet explosion really took off. For Tom, it was the answer to his prayers. Every type of porn known to man or beast – and possibly involving the two together – was available at the click of a button. With just a credit card and a laptop, he need never leave his room again.

Tom tapped a few keys on his girlfriend's laptop and a whole list of titles popped up. He selected one and set it downloading. Easy. Like candy from a baby.

He knew Carla hated him using her computer for this stuff, but what the hell. She was in the shower.

By the time she came out it would be a *fait accompli*, and Tom knew he'd be able to win her round.

His latest obsession was homemade stuff. Lately he'd found all that mass-produced crap just didn't do it for him any more. Besides, real people were dirtier than anything a film director could dream up.

The door clicked open and Tom jumped guiltily as Carla walked in. She was wrapped in a white robe, towelling her dark hair.

'Hey babe.' Carla kissed him on the forehead. 'What time are we going out?'

'I'm not sure . . .' Tom shrugged in a noncommittal way. 'Later?'

Carla glanced at the clock. 'We *are* still going, aren't we?' Tom had a habit of promising to take her somewhere nice, then changing his mind at the last minute.

'Course we are . . . I just thought we could have a little you and me time first.'

Carla sat down on the bed, leaning over his shoulder to view the computer screen. 'Tom, you know I don't like you downloading that kind of stuff . . .' She tried to keep her tone light; it pissed him off when she got all whiny. 'I thought we were going to go for a nice meal. I don't really want to watch –' she peered closer – '*Hot Asian Babe Threesome.*'

'Car-la,' Tom pleaded, doing his little-boy voice. 'It's for you and me. To enjoy together. Look, I'll delete it when we're done,' he said sulkily. She didn't answer, and he took her hands in his. 'Please baby. If you loved me you'd do it . . .'

'Tom, I *do* love you. I'm just not really into that kind of thing,' she said helplessly, willing him to change his mind. Maybe he'd just drop the subject and order them a taxi.

'You don't have to watch. I could blindfold you,'

Tom suggested hopefully. 'Come on Carla, don't get all frigid on me.'

'Tom . . .' she protested weakly. She was on the verge of tears as he began tugging at her robe. He loosened the belt and it fell open, exposing her tiny body.

Tom was instantly hard. 'Look what you've done to me, Carla,' he whispered, indicating his unimpressive erection. 'That's going to need sorting out.'

Carla looked up at him with glistening eyes, hoping she had misinterpreted what he was saying. But no, he was already sliding out of his trousers and pressing play on the computer. *Hot Asian Babe Threesome* sprang into life and Tom settled himself down on the bed beside her.

Carla hesitated. If she was lucky it wouldn't take long, and then it would all be forgotten about later in the evening as they sat in the restaurant drinking a nice bottle of red. She loved Tom, she truly did, and she knew that in his own way he loved her too. Or, at least, she hoped he did. She knew Sadie thought he was an arsehole, but they'd been together so long Carla didn't know how she'd cope without him.

She shrugged her robe off her shoulders and reluctantly knelt down on the floor. The cheap carpet scratched at her knees. She was face to face with Tom's cock, and eyed it with distaste before tentatively wrapping her lips around it.

'Oh yeah, that's right . . .' Tom said encouragingly.

Mechanically Carla slid her lips up and down, sucking half-heartedly as she tried to avoid Tom's attempts to force himself even deeper into her throat.

She could hear the noises coming from the screen behind her, as Tom groaned in unison. Somewhere at the back of her mind, she hoped none of her flatmates could hear them through the wall. Sadie's room was just next to hers, and the last thing she wanted to hear was Tom getting his rocks off.

Christ, he really was making a hell of a racket, Carla thought distractedly. He wasn't usually so vocal. She slowed down a little, but suddenly he shouted out and appeared to be trying to say something. Carla stopped and looked up, wondering if she was hurting him somehow.

'Tom?'

He could only gasp, wide-eyed and open-mouthed, as he pointed limply at the screen.

Carla twisted round, wondering what debauched image she was about to be faced with. The sight made her cry out in shock. There were three people in the frame – first was a dark-haired man, whose face was turned away from the camera. The second was an Asian woman, wearing some kind of latex fetish wear. But there was no mistaking the third woman. She was sprawled naked on the bed, legs open and dark eyes vacant as she lazily made out with the other woman. The guy stood over them, pleasuring himself.

'Oh God,' cried Carla, as she instantly recognized her best friend.

'Jesus!' yelled Tom, as he came all over Carla's freshly washed hair.

12

Jenna was packing, and the room was in chaos.

Rock music blared from the stereo, and she sang along at top volume as she raided her walk-in wardrobe. Her clothing was strewn about the bedroom, with discarded garments draped over doors and lingerie hanging half in and half out of Louis Vuitton cases.

Her head was full of daydreams of lazing around by the pool in a tiny wisp of nothing, or going on long, romantic barefoot beach walks with Nick, and she packed accordingly, her cases filling up with sexy little sundresses and bold print maxi-dresses. Then there were those bargain vest tops from Top Shop on Oxford Street, cropped cardigans with sequin embellishment and cashmere wraps for the balmy evenings. A whole case was filled with hats, from baseball caps affording blessed anonymity to the black wide-brimmed straw hat that made her look like a blonde Sophia Loren. She added them to the pile and paused for a moment, tucking a stray strand of hair behind her ears as she decided what to do next.

Shoes, she said firmly to herself, opening a door to

a separate shoe closet that would have made Carrie Bradshaw weep with envy; Jimmy Choo stilettos, sparkly mules, slingbacks by Kurt Geiger and the inevitable, inimitable Manolos all sat on the shelves.

With a sigh, Jenna reluctantly conceded that spike-heeled thigh-high boots were not going to be the most practical thing to wear by the pool, and turned her attention instead to jewelled flip-flops, gladiator sandals and stacked wedges.

Humming away to herself, her head full of limited-edition diamond-encrusted heels, it took a few seconds for Jenna to realize that her phone was ringing. Turning down the stereo, she dashed across the room to grab it.

Nick's name was flashing on the caller display.

'Nick, hi,' Jenna purred, feeling her pulse begin to race. Then a thought struck her. 'There isn't a problem, is there?' she asked nervously, praying that he wouldn't say the trip had been cancelled.

'No, no, everything's good,' he assured her in the low, Southern drawl that Jenna found so sexy. She could tell by the sound of his voice that he was smiling, and she relaxed at his reassurance. Curling up on her vast bed, among the oversized pillows and discarded scatter cushions, Jenna switched the phone to hands-free and wondered excitedly what he might be calling for.

'How's it going?' He sounded buoyant, and as confident as ever.

'Everything's fine. I'm just packing now and I can't decide what to take. I've got so much stuff and I don't want to leave anything behind,' Jenna replied, biting her lip anxiously as she surveyed the devastation of the room.

'Oh man – so you'll be the one waiting for hours for

forty suitcases to come off the carousel while the rest of us have already gone,' he teased.

'Don't even joke about it. I'm not sure the plane's even going to be able to take off, the amount of things I'm bringing.'

'I didn't realize bikinis were so heavy.'

'Neither did I,' Jenna agreed, adding, 'and mine are all so tiny you wouldn't think they'd weigh anything at all.'

She heard Nick's intake of breath and smothered a giggle. Strike one to Jenna.

'I guess naked suntanning's the only solution,' Nick said casually.

'Maybe . . . but I never sunbathe alone,' she told him. 'I need someone to rub the cream into my back.'

'I'll remember that,' Nick breathed, wondering how far he could push this. He wouldn't mind a little phone sex with Jenna Jonsson. Maybe she'd even send him some photos if he asked nicely . . .

'So, what were you calling about?' Jenna asked, abruptly shattering Nick's fantasy.

'Huh? Oh yeah . . . I wondered what you're doing about accommodation while we're out there. Have you found somewhere to stay?'

'Nick,' Jenna giggled. 'We're flying out tomorrow!'

'Yeah, I know. Sorry,' he apologized. 'I guess it was a stupid question. I just thought I'd check.'

'It's all arranged, thanks,' Jenna explained sweetly. 'Gerry's booked me in at a hotel. I've got the name around here somewhere . . .' She trailed off, looking around her for the email she'd printed out.

'Cool,' Nick interrupted, trying to sound enthusiastic. 'I just thought if you hadn't found anywhere, you could always stay at mine. I've got masses of space in my villa, and I thought it might be good for group bonding, y'know, if we all spent time together.'

'Oh, are the other guys staying with you?' Jenna faltered. Of course, she had been ridiculous to imagine it would be just her and Nick, she told herself, trying to fight her feelings of disappointment. Absentmindedly wrapping a strand of fine, blonde hair around a pale pink fingernail, she remembered her vow to make an effort to integrate herself more fully into Phoenix.

Nick paused for a split second, wondering whether to tell her the truth or to lie. He decided to lie. 'Yeah, prob'ly. I'm not sure about Zac and Amber – they might wanna stay in a hotel.'

'Oh, is Amber coming then?' Jenna cut in before she could stop herself. She had met the woman three times now, and her dislike of her grew on every occasion.

'Actually, I'm not sure,' replied Nick, wishing he'd thought his story through a little more carefully. 'She might be working overseas. So, if she is, then I guess Zac'll crash with me. He might as well, rather than staying on his own. And Ryan might stay, with all his kids,' he rushed on, his mouth working faster than his brain. ''Cos Kelly's coming out – although I'm not sure if you and Kelly . . . um . . . perhaps they're hiring their own place, I'm not sure . . .' he finished lamely.

'Yeah,' Jenna replied thoughtfully. She was feeling decidedly uncomfortable at the mention of Kelly. And why the hell was Nick acting so weird?

'So d'you wanna stay?' Nick's eager voice cut into her thoughts. 'Don might fly for a couple of days, he hasn't decided. But everyone's welcome . . .'

He sounded distant as he floundered with his story, but Jenna was only half paying attention, quickly weighing up the options in her head. She was certain of one thing – wherever Nick Taylor was, that's where she wanted to be. An opportunity like this was fate, and she didn't intend to waste it. Quickly, Jenna scanned over her packing. Oh God, she would have to completely change everything now. All the dresses she had packed looked frumpy, the sporty shorts asexual. And she wanted to look hot 24/7.

'Absolutely,' she purred. 'I'll get someone to cancel my hotel reservation.'

'Fantastic, see you tomorrow,' enthused Nick, barely able to hide the triumph in his voice. He wanted to get off the phone before she changed her mind. He knew he should probably have told her the truth, but he couldn't risk her saying no. Once he had her in the house it would be a walkover, though, he felt sure. No one could resist the famous Nick Taylor charm for long.

'Sure. Have a great night,' Jenna replied silkily, hanging up.

Nick grinned as the phone went silent. Not long now, he told himself.

The day was stormy. The half-closed blinds at the tiny window let in barely any light to Sadie's room, and she lay on her bed in semi-darkness, curled up like a child. Dark clouds scudded past outside, billowing and ominous, but Sadie hardly noticed as fat drops of rain landed on the windowpane, hitting it with force like a dozen tiny fists. Just a few miles away the rain was battering down on the gleaming tower blocks in the City, the money men who inhabited them tucked safely inside their impenetrable fortresses where nothing could harm them. Somewhere, in one of those, sat Paul Austin, surveying the world below from his ivory tower. Sadie was numb; she didn't even feel the hot tears that rolled down her cheeks and landed wetly on her pillow.

Over a week had passed and she still couldn't get the images out of her mind. She remembered Carla coming into her room, her face set with tension and guilt. 'I don't know how to tell you this hon . . .'

Sadie had demanded to see the whole thing, even though Carla had told her not to. She'd felt nauseous as she watched it, but she'd sat through the entire footage. Jesus, had she really done all that stuff? She didn't remember half of it. Afterwards she'd thrown up. She hadn't even made it to the bathroom, just hurled in Carla's wastepaper bin.

She felt so stupid, that she'd allowed herself to be used like that. She'd been falling in love with the guy; she'd sworn she wouldn't, but Paul had treated her so well, been so sweet to her. She knew he was married, but she'd managed to put that out of her mind while they were together, convinced herself it was just about the two of them. And all the time he was just playing her, using her to get what he wanted. He'd filmed her without her knowledge and put it on the net for everyone to see – she didn't even know why. For his own sordid kicks, presumably. Jesus, it was so fucking humiliating.

And it could potentially wreck her career, make her a laughing stock that nobody wanted to be associated with. Seeing herself behaving like that – besotted with Paul, doing anything he asked . . . The whole thing was a total nightmare.

At first Sadie had been angry, stabbing furiously at her phone as she tried to call that bastard. But Paul didn't pick up and, after an hour of trying, the feeling of helplessness set in. She knew he wasn't going to answer. It was as though he had no further use for her.

She'd been spat out and discarded like an old piece of gum.

First thing Monday morning she rang him at his office, determined to get answers. His PA answered.

'I'm afraid Mr Austin is in a meeting right now,' Angela Lee told her, her voice calm and impersonal. Sadie felt a stab of pure, white-hot anger, wondering how many times Angela had lied to her in the past. Lied to her, and to his wife, and to however many other women he'd had before Sadie; she wasn't naive enough to think she was the only one.

When she called for the fifth time that day, Angela wasn't quite so polite.

'Haven't you got the message yet?' she hissed. 'Mr Austin doesn't want to speak to you. Now why don't you put the phone down and stop calling here, before I report you for harassment.'

The line went dead. Sadie stared at the phone in her hand, fury pulsing through her whole body. She jumped up from the bed, determined to go round to his office and have it out with him face to face, tell all his colleagues what a lowlife piece of shit he was.

As she pulled on her jacket she realized it was futile. Even if she managed to get into the building, Paul would instantly have security eject her from the premises. Yeah, she could just imagine it – her kicking and screaming and yelling, while Paul stood there, cool and unruffled as ever, watching with a smile as some goon carted her off.

She couldn't go round to his house to confront him; she had no idea where he lived. She didn't even know if the apartment was really his – for all she knew, he could have just rented it for the afternoon. Yeah, he'd done a pretty good job of keeping his life totally separate from her, Sadie realized, furious with herself for being so fucking dumb! And he'd just walk away, scot-free, to move on to the next girl. There'd be another, she felt sure.

Sadie balled up her hands, slamming them hard into the pillow and wishing that it was Paul himself. She wanted him to suffer like she had, to be publicly shamed and humiliated, and to know that she was the one behind it. In short, she wanted revenge. She was going to destroy Paul Austin so that he had to live with the memories every day of his life, just like she would have to.

Sadie fired up her laptop and typed in Paul's name, looking for any information she could use. She was surprised she'd never done it before. A string of articles came up – a mention in *The Times*, the press release from his appointment at Willis & Bourne, details of a donation made to the Conservative Party. Then she clicked on Google Images. There was the same picture of him from the company website, looking handsome and powerful in a dark, crisp suit. Sadie hated to admit it but he looked gorgeous – she could see exactly why she'd fallen for him. But now she saw things she never had before – the steely determination in those cold blue eyes, the firm set of his jaw and the cruel mouth.

The next photo showed him at a charity fundraiser, resplendent in black tie beside an imperious looking blonde. She wore a glittering dress in palest blue that only reinforced the ice-queen image, and a dazzling diamond choker nestled at her throat. She was thin, haughty and stunningly beautiful. *Mr and Mrs Paul Austin*, read the caption.

Of course his wife would look like that, Sadie thought, swallowing hard. She obviously had money, breeding, class – the kind of woman that Sadie would never be. She understood that now; rich and powerful men only saw girls like her as playthings, not serious prospects. They could have fun, fool around, but then they'd off and marry Henrietta or Annabel with the pearls and the Alice band.

Unwittingly, Sadie thought of Jenna Jonsson. Life was working out just perfectly for her, she thought bitterly. She was gorgeous, rich and working with Phoenix. Why couldn't it happen like that for her? When was Sadie Laine going to catch a break?

She began to cry again, unable to help herself. She tried to keep it quiet, but soon broke down into big, gulping sobs, gasping for air as she cried as though her heart was broken. In a way, it was. She'd fallen for this guy big time, and now she felt utterly defeated.

Carla knocked gently on her door. 'Are you okay hon?'

Sadie looked up, wiping her bloodshot eyes with the back of her hand as Carla pushed open the door. 'Yes. No . . .'

Carla came in, closing the door behind her. Her other housemates had accepted Sadie's excuse that she had the flu and kept well away, but Carla knew the truth.

'Do you want something to eat?' she asked, her eyes full of concern as she sat down on the corner of the bed.

Sadie shook her head. 'I'm not hungry, thanks.' She couldn't remember the last time she'd had an appetite. All the pounds she'd gained after her last job had been cancelled had disappeared alarmingly quickly.

'Sadie hon, you've got to eat something. You're almost as thin as me.' Carla tried to make a joke of it, hoping to snap her out of it. It didn't work.

They sat in silence for a few moments, a rare feeling

of awkwardness between them. The rain hammered relentlessly on the window.

Suddenly Sadie's phone rang. For a split second she wondered if it was Paul; she couldn't help it, and she hated herself for it. Glancing at the screen she didn't recognize the number.

'Aren't you going to get that?' asked Carla, as Sadie threw it back down on the bed beside her.

'No,' she replied listlessly.

'It might be a job, or something exciting,' Carla suggested, trying to lift her spirits. It was days since Sadie had shown any enthusiasm about anything.

'Answer it if you want,' Sadie shrugged.

Raising an eyebrow, Carla reached across and picked it up. 'Sadie Laine's phone, her PA speaking,' Carla giggled, hoping to get a reaction from Sadie. 'Uh huh. Okay. Yeah, sure, I'll get her.' Carla put her hand over the mouthpiece and held the phone out to Sadie. 'They want to speak to you directly.'

'Who is it?' Sadie was suspicious.

'I don't know. They sounded professional.'

Sadie eyed the phone as though it might bite her. Warily, she took it from Carla. 'Hello? Yes, that's me. Yeah. Yeah. Oh, I see. That's fine. Yeah, thanks. Okay, bye.'

She hung up. Carla tried to read her face but Sadie was inscrutable. 'Anything interesting?' she couldn't resist asking.

'It was, actually,' Sadie began slowly, as though still trying to process the news. 'You remember that show I was supposed to do? *42nd Street* – the one that got cancelled?'

'Uh huh,' Carla nodded her head.

'Well, apparently we're getting some compensation for it – breach of contract, loss of earnings and so on . . .'

'Hey, that's fantastic!'

'Yeah.' Sadie paused before adding lightly, 'They're giving us almost ten grand . . .'

'Ten grand? Each?' Carla blurted out, as Sadie nodded in confirmation. 'Oh my God!'

Carla's mouth fell open but Sadie seemed strangely unaffected, as though she was still in shock.

'Just think what you could spend it on!' Carla shrieked. 'You could get a little car, or go on a massive shopping spree. Or maybe you should be sensible and invest it or something . . .' She trailed off, realizing what she'd just said. Involuntarily Paul flashed into Sadie's mind. Mr Senior Investment Manager himself. *We work with people who are rich and make them even richer.* Sadie wondered if he would think ten grand was a fortune. It would barely keep him in hookers for the month, she thought bitterly.

The memories hit her as if she'd been punched in the solar plexus, and she gasped out loud, unable to help herself.

'Are you okay?' Carla asked nervously.

'Yeah.' Sadie nodded her head automatically as she tried to get her breath. She felt the tears threaten to spill again but forced them back. She wasn't going to cry again, damn it. She was through with crying over Paul fucking Austin, and she wasn't about to let that bastard spoil this moment for her. Suddenly she felt reckless. She didn't want to invest the money or spend it sensibly; she wanted to go wild.

'Fuck it, let's do something crazy,' she burst out, grasping Carla by the arm. It was the most animated Carla had seen her for days, as though a light in her eyes had been switched on.

'Okay,' Carla agreed enthusiastically. 'Like what?'

'I don't know. Anything. Everything! We should go

away somewhere and see the world. Have an adventure. Where have you always wanted to go?'

Carla thought for a moment. 'Venice?' she suggested.

Sadie pulled a face. 'I'm not sure that's the place for a woman nursing a broken heart. Come on, we want sun and luxury and partying. Where's the craziest place you can think of?'

'I don't know,' wailed Carla.

Sadie's eyes were sparkling as she sat bolt upright with excitement. 'Vegas,' she announced decisively. 'We're going to Las Vegas!'

13

It was a scene from Jenna's nightmares.

Ushered straight from her car onto the waiting plane, she found her travelling companions for the journey out to Ibiza were to be Ryan, Kelly and their two pre-school children. The kids were already causing a riot in first class, which was – thank God – largely empty.

Jenna dropped her bag in her seat then greeted Ryan and his wife. Kelly nodded coldly at her and Jenna began to feel distinctly uncomfortable. What the hell was she supposed to say on being introduced to the woman with whose husband she had publicly been accused of having an affair? Talk about awkward. Jenna settled for a bright hello, before retreating behind the pages of a glossy magazine.

She thought about feigning tiredness, so she could simply pull down her eye mask and pretend to go to sleep, but there was no chance of that when Ryan's kids were either screaming or running up and down the aisle.

Jenna smiled politely. 'Sweet, aren't they?' she lied, as she became aware of Kelly watching her.

Kelly was dressed casually but expensively, and she

was extremely pretty – perhaps a little chunky around the hips, her body soft and untoned, but she was in great shape to say she had given birth to two kids. The outline of another bump was just about visible under the light linen trousers and white fitted T-shirt she was wearing.

Kelly smiled back, though her face showed no trace of friendliness. 'And another one on the way,' she stated coolly in that Southern drawl as she patted her stomach.

'Yeah, I heard. Congratulations. When's it due?'

'October. I'm nearly four months gone.'

'Should you be flying in your condition?' Jenna asked innocently.

'I'm pregnant, not sick,' Kelly snapped back, her voice suddenly harsh. 'Besides, Ryan and I don't want to be apart for long periods of time. His family are very important to him,' she added pointedly, placing her left hand on Ryan's knee where Jenna couldn't help but notice a huge solitaire next to a gold wedding band.

Ryan shifted uncomfortably in his seat as Jenna opened her mouth, ready to let loose with a stinging retort. Even if Kelly *was* a raging bag of hormones, she was rapidly losing Jenna's sympathy.

'Would you like a glass of champagne?' An immaculately presented stewardess appeared from nowhere at a highly opportune moment.

Jenna forced herself to stop glaring at Kelly and dragged her eyes up to the stewardess. 'That would be lovely, thank you.'

'Madam?' The stewardess turned to Kelly.

'No thank you, just an orange juice for me.'

'Of course.' Ryan asked for a Diet Pepsi, and the stewardess slipped away as discreetly as she had arrived.

Jenna let her head roll lazily to look out of the window. They were flying over northern France and the cloud covering was dense, like ghostly marshmallow. The sun shone brightly, but Jenna was too preoccupied to notice the view.

'Daddy!'

It was Ryan's eldest, a three-year-old boy called Brandon.

'Daddy, I need to pee,' Brandon insisted urgently, trying to clamber up onto Ryan's knee where he held a sleeping baby girl.

'Okay, okay,' Ryan pacified him. 'Daddy will take you – careful, mind the baby, you'll crush her. Can you hold Lea for a moment?' he asked, heaving the baby off his lap and passing her to Kelly.

Ryan smiled apologetically at Jenna and, casting a nervous look in the direction of the two women, took Brandon by the hand and led him down the aisle.

Kelly took the baby with a series of coos and clucky noises, gazing at her with a proud, albeit tired, smile. Jenna turned back to the window, determined that Kelly wasn't going to make her feel inadequate for her own lack of maternal urges. She was only 23, for Christ's sake. No way did she want sagging breasts and a torn vagina.

Kelly cleared her throat and Jenna wondered if she was trying to get her attention. She smiled tentatively, but Kelly remained stony-faced. Jenna sighed. 'Kelly . . .' she began slowly.

'What?'

Jenna paused, unsure of what she was trying to say. 'I know that things are going to be a little awkward between us, but I hope—'

'We can be friends?' cut in Kelly sarcastically.

'Well, that we can at least make an effort to get on,'

Jenna snapped back, feeling wrong-footed by Kelly's hostility.

'I'm hoping we'll be around each other as little as possible.'

'Kelly, I . . .' Jenna faltered. 'You know nothing happened,' she finished incredulously.

'Yes, I know that because Ryan is a good man. But I don't trust you further than I could throw you, and if I catch you anywhere near my husband I'll take great pleasure in rearranging that pretty face of yours. I'll make sure everyone knows what a little slut you are and your career will be destroyed,' Kelly ranted.

Jenna was open-mouthed with shock, stunned at the vitriol coming out of this tiny woman. 'You're crazy! I'm not interested in him.'

'Maybe not. But I know what girls like you are like. You don't care about families; you just do what you want. And with me like this, I . . .' Kelly broke off, her head dropping as she looked down at her pregnant belly. She had gone very pale suddenly and her eyes had welled up.

At that moment Brandon came running back down the aisle, heading straight for Kelly's bag to look for sweets as he complained that his ears hurt. Ryan was following closely behind.

'Is everything okay?' he asked cautiously, taking in the strained silence and the uneasy body language of the two women.

'Fine,' Kelly lied. She gave him a reassuring smile as he took her hand and slipped into the seat beside her.

'Jenna, would you mind holding Lea for a minute while I try and find some candy?' asked Kelly, trying to prevent Brandon from pulling everything out of her Hermès bag. 'It must have slipped to the bottom.'

'Okay . . .' said Jenna slowly, her confusion deepening. Jeez, these mood swings were extreme!

Jenna took the baby awkwardly, trying to hold her in the natural way she'd seen countless mothers do. It didn't come very naturally to Jenna and a few seconds later came the moment she was dreading as Lea turned puce and let out a long, loud wail.

'I think you should take her back,' Jenna said hurriedly, holding her out to Kelly.

'No, she'll be fine,' Kelly assured her, calmly unwrapping a sweet. 'Just rock her a little.'

'Perhaps she's hungry?' suggested Jenna desperately, but Kelly merely shook her head and did nothing.

'Maybe you should sing to her?' Ryan suggested, himself a little surprised by Kelly's behaviour.

'I don't think that would help,' put in Kelly tartly. 'Lift her up to your shoulder and rub her back a little. Maybe she's got wind.'

'I'm not sure I'm the best person to deal with this—' Jenna started to protest, but Kelly cut her off again.

'You'll be fine. Just pat her back gently.'

The baby had quietened down somewhat, and Jenna felt a growing sense of achievement as she rocked gently from side to side, rubbing her hand up and down the baby's tiny back. Perhaps Kelly had meant it as a gesture of reconciliation, Jenna thought. After all, she had trusted her with her baby, so maybe she was trying to make her feel included, even if it was a slightly odd way of going about it.

Suddenly, Jenna became aware of a slightly odd smell. Then she realized that her ridiculously expensive Marc Jacobs cashmere sweater felt wet and sticky at the shoulder.

'Oh dear,' Kelly said, in honeyed tones. 'I think someone had an accident.'

* * *

138

'Wow.'

Even Jenna couldn't fail to be impressed as the Mercedes drew to a halt after winding its way down the long, bumpy driveway leading to Casa Santos. Nick's villa was in the northwest of the island, nestled among the olive groves and pine trees, and a world away from the hedonistic nightclubs and English fried breakfasts of San Antonio further down the coast. It was a stunning location; used to luxury as Jenna was, she certainly wasn't disappointed with what was to be her home for the next few weeks.

The house was huge. It was built on only two storeys but spread over a vast area, having started off as a simple farmhouse, which had been added to and extended many times over the years. The thick, sandstone walls were painted white, with terracotta shutters enveloping the slatted windows, and the garden was immaculately landscaped, lush with palm and cypress trees swaying drowsily in the balmy breeze that was blowing in from the sea. Pink and red flowers burst from window boxes in a riot of colour, and arched wooden trellises cascading with jasmine and wisteria marked the entrance to the porch. Jenna put a hand up to her eyes to shade them from the sun, and admired the view once again.

'Beautiful,' she said to herself, taking in the heavenly scene before her from the solitude of the car. Ryan and his family had taken a separate vehicle from the airport and, after the incident on the plane, Jenna didn't care if she never saw them again.

'Jenna!' Nick descended from the porch steps and bounded over to the car to meet her, enveloping her in a crushing hug. He was wearing stone-coloured cropped trousers and his chest was bare, displaying acres of tanned flesh and a rippling six-pack.

'Nick, this is amazing. Just amazing,' Jenna marvelled, as she kissed him on the cheek, unwilling to disentangle herself from his arms. He smelt wonderful, a deliciously masculine mix of soap and aftershave, as though he'd just showered.

'Nothing but the best for you, senõrita,' Nick grinned. 'Welcome to my humble abode.'

His good mood was infectious, and Jenna could literally feel the tension ease away from her shoulders as the warm sun streamed down on her. In these gorgeous surroundings, with Nick so laid-back and charming, Jenna felt sure that everything would be all right with the band. How could anything bad happen in such a perfect place?

'Come on, let's get you inside, princess,' he said, throwing an arm around her and leading her towards the house as the car pulled away down the drive. 'I'll show you your room – I think you'll like it. Or would you rather see the back yard first?'

His American accent had become more pronounced since leaving London, Jenna noticed. She'd always been a sucker for a sexy voice. 'I don't mind. I'll leave myself in your capable hands.'

Nick raised an eyebrow. 'Okay then. Let's get you into my capable hands.' Ignoring Jenna's protesting cries, he swept her up into his arms and carried her giggling into the house. She was still laughing when Nick gently placed her down in the entrance hall. Unsteady on her feet, Jenna held on to him as she took in the house. His shoulders were broad, and her fingers lingered on the warm skin of his neck.

'Wow,' she repeated, looking around her. The terracotta-tiled floor led to a magnificent sweeping staircase cut from a rich, dark wood, and all around Jenna could see evidence of the traditional features that Nick had kept – from the period beams set into the high ceiling to the heavy, wooden furniture.

'Let's go see your room.' Nick took her hand and led her towards the main staircase. 'It's pretty special.'

Jenna followed him down a long corridor, brightly lit by the afternoon sun that streamed in through the slatted windows, as they headed towards the back of the house.

'Oh, I love it!' she exclaimed, taking in the vast room with its exquisitely carved, solid wooden four-poster bed and antique Ibizan furniture.

'Now for the best bit.' Nick looked at her intently for a moment. 'Close your eyes.'

'Nick, what—'

'Just quit arguing and do as you're told.'

'Okay,' Jenna giggled.

Gently, Nick took her hand and guided her over to the double doors that led out onto the terrace. 'Open them,' he whispered softly.

Jenna did, and for once in her life she was utterly speechless. The view from the window was absolutely stunning. 'Wow,' she said again, worrying that her vocabulary was becoming seriously reduced. 'This is your back yard?' she asked incredulously.

The window looked out over Nick's immaculately kept gardens, stretching in lush, green abundance past a large pool, all the way to a path which Jenna could see led to a tiny private beach. It was enclosed by high, rocky cliffs, and beyond that lay the sparkling, azure sea. The sunlight danced on the waves, giving the scene a magical, shimmering appearance, and, a short way out to sea, Jenna could see a dazzling white yacht, at least eighty feet in length.

Finally Nick spoke. 'Do you like it?' he asked nervously.

'Are you kidding? I love it!' Jenna tore her gaze away from the view as she turned to face him. Her brilliant green eyes were shining, and she threw her arms around him. 'Thank you so much! I can't believe you've given me this room — I feel like a princess!'

'Like I said,' Nick murmured, his eyes never leaving her face. 'Nothing but the best for you.'

Jenna felt a frisson of excitement build in her stomach as she looked at him. Her arms were still around his neck, and she could feel his solid, muscular body pressed against hers, the delicious feel of his bare skin against her thin cotton top.

Jenna started, as there was a loud hooting from downstairs.

'That's probably Ryan,' she said reluctantly.

'Uh huh.' Nick's disappointment was obvious as they untwined. 'Let's go see.'

They walked back through the villa, Jenna's heels clacking noisily on the tiles, to find that the car containing Jenna's luggage had arrived. The driver was keen to leave, but after Nick offered him a large wad of cash, he got stuck into the job of helping to carry the bags up to Jenna's room. She stayed to watch for a while, amused at the fact that Nick seemed to be attempting to carry twice as much as the burly yet overweight Ibizan.

'It's no problem for me,' he told her airily. 'I work out a lot.'

Jenna smiled indulgently, wandering onto the sunlit porch as she watched them unload the car. She figured she might as well encourage this display of machismo as it seemed to be directed at her.

Suddenly Nick's mobile began to ring, shattering the tranquil silence. Jenna recalled him leaving it on the hallway table.

'Nick,' she called, as she strode back inside.

'I'll be right there,' he shouted, his muffled voice coming from deep within the building. 'Just give me a sec.'

'It's only Ryan,' said Jenna, as she saw his name on the caller display. 'They probably got lost or something. I'll get it, it's no trouble.'

'Jenna, don't . . .' began Nick, but trailed off as he appeared at the top of the stairs, watching her face anxiously.

'Okay . . . no problem, I'll tell him. Yeah, see you tomorrow . . . Bye.' Jenna hung up, her brow furrowed in confusion. 'Nick, what's going on?'

His face was a picture of innocence, his eyes open wide to imply he didn't know what she was referring to.

'Ryan said to tell you,' Jenna began slowly, 'that they had all arrived safely, but weren't planning to come over tonight because the kids are tired and they want to get them settled in. And *then* he said to thank you for recommending the villa to them, because it's perfect.' Jenna paused, looking up uncertainly. 'I thought you told me he was staying here.'

Nick looked a little ashamed of himself as he gradually made his way down the staircase. 'Well, if I remember right, I only said he *might* be staying here . . .'

Comprehension began to dawn in Jenna. 'Right. And Zac?'

'Yeah . . . He's not arriving until later.' Nick paused. 'And he's staying in a hotel a few miles down the road.'

'So is anyone else staying here apart from you and me?'

'Not currently . . .' Nick's eyes raked over her body as they heard the heavy tread of the taxi driver upstairs. 'I can ask *him* to stay if you want?'

Jenna hit him on the arm. 'Is this some kind of set-up?' she demanded suspiciously, simultaneously pissed off and amused. While she loved the idea of being alone with Nick, she didn't want to be the butt of some joke.

'Not exactly . . . oh hell, don't get mad with me . . .' Nick pleaded, taking hold of her hands as the taxi driver came wearily down the stairs. Nick handed him another pile of notes, and with a variety of hand signals and basic Spanish, indicated that he could leave.

'I'm sorry sweetheart, I really am,' Nick began to grovel as the car drove off. 'I did invite everyone but it was all pretty last-minute. Ryan said that Kelly'd rather stay in a villa, so they could have a bit of privacy, y'know?'

Yeah, far away from me, Jenna thought darkly, the humiliation rushing back as she remembered the way Kelly had spoken to her on the plane. She hadn't deserved that.

'Zac was thinking about it, but decided to keep his hotel reservation in case Amber flies out to join him. And we don't all wanna be on top of each other, do we?' Nick pointed out, thinking how much he wanted to be on top of Jenna at that particular moment.

'Right. So it's just you and me?' Jenna could hardly bring herself to look at him, certain that her desire must be plain to see.

'Is that such a bad thing?'

Jenna didn't reply.

'I promise to behave,' he winked.

'Now that would be a shame,' Jenna shot back, the comment slipping out before she could stop it.

Nick laughed easily, enjoying her discomfort as she blushed crimson. 'And don't forget, my room's right

144

next door to yours. Just holler if you need me in the middle of the night.'

'I'll remember that,' Jenna assured him.

'Awesome!' exclaimed Nick, picking her up in his arms and swinging her round. His hands were large and strong, and she felt light as air in his grasp. 'Believe me, you won't want to leave.'

14

'I fucking love Vegas!' Sadie screeched at the top of her voice.

Hanging out of the limo sunroof, she threw her head back and took a gulp from a bottle of champagne, turning her face up to the cloudless Nevada sky.

The car sped down the Strip, flanked on either side by gigantic hotels, bigger than any Sadie had ever seen. There was the Luxor, with its giant pyramid and laser beam reaching high into the sky, followed by the New York, a replica of the Big Apple with its very own rollercoaster that encircled the building. It was wild. In the distance Sadie could see the huge Stratosphere tower, and encompassing the whole thing like a security blanket was the sun-bleached desert and the silent mountains beyond.

She felt as if she was in a movie.

Americans wearing khaki shorts and fanny packs pointed at her and some Japanese tourists took photos. A group of young guys whooped and waved. They looked like jocks, barely out of college. But they were hot, so Sadie whooped back.

She made quite a picture; her dark hair streaming out behind her as the desert sun beat down on her sinewy body, shown to perfection in the pale pink slip dress she was wearing. She had spray-tanned before she left, and now her entire body was a gorgeous shade of sun-kissed brown. She blew kisses to anyone who waved at her and felt giddy with all the champagne.

The flight to Nevada had taken ten hours. Sadie had slept for eight hours straight, then woken up and ordered a double vodka and Diet Coke. She'd barely slowed down after that, and when the VIP limo picked them up from the airport she was thrilled to discover the chilled champagne in its cavernous interior. Sadie was determined that this would be a holiday they would never forget.

'Sadie, you're drenching me!' Carla squealed, as Sadie glanced down and realized she'd tipped the bottle all inside the car. There was a puddle on one of the seats, and Carla's dress bore telltale stains.

Reluctantly, Sadie sat down, pressing her nose against the tinted glass to make sure she didn't miss any part of their arrival in Vegas. 'Look, it's the Eiffel Tower,' she yelled excitedly as they passed the Paris. Then her attention was distracted as they drove by the dancing fountains at the Bellagio, and she jumped across the limo to get a better view.

Even in the middle of the afternoon, the Vegas Strip was a blaze of neon, and the tourists were out in force. It seemed as though every nationality was out pounding the pavements, from parents with young children to teenagers to OAPs, all making their way from one casino to the next, exploring the magic the city had to offer.

Their limo swept up to the entrance of Caesars Palace, and Sadie gave the driver a stupidly generous tip as a concierge appeared to take their bags.

'Holy shit,' she swore as she walked into the enormous marble lobby. She pushed her oversized sunglasses back onto her head to get a better view as she squinted up at the painted frescoes.

'It's amazing,' Carla breathed, looking stunned. 'It's just ridiculous, gaudy—'

'And glamorous and fantastic,' Sadie finished with a grin. 'I think I've found my spiritual home.'

They checked in, and Sadie cheekily requested an upgrade. 'It's my first time in Vegas,' she purred, batting her eyelids at the cute, uniformed guy on reception.

'No problem,' he beamed back. His teeth were impossibly white. 'I've put you on the thirty-second floor. There's a fabulous view of the Strip.'

'Thank you – Kevin,' she grinned, giving him a tantalizing flash of her cleavage as she bent over the desk to read his name-tag. 'I really appreciate that.'

She shimmied off towards the elevator with a giggling Carla in tow, marvelling at her friend's chutzpah.

'If you don't ask, you don't get,' Sadie shrugged. She planned to start asking – and getting – a whole lot more from now on.

'Oh my God,' she exclaimed, as she walked into their room, which boasted two king-size beds, a separate living room and an enormous marble bathroom with a whirlpool tub big enough for three.

'Check this out,' yelled Carla, looking out of the window. The promised view of the Strip didn't disappoint, and she could see past the concrete hotels and desolate car parks to the looming mountains beyond.

'Shall we eat? I'm starving,' suggested Sadie.

'Sure,' Carla agreed easily. 'Are you sure you're okay about picking up the tab? I feel bad.'

'Oh no, don't start that again. I told you, I am going to spend this money how I damn well please, and that involves you and me in Vegas having the time of our lives. Now don't ask me again.'

They ordered room service, washed down with more vodka, while they quickly showered and dressed, eager to hit the town. Sadie pulled on denim hot pants which showed off her long legs, teamed with gladiator sandals and a black vest top with a retro print of Madonna. Carla went for a short, floral halterneck and spritzed herself with the Dior perfume she'd picked up at the airport.

'Vegas won't know what's hit it!' smiled Sadie, as they eyed their reflections in the full-length mirror.

To get out of the hotel they had to go through the casino, where they lingered watching young guys get fleeced at blackjack as they recklessly tried to impress the girls who cheered them on. Elderly women in elasticated trousers sat immobile in front of flashing one-armed bandits, their eyes locked in concentration on the spinning reels. As they passed, Sadie tried her luck. She fed in a dollar, crossed her fingers and pulled the lever. It didn't pay out.

'I thought my luck was changing,' she said forlornly.

'It is,' Carla assured her. 'We're going to have an amazing holiday. Something good is going to happen to you, after all the shit you've been through.'

'I hope so,' Sadie told her. They linked arms as they walked out of the hotel and onto the main drag itself.

'Man, it's crazy!' marvelled Carla, as their senses were immediately assaulted by the sights, sounds and smells of the city. It took their breath away. Outside the air-conditioned casino the sun beat down, the stifling heat so different to the drizzle they had left behind in London. Hundreds of people swarmed by, some dressed outrageously for stag parties and bachelorette nights. Scruffily dressed Mexicans hustled and pressed leaflets into their hands, urging them to see this show or visit that strip joint, everyone promising them discounts, offers and 'the best deal in town, *chica*', as Sadie and Carla walked joyously and aimlessly, soaking up the vibe.

They headed from bar to bar, getting steadily drunker on cocktails bought for them by hot men with names like Brad and Chad who thought their accents were just *too cute*. When Brad and Chad got too friendly, Sadie and Carla made their excuses and left. It wasn't their fault, but Sadie just didn't trust men any more, and Carla was staying faithful to Tom for reasons Sadie didn't understand.

The Vegas sky was dimming, and darkness fell quickly in the desert. Pretty soon the garish neon could be seen in all its glory. The families had disappeared and the streets had taken on a carnival-like atmosphere as gas-guzzling stretch Hummers drove past, filled with beautiful people ready to party.

The girls were heading south, aimlessly following the crowds, when a six-foot transvestite looking like an extra from *The Rocky Horror Show* grabbed Sadie by the arm.

'Hey ladies! Are you looking for the time of your lives tonight?' He peered down at them through eyes thickly rimmed with black kohl pencil. He wore a long, thick, platinum-blonde wig and zealously applied red lipstick.

'Are you the one who's going to give it to us?' Sadie

asked cheekily. She was more than a little drunk, and she clung onto him for support.

'I'm just the warm-up act,' he grinned. 'The real action's in there.' He pointed down the side street where a seedy-looking club pumped out 1980s soft-rock ballads. There were two enormous bouncers on the door and the windows were blacked out, while a red flashing sign above proclaimed it to be The Pleasuredome. 'Free entry, free drink,' the guy said.

'Free drink?' Sadie's eyes lit up. 'What is it? It better not be a shot of something disgusting,' she warned, remembering the green concoction she'd downed a few bars back.

'Anything you want.' He smiled again, showing perfect white teeth. What was it with Americans, Sadie wondered? Even their transvestites were obsessed with dentistry. 'Just tell them Tallulah sent you.'

'Thanks Tallulah,' Sadie winked, as she grabbed Carla by the hand. Security parted for them as they headed inside, tottering down a mirrored staircase where a suited guy pulled aside a faded velvet curtain and ushered them through. It took a while to adjust to the dim lighting and thick cigarette smoke, but it soon became clear that the club was filled with semi-naked women writhing on podiums as curious tourists and excitable bachelor parties watched lasciviously.

'It's a strip club!' Sadie realized.

'In Vegas? How original,' Carla returned drily.

'Do you want a table?' A blonde waitress swung by, wearing only a thong and a blue glitter star over each nipple. She was clearly on the wrong side of thirty, and even the dim lighting couldn't disguise the furrowed forehead and exhausted expression.

Sadie glanced at Carla. 'I've never been to a strip club before.'

'Me neither.'

'There's a first time for everything,' declared Sadie, turning back to the waitress. 'Yes, we'll take a table.'

'Great! I'm Glory, and I'll be your waitress for tonight,' the woman told them, as she wove through the black Perspex tables and seated them in a booth beside the runway.

'No room for the name-badge, huh?' Sadie couldn't resist saying.

'What?' Glory looked confused.

'Never mind. Oh yeah, Tallulah said we could have a free drink. Anything we wanted.'

'Friends of Tallulah's, are you? Don't worry, I'll sort you out.' She disappeared, leaving Sadie and Carla looking around in fascination. Their eyes were level with the runway, and they had an excellent view of the porn-star shoes the strippers were wearing.

'Christ, look at the size of those heels. There's no way I could dance in those,' Sadie exclaimed.

'Ooh, they're my favourite,' said Carla, cooing over a pair of clear plastic six-inchers studded with rhinestones.

Glory reappeared with their drinks. Sadie and Carla tipped her a couple of dollars, then settled back to watch the show, fascinated by the women's bodies and the reaction of the crowd. Men were stuffing twenty-dollar bills into their thongs as if they were going out of fashion.

'Look how much money they're making!' Sadie hissed. 'I need a career change.'

'There's probably some pimp in the back who takes it all, and they're on minimum wage,' Carla said cynically, popping a straw into her drink and sucking hard. It tasted delicious, sweet like bourbon.

152

'No, I'm serious. I mean, how hard can it be? I can do that!' Sadie squealed, jabbing her finger in the direction of a tiny redhead who had dropped into the splits in front of a group of very appreciative boys that didn't look old enough to be there. The stripper ruffled the hair of one of them, who looked as though he was going to come in his pants that second. His friends furiously pushed their remaining dollars into the girl's underwear, eager to see what she would do next.

Sadie was looking agitated, her eyes glittering brightly. It had been a long time since she'd been on stage, too long since she'd had the adoration of a crowd. 'Watch this!' Sadie cried suddenly, and before Carla knew what was happening, Sadie had climbed up onto the platform in front of them. Steadying herself on the nearest pole, she began to writhe against it, her body snaking from side to side as she raised her arms high above her head.

Some of the crowd realized what was happening and they whooped and cheered, turning their attention away from their own girls. Sadie lapped up the attention, spinning her body around as she bent over and pushed her breasts up against the pole. The onlookers yelled for more, as Carla shook her head and shouted at Sadie to get down. Sadie ignored her. The other girls on the podium had turned to see what was going on, and they didn't look happy. Over by the door, the security guys were conferring. One lifted his walkie-talkie.

'Strip! Strip! Strip!' chanted the crowd. Sadie flicked her hair and looked teasingly at the group of men below her. Pursing her lips, she ran her hand down to the bottom of her T-shirt, sliding it slowly up her body to reveal a glimpse of the black lace bra she was wearing underneath. The crowd hollered in approval. Then, holding her arms above her head, she slid down into perfect splits. The onlookers went crazy. Security left their post by the door and began walking over. Carla grabbed Sadie's arm and hauled her off stage, to a chorus of boos and braying.

'What did you pull me down for?' Sadie snapped at Carla. She was drunk and angry. 'I'm going to get another drink.' Without giving Carla time to reply, she marched off in the direction of the bar. 'Bourbon and coke. Large.' Her breath was coming fast, and she still felt pissed off.

'That was quite some show up there,' the barman grinned. He was cute. Sadie grinned back. 'You want a job here?' he asked, as Sadie laughed.

As he turned away to mix her drink, a pair of breasts appeared beside her. High, round and clearly fake, the perky nipples rested on the countertop just next to Sadie's elbow.

'Nice work up there,' said the owner of the breasts, in a heavy West Coast accent.

Sadie turned to look at her, taking care to focus on her face. The girl had poker-straight, bleached-blonde hair, heavy make-up and dark fake tan – typical Vegas style. Yet Sadie could see that beneath all that she had a natural prettiness. She was young – probably about the same age as Sadie herself. She wore nothing except a red glitter G-string and matching platform heels, but she seemed completely unselfconscious.

'Thanks,' Sadie replied cautiously, wondering if she was taking the piss.

'I mean it.' Sadie's drink arrived, and the girl said, 'Don't worry Joe, I'll cover this.' She brandished a crumpled twenty and added, 'And get me one of whatever she's having.'

'Thanks,' Sadie repeated as she took her bourbon.

'No problem. Are you British?' she asked curiously.

'Yeah. From London.'

'Gee, I thought you guys were meant to be repressed. I'm Brooke, by the way.'

'Hi Brooke. I'm Sadie.' There was a pause as Brooke took her drink, and for something to say Sadie asked, 'So you work here?'

'Regular detective, aren't you?' Brooke shot back, indicating her state of undress. Through her alcoholic haze, Sadie felt embarrassed.

'Sorry,' Brooke apologized. 'But I meant what I said before. You've got an amazing body, you know. You move really well.'

'I'm a dancer.'

'Really? Exotic?'

'Nah,' Sadie shook her head. 'I specialized in jazz. And hip-hop for fun.'

'Right.' Brooke looked thoughtful. 'You know, you should try out for this.' She reached behind the bar and picked up a flyer. It was hot pink, with bold black text that read:

Only the Hottest Girls need apply for the Sexiest new show in Vegas!

Beneath was an address and tomorrow's date.

'My friend's running it. He's the best. He's gay, so no funny business,' Brooke explained seriously.

'What is it?'

'A cabaret troupe. Burlesque. Dancing, entertainment. He's holding open auditions tomorrow. We're gonna be the next Pussycat Dolls.' Brooke's eyes were sparkling. She clearly believed whatever hype her friend had sold her.

Sadie looked doubtful. 'Sounds interesting but—'

'Oh, it's not like this,' Brooke cut her off quickly, waving her arm to indicate the grimy club around her. 'This guy's big time. Karl Madison – you heard of him?'

'Sounds familiar,' Sadie told her truthfully.

'He's a choreographer. He's worked with all the big stars – Beyoncé, Lady Gaga, Justin Timberlake . . . He's always in Vegas, he loves it, and he wants to start up a little side project here. He's got a good club lined up – The Play Rooms, you know it?'

Sadie shook her head.

'It's good. Sophisticated. Not like this place.' Brooke looked around her distastefully.

'Are you trying out for it?'

'I don't have to,' Brooke announced proudly. 'My place is guaranteed.'

'Cool. Well, I'll think about it.' Unsteadily, Sadie folded the leaflet into quarters and popped it in her purse.

'What's your cell number?' Brooke asked.

'I don't have one here,' Sadie explained. She told her she was staying at Caesars and gave Brooke her room number.

'Cool. Yeah, yeah, I'm coming,' she yelled, waving distractedly at an irate-looking guy who had stuck his head out of a back room. 'My break's over,' Brooke explained reluctantly, as she reapplied her pink lip gloss in the mirror above the bar. 'Time for me to get back up there. It was nice to meet you, Sadie.' She gave her a big grin and walked off. The thong she wore was barely more than dental floss, but her body was toned and firm, her butt smooth and peachy.

With barely focused eyes, Sadie watched her go. Her

brain was foggy, her body exhausted through a combination of jet lag and alcohol. Yet she couldn't shake the weirdest feeling that her life was about to change forever.

15

Jenna was woken by the glorious sun streaming through her curtains, and for a moment her sleep-fogged brain couldn't place where she was. But as she opened her eyes and saw the heavenly room, it all came flooding back.

Despite being tired after the flight, Jenna had stayed up talking late into the night with Nick and consequently she had woken late this morning. It was the first time they had spent so much time alone together and they were both acutely aware of the fact. Nick had been courteous and attentive, tactile without overstepping the boundaries. Almost *too* courteous, Jenna thought with disappointment. They'd shared a bottle of wine or two last night, and in the relaxed, heady atmosphere she had been certain that he would kiss her. Her body had been on fire for him, literally aching as she longed for him to reach across and take her in his arms. But he'd held off.

Was it possible she'd misread the signs? No, that was ridiculous, she assured herself. He was probably playing it cool out of respect for her. Not rushing into anything. Jenna Jonsson wasn't just some one-night stand and they both knew it.

Stifling a yawn, she got out of bed. It was so high off the ground she practically had to climb down. Wrapping herself in a sheet, Jenna padded across the room to the window, the floor tiles feeling deliciously cold on her warm feet. Pulling back the white voile curtains, she felt the same rush of excitement she had experienced yesterday as she looked out across Nick's extensive gardens, stretching all the way down to the tranquil sea.

It was going to be a scorching day; the sky was almost pure blue, with only the occasional fluffy white cloud drifting lazily across it. The Mediterranean was a dazzling turquoise colour, with the sunlight reflecting off it so brightly that if Jenna screwed up her eyes it appeared almost silver. Nick's boat, *Nightfinch*, bobbed regally in the distance. White and gleaming, it was the perfect millionaire's plaything.

Realizing that she hadn't eaten since yesterday evening and it was now almost lunchtime, Jenna showered quickly then pulled on a vest top and a pair of knickers before padding downstairs to see what she could find.

'Oh!' she exclaimed, letting out a cry of surprise as she rounded the bottom of the staircase and crashed into a complete stranger. 'I'm so sorry,' she apologized breathlessly, painfully aware of how exposed she felt in what amounted to little more than her underwear.

Her cheeks began to colour as the man looked her up and down, his heavily lined face creasing into an expression of disapproval. He looked quite old – in his sixties at least, Jenna thought – and he was wearing a T-shirt and a light pair of trousers. He was extremely tanned, and looked as though he spent much of his time outdoors.

'*Senõr Taylor está en la cocina,*' the old man told her sourly.

'*Gracias,*' Jenna told him, mustering her dignity, and hoping her Spanish hadn't let her down as she headed in the direction of the kitchen.

'Hey!' Nick greeted her. 'You've spoilt my surprise.'

Jenna barely registered the food he was preparing as she burst out, 'Nick, who the hell was that old guy out there?'

Nick threw back his head and roared with laughter. 'I see you've met Carlos,' he observed. 'I'm amazed you didn't give the poor old guy a heart attack. You've practically given me one,' he told her, eyeing the skimpy panties and tight-fitting vest.

'But who is he?' Jenna pressed, determined not to get distracted. Nick was wearing a pair of loose-fitting khaki shorts, and nothing else. His bare chest was tanned, with just a smattering of curly blond hair, and it was obvious that he worked out a lot.

Nick smiled lazily, knowing he was looking good. 'Carlos? I guess you could say he's my handyman. He's been here forever from what I hear, and kinda came with the house. He looks after the joint when I'm not here and does what needs doing – repairs things, gardens, whatever. He's completely unimpressed by this place. And by its guests,' he added, correctly guessing that Jenna was a little surprised by the lack of recognition Carlos had shown her.

'He's not the most . . . talkative of guys though,' Nick continued. 'But we seem to get on okay. I think he disapproves of semi-naked pop stars, though,' added Nick wickedly, as Jenna glared at him.

'If I were you, Mr Taylor, I'd shut up and start pouring me some juice.'

'Well, if you hadn't been so desperate to parade

yourself in front of old Carlos there, I'd have brought this to you in bed,' Nick told her, raising an eyebrow suggestively.

'It's a good job you didn't,' Jenna teased. 'I sleep naked.'

'Really? Hey, tomorrow morning – I'm there!' Nick joked, as Jenna began to laugh. He picked up a tray of fantastic-looking food – fresh bread rolls, creamy yellow butter, locally made jams and *ensaïmadas*, the traditional island pastry. 'Don't even think about the calories,' Nick warned her, 'otherwise you'll miss out on one of the most delicious things you've ever eaten.'

'Mmm, they smell fabulous,' Jenna told him, breathing in the mouthwatering scent. 'And don't worry, I'm planning to take it easy on myself for a few days. I don't want any punishing exercise regime, just a lot of lounging around, stuffing myself full of *ensaïmadas*.'

'That's my girl,' Nick told her, as he picked up the food. 'C'mon, let's take all this stuff and eat outside.'

'This is heavenly,' sighed Jenna contentedly, as she lounged in one of the easy chairs on the terrace, shaded from the fiercest of the midday sun by a large white parasol. 'I've eaten so much I don't think I can move,' she groaned.

'Well, you don't have to, princess. Nothing to do all day but lie here and chill,' Nick told her, pouring them both another glass of freshly squeezed orange juice.

'But shouldn't we work on some material or something?' Jenna protested feebly.

'No need,' Nick replied easily. 'Zac's flying out today and won't be here until later. You've got all afternoon to relax and settle in.'

'Okay, you've convinced me,' Jenna told him, lazily

batting away a bright blue dragonfly that buzzed around the trailing bougainvillea. The heat was heavy, but not oppressive, and Jenna was grateful for the gentle breeze blowing off the sea, which kept the temperature bearable.

She stretched luxuriously in her seat, and Nick watched her and smiled.

'I think I might get changed and go for a swim,' Jenna told him. 'Then just spend a couple of hours by the pool.'

'Yeah, well, don't get too used to it,' Nick warned. 'When the others get out here I'm gonna start cracking the whip.'

'Really?' Jenna raised an eyebrow. 'Sounds fun.'

'Oh it is. But I'd better warn you – I'm merciless.'

Jenna smiled. 'I'll see you back here in ten minutes, Nick,' she told him firmly.

'It's a date,' he winked, as Jenna headed back to the house. She felt ridiculously happy as she walked back to her room, unable to stop herself from smiling.

It must be the hot weather, she told herself, as she began to gather the things she needed into a large canvas beach bag; sun cream, sunglasses, a thick, glossy novel, iPod, a selection of magazines and a large Gucci beach towel.

Yeah, either that or the gorgeous guy waiting for you by the pool, she realized with a giggle. Still smiling, she undressed and slipped into a Missoni print bikini, checking out her reflection in the mirror.

Perfect.

If this didn't hook Nick Taylor, nothing would.

When Jenna returned to the pool she found Nick wasn't there. Unconcerned, she dumped her bag on a sun lounger and impulsively dived into the pool. After the hot sun on her body, the water felt freezing cold, but Jenna welcomed the shock to her system. She gasped as she broke the surface, smoothing back her long golden hair.

Jenna began to swim a few laps of the pool, basking in the deliciously refreshing water, which made her skin tingle and invigorated her whole body. She rolled over and closed her eyes, letting her mind drift as she floated on the surface, basking in the sun's warmth.

As a shadow fell across her face, she opened her eyes to see Nick standing by the side of the pool, his muscular body directly in the sun's path. She wondered how long he'd been watching her.

'Hey,' he said softly.

'Hey.'

'No need to get out on my account,' Nick told her, his voice low and husky, as Jenna swam to the edge.

'I've been in too long anyway,' she replied, easing herself out of the pool.

Nick groaned inwardly. Man, this was torture! Halle Berry had nothing on Jenna Jonsson, he thought to himself as he watched Jenna emerge, dripping wet. Her skin was shiny, her muscles toned, and droplets of water streamed down her arms, down her thighs, between her breasts . . .

Nick swallowed as Jenna ran her hands through her hair, pushing it back from her face. It was like being in some clichéd soft-focus movie scene, Nick thought, but he certainly wasn't complaining.

Jenna began to towel her hair, then searched through her bag for her sun cream – anything to take her eyes off Nick. She couldn't stop checking him out, and desperately hoped he hadn't noticed. She needed to play this one cool, not throw herself at him like some love-struck teenager.

But could any woman help herself, she reasoned? Dressed in just black swimming trunks and dark Gucci sunglasses, there was so much perfectly honed body on show. His shoulders were muscular, his chest toned and broad. And his thighs . . . With a sudden burst of lust, Jenna found herself imagining what it would be like to make love to him, crushed beneath his powerful frame, their bodies matted with perspiration as they writhed together. Unable to stop, she began wondering how he would make love to her – would he be slow and gentle, with a confident, teasing touch, or would he be urgent and thrusting, unable to hold back in his desire for her?

'I brought you some water.' Nick's voice broke into her thoughts as he held out the chilled bottle of San Pellegrino.

'Thanks,' said Jenna, hardly daring to look at him as she took the bottle. She felt as though she must be blushing furiously and desperately hoped Nick wouldn't be able to detect the way she was squirming with lust beside him. *Get a grip*, she warned herself, as she began to get slick between the legs. 'I think I'm just going to chill here for a while now,' she told him, trying to keep her voice even.

'Sure,' he replied easily, in that sexy Southern drawl.

Jenna began to apply lotion as Nick stretched out on his sun lounger, folding his hands behind his head. There was a long silence.

'So, d'you like it here?' Nick asked finally.

'I love it! It's like paradise,' Jenna gushed, overcompensating madly as she spread lotion across her stomach and chest.

'So it wasn't a bad decision then, staying here?' Nick couldn't resist asking.

'Nick,' began Jenna warningly. 'I'd quit while I'm ahead

if I were you,' she joked, threatening him with the tube of sun cream.

Nick reached over and plucked it out of her hand.

'Don't take that tone with me, Jonsson,' he said sternly. 'Now turn over while I do your back.'

Meekly, Jenna obliged, rolling over onto her stomach. Nick moved to sit on the edge of the wooden lounger and clicked the cap off the cream, squeezing it gently onto Jenna's flawless skin.

Jenna inhaled sharply. 'It's cold!'

'Is that better?' Nick asked softly. He began to smear the cream smoothly, his hands slipping over her shoulder blades, over the toned muscles and all the way down to her lower back. He rubbed gently, his palms making a circular motion in the hollow at the base of her spine as his fingertips gripped her waist.

'Mmmmm,' she murmured.

Not letting go of her waist, he swung his leg across her body and straddled her, his feet either side of the sun lounger. Gently, he rested himself on her back. 'Does that hurt?' he asked her worriedly.

'A little,' Jenna told him truthfully. He was a big guy.

Nick raised himself off her, and Jenna spread her legs a little wider, giving him more room to sit down. 'Is that better?' he asked, lowering himself back down.

'Mmm hmmm . . .' she replied, not trusting herself to say anything more.

Nick continued to slide his hands up and down her body, gradually applying more pressure. He was unbelievably hard; his cock was so swollen it hurt, as he slid his hands under the string that fastened her bikini.

'You're gonna get tan lines,' he whispered hoarsely.

Jenna didn't speak, but simply reached round to her back with one hand and pulled the tie gently, letting her top fall away to the side. She was acting purely on instinct now, too horny to think straight.

Nick shifted position, feeling his erection straining against his shorts, and applied more lotion, making Jenna's body slippery underneath his hands. He massaged her shoulders, his fingertips reaching far over her collarbone and down towards her breasts. Jenna felt her nipples tighten almost painfully, and hardly dared move, she was so turned on. She felt sure that if she so much as rubbed against the fabric of the sun lounger she would come. Then Nick's fingers withdrew, sliding back over her shoulder blades, down towards her butt, and out to the sides as he began to caress her waist, his hands steadily moving along her body until they were cupping the sides of her breasts. The rest of her chest was hidden from him, crushed into the soft material of the sun lounger.

'Jenna . . .' breathed Nick. He couldn't hold on any longer, he was going to have to kiss her, he—

'How's it going guys?'

Jenna and Nick looked up sharply to see a stony-faced Zac standing a few feet away. Dressed casually in combats and a sleeveless white top, he cut a strikingly handsome figure in the glamorous surroundings of Nick's villa.

'I can leave if you're busy,' he said, his voice heavy with sarcasm.

'No need to do that,' replied Nick smoothly, climbing off Jenna's back. His erection was still clearly visible and, although Nick didn't seem to find this a problem, Jenna felt decidedly uncomfortable. She knew exactly what the scene must have looked like to Zac, and this was not the way she would have wanted him to find them. The move to Ibiza was supposed to herald a new

166

start for the Phoenix project; fooling around with Nick didn't exactly signal a committed attitude to her work.

'Hey,' she greeted him awkwardly, not daring to move in case she exposed her breasts to them both.

'Hey,' replied Zac neutrally.

Jenna sat up carefully, holding her top in place as she retied it at the back.

'Carlos let me in,' Zac told them, by way of explanation. His voice sounded stilted and carefully controlled. 'I arrived a couple of hours ago and thought I'd come round and see how you both were. But I see you're settling in just fine,' he said pointedly.

Jenna felt herself redden, hating Zac for the way he was making her feel. Mutinously, she looked up at him from underneath her long lashes, her green eyes defiant. 'Yeah,' she said brightly, deliberately not picking up on his inference. 'Nick's been the perfect host, and the house is just gorgeous.'

'Gorgeous,' Zac echoed tonelessly. 'Anyway, I'm gonna head off. Like I said, I just thought I'd drop in.'

'You don't have to leave. We weren't doing anything that won't wait until later,' Nick grinned, and Jenna felt an unexpected stab of annoyance at his cavalier attitude.

'Look, why don't you stay?' she said warmly to Zac. 'It's so nice just sitting out in the sun and chilling. We can talk about our plans for the music.'

Zac considered her for a moment, but Jenna couldn't quite read his expression as his eyes were hidden behind his sunglasses.

'How about if I leave you two out here to catch up while I head back inside and get us some drinks,' she offered. 'Maybe make a spot of lunch or something?'

'Jenna Jonsson cooks?' remarked Zac cynically, raising an eyebrow.

'Well I can manage pasta and salad,' she told him defensively, feeling her guard come up the way it always did when Zac teased her.

'Then I guess pasta and salad it'll have to be then,' he said lightly.

'You're staying?' she burst out, unable to hide her surprise.

'Yeah,' he said neutrally. 'I'll stay.'

'Cool,' said Jenna, trying to subdue the emotions churning through her. She suddenly felt desperate to escape. There was a trace of a smile on Zac's face and she couldn't help but feel he was laughing at her, that once again she was the butt of some private joke.

'You don't have to do that,' Nick told her, as Zac settled himself on a chair beside the pool. 'I'll ask Carlos to bring something out here.'

'It's fine,' Jenna snapped, the words coming out more harshly than she'd intended in her haste to leave. She felt inexplicably annoyed with Nick, as though she was blaming him for Zac discovering the two of them like that. Pulling a light silk kaftan over her bikini, she turned on her heel, walking towards the house as fast as she dared.

16

The telephone rang loudly and insistently. Sadie felt as though the noise was right inside her head, hammering into her brain. With a groan, she rolled over and pulled the pillow over her ears in a futile attempt to block out the sound.

'Phone,' she croaked pathetically. Her throat was parched and her mouth tasted as though she'd been licking out Usain Bolt's running shoes. 'Phone's ringing,' she tried again. 'Carla, can you get it?' Sadie pleaded. She didn't seem to be able to open her eyes; the light was painful.

From across the room came bad-tempered muttering, but eventually Sadie heard the sound of Carla's sheets being pulled back and bed springs creaking as she moved across to finally, blessedly, stop the ringing.

Being woken quickly hadn't agreed with Sadie. Before she could even find out who was calling, she felt an insistent, nauseous churning in her stomach. It wasn't pleasant and she dashed to the bathroom, bolting across the unfamiliar carpet. Hanging over the toilet bowl, there came a gentle knock at the door.

'Sadie?'

Sadie raised her head. 'Yeah?'

'You okay?'

'Um . . . not great.'

'Oh.' Carla didn't sound hugely sympathetic. 'There's some girl on the phone for you.'

'Huh?'

She heard Carla sigh in exasperation. 'I said there's some—'

'Yeah, yeah, I heard you. What girl? I don't know any girl here.'

'I don't know.' Carla sounded as if she was speaking through clenched teeth. 'She asked for you. Are you gonna take the call or not, 'cos she's waiting.'

Something, somewhere, seemed vaguely familiar to Sadie. 'Yeah, I'm coming,' she said irritably, hauling herself up from the bathroom floor and flushing the toilet. Wrapping herself in one of the delightfully fluffy and comforting robes, she crawled onto the bed and weakly picked up the receiver.

'Hello?'

'Sadie? Hi, it's Brooke! I'm so glad I found you – I didn't think I was gonna remember your room number 'cos I just have, like, the worst memory, but I found you! So what time are you coming to try out today?'

Sadie held the phone away from her ear. She couldn't cope with so much exuberance when she had just woken up, and she'd barely made it past the first sentence. 'Brooke?' she repeated in confusion.

'Yeah. From last night,' Brooke clarified, sounding a little deflated. 'The Pleasuredome, remember?'

'Umm . . .' Sadie squinted across at Carla, hoping she might provide some clue. Carla pursed her lips and looked extremely pissed off. Sadie swallowed. Snatches of last night began to come back to her, the occasional image flitting across her mind like a movie montage. Garish coloured cocktails with Brad and Chad. A strapping transvestite in corset and suspenders. Topless women and then . . . Oh God, Sadie had a vague recollection of being up on stage herself, giving a steamy performance as she tried to take her clothes off. Shit, that was so embarrassing. And then talking to some stripper . . . 'Brooke?' she tried again.

'Oh, now it's all coming back,' Brooke cackled. 'How are you feeling today?'

'Shit,' Sadie told her bluntly.

'Oh, that's too bad. But you're still coming for the audition, yeah?'

Sadie fell silent again, dredging the depths of her brain for something to help her understand what Brooke was talking about. She remembered a pink flyer, and Brooke's excited talk of a new burlesque troupe. Right, like Vegas needed another one of those. 'Brooke, I don't think—'

'Sadie!' Brooke immediately cut her off, and her tone was petulant. 'But you promised me!'

Had she promised? Sadie couldn't remember. Brooke could have told her she'd lap-danced for Barack Obama, and she wouldn't have known whether to believe her.

'Brooke,' Sadie began tiredly, wishing the banging in her head would stop for just one second, 'I'm really sorry. To be honest, I can't remember what I said last night, but I'm in no fit state to do anything today except crash out by the pool.'

'But you *gotta* come! You were totally amazing last night. I've told Karl all about you, he's dying to meet you!'

'Brooke, I'm on holiday! I came here to party and to shop and to gamble – not to audition for a show.'

171

But Brooke was insistent, and a weak and exhausted Sadie was no match for her tenacity. 'Look, I know where you're staying and I've got friends who work there who owe me favours. I can get them to evacuate you from your room in no time.'

'Why are you doing this?' Sadie groaned.

'Because I think you'll have fun!' Brooke was infuriatingly perky. 'I think you've really got something, and I think you should meet Karl. Get yourself in a cab and get over here as soon as possible. You still got the flyer I gave you?'

Sadie checked her purse. 'Yeah, I've got it.'

'Awesome! See you in an hour.' Brooke hung up.

Sadie rolled over, burying her face in the blissful softness of her warm bed before letting out a long, low moan. 'I think I have an audition,' she told Carla.

'I know, you wouldn't shut up about it last night.'

'Really?' Sadie sat up, worried by Carla's tone.

Carla nodded then walked over to the windows, flinging the curtains wide open to let the bright light flood in. It was almost midday and the sun was high in the sky. The weather was glorious; in the distance the heat shimmered over the mountain tops.

'Aargh,' Sadie cried out. She fell back onto the bed, shielding her eyes dramatically. 'Please help me,' she begged. 'I can't do this alone. Help me, Carla.'

Carla sighed. 'I'll ring room service and order a large pot of coffee.'

'And a round of toast?' Sadie asked hopefully, raising her head to smile winningly.

Carla rolled her eyes as she picked up the phone.

'Hey, you wanna come with me today?' Sadie suggested, brightening at the idea.

'Oh no. No way. This is your mess. I'm going to sit out by the pool and catch me some rays.'

'Really supportive, thanks,' Sadie muttered, as Carla grinned sweetly and ordered breakfast for the two of them.

Paul Austin stood in front of the floor-to-ceiling windows in his office, staring out at the city. It was late evening and the buildings across the capital were illuminated, a stark contrast to the blackness of the night sky. Far below him the streets were empty – most of the office workers had gone home, and the area was deserted.

The bleakness matched Paul's frame of mind. He was not in a good mood. He'd been taking it a little easy at work recently, taken his eye off the ball, and the chief exec had noticed. Paul reported directly to William Davis-Wright, the CEO of Willis & Bourne, a ruthless, results-driven guy who left you alone as long as you were performing but savaged you if you weren't. Paul had been called in to discuss the productivity of all those long lunches and external meetings he had been taking, all on the company expense account, naturally. He hoped the meeting would have been kept quiet, but the gossip network in this place was notorious. William's PA, Anna, was on the phone the second he left the office, the loose-lipped bitch. And now the sharks would be circling; any one of those on the office floor was just waiting for the chance to take his office and his position.

Paul exhaled sharply as he watched a single droplet of rain make its way down the polished glass. It was true that he hadn't been performing well recently, but he was sure it was just a temporary glitch. Paul had the Midas touch when it came to investments. Everyone knew it. He knew it and William Davis-Wright knew it. He just needed to rediscover it. Sure, he'd gone in for some high-risk deals recently, but how the hell was he expected to keep making returns that blew the competition out of the water if he didn't?

At least that silly slut Sadie had stopped phoning him. She was the reason he'd spent so many afternoons away from work; the reason he was deep in the shit now. It had been fun while it lasted, but these things had to end, surely she realized that? And boy, had she gone out with a bang . . .

Oh yeah, she'd been hot, Paul smiled, allowing himself a moment to remember that perfectly flexible body, the way she'd been instantly responsive with fire in her eyes. There'd certainly been a buzz when he'd posted that footage online, with other users falling over themselves to download it. It gave him an intoxicating rush of power, an almost sexual thrill from knowing he could film the girls without their knowledge while he dominated them completely, then put it out there for the whole world to see. Sadie had been one of his best yet. She'd been eager to please, up for anything.

But he was a married man – there was no way it could continue. He'd never promised her anything, never shown any signs of commitment. So what the hell did she think she was playing at, ringing him repeatedly, leaving hysterical voicemails? He knew she'd been calling the office too, but Angela had dealt with her. Paul smiled. Maybe he should give his PA more credit – she was always good at getting rid of the women who were bothering him. Now this one would just crawl back to whichever hovel she came from, like the rest of them.

Allowing himself a satisfied smile, Paul turned back to his computer. What the . . .? His jaw tightened, the muscle above his left eyebrow pulsating with anger.

That fledgling finance company in Qatar that he'd thought was such a good investment – the whole fucking thing had gone under. Paul smashed his fist on the desk so hard that the framed photograph of his children toppled over. He'd invested thousands in that. Jesus, why did this keep happening to him? Quickly, he checked his client portfolios. They were looking pretty awful. Fuck, he was down on nearly every transaction.

Paul glanced quickly round the office, looking for a way to vent his anger. His gaze landed on the crystal tumbler on his desk. Snatching it up, he threw it as hard as he could against the far wall. It shattered into jagged pieces, the crash eerily loud in the silent building.

Paul slammed his hands down on the desk, bending over as he tried to slow his ragged breathing. Almost instantly there was a knock at the door. 'Mr Austin?' asked a worried voice. 'Is everything okay?'

It was Angela. She opened the door a crack and peered in. 'I heard a noise . . .' she explained awkwardly.

'Angela.' Paul collected himself. 'I didn't realize you were still here.'

'Yes,' she nodded. 'I always stay until you go home, just in case you need anything.'

'Right.' Paul exhaled slowly, digesting the information. 'That's very dedicated.'

'I am very dedicated,' she assured him. Her eyes were wide, her voice breathy.

Paul watched her with amusement. She couldn't have been any more obvious if she'd lain down naked on the office floor and spread her legs wide open.

'Is everyone . . . Is there anyone else around, Angela?' he asked casually.

'I think this floor's empty, sir,' she murmured, her gaze downcast. 'You and I are the only ones left.'

Paul could feel his pulse racing, the adrenaline still pumping from his earlier fury. He knew of one certain way to subdue his rage, something guaranteed to distract him from his problems.

'Come in, Angela,' he told her. She stepped inside and saw the smashed glass, her mouth falling open in shock.

'What happened? Should I clean it up?'

'Not now,' Paul shook his head. 'Don't worry about it. Close the door behind you.' Angela did as she was told. 'Lock it,' he commanded.

Angela clicked the lock, her cheeks flaming.

'Good.' Paul seemed pleased, his blue eyes glittering dangerously. 'Now come over here, Angela.'

Angela gazed up at him, her heart thumping. They both knew she would do anything he wanted.

Slowly, she began to walk across the office towards him.

17

Sadie staggered through the door of The Play Rooms
wearing enormous dark sunglasses and clutching a
Starbucks. She'd been surprised to see a long line of
girls outside the building, all super-groomed and
dressed to the nines. The queue snaked round the
block, and Sadie had had to sweet-talk the guy on the
door, using Brooke's name to jump to the front. Seeing
the way some of the women were dressed, Sadie began
to wish she'd made more of an effort. She hadn't
brought any dance gear to Vegas, so she was wearing
a pair of black leggings over which she had layered a
couple of vest tops. On her feet were silver flip-flops;
she planned to dance barefoot. The look was casual
but sexy, showing off the curved lines of her slim
figure.

Inside, the club was spectacular. The overhead lights
were on, but it must have looked amazing at night,
Sadie realized. It was decorated in shades of chocolate
and burgundy, giving it a dark, decadent feel. The
seating was low, plush red velvet with dark wooden
tables and beautiful silver lanterns to hold candles.
Gilt chandeliers hung from the ceiling, and every wall

was decorated with huge mirrors framed by crystals that sparkled in the light. It was like being in a very glamorous boudoir. As Brooke had said, it was in a different league to The Pleasuredome: sexy, sophisticated and intimate. Sadie was impressed. This was much bigger than the seedy strip show she had expected. She began to feel a little nervous.

'Sadie!' Brooke screeched as soon as she saw her. 'You came!'

Sadie gave her a little wave, then walked across the room to introduce herself.

The set-up looked like a TV talent show, with Brooke, a short bald guy she assumed must be Karl, and a woman she didn't recognize at all, sitting behind a long table. Piles of notes, résumés and headshots were stacked up in front of them, and they each sipped from a can of Diet Pepsi.

'So this is the famous Sadie Laine,' Karl commented, in his nasal San Francisco accent, as Sadie shook his hand. 'I hope you're as good as your reputation,' he sniped, and Sadie wasn't entirely sure whether he was being friendly.

'Just ignore him,' Brooke told her. 'He's the bitchiest queen around.'

Even sitting down, Sadie could tell that Karl Madison was not a tall man. In fact, he was all of five foot five, but what he lacked in height he made up for in acidic put-downs. He was as lean as a whippet and dressed immaculately with a real sense of flair. A self-confessed star-fucker, Karl was as camp as they came but was a total pussycat behind the tigress exterior.

'How's your head, darling?' he yelled loudly in Sadie's direction.

Sadie made a noncommittal gesture, hoping he wasn't planning on doing any more shouting.

'Oh, I heard *all* about it. Your reputation precedes you my dear,' he drawled smugly, before introducing the attractive black woman beside him. 'This is Desiree Jones. She's an amazing choreographer and we've worked together many times over the years. I adore her vision,' he told Sadie, 'And I trust her judgement implicitly. It's almost as flawless as mine.'

Sadie and Desiree shook hands, then Karl said, 'Okay, show me what you can do. Astound me.'

'But . . . I don't have anything prepared,' Sadie faltered, immediately forgetting all of her training. The first rule of auditioning was that you never said no.

'Are you wasting my time?' Karl asked sharply, narrowing his eyes.

'No. I'm on holiday. I don't have my music with me,' Sadie retorted stubbornly, wondering why she had even bothered to turn up. This was all a big mistake. Brooke had made it sound fun and casual, but it was clearly more serious than that.

'Maybe she could freestyle,' Brooke suggested, looking worried. She'd gone out on a limb to get Karl interested in this girl, and she didn't want him to think she was stupid.

'Okay,' Karl agreed with a theatrical sigh. 'Desiree, could you put on some music?'

'What style do you want to see?' asked Sadie, as she put down her coffee and kicked off her flip-flops.

'Whatever you prefer,' Karl said magnanimously.

The music started and Sadie could have laughed out loud at the irony; it was *Feel It* by Jenna Jonsson.

Karl noted the look on her face. 'What's the matter,

Miss Sour Puss? Don't you like the music? Jenna's one of my favourite clients, I totally adore her.'

'*You're* Jenna's choreographer?' Sadie burst out. Great. This was just totally fucking perfect.

'You want to discuss it or you want to dance?' Karl shot back.

His attitude fired up Sadie with the adrenaline she needed. She could have walked out, but she knew there were five hundred girls outside who would kill for this opportunity. Despite everything, she still couldn't fight her competitive instincts. Defiantly, Sadie began to move, feeling herself get into the rhythm of the song. She'd always tried to avoid listening to Jenna's music, but she couldn't deny that the beat on this was hot. Desiree turned it up loud so that the building throbbed, as Sadie broke into hip-hop. It was her favourite style so she concentrated on that, but she sexed up her moves, giving it pace and attitude.

After a minute or so, Karl signalled for her to stop. 'I want to see how you take choreography,' he said, his face giving nothing away.

'Okay.' Sadie ran her hands over her hair, smoothing back the loose strands. She hadn't had time to dry it properly before she left, so had just pulled it back in a ponytail.

Karl got up from behind the table and ran over a short routine with her. It had strong elements of burlesque, and was different to anything that Sadie had ever done. To her surprise, she found herself wanting to do well. Karl was clearly an amazing dancer, undeniably dedicated to what he did, and she wanted to please him. There was a tricky section in the final eight, where the steps were fast and complicated. Sadie gave it her all and began to break a sweat.

Finally Karl stood back and it was left to Sadie to

perform alone. She knew she had to step it up a notch, and she made sure her moves were clean and sharp, that she made it her own. Her face expressed everything she was feeling; she was intense, strong and passionate. Most of all, she was enjoying it.

Karl was clapping along with the music, keeping pace, unable to stay still as he bounced from side to side. He kept up a constant stream of encouragement and direction. 'Yes, that's it, give me attitude, give me sexy . . . Work it girl, you look hot, hot, hot . . . I love it!'

When Sadie finished she felt elated. She'd been good and she knew it. She assumed the audition was over, but then Karl unexpectedly asked if she could sing.

'Sing?' she repeated dumbly.

'Yes, sing. You know, as in la la la,' he said tartly.

'Not outside the shower,' she fired back.

Karl was amused. Despite his cutting attitude, he loved it when someone took him on and gave as good as they got. 'I'm not interested in your opinion, only mine,' he bitched. 'Now, give me a few bars of something.'

Sadie went blank. Dancing she could do, but singing was outside her comfort zone. She glanced across at Brooke, hoping for inspiration.

'What about Madonna?' Brooke suggested brightly. 'You were wearing the T-shirt last night.'

Sadie grinned, mentally running through the track listings on her iPod. She decided on 'Like a Prayer'. It was her favourite; she loved the song, the image, the video – everything about it. She had no idea whether or not she could sing it, but she was going to damn well try.

Sadie closed her eyes for a second, trying to get into the moment, but Karl told her to open them.

'They're the windows to the soul, baby,' he chanted. 'You've gotta communicate with the audience, lay yourself open to them. How're you gonna do that if you're shutting yourself off? People lose interest if they can't see your eyes.'

Sadie nodded. She understood. Like dancing, it was all about feeling the emotion and communicating it. She fixed Karl with her gaze and began to sing. Her voice was good, tuneful and powerful, with a slight husky quality that was a legacy from last night's drinking in smoky bars. She made it through a verse and a chorus and Karl looked impressed for the first time that day.

'Ooh, what else are you hiding in there, Miss Laine?'

Sadie felt triumphant, wondering what else he was going to ask her to do. *Bring it on, bitch!* She was starting to feel invincible.

'Okay, Sadie, thank you for coming. We'll be in touch,' Karl said suddenly, and his tone was dismissive.

'That's it?' Sadie exclaimed in surprise, wondering what she'd done wrong.

'Hey, you've already had twice as long as any other girl I've seen, and you didn't even have to queue thanks to your number one fan here,' he said, indicating Brooke. 'Now, we have your cell number, yes?'

Sadie explained that she was staying at Caesars but they could reach her there.

'Great. Thank you. Next!' Karl called out sharply.

A stunning South American girl wearing little more than hot pants and a bra strutted in. Her body was amazing; she had the longest legs Sadie had ever seen and her abs were so toned you could see the outline of a six-pack. She wore black fishnet hold-ups with biker boots, and had such a sassy attitude that an onlooker would think her place in the group was a God-given right. Sadie felt ridiculous in her leggings and flip-flops, wondering how on earth she'd ever expected to be taken seriously.

She glanced at Brooke, hoping for some reassurance. Brooke gave her an excited thumbs-up before turning her attention to the new arrival who was announcing herself as Adriana. Everyone seemed to have totally forgotten Sadie's existence. As discreetly as possible, she picked up her now cold coffee and slunk out of the door.

18

Jenna stood in front of the antique mirror in her room in Casa Santos, scrutinizing her appearance. She was wearing denim hot pants and a white triangle bikini top which showed off her fabulous tan. Her long, thick hair was pulled up into a loose knot on top of her head, with a few wispy tendrils breaking loose to perfectly frame her pretty face, and she had applied just a slick of lip gloss and a little waterproof mascara. The look was simple and uncomplicated, and showed her natural beauty to perfection. Yet she felt on edge.

It was her second day at the villa and Nick had decided to throw a barbecue. Very shortly, Zac, Ryan, and his family would be arriving for a pleasant afternoon's socializing on the beach. Except it wasn't going to turn out that way, because Kelly was an insecure, hormonal mess, and Zac acted like he found Jenna ridiculous and immature, and couldn't stand being around her for any longer than he had to. Jenna bit her lip. She knew Nick was just being his sociable, easy-going self, but it was fine for him – this was his world, his friends. She wished it could be just the two of them, so they might finally get a chance to finish what they'd started . . .

She heard a tap at the door, and it swung open just a little. 'Are you ready?' asked Nick. 'Everyone'll be here soon.'

'Not quite. Go ahead, I'll be down in a minute.'

'Nah, come down now – you look incredible.'

'I'm not ready yet,' Jenna repeated unconvincingly.

Seeing that something was wrong, Nick stepped into her room, closing the door behind him. 'Are you okay?'

'I'm fine,' Jenna lied, avoiding his gaze.

'Hey, what's wrong?' Nick asked, evidently concerned.

Jenna thought back to the way Kelly had spoken to her on the plane, the look of hostility in her eyes. 'It's nothing,' she said dismissively. 'I'm just being silly.' She felt increasingly annoyed with herself. It wasn't like her to let a little thing like this get under her skin.

Nick sighed as he stepped towards her, wrapping his arms around her and pulling her close. His embrace was strong and reassuring as Jenna sank against him. 'What am I going to do with you, Jonsson?' he asked hoarsely, holding her tightly as he rested his chin on the top of her head, feeling her silky hair beneath his rugged stubble.

Jenna didn't reply but let herself melt into his arms, smelling the glorious, musky scent of the aftershave he was wearing. She closed her eyes, wishing she could stay protected in his arms and not have to go downstairs and face Kelly's wrath or Zac's disapproval. Jenna was crushed against Nick's bare chest, acutely aware of the intense skin-on-skin contact. She couldn't fail to be; her body made it unmistakable as she felt the heat flood into her belly, moving lower, all too aware of how easy it would be to just—

The doorbell rang, and they heard Carlos shout from downstairs, 'Señor Taylor?'

'Yeah, I'm coming,' Nick hollered back, reluctantly pulling away. 'Are you gonna be okay?' he asked her seriously, wanting to make sure but knowing they had to go.

'Yeah.' Jenna nodded. 'Yeah, I'll be fine.' She smiled up at him as he placed a hand lightly on her back and steered her towards the door.

'Come on, let's go.'

In the hallway Jenna quickly checked her appearance in the mahogany-framed mirror. The better she looked, the more confident she felt – and she looked sensational. Any bullshit from Kelly or Zac, and Jenna couldn't be held responsible for her actions.

Nick opened the door and the first people she saw were Ryan and Kelly. Ryan stood with Brandon wound round his legs, as Kelly held the baby in her arms. The overall effect was as though this perfect family had just stepped out of the pages of a glossy magazine, straight out of a fragrance ad. It was nauseating, thought Jenna spitefully, forcing herself to smile at them.

Behind them was Zac. He looked fantastic in a white Paul Smith shirt, open at the neck to show off his light tan.

Then Jenna noticed – Amber was standing beside him.

'Amber, hi! I didn't know you were coming,' Jenna faltered, her surprise all too obvious. Could it possibly get any worse, she wondered? Kelly and Amber all in the same afternoon. Fan-fucking-tastic.

'I flew out late last night,' Amber explained coolly. 'I have to fly back to New York tomorrow afternoon, but I thought I'd come and see my baby while I've got a couple of days off,' she added, as she slipped a skinny arm possessively around Zac.

Nick stepped forward to kiss Amber on the cheek.

'Well, it's great to have you here,' he told her warmly. Whether he was being genuine or not, Jenna couldn't tell, but he was enthusiastic enough to make it believable and Jenna didn't want to ruin his party.

Faking a bright smile, she turned to Amber. 'I love your hair,' she lied effusively. 'It looks fabulous.' Amber had had her long copper hair chopped into a stylish, graduated bob, complete with blonde streaks. Fortunately for her, Amber had the skyscraper cheekbones to carry it off, but Jenna wasn't keen on the style. It was undeniably cutting edge, but Jenna preferred to look a little more classic – a little more timeless, in the iconic Bardot mould.

'Thanks,' drawled Amber. 'Zac doesn't like it, do you honey?' she asked, her movements strangely exaggerated as she turned to look at him.

'It's not that, it's just—'

'He prefers it long,' Amber announced loudly as she cut Zac off, her voice high and shrill. Zac looked at the floor, his cheeks blazing in embarrassment. He looked furious, his fists balled up tightly at his sides. Yet Jenna was surprised to see that he kept his temper in check and said nothing.

The others looked at each other somewhat nervously, trying to work out what was going on. The atmosphere seemed strained, as they all stood in uncomfortable silence in the expansive entrance hall. Despite its high ceilings and wide, sweeping staircase, it suddenly seemed unbearably claustrophobic.

'Shall we head out back?' Nick asked brightly, as though nothing was wrong. 'Carlos has been working like crazy all morning, and the beach looks awesome.'

With Nick at the head of the group, keeping up a constant stream of chat to ensure that there were no awkward pauses, and the two couples walking side by side, Jenna hung back, walking behind Zac and Amber. She eyed her critically; Amber was wearing a pleated white minidress by Chloe, and she was so thin she was practically skeletal. Her stomach was concave, and her rib cage protruded visibly through her skin. Her arms were so lean that the shape of the muscles could be clearly seen – there wasn't an ounce of spare flesh to cover them. She seemed to be having difficulty walking, and clung onto Zac for support. Occasionally she would stumble on one of the flag-stones, then swear violently at Zac as he tried to hold her up.

Jenna felt sickened. It was obvious what Amber's problem was, and it made Jenna hate her more than she ever had. Not simply because, from all Jenna's experience of her, Amber seemed to be a Class-A bitch – it was her Class-A habit that really pissed off Jenna. She had had first-hand experience of how coke could wreck lives, and she still couldn't believe people were dumb enough to take it. Amber was a mess – one look at her made it plain for anyone to see. Why Zac was with her, Jenna couldn't begin to understand.

They made it down to the beach without incident, and, as Nick had said, it looked fabulous. There was enough food to feed them all for weeks, and Carlos and his men had got the barbecue blazing nicely. They'd rigged a system of lights all the way along the path and onto the sand itself, so the party could continue even after it got dark, and an iPod dock had been set up on the food table, pumping music from the speakers.

Little Brandon was wild with excitement, running excitedly from the sea to the barbecue and back again. Nick was handling the cooking, and Jenna picked slowly at a vegetable skewer, feeling a little excluded as she watched the couples around her, increasingly intrigued by the strained relationship between Amber and Zac.

At times they would look like any other loving couple, as Amber curled up on Zac's lap, nestling into his shoulder while the two of them whispered to each other and giggled at private jokes only they understood. But at other times, Amber seemed irritated by his very presence, snapping viciously at him and causing everyone to look away uncomfortably as Zac grew mad and struggled to hold his tongue. Her behaviour infuriated Jenna – she felt outraged on behalf of Zac, at the way Amber was humiliating him. Okay, so Zac had never exactly been her favourite person, but he didn't deserve to be treated that way. More than anything, Jenna wanted to give Amber a good, hard slap, and tell her to grow up.

It was inevitable that Jenna should end up talking to Nick for most of the afternoon. Being surrounded by couples they were naturally drawn together, and because she was living with him she undoubtedly felt closer to him than the other members of Phoenix. At least, that was what she *told* herself. The fact that she fancied him like crazy was just pure coincidence.

Jenna stretched out on the sand, feeling the hot sun caress her body as she watched Nick expertly handle the barbecue. It wasn't just the Mediterranean heat that was making her body temperature soar, she realized. She wanted him badly. It was excruciating, being in such close proximity to the guy she wanted most in the whole world twenty-four hours a day. And it wasn't as though Jenna Jonsson had any trouble getting guys. But she knew this was different. They worked together, which was always going to make things difficult. And he had a reputation. Nick Taylor was one of the industry's biggest players, and Jenna wasn't stupid. She read the papers. She knew he had a different girl every week. But still . . .

She had seen the other side to him – the caring, affectionate side which was always absent from the way the press painted him. According to the papers, Nick was merely an arrogant playboy with a string of beautiful women all over the world and an irresponsible lifestyle. But they didn't *know* him, thought Jenna affectionately, watching the way his muscular body glistened in the sunlight. She didn't think she'd seen him wear a shirt the whole time they'd been in Ibiza.

'Hey!' came a loud shout. Jenna turned to see Amber tottering unsteadily down the steep steps cut into the rock face. She'd been back up to the house and had clearly just indulged. Everyone looked over as she yelled; she had their full, horrified attention. 'You guys,' she announced loudly, 'are *sooo* fucking boring. Let's liven the place up a little. Put some music on we can dance to or something. *Anything*,' she drawled, as she slid down the last couple of steps and stumbled onto the sand.

Zac sprang to his feet, his face contorted with rage. 'Amber—' he began, but Nick stopped him.

'Hey man, it's fine. Everything's fine,' he said carefully. 'Sure, come and pick another track,' Nick told Amber, speaking gently, as though she were a difficult child. 'There's loads on here.'

'Nick, you don't have to . . .' began Zac apologetically.

'Don't worry, it's no problem.'

Amber made her way over to the table, the uneven sand causing her to walk unsteadily like some grotesque parody of her catwalk strut. It was embarrassing to watch, and it must have been heartbreaking for Zac, Jenna thought unhappily.

Amber quickly scrolled through the playlist. 'They're all shit,' she snapped dismissively, as she clumsily prodded at the buttons. She chose a Faithless track, dance music with a heavy, insistent bass line. Amber whacked the volume up to full and began to move, kicking off her sandals. 'Come on you guys,' she laughed, now seeming to be enjoying herself.

'Jesus,' muttered Nick under his breath, watching her dance maniacally on the sand, lost in her own world as she span around and swayed from side to side, waving her arms above her head.

'Would you care to dance?' asked Nick, offering his hand to Jenna in an attempt to lighten the appalling situation and draw the group's attention away from Amber. She had now closed her eyes and was running her hands sensually over her body. Zac's cheeks were flaming as he watched her dancing provocatively, all inhibitions lost in her drug-fuelled haze.

'Sure,' Jenna smiled. 'You're a good mover,' she teased him, as he took her by the hand and spun her around. 'You should have been in a boy band.'

Nick laughed, and after a couple of songs the tension seemed to have eased a little. Zac blankly raked the hot coals of the barbecue, as they all pretended not to have noticed Amber dancing by herself further down the beach.

Ryan and Kelly sat curled up together, proud, loving smiles on their faces as they watched Brandon dancing by himself on the sand, blissfully unaware of the strangeness of the situation. Ryan sat with one arm protectively around Kelly, the other hand resting on her stomach. She looked tired but happy as she rested her head on Ryan's shoulder. When she caught Jenna watching them, her face hardened, and Jenna quickly glanced away.

The music changed to a chill-out song by Groove Armada and Nick automatically pulled Jenna closer. Smiling, she slipped her arms around his neck, throwing her hair out behind her. It had dried now, and Jenna could tell that the sea water had sent it dry and lanky. It must look awful, she thought.

She's so beautiful, thought Nick, as he pulled her close and rested one hand on her lower back. His touch was warm and it made Jenna's skin tingle. Her breasts were crushed against his chest, and Nick was getting horny as hell. But his gaze never wavered from her face as they looked at each other, locked in a silent game of daring the other to look away first. Neither of them did. Jenna felt her cheeks start to flush. Her body was hot and she felt her nipples tighten, wondering if Nick could feel them through the thin material of her bikini top. But still she didn't look away. She knew the others would be watching them and she didn't care. She didn't care about anything except Nick and those dizzying blue eyes as he drew her closer . . .

'Fuck!'

Jenna started, pulling away from Nick as there was a piercing scream from nearby. She looked around to see Amber in a heap on the sand, one leg badly twisted under her. Pandemonium broke loose as everyone ran towards her.

Zac got there first, shortly followed by Ryan.

'What happened?'

'She lost her balance,' said Zac quietly.

'I fell, you stupid fuck! I fell over, and now my fucking leg is broken,' Amber shouted, letting out another yell.

She was close to tears as Zac smoothed her hair, trying to calm her down.

'Can you stand?' he asked her.

'Of course I can't fucking stand,' she screeched. 'My fucking leg is broken. Don't you understand, you stupid bastard?'

'It might not be so bad,' said Nick. 'Try and lean on me, see if you can stand.'

'Get your hands off me,' Amber screamed at him, flailing her arms wildly as she pushed him away. 'Get me a helicopter or something, I need to go to hospital.'

Kelly knelt down by Amber's foot, pressing it lightly and gently moving it from side to side. Amber screamed in pain.

'Does that hurt?' asked Kelly, looking at her worriedly.

'Would I be screaming if it didn't?' she hissed.

'Look honey, I'm sure it's just a sprain,' Zac told her firmly, struggling to control his temper.

'What the hell would you know? You're not a fucking doctor, are you?' Amber rasped, her voice low and harsh. 'It's all your fault anyway. I never wanted to come here and spend a miserable afternoon with your boring friends. I don't know any of these people.'

'Amber,' Zac began sharply, but she ignored him, continuing to spit insults.

'I want to go back to New York with *my* friends. I want to have fun with them, not waste my life here.' She began crying again, snapping at Zac. 'Ow, my leg! It's all your fault. I'll never work again, do you know that? How the hell can I work with my leg in this fucked-up state? It's all your fault, you stupid cunt.'

Zac looked as though he'd been slapped. He blinked slowly, his face a picture of utter misery. 'We need to go,' he said quietly to Nick. 'Help me get her up.'

Together the two of them managed to get the screaming Amber to her feet. She had calmed down a little after her outburst and, by leaning on Zac, she was able to take a few slow steps.

'This is ridiculous,' snapped Zac, as he scooped Amber up in his arms and carried her across the sand. Amber clung to his neck, crying hysterically and repeatedly apologizing.

'I'm sorry baby, I'm so sorry . . .' she sobbed.

Zac said nothing, and the group on the sand simply watched them leave. They stood uselessly, impotent with shock. No one spoke. They watched until Zac and Amber had ascended the stairs and were out of sight, swallowed up by the lush foliage of Nick's garden.

19

'Jesus,' swore Nick. The group stood motionless, watching the spot where they had last seen Zac and Amber.

'Do you think she'll be okay?' asked Kelly, after a pause.

'I don't know. I really don't.' Ryan shook his head ruefully. 'That girl needs help.'

'Is she always like that?' Jenna asked curiously.

'Hell, no.' Nick shook his head. 'I've never seen her like that before. She's always been great, a really sweet girl. Her and Zac always seemed totally solid, y'know? Then again, I guess I haven't seen her in a while . . .'

'It's such a shame,' sighed Kelly. 'I've seen it so many times before. People get messed up with drugs and it just ruins them.'

Jenna said nothing.

Ryan glanced sharply at Kelly, and she clapped a hand over her mouth. 'Oh, I . . .' Her cheeks had turned bright red and she was clearly flustered. 'I didn't mean . . . Just forget I said . . .' she stammered awkwardly.

'It's okay,' said Jenna. She shrugged her shoulders slightly, a tiny movement. 'It's fine.'

There was an excruciating silence as they all remembered how Jenna's mother had died, killed by a helicopter pilot high on coke.

'I think we oughta be heading back now,' said Ryan, looking pointedly at Kelly as he swung Brandon into his arms.

'Yeah, the kids are getting tired,' she added quickly.

'It's probably best if we call it a night,' agreed Nick. It was early evening; the heat of the day was finally cooling, giving way to a fresh breeze. Their shadows were lengthening across the golden sand and it would soon be sunset.

They all made their way back up the steps and through the house, standing on the front porch as Kelly got the kids settled into the SUV they'd hired. Nick casually slipped an arm around Jenna's waist, his fingers splaying over her ribcage. She was still wearing just the bikini top and shorts she'd had on earlier, and the skin on her stomach was bare. She could feel the pressure from his fingertips, instantly aware of even the slightest movement he made as she gently leaned against him.

'D'you reckon we'll still be on for recording tomorrow?' asked Ryan as he climbed into the car.

Nick blew out the air in his cheeks. 'I've no idea, after tonight,' he shrugged. 'I guess it all depends on Zac. I'll call you, yeah? Let you know if he turns up.'

'Cool. See you soon. And thanks for this afternoon.'

'No problem. Drive safely, yeah?'

Ryan slammed the door and the car pulled away, bumping down Nick's uneven drive.

'Man, what a day!' exclaimed Nick, as he closed the

heavy wooden door. It banged shut behind them, echoing in the silence of the entrance hall. Once again it was just the two of them, Jenna realized, feeling little butterflies of excitement dance in her stomach.

'So . . .' Nick ran his gaze over her body, making no attempt to hide it. His eyes lingered on her full breasts, that hand-span waist, the tight little shorts fitting snugly over her butt. 'The night's still young. Seems a shame to waste it.'

Jenna could only nod in agreement – she seemed to have forgotten how to speak. She flashed back to the first time they'd met, at the MTV Awards, where Nick had left her tongue-tied with a single glance. It looked like nothing had changed.

Nick grinned. He seemed to be well aware of the effect he was having on her. 'Shall we get a drink?'

'That'd be . . . nice,' Jenna said carefully, then instantly felt stupid. *Nice?* Was that the best she could come up with?

'Lead the way,' Nick invited, indicating she should go ahead of him.

Self-consciously, Jenna set off along the corridor. Nick followed close behind and Jenna could tell that he was enjoying the view, watching the way her ass moved as she walked, her hips swaying from side to side.

They reached the kitchen and Jenna slid onto a bar stool while Nick got them both a drink. He took his time, moving unhurriedly as he cracked open a beer and poured a glass of wine for Jenna.

'Ice?'

'Please,' Jenna nodded. She watched Nick pull open the freezer, his arms tanned and muscular, a six-pack rippling at his stomach. It wasn't an exaggeration to say he had the best body she'd ever seen.

He dropped a couple of cubes into her glass, keeping a third one clutched in his hand. The ice-cold water dripped over his fingers, trickling down his wrist. Jenna had the overwhelming urge to lean across and lick it off. She took a sip of wine to distract her. The alcohol was good; she felt it hit her system almost immediately, the comforting warmth relaxing her body.

Nick saw her looking at him, noticing the way her pupils had dilated, her skin flushed. Then he reached across and lightly ran the ice cube along the full length of her arm, leaving a thin trail of water. He came to rest at her wrist, holding it against the delicate skin.

'It cools your body down quicker,' he explained hoarsely.

Jenna nodded, unable to take her eyes off him.

He moved round behind her, so close that she could feel his body brush against hers. Her hair was loose and he gathered it up, sweeping it over her shoulder to leave her back exposed. Gently, and with excruciating slowness, Nick ran the ice cube all the way down her back to the base of her spine. Jenna gasped. The hairs on the nape of her neck sprang up; every sense had gone into overdrive.

'Feels good after a crazy day, huh?'

Jenna shivered. The tension between them was off the scale, the air around them positively crackled with electricity. 'It's been kind of . . . intense . . .'

'Time to slow the pace a little . . .' Nick said softy. 'Kick back with a beer and a beautiful girl, on a warm night when there's just the two of you and no one else for miles around . . .' He sat down on the stool beside her, leaning in close. 'I don't think life gets any better than that.'

Jenna's eyes were half closed as she listened to him, his breath caressing the skin on her neck. 'Nick . . .'

'Let's go outside,' he suggested, his voice low.

Jenna opened her eyes. 'Nick, what . . .?'

'Trust me.' He took her hand, his strong fingers closing round hers as he helped her up from her seat. They headed out through the terrace doors and Jenna was instantly hit by the balmy evening air, the heady scent of wisteria and jasmine infusing the darkness. Sweeping fig trees hung over the pathway, and from deep within the rhododendron bushes she could hear the distinctive call of cicadas.

'It's beautiful,' Jenna breathed. 'So romantic.'

Nick turned to face her, wrapping his arms around her as he drew her close.

'Not as beautiful as you,' he murmured, brushing a loose strand of hair from her forehead. He let his fingers dance lightly over her skin, stroking her cheeks, her mouth, her neck.

'Nick . . .' Jenna sighed again. But she never got the chance to finish her sentence as the next moment he bent his head towards her and his mouth was on hers, his lips brushing her own with the lightest of touches, teasing and exploring. Jenna thought she might explode with happiness. This was what she'd dreamed about for so long – Nick Taylor, his mouth warm and inviting, his tongue gently exploring. He tasted so delicious she didn't ever want to stop, her body taking over as she felt a sweet rush of heat to her groin.

Unexpectedly, Nick pulled away. Jenna stood anxiously in front of him, wondering if she'd done something wrong. She was shaking with desire, desperate for him to kiss her again.

When Nick spoke, his voice was thick with longing. 'Let's go down to the beach.' He grabbed her by the hand and Jenna stumbled after him.

They wound along the narrow path as it led them

into the heart of the garden. The solar lamps had come on and the whole scene looked magical, dozens of tiny lights scattered along the rocky cliff edge. Ahead of them stretched a vast expanse of blackness, only the occasional glow of a ship far out at sea to illuminate it.

Nick helped her down the steps, lifting her onto the sand as she neared the bottom. His arms were strong, and she felt light as air in his grasp as he placed her down gently in front of him. They kissed again, more urgently this time. Nick was instantly hard; Jenna could feel him pressing against her and she ran her fingers over his chest, caressing the rock-hard muscles of his stomach, her hands working lower . . .

Suddenly Jenna squealed as the sea rushed in, lapping at her ankles. She gasped in shock, holding on to Nick to keep her balance.

Nick looked thoughtfully at his feet. 'Feel like a late-night dip?'

Jenna laughed nervously, wondering if he was serious. 'You're crazy!'

Nick shook his head, a challenging glint in his eye. 'You only live once, right?'

Before Jenna even had time to reply, Nick reached down and pulled off his shorts, throwing them down on the sand. Jenna caught her breath, a bolt of desire surging through her. God, he looked amazing. Someone should make a sculpture of that body, she marvelled, taking in the broad chest, ripped stomach and . . . Jenna let her gaze trail downwards and flushed. He was big; long and thick. She wondered how she must look, squirming with desire on the sand beside him, desperate to have him inside of her.

Nick turned away, striding into the water and swimming powerfully out until he was a short distance from the shore. The water came to his chest, his broad shoulders glistening in the moonlight.

They stared at each other for a long moment. Then Nick broke the silence. 'Are you coming in? Or do I have to swim alone?'

Jenna paused for a fraction of a second. *Fuck it!* She wanted to do something crazy. This was what she loved about Nick, the way he lived life to the full. The guy she wanted most in the world was just a few metres away from her, basking in a warm sea in the darkness of a summer's evening, waiting for her . . .

Jenna pulled the string of her bikini and let it fall away.

Out in the water, Nick groaned. Jesus, her body was sensational! So ripe and full, with curves that could drive a man insane just by thinking about them. As he watched, she wriggled out of her shorts and he saw that she was waxed, just a tiny triangle of neat blonde hair between her legs. Man, she made him feel like some horny schoolboy. It took all his effort not to swim straight back and take her right there on the sand.

Jenna walked hesitantly into the dark sea. It was cooler than she'd expected, and she shivered.

'Scared?' Nick called, taunting her.

'I'm not scared of anything.'

She plunged into the water, surfacing just in front of him. She looked like a glorious mermaid, her long, blonde hair slicked back and hanging damply down her neck.

And then Nick reached for her, his mouth crushing down upon hers as they were lost in a tangle of water and hands and bodies and tongues. Jenna heard herself moan as her hands slid over his body, throwing back her head as Nick began to kiss her neck. They moved instinctively, her hands caressing him, feeling him hard as flint beneath her fingers. Nick reached for her breasts, his mouth moving down, his tongue flickering over the tight nipples. Jenna groaned. She desperately wanted to take her time, to savour this moment, but she had been waiting for it for so long that her body took over. She felt out of control, primitive.

She reached for him, guiding him into her as Nick moaned and she felt him fill every inch of her, waves of pleasure rocking through her body as she moved insistently against him. Jenna was close already, she could feel it, as Nick wrapped his hands around her hips and pulled her down onto him, forcing himself deeper. She didn't ever want him to stop as he stroked her teasingly, moving smoothly and relentlessly inside of her. She wanted this feeling to last forever, but the pressure was building and she knew it couldn't last. Something was going to have to give, or else her body was going to explode, and then finally it did, and she threw back her head, arching her back as the starry night sky became blurred and she could think of nothing except the pleasure that was spreading through her whole body. And as she moved she felt Nick come inside of her, shaking as he clasped her tightly to him, burying his head in the curve of her neck.

Jenna closed her eyes, running a shaky hand across his back. He held her for so long she began to think he might never let go. But finally he eased his grip and Jenna leaned back to look at him.

She smiled at him, and he kissed her gently.

'You're so beautiful,' he murmured, looking at her with such tenderness that Jenna suddenly felt close to tears.

It was fully dark by the time the pair crept back onto the beach, just an unclouded crescent moon casting a pale light across the inky night sky.

'Can we rest here for a minute?' asked Jenna, as they emerged from the shallows. She was still shaking, and she wasn't sure it was entirely due to the cold.

They collapsed onto the soft sand at the base of the cliff face, and Nick wrapped his arms around her as they kissed again. They moved slowly now, tentatively, taking time to explore each other in a way that there had been no time for in their earlier frenzied urgency.

'Wait here a moment.' Nick jumped to his feet, jogging over to where the barbecue had been. He returned a few seconds later with a large, cashmere blanket, slipping it around Jenna's shoulders as the two of them snuggled up beneath the warm wrap.

Unbelievably, Nick felt himself growing hard again as their kisses grew deeper, their hands raking over each other's bodies. But they both knew that this time there was no rush; they could take all night if they wanted.

Slowly, Nick began to kiss Jenna's naked body, tiny butterfly kisses trailing down her chin, her neck, between her breasts and all the way down her stomach. Then he moved lower, using his tongue, sliding gently over her in the most intimate of places, doing exactly what she'd fantasized about for so long. The pressure was light at first, teasing, gradually growing more and more intense until Jenna arched her back and surrendered to it. Her orgasm was light and sweet, her soft cries carrying across the night sky. She drew Nick to her, breathing in the scent of him, delighting in the feel of his skin next to hers. She felt the hardness of him against her and she lazily parted her legs as he slipped inside of her. They moved together slowly, insistently, until he too was satisfied. Nick came with a groan and they collapsed against each other, staring up at the starry night sky.

Nick propped himself up on one elbow, stroking her hair as he marvelled at how stunning she was. 'Do you wanna go up to the house?'

'No, not yet,' Jenna replied sleepily. She lay down on the sand as Nick spooned around her, pulling the blanket tightly to them and wrapping an arm around her waist.

Jenna closed her eyes and relaxed against him, her back to his broad chest as she rested a hand on his thigh. Her heart rate had slowed to normal, and her breathing was deep and regular, settling into sleep.

But Nick was still wide awake and his mind was racing. Jenna Jonsson! *He had just fucked Jenna Jonsson!* And now she was lying in his arms, her blonde hair spilling across his biceps. She was so beautiful, so sexy. She was what every man wanted – and now she was his.

Under the dark, Mediterranean sky, as the sea crashed just a few metres away from them, Nick Taylor smiled to himself.

20

For Sadie and Carla, the drive back to McCarran International was far more subdued than the journey there had been. This time they weren't even travelling in a limo — Sadie had ordered a regular cab. She sat quietly in the back beside Carla, staring out of the window as she watched the world-famous sights pass by, the enormous hotels and neon signs all slipping past without comment. She had got used to it so quickly that it had begun to feel like a second home.

Yeah, she really loved it here, she realized. She adored the excess, the crazy people and the anything-goes attitude. The weather was fabulous, the shows were amazing and the shopping was out of this world — what was there not to love?

The two of them had had the most fabulous time in Sin City; they'd chilled out by the pool, partied at Pure and Studio 54, and eaten portion sizes so big in some of the restaurants that Sadie didn't think she'd ever be able to move again, let alone dance. Even Carla had been tempted by pancakes with maple syrup, and huge plates of greasy fries. They'd been so busy that Sadie had almost managed to put the audition out of her mind.

Almost. Every day she'd expected Brooke to call, but she'd heard nothing until yesterday evening.

'I can't believe how quickly this holiday's gone,' Carla remarked sadly, breaking into Sadie's thoughts.

'I know. Five nights – just like that.' Sadie clicked her manicured fingers as they drove past an enormous billboard advertising Bette Midler. *Vegas, the home of showgirls*, thought Sadie with a wry smile.

The traffic was light, and it wasn't long before they pulled up outside the departures lounge. The driver was thrilled to be driving two such good-looking women, and he couldn't stop checking them out as they climbed out of his cab. He loved their British accents too – it instantly gave them a certain class. 'Have a nice day now ladies,' he told them, taking the suitcases out of the trunk.

'You too,' grinned Sadie, as they strode through the doors into the manic bustle of LAS. They checked in the luggage and headed towards security control. 'Do you want to go through yet?' Sadie asked Carla.

'No, not yet. Let's get a coffee or something first.'

As they queued in Starbucks, Sadie's attention was taken by the giant TV screen in the corner. It was showing American football, and even the young girl behind the counter seemed glued to it.

'Who's playing?' Sadie asked.

'Chargers versus the Broncos,' the girl explained, as she turned away to make the drinks.

'And who's *that?*' Sadie drooled, as a stunning black guy appeared on the screen, pulling off his helmet to show a vigorous, passionate face. Even with all the padding, Sadie could tell that his body was amazing, with a broad chest and strong, powerful thighs.

'That's Tyrone Cole. He's the quarterback for the Chargers, and he's *gorgeous*. He comes to Vegas all the time with his team-mates, but I've never seen him. One of my friends has though,' the barista gushed, as she handed over two steaming mugs of cappuccino. 'She works at the Palms, and he always stays there.'

'Thanks. Have a nice day,' Sadie grinned, trying out the phrase for herself as she and Carla found a table.

It wasn't until they were finally seated that Carla stared hard at Sadie and burst out, 'Oh my God, I can't believe you're not coming back with me!'

'Me neither,' squealed Sadie, as the two girls clasped hands.

'It's brilliant that they chose you though, you did so well. This could be it, Sadie – this could finally be the break you've been waiting for.'

In spite of herself, Sadie couldn't hide her excitement at Carla's words. It was exactly what she'd been thinking herself. When Karl and Brooke had rung her the previous night to say they wanted her to become a Kandy Girl, Sadie had had less than twenty-four hours to decide. She didn't need that long – she knew instantly what her decision was. She loved it here, and knew that if she passed on this opportunity she would regret it forever. Perhaps she was crazy – but what did she have to go home for? London held bad memories for her now. A fresh start in a new city – hell, a new country – was exactly what she needed. Maybe things were finally starting to work out for her, and all that shit she'd gone through recently was for a reason.

Carla blew across the foam on her drink and asked, 'How long are you going to stay for? I mean, are you ever going to come back? I'd miss you so much if you didn't.'

'I don't know,' Sadie told her honestly.

'But what if it all goes wrong?' Carla whispered, as

though she daren't voice the thought out loud. 'What will you do then?'

'I'll come home,' Sadie said simply. 'I've got no idea if this is going to work, but I have to try. The way I see it, there's nothing to lose.'

'You're so brave,' Carla told her admiringly.

Sadie shook her head. 'I'm running away. What better way to forget my problems than to lose myself in a magical city where everything's a fantasy and nothing's real? You know they call this place Disneyland for adults?'

Carla smiled sadly, then drained her mug. 'Shit, is that the time?' she exclaimed, noticing the clock on the wall.

As she spoke, the announcement came over the tannoy. 'Flight VIR44W to London Gatwick is now boarding.'

'I've got to go,' Carla wailed, as she threw her arms around Sadie. 'Take care of yourself, honey.'

'I will,' Sadie nodded, as her eyes began to well up.

'Oh, don't cry, you'll set me off,' Carla sniffed, as the tears began to roll down her cheeks.

'I'm not crying – I'm just emotional,' Sadie argued illogically. 'I'm going to miss you so much.'

'Me too. Skype me as soon as you get set up.'

'I will. I promise. And Carla, do one thing for me.'

'What's that?' asked Carla. She'd already agreed to speak to the landlord about Sadie's tenancy, and to clear out her room for her. She was planning to ship out some of Sadie's belongings and store the rest.

'Dump Tom,' Sadie said shortly. 'He's a total and utter *asshole*, as they say out here. You can do so much better, I know you can.'

'I know, I know,' Carla nodded, wiping her eyes. 'I'd

already decided that. Just seeing you make the break and go for what you want – I'm going to do the same.'

The tannoy crackled into life once more. 'Final call for flight VIR44W to London Gatwick.'

'Shit, I've really got to go,' swore Carla as she picked up her bag. They hugged tightly, before Carla ran through the security control gate. She turned and waved, then was gone.

Sadie walked back through the airport wiping her eyes. She hoped she hadn't messed up her make-up. As she strolled out of the air-conditioned building to the cab rank, she was struck by the heat and the sunshine, the sense of exhilaration in the air. For a moment she stood dazed as she watched a plane take off, climbing high above the desert and leaving a vapour trail across the cloudless blue sky. Sadie pulled down her sunglasses and wondered if Carla was on board.

She was on her own now but she was excited at the prospect, full of optimism for what the future held. Being away from London had given her a much-needed sense of perspective – she realized how much bigger the world was than her own tiny corner of it. What did it matter if she'd taken a few knocks along the way? Out here she could start again. She might have lost out to Jenna Jonsson once before, but this time no one was going to snatch the opportunity away from her, Sadie thought fiercely. She'd been given a second chance and she intended to grab it with both hands.

She climbed into a taxi and was soon heading back down the Strip towards The Play Rooms, where she had arranged to meet Karl. Las Vegas stretched out before her, dazzling in its ostentation and brazen excess. She was going to take this town, she vowed, feeling her heart start to beat faster with excitement. Vegas had better watch out – Sadie Laine was on her way.

Only a few miles away from where Jenna and Nick lay curled together on the beach at Casa Santos, Zac and Amber's relationship was falling apart.

During the short journey home Amber had become hysterical, sobbing wildly one moment and screaming at Zac the next. At times she would grow quiet, repeatedly apologizing to Zac for her behaviour and insisting that she loved him. The next moment she was savage, pounding him with her fists as he struggled to keep the car on the road. It was largely done to get a reaction out of him. Zac was so angry he didn't trust himself to speak, so he said nothing.

They pulled up outside the hotel and Zac attempted to get Amber to their room as quickly as possible – not an easy task when she was insisting that her leg was broken and that she couldn't walk. The discreet hotel staff turned a blind eye when Amber once again began shouting at Zac in the lobby, and he simply picked her up and carried her to their suite.

Zac rang down to reception and they sent a doctor to examine Amber's leg. He pronounced it sprained, but not broken, and Amber sat meekly as he strapped up her ankle, only her bright red eyes and blotchy complexion betraying the fact that something was not quite right.

'I'm going to bed,' Zac announced curtly, as soon as the doctor had left. He knew that he and Amber needed to talk, but he didn't know if he could deal with that now. He had a lot to think about.

'Are you mad with me, baby?' Amber asked demurely, widening her eyes.

Zac didn't answer. He went into the bathroom and locked the door.

'Zac?' asked Amber uncertainly. Then she began to scream. 'You bastard, how dare you fucking ignore me? Get out of there *now*. What's the matter, are you too scared to face me? You cowardly shit, you—'

Zac turned the shower on full, trying to block out the sound of Amber's relentless tirade. Placing a hand on either side of the washbasin, he hung his head in defeat. He felt sick.

He lifted his head to look at himself in the mirror. The harsh lights of the bathroom were unforgiving. He ran the cold tap until it felt icy, then plunged his head underneath. The freezing water was a shock to his skin, but it felt good. As he towelled himself off, he realized Amber had gone quiet.

Zac sighed heavily. How had it all come to this?

When he'd left his wife, Jessica, three years ago, he'd been convinced that it was the right thing to do, that he and Amber would stay together for keeps. The media had written them off as yet another celeb couple, bound to split up once the gloss had worn off, but Zac was sure they'd be proved wrong. He'd been through the wringer for this girl and was determined to make it work.

He'd been too young when he'd married Jessica, he told himself. Just 18 years old, a good Southern boy eager to wed his childhood sweetheart and start a family. Then Phoenix went nuclear and suddenly he was barely home, travelling the globe and partying every night. Arizona seemed a very long way away. Zac tried his best to be a good husband, but he was confused. Life wasn't working out the way it was supposed to, and in doing best by everyone else he was losing his sense of self.

It was obvious the marriage was over by the time he met Amber at a party in New York. She had taken his breath away, and he was entranced. He'd kicked and screamed against it, trying to reconcile what his head and his heart were telling him, but in the end there was no way to fight it. He was absolutely, irrevocably in love with Amber. They both had heady, successful careers, which meant they had to spend long periods apart, but they understood that was the nature of their work. In the early days it had been a turn-on, the thrill of being part of a celebrated power couple riding high at the top of their chosen professions. But maybe it would ultimately be their downfall, Zac realized sadly.

He unlocked the bathroom door. It opened with a gentle click.

Amber was sitting on the bed with her back to him. Zac hesitated. He knew they needed to sort this out. He just didn't know if he wanted to.

Slowly, Zac crossed the room and knelt on the bed, putting his hands lovingly on Amber's shoulders.

'Don't touch me,' she hissed.

Zac closed his eyes. 'Amber,' he began gently, 'we need to talk.' He paused. 'I think you have a problem.'

Amber rounded on him, eyes blazing. She had a rolled-up fifty-euro note clutched in her hand. '*I* have a problem?' she screeched. 'It always has to be my fault, doesn't it? Everything's always my fucking fault. Well, news flash for you baby – you're the one with the fucking problem.'

'Me?' returned Zac incredulously, stung by her anger. 'What have I done? I'm trying to make it better between us.'

'You think I'm stupid,' spat Amber. 'You think I don't notice? You and that slut. Do you think I didn't see the way you looked at her?'

'What're you talking about?' asked Zac helplessly, genuinely clueless about what she was referring to.

'That Jonsson bitch, flaunting herself in front of you. I was talking to Kelly and she agrees with me. She's nothing more than a dirty little slag. Everyone's had a piece of her, and now you're getting your bit.'

'That's not true,' Zac said quietly, his voice carefully controlled as he fought to keep his temper in check. Of course he wasn't sleeping with Jenna. She was hooking up with one of his best friends. The idea was ridiculous. Hell, he wasn't even sure he liked the girl – if you looked in the dictionary under 'high maintenance', he was confident you'd find Jenna Jonsson's photo.

Okay, so she was undeniably a sexy chick, and it was natural that he should feel a little horny when he caught sight of her breasts bouncing slightly as she danced, or the way her ass wiggled when she was walking across the studio. But the idea of the two of them having a relationship? It was just . . . it was ludicrous.

'It's not true,' Zac yelled. He was shouting this time; he suddenly felt absolutely furious, rage pumping through him.

The look in his eyes scared Amber. High as she was, she knew she had pushed it too far. She began to cry.

'I'm sorry,' she sobbed. 'I'm so sorry, I didn't know what I was saying.' She opened her arms for Zac and he held her, relieved that, for a while at least, his Amber was back.

'I know it's not true,' she continued to sob. 'I just love you so much, I get jealous sometimes. I'm sorry.' She cried quietly for a while, gradually calming down as Zac held her. Neither of them spoke for a few moments, until Amber pulled away from him. She clung

213

to his neck as she looked up at him. Her eyes were red, her face tear-streaked.

She ran one finger down his cheek and suddenly, without warning, kissed him fiercely. Zac instantly responded, his body bearing down on her fragile frame. His head was a whirl of emotions and they clung to each other desperately, hungrily. With shaking fingers Zac wrenched up her skirt, plunging into her as Amber clawed at his back like a wild animal. The sex was frenzied and urgent, both of them needing to make a connection and find a release.

Zac thrust hard, feeling the pressure of his orgasm build up inside him as instinct took over. He wanted his mind to go blank, to forget everything except how good it felt to be inside his girl and have her bucking and writhing in pleasure beneath him. This would show her, he thought distantly. Show Amber that all that talk about Jenna was just ridiculous. Where the hell had that come from anyway?, Zac wondered, before dismissing the thought.

The last thing he wanted to think about now was Jenna. No, he didn't want to think about those wicked, cat-like green eyes, or the way she looked up at him when he called her out on something, her cheeks flushed, her lips wet and slightly parted. He didn't want to think about what it would be like to put his cock between those full, soft lips and let her suck him until he exploded. And he wasn't going to think about the hard pink nipples he couldn't help but notice, outlined against the material of those tight little tops she always wore. The perfect nipples on those full breasts, and what it would be like to take them in his mouth, then take her, pushing into her, his hands on that rounded butt, and just ride away . . .

Zac moaned loudly as he came, the waves of pleasure

relentlessly washing over him in sweet release. He held Amber tightly as she pressed against him, lost in the intensity of her own orgasm. They clung to each other, motionless for a few moments, until Zac rolled off her and took her in his arms; then they lay together in silence as their heart rates gradually slowed.

Amber propped herself up on one elbow and turned to look at him. 'Do you still love me?' she asked seriously, hardly daring to hear the reply.

A solitary tear rolled down her cheek and Zac wiped it away with his thumb. 'Of course I do,' he told her, kissing her gently. 'Of course I do.'

He hoped he'd sounded convincing, because the truth was he didn't know what the hell to think. Somehow, somewhere, Amber had hit a nerve, recognizing something that Zac hadn't even realized himself. Jenna Jonsson – the girl his best friend was crazy about; the woman he was supposed to be making a record with; hell, probably the most famous pop star on the planet . . .

It was too fucked-up to think about.

Zac was falling for Jenna Jonsson.

PART TWO

21

'Diamonds . . .' Sadie purred into the microphone, as she crooned the opening chorus of 'Diamonds Are a Girl's Best Friend'. Giving a Marilyn-style wiggle, she surveyed the crowd before her through smouldering, half-closed eyes. The room was dark and tightly packed, arranged cabaret-style as the young, moneyed clientele lounged around small candlelit tables on velvet-covered faux-Louis XIV chairs. The air was thick with curling cigarette smoke, making Sadie feel as though she was in some decadent 1920s Berlin club, not The Play Rooms just off the Strip. Everyone was drinking, laughing, having a good time as the champagne flowed; it was pure hedonism, exactly what Las Vegas was famous for.

As she sang, Sadie tugged gently at each fingertip of the long, white gloves she was wearing, before pulling them off with her teeth and throwing them into the crowd to raucous applause.

The big band musical soundtrack rose to a crescendo, and Sadie prepared for her grand finale, belting out the well-known lyrics. With one swift movement she ripped aside the full-length pink satin dress she was wearing to reveal a dazzling silver corset, dripping with diamonds – fake, unfortunately for Sadie. The crowd went crazy, on their feet applauding as Sadie gave a little shimmy before blowing a kiss and tottering off stage on her silver glitter heels.

As soon as she reached the wings she pulled off her blonde wig, shaking out her own glossy, dark hair. She could still hear the cheers and wolf-whistles of the crowd a few feet away. Out of nowhere, a pair of hands appeared to help her on with her final outfit.

'Thanks Brooke,' Sadie grinned, as she pulled the dress down over her corset; the change for the encore needed split-second timing, so there was no time to remove it.

Quickly, Sadie applied a coat of glossy red lipstick before smoothing down her white stockings.

'Is my hat straight?' she asked Brooke, as she pulled it on.

Brooke reached up and made a couple of adjustments, fastening it on with a hairpin. 'Perfect.'

Outside the applause was starting to die down, and shouts of 'More' and 'Encore' could be heard.

'Is everyone ready?' Sadie hissed into the darkness, as she slipped into a pair of red skyscraper heels. There were assenting murmurs from the other girls, and then the music started up. Sadie strutted out into the dazzling glare of the lights as the others filed out behind her.

The energy of the crowd stepped up a notch – Sadie could feel it, as though it was a living, breathing being. Many of them had seen the show before, or read about it, and they knew what was coming. The anticipation in the air was tangible. *This* was how the Kandy Girls had got their name. All five of them were dressed in very short, very sexy red and white striped uniforms, slashed low at the front to show their corseted cleavages. They wore matching red and white striped hats, white stockings and a red garter belt. It was a sexed-up version of the traditional Candy Stripers outfit, worn by the young American women who used to volunteer in hospitals. In a fit of narcissism Karl had changed the spelling, and thus the Kandy Girls were born.

Lola, an Amazonian redhead with a body to die for, was stalking up and down the front of the stage, microphone in hand. She had enormous fake breasts that weren't even trying to look natural, and a take-no-shit attitude that made her a perfect candidate to deal with the rowdy crowd.

'How y'all doin' tonight? You enjoyed the show?' she demanded. A roar of approval greeted her words. 'Gooood,' she drawled seductively. 'We aim to please.'

Now it was Heidi's turn to take centre stage. She had legs that went on forever, cropped platinum-blonde hair and the offbeat, angular features of a model, with high cheekbones and an imperious bearing. Sadie thought she was a bitch.

'So are any of you guys feeling dirty tonight?' Heidi asked, receiving a volley of whoops and whistles in reply. Her blue eyes sparkled as she asked, 'Well, who's the dirtiest of all of you, huh? Who's the filthiest?'

A number of guys waved their hands in the air, and there were shouts of 'Hell, yeah!'

Heidi lowered her voice and asked in a husky tone, 'Who's so dirrrrty . . . that they need a bed bath?'

The crowd went wild at her words as a full-size four-poster bed descended from the ceiling, fully made up with red silk sheets, soft pillows and feather cushions. The girls stood to the side as it was lowered into place, pretending to scrutinize the room to choose the lucky volunteer.

The audience was predominantly male, with a scattering of couples and mixed groups. Many of them were the rich, young, LA set, who lived off their parents' money and flew up to Vegas to party on a weekend. There were a handful of celebrities, and half the San Diego football team in tonight, Sadie noticed, as she raised a hand to her eyes and scanned the crowd. Kandy Girls was fast becoming the ultimate show to see and be seen at.

'Hey Vanessa,' drawled Heidi to the fifth member of the troupe, a stunning African American girl. 'Would you like to choose tonight?'

Vanessa smugly looked out at the crowd, where a number of guys were vying for her attention. Her body was slim but with curves in all the right places, a high, round booty that would have put J-Lo to shame, and large, all-natural breasts. She and Sadie were the only girls that weren't surgically enhanced, and Sadie felt positively flat-chested beside the rest of them.

Vanessa pretended to weigh up the options, but Sadie knew that tonight's 'volunteer' was a foregone conclusion. A lot of money had changed hands to ensure that one particular guy would be picked; his friends had set him up for a bachelor night he would never forget.

'You!' Vanessa exclaimed breathlessly, pointing at a dark-haired man in his late twenties who was sitting at the front table. 'Don't be shy, come on up here,' she beckoned him encouragingly, as he was pushed onto the stage by his buddies. Everyone was going crazy now, on their feet and screaming. They knew what came next.

'Hey baby, what's your name?' Vanessa asked, as she put her arm around him and passed him the microphone.

'Oh, man.' He covered his face in embarrassment,

his curly hair falling across his forehead. He was cute, Sadie realized. Light tan, good skin, hot body. 'My name's Dexter and I'm going to fucking kill those guys!'

'Well, you can do that later, but first I think we need to get you out of those clothes. What do you think ladies?'

The audience whooped as the girls pounced, Sadie tugging at his jacket while Lola and Vanessa went to work on his shirt buttons. Brooke pulled off his belt while Heidi went straight for his fly. Moments later, Dexter was standing centre stage wearing only his Armani boxers. He didn't look at all fazed by the experience. In fact, he was loving the attention as he struck a variety of poses, flexing his impressive muscles. He had a rock-hard body, and he wasn't afraid to show it off.

Heidi raised her leg in a high kick, pushing him sharply backwards with her stiletto heel. He stumbled drunkenly and fell onto the bed, where all five girls immediately leapt up to join him.

'Bed bath!' yelled the crowd, as the Kandy Girls gave Dexter the sexiest rub-down he'd ever had in his life. Lola raised her hands above her head and squeezed a large sponge over her body, causing water and bubble bath to trickle down between her breasts as she soaped herself provocatively. Then she began to wash Dexter, smoothing the sponge in long, slow circles across his chest until the two of them were slippery wet with soapy bubbles.

The others bent over his body, giving the audience a tantalizing flash of underwear as they got to work with oils and lotions. They each took a limb, massaging the warm oil into Dexter's skin, their fingertips pressing and probing every inch of his body. Sadie could see he was doing his best not to get aroused, but it was practically impossible. After the amount of Patrón his friends had made him down, his dick was working independently of his brain. Hell, the two were uncooperative at the best of times.

Sadie tried not to giggle as she watched him close his eyes and bite down on his lip in a lame attempt to distract himself. She knew it wouldn't work. The Kandy Girls were *very* good at what they did, and always tried to ensure the guy left with a full-on erection for maximum embarrassment. 'I want completely unsatisfied customers!' Karl had instructed them. It was amazing how popular this ritual humiliation had become, with guys lining up to be picked.

The music was nearing the end and, without warning, the five girls suddenly jumped off the bed leaving Dexter alone and vulnerable. They took their bows to a standing ovation, and once again Sadie felt the sheer thrill of performance. She didn't think she could ever tire of it – the adrenaline and the adulation of doing a live show.

'Vegas, give it up for Dexter!' Heidi yelled into the microphone. Sheepishly, he crawled off the bed, hunching over as he awkwardly acknowledged the cheers. Heidi grabbed his hand and thrust it into the air as though he'd just won gold at the Olympics, before sending him back to his seat wet, greasy and barely dressed.

The Kandy Girls took one final bow before they sashayed off stage. In the wings they grasped each other's hands and squealed, thrilled with their performance.

'That was the best one yet,' shrieked Brooke.

'Man, it was awesome up there,' agreed Lola. 'Did you see Sam White?' she asked, naming the hot new

TV actor and star of the CW Network's latest teen drama.

'No! Was he out there?' asked Vanessa in disbelief.

'Uh huh. And he liked what he saw!'

Giggling and talking, the girls fell back into their dressing room where they opened a bottle of champagne and toasted the show. Each of them had their own mirror and vanity table, with a large bunch of flowers on every one – Karl sent them each week without fail. Sadie thought it was sweet.

She still couldn't believe how quickly everything had happened. Karl had rented a house for her and the other girls in Henderson, Clark County, a little way south of the Strip. The idea was for them all to bond, and to this end Sadie and Brooke were sharing a room, as were Vanessa and Lola. Heidi had managed to bag the third room all to herself, which pissed Sadie off. Not that she minded sharing with Brooke, but the lack of privacy took a little getting used to and she hated seeing Heidi strutting round as if she was the queen of the place.

The house itself was beautiful – a luxurious family home with a gym set up in what would have been the dining room and even a small swimming pool in the back yard. Not that they'd had time to use it. Karl had worked them like slaves and the rehearsal period had been ridiculously intensive: twelve-hour days, with Karl masterminding and Desiree filling in when he had to fly off to attend to his other clients.

Their first gig was a month to the day after they moved into the house. Their ninety-minute set incorporated singing, dancing, banter and burlesque, and the Kandy Girls had gone down a storm. They danced to 'Hit Me Baby One More Time' in pigtails and jail-bait school uniforms, and Christina Aguilera's 'Candyman' wearing hot little Forties' outfits. They performed 'Like a Virgin' in tiny white-lace dresses that looked like sexed-up wedding gowns, and 'Mein Herr' from *Cabaret* with a raunchy routine featuring top hats and canes.

They were booked for three nights a week at The Play Rooms, but Karl wanted them to cut down to two.

'That's crazy,' Heidi complained. 'We could triple what we're making now if we played every night.'

'*Au contraire*, my dear,' Karl contradicted her, wagging a finger in her face. 'Always leave them wanting more. The more popular we get, the more exclusive we become.'

And he knew what he was talking about. The reviews were unbelievable:

'The sexiest show in town', screamed *Las Vegas Weekly*.

'Glamorous, glossy and downright dirty', purred *Luxury Las Vegas*.

Las Vegas Magazine said that, 'Whilst the Kandy Girls may not be the most original idea out there, they sure as hell do it bigger, better and harder than anyone else. Unmissable.'

They'd even done a profile on Sadie, with a two-page interview and photo shoot at The Mirage, entitled: 'Sadie Laine, A Star Is Born'. She had quickly emerged as the Kandy Girls' main attraction, something which she could see had the potential to cause friction within the group. The truth was that Sadie was the only girl who was a trained dancer – the rest of them were wait-ressing wannabes, stars in their provincial home town who'd made the long journey to Nevada in the hope of making it. Along with Lola, Sadie also had the best singing voice, and the crowd went wild for her British accent when she spoke over the microphone.

As she pulled off her Candy Striper dress and wrig-gled out of her corset, there was a knock at the door.

Amanda, who was staff at The Play Rooms, stuck her head round.

'Great job girls, you rocked!' she told them.

'The audience were wild tonight, huh?' said Lola.

'Yeah, and some of them are dying to meet you. There are six of the Chargers guys out there waiting for you.'

'Six? I guess one of us will have to double up,' giggled Brooke.

'They sent you this, with their compliments,' explained Amanda, holding out an enormous bottle of Cristal, 'and they were wondering if you'd like to join them for dinner afterwards.'

'Oh my God!' shrieked Vanessa. 'Those guys are hot!'

'Yeah, I love a bit of athletc action,' smirked Heidi. 'Especially Tyrone Cole. I could give him a night he'd never forget. He'd be too exhausted to play football the next day, I guarantee it.'

'Well, he's out there,' Amanda confirmed excitedly, 'and he specially wanted to know if Sadie was going to join them tonight.'

'Me?' Sadie's head snapped up from where she was pulling on her battered old jeans.

'Oh my God, Sadie, you *have* to come out tonight,' Brooke insisted.

Sadie waved a hand dismissively. 'I don't even know who he is.'

'He's *gorgeous*,' Lola filled her in, as though that explained everything. '*So* hot. He's the Chargers' quarterback and he's divine.'

Something seemed vaguely familiar to Sadie. Briefly, she flashed back to the Starbucks at LAS, the TV screen with the handsome black guy, and the barista's comments. 'Sorry, not interested,' she shrugged, as she turned away and hooked her bra.

'Sadie, are you *insane*?'

'Are you a lesbian?' bitched Heidi, peering at her as though she was a different species.

'I'm tired tonight,' she shot back irritably. 'I just want to go home and chill.'

'Freak,' Heidi said lightly, but Brooke glared at her. She could tell that there was something else – something Sadie wasn't letting on.

'Are you sure you don't want to come tonight?' she asked gently. 'If it's money you're worried about, they'll pay for everything. And they'll take us somewhere amazing, VIP all the way.'

Sadie smiled wryly. Oh yeah, she knew all about rich men who turned up bearing extravagant gifts and took her to fabulous places. She found herself wondering whether Tyrone Cole had a wife back in San Diego. 'Not tonight. But you guys go, have an amazing time.'

'Don't wait up,' Heidi quipped, as she swung her bag over her shoulder and walked out of the door, followed by the others.

Sadie watched them go.

She would go home, soak in a hot bath then curl up in her pyjamas and watch trash TV. It would be so nice to have the house to herself for a while, a little breathing space to clear her head. Yeah, she was just concentrating on her career right now, she told herself – and that was working out fantastically. Turning down tonight's invitation definitely wasn't anything to do with how Paul Austin had treated her.

Okay, so Tyrone was undoubtedly hot, but she knew next to nothing about him – and everything she did know marked him out as trouble. There was only one reason an absurdly rich, stunningly gorgeous athlete made a play for a cabaret dancer, and it certainly wasn't for her conversation.

Sadie stood up and glanced around the now empty dressing room. It seemed bare and lifeless without the exuberant chatter of the other girls, empty and still. Through the wall she could hear the distant sound of music playing in the club and the hum of conversation and laughter – the sound of other people having fun. Without giving herself time to think, Sadie picked up her bag, switched off the light and headed outside to hail a cab.

22

High above Las Vegas in the inky night sky, the Virgin Atlantic flight from London was beginning its final descent into McCarran. Comfortably ensconced in upper class were Jenna Jonsson and Nick Taylor, whose arrival at Gatwick had caused a sensation. They were now officially an established, superstar couple, with all the gossip, speculation and paparazzi craziness that entailed. It was only now that Jenna was realizing the press attention she'd dealt with in the past was nothing. Dating a fellow celebrity hadn't just doubled people's interest in her − it had blown it off the scale.

She settled back in her seat, gazing idly out of the window at the stunning view below. Vegas looked spectacular at night, as the gambling city loomed unexpectedly out of the miles of barren Nevada desert that surrounded it, a blaze of neon in the dark sky.

'Excited?' Nick asked her with a grin.

'Absolutely,' Jenna assured him, as she ran a French-manicured hand along his thigh and thought how gorgeous he looked. He was wearing loose-fitting jeans and a light shirt, open at the neck. Both of them had baulked at the unflattering sleep-suits provided by the airline. It was like wearing a polyester body bag tied up with a shoelace.

The pair of them were heading to Sin City for The Night of a Thousand Stars, a huge one-off concert that looked set to be the music world's biggest event of the year. Millions would be watching around the globe, and there had been a furious bidding war for screening rights, with NBC emerging as eventual winners.

The Night of a Thousand Stars was being held at The Colosseum, and Jenna and Phoenix had both been asked to appear. The official line was that they were performing as separate acts, but in fact the plan was to finally debut their single 'Without You'. Details were supposed to be kept confidential for maximum impact on the night, but inevitably the story had leaked. Someone had talked – a roadie or a make-up artist had sold them out for an exclusive with *US Weekly*, and now the rumours were spreading like wildfire.

Although Jenna hadn't exactly lied when she told Nick she was excited about the show, she hadn't mentioned that she was also absolutely terrified. She had the ridiculous sensation that her whole career was on the line. Everything she'd done until now, professionally, had always gone down a storm – there had been number one singles, sell-out tours, adulation and adoration. But now she wanted to step it up a level and run with the big boys. She was moving out of her comfort zone, from bubble-gum, mass-market pop to a major collaboration with an established band. She wanted to prove to people that she would be around for the long term; that she was more than just a manufactured pop star with a limited shelf life. More than anything, she wanted credibility and respect.

But she was confident that the music was good. She knew the critics weren't expecting it to work – a pop vocal on a storming rock track – but it did, and together they'd delivered a piece of music that was sassy, sexy and bang on trend.

After the incident with Amber, which they'd all tactfully pretended to have forgotten, the band had stayed on the island for another couple of weeks. The atmosphere had been a little weird, and Zac in particular had been tense and snappy for a while – because of what had happened with Amber, Jenna presumed. But the creative juices were flowing and they'd made a fantastic record. It had been sent to Don back in London for final production, and he'd done them proud. They all knew they were looking at a sure-fire hit.

On a personal level, Jenna was walking around with a ridiculous grin on her face and a constant, insatiable heat between her legs. She was crazy about Nick Taylor, and the sex was incredible. They'd tried to keep their relationship under wraps, worried about what the rest of the band might think, but it was obvious to anyone who saw them together. Nick couldn't keep his hands off her. His gestures were possessive and more than a little smug – for a playboy like him, dating Jenna Jonsson was like winning the pussy lottery.

With some trepidation, Jenna had rung Gerry to tell him. She knew that they couldn't keep it a secret forever. Casa Santos was incredibly private, but the second they left the house the paparazzi would be crawling.

When she told Gerry there was a long silence. So long, in fact, that Jenna began to worry the connection had been cut off.

'Gerry?' she asked hesitantly.

Gerry sighed, and Jenna could almost picture him massaging his brow. 'Is that really a good idea, Jenna?' he asked finally.

'What do you mean by that?' she snapped, furious at him for puncturing her good mood. She'd been living in a blissful bubble for a week now – she didn't want Gerry's reality check bringing her down.

Gerry didn't pull any punches. 'People already think you've slept with Ryan. Do you want them to think you're working your way through the whole band?'

'Screw you,' she retorted. 'I don't care what people think. This is serious Gerry – he's the one for me.'

'But are you the one for him?' Gerry had asked maddeningly. Jenna knew exactly what he was alluding to – Nick's womanizing reputation.

'Jesus, why will no one give him a break?' Jenna burst out in frustration. 'This is different, Gerry. He's told me so himself, and I believe him.' It was true – Nick had lavished her with praise, telling her he'd never met anyone like her; that he'd never felt like this before. He'd talked about their future together, mentioning kids, marriage – the full works.

'Well, as long as you're sure,' Gerry said witheringly, sounding as far from sure as it was possible to be.

'I am,' Jenna retorted. 'Just organize it, Gerry.' She hung up the phone and angrily threw it onto the bed. She didn't want to admit that the reason he'd riled her so much was that she'd had exactly the same worries herself.

But Gerry knew better than to interfere in Jenna's personal life and, despite his reservations, he did as she'd requested. A staged paparazzi shoot was organized on Nick's private beach. They invited a friendly photographer with links to Gerry's agency, and worked out a contract to split the profits from the sale. It was par for the course and meant everyone won – the papers got their story, and Jenna got to control the output and ensure she looked fabulous in the pictures. And she did – her body was tanned and toned in a minuscule bikini, while Nick looked hot in black board shorts, his finely honed six-pack rippling in the sunlight. They were young, gorgeous and sexy as hell, frolicking in the surf. It was a publicist's wet dream.

The plane hit the runway and Jenna was jolted out of her daydreams by the bumpy landing. As they taxied towards the arrivals terminal, Nick leaned over and squeezed Jenna's hand. She felt his breath, warm and delicious against her ear, and noticed a stewardess watching them with barely concealed envy.

'Don't you worry about anyone else,' he reassured her. 'Anything they can do, we can do better. Our act is gonna blow them away.'

Jenna stared straight ahead, her face set with the determined look that Nick recognized and knew not to argue with. 'Let's go get 'em,' she declared.

Sadie was up early. She'd already spent thirty minutes in the gym, swum laps in the pool, and made herself a dubious-looking smoothie containing carrots, orange and spinach. She reminded herself of its nutritional value as she forced herself not to gag.

She padded outside to the garden, feeling the warm flagstones beneath her bare feet. Another scorching day, she realized, as she turned her face up to the cloudless blue sky and shielded her eyes. They hadn't had a drop of rain the whole time she'd been in Vegas. Maybe she'd sunbathe out here for a while, she decided, until the other girls got up. She'd heard them roll in about five that morning. Brooke had stumbled into their shared room, recking of cigarette smoke and alcohol, crashing into the furniture and giggling to herself in a failed effort to be discreet. The Kandy Girls didn't have a show tonight so they could afford to slack off, and Sadie was rapidly learning that these women liked to party hard.

As she settled herself beside the pool, she heard the doorbell ring at the front of the house. *Typical, dammit.* She wondered who it could be – maybe a neighbour coming to complain about all the noise they'd made last night. It certainly wouldn't be the first time.

Sadie opened the door to see a young, skinny guy dressed in a FedEx uniform.

'Package for Miss Sadie Laine?' he asked, squinting up at her from beneath his baseball cap.

'That's me.'

'Sign here please.'

Sadie did as she was told, wondering what on earth was in the box. For a brief moment she thought maybe Tyrone Cole had sent her something, then realized that was crazy. Why the hell was she thinking about him?

As she carried it through to the lounge, she saw Carla's name on the sender's details and grinned, ripping it open excitedly. Carla had promised to send over the possessions Sadie had requested, but looking at them now they seemed rather pathetic. The box was barely even full as Sadie had got rid of all her winter coats and thick jumpers, knowing she wouldn't need them out here. She'd told Carla to take what she wanted, and to send the rest to a charity shop. She imagined Carla had kept very little – she was so tiny that Sadie's clothes would probably swamp her.

She wondered briefly how Carla was. They'd exchanged a few emails and texts, spoken a couple of times on Skype, but Sadie had been so busy she'd barely had a chance to contact her, she realized guiltily. She knew Carla had split up with Tom, and for that she was grateful. Carla was currently single, tentatively dating, but Sadie felt sure she'd find a good guy soon. She just hoped it was that easy for her too . . .

Curiously, she began sorting through the box. It was strange, seeing the remnants of her old life out here in Vegas, like a merging of two very different worlds. There wasn't much – a couple of light jumpers, some skinny jeans and half a dozen vest tops that looked faded and dated. She'd bought loads of new stuff out here, and doubted she'd ever wear them again. She lifted out her black cocktail dress and a summer jacket to reveal framed photos of her family and friends. Out of nowhere, she felt tears of homesickness start to prick at the corners of her eyes and quickly placed the photos on the pile, reaching into the box to see what came next. Her hands closed on a large black notebook and she smiled in recognition. Carla had included the jotter in which Sadie had meticulously made notes after every dance class. She flicked through slowly, glancing at page after page of her neat, sloping handwriting, the hours of work that had gone into it, proving her dedication to her craft.

She heard a noise on the stairs and glanced up to see Brooke making her way into the room. She was wearing Disney pyjamas, and her bushy blonde hair was out of control. She yawned widely, stretching her fingertips up to the ceiling, and her shirt rode up to reveal her tiny, flat stomach.

'Good night?' Sadie asked.

'Yeah, it was amazing. You really missed out,' Brooke said lazily, throwing herself down on one of the squashy sofas. 'We ate at Joël Robuchon then partied at Tao. I seriously think it was the most amazing night of my life.'

Sadie smiled. 'Maybe I should have come.'

'Hey, it was your call. We did warn you,' Brooke said easily. She glanced down at the FedEx box and the heap of clothes scattered beside Sadie. 'What's that?'

'My life,' Sadie replied wryly.

'Huh?'

'Everything I needed from home. My friend's just sent it all over from London.'

'Oh wow!' Brooke plopped down beside her and began searching through the pile. 'Is this your family?' she asked, holding up a picture taken at a long-ago birthday party. Sadie nodded. 'Your mom's so pretty. I can see where you get it from.'

'Thanks,' Sadie grinned, as Brooke picked up another photo.

'Who's this?'

'My best friend.' It showed her and Carla in their dance gear, taken backstage at some terrible show they'd only done for the money. They looked so different, Sadie marvelled. It had only been taken a couple of years ago, but they seemed so young, their faces full of optimism.

'She's very thin,' Brooke commented, wrinkling her nose.

'Yeah. She sometimes forgets to eat,' Sadie said lightly.

'Wow. Bad memory.'

'Yeah . . . So is there any gossip from last night?' Sadie asked, changing the subject.

'Well, Tyrone wouldn't stop asking about you,' Brooke teased, as Sadie pulled a face.

'I expect Heidi proved to be ample company.'

Brooke clapped a hand over her mouth. 'Oh my God, I totally forgot. Heidi came home with Dexter!'

'Dexter?' Sadie looked puzzled. 'Is he one of the football players?'

'No, Dexter, the guy from the show,' Brooke hissed under her breath, glancing around as though worried he might appear at any moment.

'The engaged guy?'

Brooke nodded vigorously. 'I guess at least he can say he slept with a Vegas stripper at his bachelor party. Kind of a cliché, huh?'

'We're not strippers,' Sadie said defensively. 'We're burlesque dancers.'

Brooke shrugged. 'Hey, you say tomato . . . anyway, there's nothing wrong with being a stripper,' she said, her expression growing wistful.

'Oh no, don't tell me you're missing The Pleasuredome.'

'Hell, no. I love my new life. I wanna be a Kandy Girl forever.'

'Forever?'

'Uh huh,' Brooke nodded.

'I think in this profession there's kind of an age limit,' Sadie told her sadly.

'There's always surgery. I'm gonna have everything nipped, tucked, squeezed and pulled. I'll tell the surgeon to just grab hold of my scalp and yank everything upwards until it's all stretched out and there's no more wrinkles.'

'Sounds beautiful.'

'It will be or else I'll sue,' Brooke grinned.

'So what happened with Tyrone Cole?' Sadie asked,

curious in spite of herself. 'Did he go home with anyone?'

'Nah, he left early. Didn't look like he was enjoying himself.'

'Really?' Sadie arched an eyebrow. 'He probably had some girl waiting back at his hotel room.'

Brooke stared hard at Sadie. 'Why are you so down on the guy? I mean, what did he do to you?'

Sadie sighed. 'Sorry, I know I'm being unfair. My track record with men isn't very good. I guess you could say I've lost my trust in them.'

'Bad experience?'

Sadie nodded.

'Well, you need a good experience to get you over that.'

'I guess so,' Sadie smiled. She couldn't fault Brooke's logic.

'I'm glad you agree 'cos I gave Tyrone your phone number,' Brooke mentioned casually.

'You did what?' Sadie exploded. 'What the fuck did you do that for, Brooke?'

'Woah, calm down, girl. I did it because I thought it would be good for you. You haven't been out on one date the whole time we've lived here, and he seems like a nice guy.'

'I've had plenty of guys offering me their phone number,' Sadie retorted hotly. 'It's not like I can't get a date. I just don't want one.'

'It's like this,' Brooke began, slowly and patronizingly. 'Sometimes people don't know what's best for them, and their friends need to give them a push in the right direction.'

'Of all the people you could have set me up with, you decide on an NFL player? Yeah, they're really known for being loyal and committed.'

'Just give him a chance,' Brooke insisted.

'How can I? He hasn't even rung me and I bet he's not going to.'

'He just doesn't want to look too eager. Give him time,' Brooke stated confidently. 'He'll call. I guarantee it.'

23

The Colosseum at Caesars Palace is a spectacular building at the best of times, but for The Night of a Thousand Stars they had really pulled out all the stops. A 4,000-seater Roman amphitheatre, decorated in red and gold with state-of-the-art equipment, it had played host to some of the world's biggest superstars since it had opened. But Vegas had never seen anything quite like the show planned for that evening. One megastar after another would take to the stage for their 15-minute set, each aiming to be bigger, better and more fabulous than the last.

Already they were competing to see who could make the most outrageous demands, and some poor flunkie had been despatched to find a dozen white kittens for an R'n'B diva that no one was allowed to look in the eye. Rumour had it that rap mogul TJ Daze had refused to come out of his dressing room without an assistant walking in front of him scattering hundred-dollar bills, but no one had been able to verify that.

Out front, technical rehearsals had been taking place all day. Each act had thirty minutes to sound-check and set their lights. Some were using pyrotechnics, others had enormous video screens, backdrops, projectors and holograms. Even the air humidity in the arena was controlled, to protect the performers' delicate vocal chords. The whole thing was a logistical nightmare. It was now mid-afternoon and they were inevitably running way over schedule.

Jenna was nervous as hell and trying not to explode. Things kept going wrong. A quaking assistant had been sent over to tell her that the shoes she'd planned to wear on the red carpet couldn't be flown in from Paris on time, and an alternative would have to be provided. Then Karl discovered he'd been given the wrong dimensions for the stage, meaning their carefully choreographed routine didn't work right in the space. The dancers were tense and bitching, Karl was flapping, and Jenna thought how ironic it was that she was the one who was labelled a diva.

And where the fuck was Nick?, she wondered irritably. He'd promised he'd be there to support her, and she hated it when people let her down. He knew how nervous she was, and she really wanted him there. Hell, Phoenix's tech slot was up next, so he'd better get his arse in gear, she thought, chewing on her nail as she moved across the stage so they could focus the spotlight. She hadn't bitten her nails since high school. Fuck, she was nervous.

All of the problems meant Jenna was too distracted to notice the solitary figure in the darkness of the auditorium. It was Zac. He was sitting on the mezzanine level, looking down at the stage where Jenna was running through her routine, and wondering what the hell he was doing there. But he couldn't help himself. He watched, mesmerized, as the intro to 'Sexual Rush' blasted out and Jenna began to dance. The suggestive lyrics kicked in and Zac found himself enthralled, just watching the way her body moved. She had such guts, such presence, such . . . in-your-face sexuality.

This was a mess – he was under no illusions about that. After leaving Ibiza he knew he wouldn't see Jenna again until the rehearsals for Vegas began, a good two months away. Zac had thought this would be a good thing. It turned out to be torture. With Amber back in New York and the two of them barely speaking, he'd been rattling round his Arizona ranch, taking solace in his guitar and writing miserable songs about lost love. He'd spent hours in the gym, which had left him with a hard, ripped body, but had done surprisingly little to work out his frustrations. It had been a truly depressing time.

To really stick the knife in he'd started reading the papers. Usually he didn't touch those rags, but he couldn't help himself. Day after day he pored over the tormenting images, watching Jenna and Nick's blossoming relationship play out in the gossip pages. The papers speculated that Nick's womanizing days were over. Zac wasn't so sure. He'd heard rumours and he hoped for Jenna's sake they weren't true.

Zac had barely seen Amber either. She'd been working in New York fronting the Guess Jeans campaign, and he'd made lame excuses about being too busy to visit. She didn't seem too heartbroken. They talked dutifully on the phone a couple of times a week, but both claimed their schedules made it hard to find an opportunity. He felt as if they were putting off the inevitable.

And now she was here, in Las Vegas. She'd turned up unannounced at his hotel suite. She was developing a habit of doing that. Once upon a time it would have seemed romantic, but now it felt disturbingly like she was trying to catch him out.

Zac had currently left her behind in the dressing room, tiring of her sarcasm and her insults and the loud, grating voice she used when she was smashed off her face. He'd left her flirting with TJ Daze, and he couldn't have cared less. He'd told himself that he wanted to get to the stage early – that Phoenix's sound-check was up next and he wanted to be ready.

But if Zac was being honest with himself, he knew it was more than that. During the time he'd been away from Jenna he hadn't been able to stop thinking about her. All the things that had driven him crazy in the first place – the inappropriate clothing, the fact that she always needed a second take, the way she flirted to get herself out of trouble – he'd started to miss them. The first day they'd got together to rehearse for this show had been like a slap in the face – she was even more beautiful, feisty and vivacious than he'd remembered. And she was dating his best friend. She was all over his best friend, in fact, and clearly bliss-fully happy. Zac's thinking wasn't rational – he wanted to take Nick outside and beat him into the ground.

And now Zac had come to watch Jenna rehearse, knowing full well that he was going to see her at her most seductive, her most provocative. It didn't bear thinking about. He knew he was playing with fire. She was his mate's girl, the ultimate taboo. He would have to forget about her, learn to handle it and—

His thoughts were broken by a sudden commotion taking place on stage. Zac sat bolt upright, trying to work out what was going on. He could see the dancers all huddled together in one spot, as though surrounding something. Karl was flinging his hands in the air dramat-ically, and Jenna had pushed through to the centre of the group, looking worried. One of the runners, self-important with a headset and clipboard, went dashing into the wings.

'We need a medic over here people,' Karl screeched. 'We've got a fainter. Give her some air.'

The crowd reluctantly stood back a little, and Zac saw one of the dancers lying on the ground. Her eyes were closed, and someone had put a sweater under her head. Then a man in a green jumpsuit ran onto the stage, followed by the assistant who had been sent to get him. His authority was enough to disperse the others, as he quickly knelt down and began examining her.

'Is she okay?' Jenna asked. Her eyes were wide with concern, and she had started biting her nails again.

The girl was starting to come round now. She moaned and tried to sit up, but the medic told her to lie still for a moment while he checked her vital signs and shone a light into her eyes. He placed a hand to her forehead and looked up worriedly.

'She's running a hell of a fever,' he told them. 'She needs to drink plenty of fluids and go straight to bed for at least forty-eight hours.'

'But she can still do the show, can't she?' Karl asked manically.

The medic laughed in amazement. 'This girl's going nowhere except her room. I'm amazed she's kept going this long. She's running a temperature of one hundred and four.'

'But we need her for the show!' Karl repeated obstinately, seemingly unable to comprehend what he was being told.

The medic ignored him. 'Is there someone here who can take her back to her room?'

'We'll just have to cut that couple,' Jenna whispered to Karl. 'There's no alternative.'

'We can't cut them!' Karl insisted. The dancers were paired up for a sexy salsa routine, and had been choreographed to within an inch of their lives. Karl was determined that Jenna's solo show would be the best of the night, and was taking her success personally. 'It will look all wrong, totally unbalanced!'

'Well, what are we going to do then?' Jenna demanded. 'We don't have anyone else who knows the steps – unless you want to dance with Juan?'

'I wouldn't mind . . .' Karl drawled, making eyes at the luscious South American.

'Karl . . .' Jenna warned, as she began to massage her temples. 'This is not helping.'

'Well, I might not be able to take over, but I do have a hell of a lot of contacts in this city.'

'So what? No one can learn the routine that quickly. We've only got a few hours before the show.'

Karl smiled smugly. 'I know someone who can.' He raised an eyebrow at a disbelieving Jenna, and reached into his pocket for his cell phone.

Backstage it was pandemonium. Nick didn't think he'd ever seen so many people crammed into one space, each convinced that they were the most important, that their job was the most urgent. The corridors were awash with people: PAs running up and down with messages for the star they worked for; stylists trailing essential pieces of costume; inexperienced runners trying to find their way around the backstage maze.

Nick moved easily through the throng. He walked with the confidence of a man who knew just how desperately good-looking he was. The longing stares of the women he encountered were testament to that; the phone numbers pressed into his hand by eager groupies was all the proof he needed that he was one fine specimen of manhood. And now he and Jenna were the golden couple. She was the perfect comple-ment to his handsome looks and alpha male status. Jenna was young, sexy and adored the world over – only the best would do for Nick Taylor.

'Shit,' he swore, as he checked his Rolex. She would be sound-checking around now, and she'd asked him to be there. He stepped up his pace a little, not wanting to look as if he was in a hurry, as he flashed his dazzling smile at any attractive woman he passed.

The further Nick walked, the more the crowd thinned out and, as he turned down a deserted corridor, he realized he was lost. How the hell had that happened? He'd been following the signs to the stage, hadn't he? Maybe he'd been distracted by a particularly fine pair of legs walking past him. He'd lost count of the number of stunning women wandering around The Colosseum today.

He was about to turn back when he saw someone he recognized stagger out of a door a little further down the poorly lit corridor. It was Amber. As he watched, she was followed out by a well-built black guy, one of TJ Daze's entourage, who was zipping up his jacket.

Nick hesitated, wondering what to do. Probably best to get the hell out of there and pretend he'd never seen them . . .

'Nick!' Amber screeched.

He sighed, turning back to look at her. She tottered towards him, sniffing heavily. Her eyes were bloodshot and she took a moment to focus on him.

'Hey, Amber. Who's your friend?' he asked coldly, jerking his head in the direction of the guy.

Amber walked slowly towards him. Her thin lips curled into a ridiculous, smug smile that irritated the hell out of Nick.

'Him? Oh, that's just Reggie. He's a friend of TJ's,' Amber drawled, giggling, 'Say hello, Reggie.'

''Sup,' Reggie greeted Nick. Nick didn't reply.

'He's just been helping me out with a little something,' Amber confided. 'You want any? Reggie's very generous.'

'You're a mess, Amber,' Nick told her harshly. 'I don't know how the hell Zac puts up with you.'

Amber threw back her head and shrieked with laughter. Jesus, she was really out of it, thought Nick agitatedly, glancing down the corridor for someone to help him.

'Zac?' Amber repeated. 'I'm old news. He's got a new obsession in his life now.'

'What the fuck are you talking about?'

'Jenna,' Amber rasped, making the name sound like a curse. 'He wants Jenna now. He wants your girlfriend.'

'You're crazy,' Nick sneered.

'Am I? Think about it Nick. Open your eyes.'

Nick's breath was coming fast as he struggled to keep calm. Whatever she was on was clearly some good shit – she was out of her mind. 'You've already ruined one relationship, Amber,' he said grimly, a blatant reference to Zac and Jessica. 'Leave me and Jenna alone.'

But Amber only laughed harder as Reggie looked on, enjoying the spectacle. 'You poor, sad fucker. I was only trying to offer you some advice. You know – *as friends*,' she added sarcastically, leaning in close to Nick. 'Just wait and see if I'm right.'

'Amber,' Nick began, feigning exhaustion. 'Stop being a spiteful bitch, okay? It's getting boring.'

Amber's hazel eyes blazed suddenly, as she felt pure venom shoot through her. 'I've always thought you were a cocky little cunt,' she spat. 'Perhaps I was wrong about you two – you and your slut of a girlfriend make a great team.'

Amber shot him a look of hate and went to walk off, but Nick grabbed her by the arm. He was a well-built guy, and his grip was strong. Amber's face contorted in pain.

'Get your fucking hands off me,' she hissed, adrenaline pumping through her from the heady combination of fear, anger and coke.

'Yeah man, what the fuck?' was Reggie's contribution.

Nick didn't loosen his grip, and the skin on Amber's arm began to turn white as the blood drained from where he held it.

'Don't you *ever* say that about her,' he roared at Amber.

'Get off me before I scream this fucking place down and get you done for fucking assault,' she rasped, her voice low and unsteady.

Nick pushed her aside in disgust, flinging her away like a rag doll. Amber stumbled as he threw her, banging her hip on the wall. Then, out of the corner of his eye, Nick saw Reggie launch himself towards him. Instantly, Nick lashed out, his fist colliding with Reggie's jaw. Fuck, that was going to hurt later. He hoped he'd be able to drum. Reggie staggered backwards, looking shocked.

'Man, you gonna regret that shit,' he threatened, squaring up to a furious Nick.

Nick was fired up, ready for a fight. He'd launch that wannabe gangsta into orbit if he so much as laid a finger on him.

'Reggie, leave it,' Amber snapped, recognizing the rage in Nick's eyes as she limped off down the corridor. Reggie glared at Nick, then spat on the ground at his feet. Phlegm mixed with blood from his bleeding gums. Nick stared him down, unmoving, as Reggie set his shoulders and walked off after Amber.

As they reached the top of the corridor, Amber spun around. 'Just you fucking wait,' she warned, before they disappeared out of sight.

Nick stood, breathing heavily. He couldn't work out what had happened. He'd never hit a woman before, and he despised men who did . . . but he'd been so close with Amber. Christ, he'd been so mad he couldn't even see straight – there was just a red haze in front of his eyes.

All he knew was that he would have done anything to protect Jenna, regardless of the consequences. And to have that fucked-up junkie speaking about his girl like that, to call her those names . . .

As Nick stood shaking with anger, his fists clenched and his knuckles white, he suddenly knew that all he wanted was Jenna. He wanted to put his arms around her and protect her. With a flash of realization, Nick understood that he wanted to do that forever – to take care of her and keep her safe from the world. He didn't ever want to let her go.

He wanted to marry her.

24

'No fucking way.' Sadie paced up and down beside the pool, gesticulating angrily with her free hand. She was wearing a blue and white striped bikini, and her bronzed skin was slick with sun cream. 'I'm not doing it.'

At the other end of the phone, Karl Madison winced at her vehemence. 'Sadie, honey—' he began, but Sadie cut him off.

'How can I learn the routine that quickly? I'll look like an idiot.'

'I wouldn't have asked you if I didn't totally believe, one hundred per cent, that you could—'

'There'll be four thousand people – and God knows how many watching on TV – looking at me wondering why the hell some amateur who can't even do the steps properly was given a job,' Sadie went on, as though Karl hadn't spoken.

'It'll be easy for you, you're a fabulous dancer—'

'No,' Sadie replied resolutely.

Karl paused. He had ducked out of a fire exit behind the stage and was now leaning against the smooth stone wall of The Colosseum. The brightness was blinding after the darkness of the interior, and the hot sun blazed down on him. Karl was inhaling petrol fumes from the endless convoy of trucks that were reversing up to the goods entrance, their cargo unloaded speedily and efficiently by sweaty roadies wearing grease-stained wife-beaters and stonewash jeans. There was a hell of a lot of muscled, oily flesh on display. *Rough trade, yum.* Karl forced himself to stop staring and focus on Sadie.

He'd been in the business for a long time – as a dancer for seven years, and now as a choreographer for a further twelve. For the past five years he'd been at the very top of his profession, the go-to guy for celebs who wanted a sexy, spectacular routine for their concerts, videos, whatever. He'd seen endless clients have major breakdowns, panic attacks or suffer crippling stage fright and claim that they couldn't go on, that the routine was too hard and they'd never be able to do it. In addition to dancing, Karl reckoned he could have a pretty lucrative sideline in motivational speaking.

But he knew there was always an underlying cause to their anxiety – he just had to figure out what it was.

'Sadie, do me a favour and level with me.'

'I don't know what you mean,' she replied, instantly defensive, and Karl knew he was on to something.

'What I mean is that this would be a phenomenal experience for anyone. Both you and I know that you're one of the most talented dancers around and the steps are not going to be a problem for you – even if the situation is gonna be a little . . . pressured. So what's the real reason?'

Sadie sighed. She stopped pacing and sat down on a sun lounger, feeling cornered. 'I know her,' she admitted finally. 'Jenna.'

'Oh *really?*' Karl raised his eyebrows so high they nearly fell off his face.

'Yeah. When we were younger – we were on the same competition circuit.'

'But that was years ago,' Karl said dismissively.

'I don't like her, Karl.'

'Look, I'll make sure you get really well paid. Enough to get you over a little personal dislike.'

'It's not about that,' Sadie burst out in frustration, wondering how to explain herself. 'Look, this is kind of embarrassing for me. And a little awkward, given that she's your number one favourite client or whatever,' she added sourly.

Karl stayed silent for once, giving her the chance to explain.

'A few years ago we were in the same competition, and it was a big one. A really big deal. She danced well, yeah, but nothing special. But Karl, I blew everyone away. It was one of those moments where everything came together – I couldn't have wished for it to go any better. It was like the perfect storm, you know?'

'So what happened?'

'Jenna won,' Sadie stated flatly.

'Okay . . .' Karl began slowly. 'Well . . . maybe you just weren't as good as you thought you were. I mean, sometimes it *feels* like you've done an awesome job, but it just doesn't communicate—'

'*No* Karl.' Sadie could feel herself getting angry. 'I *should* have won. Everyone told me I should have. And you know why I didn't?'

At the other end of the phone, Karl shook his head. Sadie didn't wait for an answer.

'Because she fucking cheated. Her mother was screwing the head judge.'

253

'For real?' Karl's jaw dropped.

'Yes Karl, for real. I *saw* them together. And you know what happened? The prize was a trip to LA to work with Ghetto Angels. While Jenna was out there she got discovered by Ultimate Management, then a few months later she's this huge star. That was *my* chance,' Sadie wailed, all the repressed feelings of injustice that she'd tried to keep locked away came spilling out. '*My* opportunity to kick-start my career. If I'd gone to LA that could have been it for me – straight into the big league, working on projects that I love. Instead I've spent the last three years dragging myself round London doing shitty auditions for half-assed shows I don't even want to be in.'

Sadie could feel herself getting upset and that frustrated her more than anything. She hadn't even wanted to tell Karl in the first place. The move to Vegas had been meant to herald a fresh start, a chance to put everything behind her. Now, with the arrival of Jenna, she felt as though her past had followed her.

'Can you understand why I don't want to do it, Karl?' Sadie pleaded. 'I've had to watch her take the chance that should have been mine and then when I've finally started to do something with my life, to make something of myself out here, she rocks up and you want me to drop everything just to be her backing dancer? To stand in her shadow and make her look good while she takes all the glory? I can't do it,' she finished.

Karl hesitated, wondering how to play it. 'Look Sadie,' he said finally, his voice soft. 'I understand, I really do. But I'm not asking you to do it for Jenna. I'm not even asking you to do it for yourself. I'm asking you to do it for me.'

'But—'

'Don't interrupt,' he chastised her gently. 'You're an

amazing dancer. You're superb at what you do and your career is about to sky-rocket. There's a lot of buzz about you out here.'

'I bet you say that to all the girls,' Sadie muttered, but she couldn't help but feel pleased.

'No Sadie, I don't,' Karl said firmly, his tone serious. 'Look, don't tell the others anything about this yet, because it's not confirmed, but I want to take the Kandy Girls global. I'm already getting calls from friends in other cities – New York, LA, New Orleans. And I reckon we could make a huge impact in Europe – the Crazy Horse, the Lido, the KitKatClub . . .'

'Really?'

'Honestly. That could be your future, Sadie. What does one little gig matter?'

Sadie said nothing.

'I mean, who knows what's meant to be,' Karl went on. 'Maybe you were never supposed to win the competition. Maybe your destiny was always to come to Vegas and meet the faaaabulous Karl Madison.'

In spite of herself, Sadie smiled.

'I'm asking you as a favour to me because you're the only one who can do this. You know that. None of the others could manage it.'

'That's emotional blackmail!' Sadie cried, feeling herself start to weaken and hating herself for it.

'It's the truth. You're the best and I need you for this.'

'Enough already with the flattery!'

'Okay, but I just want to say one more thing – don't you want to be part of this show? The Night of a Thousand Stars,' Karl whispered, making it sound magical. 'Do you know how many big names are inside The Colosseum right now? This is history in the making, Sadie, and you could be part of it . . .'

'All right, all right, you've worn me down. I'll do it!'

Karl let out a shriek that caused the truckers to look curiously in his direction. He gave them a little wave, and they quickly went back to work. 'You will?'

'I don't know why, but yes. For you. You owe me big for this, Karl, I mean it.'

'I do. I know. Sadie Laine, you are one fabulous diva.'

'Thank you.' Sadie let out a deep breath, trying to release the tension. Maybe it wouldn't be so bad. *Yeah, right.* 'What do I need to do?'

'I'll take care of everything. Just get yourself here.'

'Should I call a cab?'

'There's one coming over for you. In fact, I called them before I called you, so it should be there any second.'

From outside the front of the house, Sadie heard a car horn.

'You bastard,' she swore.

'See you in ten,' Karl said sweetly, before hanging up.

Five minutes later she was on Boulder Highway, heading north towards the Strip. The cab driver had obviously been promised extra if he could get her there quicker as he was weaving in and out of the traffic like a maniac. Sadie was starting to feel sick. She hung onto the door handle as he swerved in front of a huge truck; the driver pressed down on his horn as the cab sped away.

She was already pretty stressed when her phone rang. Unknown number. She snatched it up angrily. 'For fuck's sake, Karl, I'm on my way.'

'Uh . . . Sadie?' It was a male voice she didn't recognize. Deep, with an American accent.

'Yeah. Who's this?'

'This is Tyrone.' He cleared his throat. 'Tyrone Cole.'

Sadie wanted the car seat to open up and swallow her. 'Hi,' she managed to squeak. She tried to picture the guy she'd seen on the TV screen in Starbucks. Gorgeous face, broad shoulders, strong thighs.

'Your friend Brooke gave me your number.'

'Yeah, she told me,' Sadie replied, and it came out harsher than she'd intended.

'Have I caught you at a bad time?' Tyrone was all politeness and Sadie immediately felt guilty.

Just give the guy a chance.

'Kind of . . . But it's fine. I'm in a cab, so I can talk.'

Another truck driver blasted his horn as the taxi veered across a lane.

'Is it a runaway cab?' Tyrone asked.

Sadie smiled. 'You could say that. I think the driver thinks he's Robert De Niro.'

Tyrone laughed, a rich, warm sound. 'Listen, I really enjoyed the show the other night – you were great.'

'Thanks, I'm glad you did. We had a really good night – it was one of our favourite shows,' she rambled on.

'I love your accent too,' he told her. He sounded genuine, as if it wasn't just a line. 'It's really cute.'

'Thanks. It comes completely naturally to me,' Sadie teased, and Tyrone laughed again.

'Uh, Sadie, the reason I was calling – I've got tickets for that big concert at Caesars tonight. I wondered if you wanted to go. It should be pretty awesome.'

Sadie could have laughed out loud at the irony. 'You'll never believe this, but I'm actually performing in it.'

'Really? Wow. I didn't know the Kandy Girls were on the bill.'

'Oh, we're not. It's just me – I'm doing backing

for . . . It's a long story.' Sadie realized she didn't want to go into it. 'I only found out myself about ten minutes ago.'

'Jeez, talk about pressure,' Tyrone sympathized.

'I know. Crazy, huh?' The traffic was stationary and Sadie relaxed into her seat. Tyrone was easy to talk to. He seemed quiet and polite – a little shy even – and in spite of herself Sadie felt herself warming to him.

'Well, that's perfect. We can have dinner afterwards,' he suggested. 'What do you like? Steak? Italian? Or I know a great sushi place—'

'I'm really sorry, but I don't think I'll be able to make it,' Sadie apologized.

'Oh.' He sounded disappointed. 'You already have plans?'

'Not exactly,' Sadie admitted. 'But I'm gonna be exhausted. I'll be working all day, and then the show tonight . . .'

'But you've still got to eat, right?' Tyrone said easily. 'We don't have to make it a late one.'

'I . . .' Sadie found she was all out of excuses. 'That'd be great, thank you.'

'Hey, no problem. I'm really looking forward to it.'

'Me too,' Sadie said automatically.

'Best of luck for the show, yeah? I'll be watching. I know you'll be amazing.'

'I hope so.'

'I know so.'

He hung up the phone, and Sadie sat motionless for a few moments, gazing out of the window at the sun-bleached desert. She had a date. With Tyrone Cole – a rich, gorgeous football player. He could have any girl he wanted, but he'd chosen her.

For the first time since all that shit with Paul Austin,

Sadie felt a frisson of excitement, a glimpse of her old self. She was going to have a good time tonight. She deserved it. All she had to do first was get through this show.

Sadie raced through the maze of corridors backstage at The Colosseum. It was absolute bedlam. Karl had been right – there were more stars here than at a pre-Oscar gifting suite. She'd already passed a host of famous names and had to force herself not to stare as she caught a glimpse of Madonna being shepherded to her dressing room surrounded by six enormous bodyguards.

'Oh, sorry!' she apologized breathlessly, as she collided with someone. A tall, masculine, broad-chested someone. She glanced up, flushing bright red as she realized who it was.

'Don't worry, no harm done,' Nick Taylor said, in that glorious Southern accent. He held his hands up in a playful gesture and broke into a wide grin. 'Are you okay? No broken bones?' His eyes scanned over her slowly, and Sadie got the impression he was looking at more than potential cuts and bruises.

'I'm fine,' Sadie mumbled. God, he was so handsome in the flesh, all rugged cowboy good looks and twinkly eyes. She'd seen him on TV and in the papers, of course, but up close he was something else. Her first thought was that she wished she was wearing something a little more glamorous; she'd barely had time to fling on cropped sweats and a tank top before hurling herself into the taxi. Her second thought was that Jenna Jonsson's boyfriend was currently looking at her like he wanted to throw her against the wall and bang her brains out.

'You sure you're okay . . . um . . .?'

'Sadie,' she answered the unspoken question. 'Yeah, I'm fine. Don't worry about it.'

'Sadie,' he repeated languorously. 'Hot accent by the way. Are you British?' His manner was laid-back and easy-going, his smile effortlessly sexy. A woman walked by and stared at them, then glanced jealously at Sadie.

'Yeah. Yeah, I am,' Sadie purred. Maybe a little flirting could be fun.

'Really? That's awesome.' He let his gaze run over her once again. He was blatant about it, didn't even try to hide it. After his run-in with Amber, Nick felt he could do with a little ego-massaging. 'So how come you're in Vegas?' He leaned casually against the wall, angling his body closer to hers. It was an intimate gesture, cutting off the craziness in the rest of the corridor.

'I live out here now. I'm a dancer with the Kandy Girls. We perform at The Play Rooms and we're pretty amazing,' she told him boldly.

'Maybe I should come check you out.' That look again, straight into her eyes like he was picturing her naked.

'Maybe you should.' Sadie held his gaze.

'You know, I'm around for another couple of days,' he began lazily. 'Maybe you and I should find a window to hook up.'

A flicker of confusion crossed Sadie's brow. Was he suggesting . . .? 'Aren't you dating Jenna Jonsson?' The words came out before she had chance to think what she was saying.

Nick shrugged. 'It's not serious.' The lie came automatically.

'That's not what the papers are saying.'

'Don't believe everything you read,' Nick smirked. She was playing hardball but he was confident he'd close the deal. It was like a game for him. Flirting with women came instinctively; he couldn't help it. It was in his genes, after all. The occasional other girl on the side didn't mean he loved Jenna any less – it was just that women got hung up about that whole fidelity thing. They didn't understand the way men worked. If Nick was going to get married then he needed a final fling – and this girl looked like a pretty perfect candidate. Beautiful face, superb body, natural breasts. 'So, how about it?' he asked, sounding entirely sure of himself.

Sadie was taken aback. Jeez, could no guy keep it in their pants any more? They were all disgusting, every single one of them. Out of nowhere, she felt a sudden stab of sympathy for Jenna – the last emotion she'd ever expected to feel where she was concerned. From everything Sadie had seen and read, Jenna was clearly head over heels for Nick. Sadie had thought he felt the same about Jenna, but apparently not. She smiled to herself. Time to have a little fun.

'Actually the reason I'm here is that I'm going to be working with Jenna.'

Nick's face dropped, his smile slowly fading as he realized what she was saying. Beneath his tan he turned pale. 'With Jenna Jonsson?' he stammered.

'Yeah. As one of her dancers. Good thing you two aren't serious, isn't it? Hope you don't mind if I don't give you my number but, you know, I think you should go fuck yourself. Have a good show.'

Sadie grinned as she walked off, leaving a stunned Nick Taylor gaping after her.

25

The Night of a Thousand Stars had exploded into life. Backstage Sadie could hear the deafening screams from out front as yet another megastar tore up the place and the entire building throbbed to the pounding beat of the music. The excitement in the air was tangible.

Sadie had spent the last five hours locked in a tiny, makeshift rehearsal room, with just a couple of breaks to catch her breath and eat a banana for energy. No run-through on the main stage meant she was going to be winging it out there, but she was feeling confident. Her partner, Juan, was a sweetie, the whole troupe was fantastic and Karl was a genius. Despite her earlier reservations, she was excited. This was the big league and she could feel it.

Unconsciously, Sadie smoothed down her outfit – a tiny, red silk skirt that draped round her body and flared when she danced, paired with a jewelled bikini-style top in brilliant shades of jade and mango, displaying acres of honey-brown stomach. The theme of Jenna's set was Brazilian carnival, and Sadie's outfit was a dazzling riot of colour, intended to evoke images of hot, lazy days on Copacabana beach and long, sensual nights of erotically charged dancing.

Her dark hair was loose, curled and backcombed for a wild, gypsy look. The make-up artist had painted on thick black eyeliner, with bold coloured make-up in blues and oranges. The brash, strong look suited Sadie, especially with the tan she'd acquired since living in sunny Vegas. She looked like a tempestuous Latina, a glorious Carmen.

And now she was standing outside Jenna Jonsson's dressing room, having been summoned to see the woman herself. Karl had told her that Jenna personally wanted to thank Sadie for saving their skin. Too bad she hadn't turned up at rehearsals to say it herself, Sadie thought tartly, resenting the fact that she was expected to dance attendance on Jenna the way the rest of the world did. It wasn't as if she had nothing better to do. She could really use a break to rest her body, maybe grab a sandwich and refuel . . .

Yet she couldn't deny that she was curious. More than curious – she was keyed up, totally on edge as she wondered how Jenna would react. Sadie could hardly believe that she was going to see her again after all this time. Would Jenna be ashamed, embarrassed about what had happened? Maybe she would break down and apologize. Perhaps, Sadie thought uncomfortably, Jenna wouldn't even remember her. Maybe she'd never registered on Jenna's radar – just another minor irritant to be stamped on and dismissed as she clawed her way to the top.

Well, whatever happened, Sadie was ready for it. *Bring on the showdown.*

Without giving herself time to hesitate, she knocked firmly on the door. It was opened by an enormous security guy who eyed her suspiciously.

'It's fine,' she heard Jenna call out. The goon grunted, standing aside to let her in.

Sadie stepped through the door, her eyes sweeping quickly around the enormous dressing room as she took in the scene before her. Jenna was standing in front of a full-length mirror, wearing a tinier, sexier version of Sadie's costume, and surrounded by a small army of stylists. One girl knelt at her feet, fastening the straps on her stacked heels. Another was frantically fixing her hair, while a third applied blusher with all the skill of a fine-art specialist. It was as though they were playing dress-up with a life-sized Barbie.

Sadie was shocked to see how stunning Jenna was in the flesh, without airbrushing or touch-ups. Even all those years ago she'd been pretty, but now she was glossy and groomed to within an inch of her life. She had that natural radiant glow that was anything but natural – it took a truckload of time and money, and was impossible for mere civilians to achieve. She looked every inch the superstar she was.

'I'll be with you in a minute,' Jenna apologized, barely glancing in her direction. 'Take a seat. Help yourself to anything.'

Mutinously, Sadie remained standing as she glanced round the luxurious dressing room. She'd thought they had a pretty good deal at The Play Rooms, compared to some of the dives she'd worked in, but this was another level. She stared round at the soft, white couches, marvelling at the freshly cut flowers and the giant fruit platter on the coffee table. There were plates of sandwiches, a stand of beautifully decorated cupcakes and endless bottles of Bling H_2O and Cristal. Jenna had restricted herself to water and a little fruit, Sadie noted, feeling pangs of envy sweep through her once more. *This* was what she wanted! This was what her life could have been like if it hadn't been for that cheating . . .

She balled her fists in fury, beginning to wonder if Jenna was on some sort of ego trip. *How dare she make me wait around like this*, thought Sadie, feeling a tight knot of rage begin to build in her stomach. She hadn't come here to be some sort of spectator to Jenna's sickeningly perfect life. She was on the verge of walking out when Jenna waved away the huddle of people and turned to Sadie with a disarmingly genuine smile.

'Sadie Laine.' Jenna looked her over appraisingly. Sadie felt pleased that she wouldn't find anything negative. She looked good, and she knew it. 'It's been a while,' Jenna said lightly.

The hovering assistants pretended to be engrossed in their own conversations, but Sadie could tell they were eagerly listening in. There was a crackle of animosity in the air, an unexplained tension, and they sensed something was going to happen.

'You're doing pretty well for yourself I hear,' Jenna continued.

'Not as well as you,' Sadie acknowledged, unable to keep the note of bitterness out of her voice. Jenna might be all sweetness and light, but Sadie didn't buy it.

'Karl Madison worships the ground you walk on. He always tells me I'm hopeless,' Jenna smiled, trying to lighten the atmosphere.

'I'm sure he doesn't mean it,' Sadie said tightly. She couldn't help it. Seeing Jenna like this brought it home to her that while she thought she was doing well for herself, Jenna was in a different league. She had the glittering career, the shelf of awards and the superstar boyfriend – even if he was a total sleaze. All Sadie had was a job as a glorified stripper and a growing distrust of men.

Jenna's brow creased in confusion, a flicker of hurt passing across her eyes. Aware that the conversation was not going how she'd expected, she turned to the gaggle of people surrounding her. 'Give me five minutes here, guys.' Her tone was pleasant, but insistent. Without a word, they quickly filed out of the room, leaving the two women alone. Sadie stood her ground, determined not to feel intimidated.

'Sadie,' Jenna tottered across the room towards her. 'I know this is a little awkward, but I'm so grateful to you for doing this. And I know Karl is too — he was going frantic.'

'Well . . . thanks for giving me the opportunity,' Sadie managed grudgingly, aware that she was behaving like a bitch.

'No problem.' Jenna smiled, a sweet, angelic expression that made Sadie long to slap her. Did this girl ever do anything that was less than perfect? 'I'm so glad you're okay about all of this. I just wanted to speak to you and clear the air — Karl said you were still kind of mad over what happened . . .'

'Did he?' Sadie's tone was sharp. Jenna didn't notice.

'Yeah . . . But it was a long time ago and I guess we've both moved on, right?'

Patronizing bitch, Sadie thought furiously.

'I mean, I know it was probably disappointing for you at the time,' Jenna gabbled on, 'but I won fair and square so—'

'*Fair and square?*' Sadie burst out, unable to hold back any longer.

'Yes,' Jenna nodded. 'Why, what are you—'

'Why do you think you won that competition?' Sadie's lips were pressed into a tight line, her voice dangerously controlled.

'Because I was the best dancer,' Jenna stated

266

incredulously, unable to understand why Sadie was behaving like she was. 'You're obviously still pretty hung up about it, but I really think that by now—'

'Are you for real?' Sadie asked in disbelief.

'Sadie, I don't understand why you—'

'Save it, Jenna,' snapped Sadie. 'I don't know if this is all some act, or if you've brainwashed yourself into believing this but—'

'I've got no idea what you're talking about,' Jenna protested helplessly.

'Do you really think that's why you won?' Sadie demanded, growing angrier by the second. *Time for a few home truths.*

'Yes!'

'No, Jenna,' Sadie yelled. 'It's because your mother was sleeping with the head judge. She was screwing Dickie Masters!' Her breath was coming fast and she felt her stomach lurch, wondering if she'd gone too far. Jenna seemed to crumple before her, and for a moment Sadie thought she might cry. Then she pulled it together, her eyes narrowing as she glared at Sadie.

'That's not true,' Jenna whispered.

'Isn't it?'

'You're lying,' Jenna insisted. Her tone was cold, the sweet demeanour gone. But the catch in her voice gave away her uncertainty.

'I'm *not* lying. I saw them.'

Jenna's face clouded with confusion, her mind working furiously. Something, somewhere was making sense. She'd watched Sadie perform. She had known Sadie had been good – amazing, in fact – and she hadn't thought she stood a hope in hell. She remembered moving awkwardly, messing up a few of the steps as nerves got the better of her. She'd been as astonished as anyone when her name had been called and the trophy thrust into her hand. Even more surprising was when Dickie Masters had turned up in LA to spend a few days with her mother while she rehearsed with Ghetto Angels . . .

'You're just jealous,' Jenna rounded on her furiously, the anger rising in her chest. She'd rather die than admit that Sadie might be right.

'Oh grow up, Jenna. You're not in high school any more.'

'It's true. What is it you're doing with your life now?' Jenna sneered. 'Stripping in Karl's little group? Pathetic.'

'Nick Taylor didn't seem to think so . . .' The words were out of her mouth before Sadie could stop them.

Jenna started. 'What the hell is that supposed to mean?'

Sadie shrugged. 'I bumped into him earlier – literally, in fact. He's a friendly guy, isn't he?'

'Screw you,' Jenna swore. 'You don't know anything about him.'

'True. But he seemed very interested in getting to know me. He suggested we hook up. He was pretty blatant about it in fact.'

'Bullshit.'

'Oh, change the fucking record. Why don't you open your eyes for once, Jenna? You're exactly like I remember – a spoilt little brat who believes the world revolves around her.'

'Yeah? And you know what I remember about you? You're a loser, Sadie. You're jealous of me because you want what I have – *my* career, *my* boyfriend, *my* life. And you'll never have it. Face it, you're just not good enough.'

'You're wrong. I *am* good enough. I was better than you and you know it. And at least I can say that every-thing I've got is because I worked for it – not because I fucked my way there.'

Jenna drew herself up, standing tall on her heels. She looked pityingly at Sadie. 'You're deluded, you know that? Really messed up. You're desperate to have what I've got and now you want my boyfriend. You probably threw yourself at him.'

'Oh please,' Sadie scoffed.

'He probably thought you were desperate. I mean, do you even *have* a boyfriend?'

Sadie coloured – it was all the answer Jenna needed.

'I didn't think so,' she crowed triumphantly. 'I'll let you into a little secret – men don't like crazy-ass bunny boilers.'

Sadie let rip, all the frustration that she'd lived with for so long spilling out. 'You know what? Your mother would be so proud of you, following in her footsteps like that. How did you end up working with Phoenix? Oh yeah, you slept with Ryan and Nick. When's Zac's turn, Jenna?'

'Fuck you,' Jenna spat.

They were inches apart, close enough for Jenna to see the cold fury in Sadie's eyes. Suddenly Jenna's mobile rang, shattering the tension.

'Get out or I'm calling security,' Jenna hissed.

'Fine with me,' Sadie shot back.

Jenna threw her a final look of disgust, then stalked across the room to grab her BlackBerry.

'I'm not a liar, Jenna,' Sadie warned ominously. 'Remember that.'

Jenna ignored her, turning her back as she picked up her phone. 'Hello?'

It took all of Sadie's self-control not to tell Jenna to go fuck herself and walk straight out of the building, just forget about the whole show. But she had promised Karl. She knew how much tonight meant to him and, after the opportunities he'd given her, she was damned if she was going to be the one to mess it up. Let his precious Jenna be the one to throw her toys out of the pram.

Sadie turned to go, in her haste snagging her skirt on the edge of a clothes rail. 'Shit,' she swore. The material was caught around a small screw. Sadie tugged it hard. The skirt ripped, tearing the silk. Sadie was past caring – she just wanted to be out of there. Let wardrobe deal with it.

'What?' Jenna yelled suddenly. Sadie jumped. It was impossible not to overhear the conversation. 'What do you mean it's all gone? How can that happen?' Even with her back to her, Sadie could tell Jenna was livid. 'I don't need this right now. I'm about to go on stage. Can't you sort it out yourself?'

Sadie had heard enough. She made her way to the door, grasping the handle, when Jenna said something that made her stop dead.

'That's impossible. Put me through to him,' Jenna demanded furiously. 'I don't care what fucking time it is over there, just get Paul Austin on the phone. *Now.*'

26

Sadie froze. Her heart rate tripled. Had Jenna just said . . .?

'I don't give a shit, just do it!'

Sadie tried to speak but her mouth felt dry, as if it was full of sand. 'Paul Austin?' she croaked.

Jenna glanced up. She looked startled, as though she had forgotten that Sadie was there. 'I thought I told you to get out.'

Sadie's eyes glittered dangerously. 'Paul Austin of Willis & Bourne?' Now she had Jenna's attention.

'You know him?' Jenna whispered. The blood had drained from her face, and she eyed Sadie suspiciously. 'Do you work with him? Is this some kind of set-up?'

Sadie snorted. 'Don't get carried away. All I know about him is that he's a lying, cheating, piece of shit. Does that seem familiar?'

Jenna stared hard at Sadie. Then she raised the phone to her ear again. Sadie noticed her hands were shaking. 'Call me as soon as you have news.' Jenna hung up. 'What do you know about him?' she demanded.

'I already told you,' Sadie snapped, irritated by Jenna's tone.

'But how do you know him?'

'None of your fucking business!'

Jenna paused, realizing that she needed to calm down if she was going to get Sadie on side. She let out a long, shaky breath. When she spoke again, her tone was gentler. 'Look, Sadie, I'm in such a mess here. If you know anything – any information about Paul Austin – I'd really appreciate it if you could help me.'

Sadie remained silent, defiantly refusing to meet Jenna's gaze.

'*Please.*' Jenna was close to tears. 'I'm so sorry about what I said before, I didn't mean—'

'What do you want to know?'

'Anything.' Jenna leapt eagerly on Sadie's words. 'Anything you know about him, that you think I could—'

'Why?'

'What do you mean?'

'Why,' Sadie repeated. 'I don't know what'll be useful for you unless you tell me why you need to know about him.'

Jenna looked at her intently, wondering whether to trust her. She knew she had no option if she wanted her help.

'He's my investment manager,' she explained awkwardly. 'I've been giving him money. A lot of it.'

'How much?'

'I don't know!' Jenna looked panicked as she tried to calculate. There was the initial investment of half a million – the minimum Paul would accept. Then there had been further, regular transactions running into hundreds of thousands. 'Around a couple of million – maybe more.'

'Jesus,' Sadie inhaled sharply.

'I know. Oh fuck, I've been so stupid,' Jenna wailed. She'd thought she was being so in control, so grown-up, trying to manage her money like this. Paul had been charming and intelligent; he seemed so trust-worthy, she thought, furious at herself for being taken in like this. He'd sent her regular reports, long and detailed, full of figures, calculations and spreadsheets. If she was being honest, she'd never read them. She'd just believed him when he said her portfolio was doing well and asked for a further hundred grand to invest in Bulgarian property or whatever.

'But he can't just lose it, can he? I mean, surely you can't just take someone's money and give them nothing in return?' She sounded desperate.

Sadie thought about it. She remembered his words, *Whether they win or lose, I always win.* She knew he took a fee out of every payment that was made to him, plus a percentage of the profits – if there were any. Sadie recalled ads in the papers, the microscopically printed caveat warning investors that *the value of your shares can go down as well as up.*

'It doesn't sound good,' she admitted.

'Shit,' Jenna swore. 'You've *got* to help me, Sadie. Did he take your money too?'

'He was . . . I didn't know him in a professional capacity,' Sadie began carefully.

'Then what . . .?'

'We had a relationship.'

Jenna looked puzzled. She remembered a wedding ring, a photo of his kids. 'I thought he was married.'

'He is. It didn't end well.'

'Right,' Jenna said lightly, and Sadie knew she'd just confirmed everything Jenna suspected about her.

'It's not what you think,' she said quickly.

'No?' Jenna's tone was mocking.

'I'm not some slut, you know,' Sadie defended herself hotly. 'Some home-wrecker after another woman's husband.'

'I didn't say that.' Jenna's expression implied that's exactly what she'd thought.

'Well, you know what?' Sadie began fiercely. 'I got what was coming to me. You asked how I know him – like I said, we had a relationship. We'd been seeing each other for a few months when he brought round another girl for a threesome – a prostitute, actually.'

Sadie saw the look on Jenna's face, but carried on speaking. She knew if she stopped, she'd lose her nerve. 'I went along with it because he wanted to. I was crazy about him and would have done anything for him. But he secretly filmed us – I didn't know anything about it. He filmed us, and then he put the footage on the Internet for everyone to watch. My family could have seen that. It could have destroyed my career. But I guess that's what I deserve, right? I guess that was just karma coming round to bite me on the ass,' she finished furiously, her eyes stinging with tears.

'My God,' Jenna whispered, her mouth falling open in shock. 'He really did that?'

'Yes, he did,' Sadie confirmed bitterly. 'I've never seen him since and I hate that bastard more than you can possibly imagine.'

Sadie suddenly felt the overwhelming urge to confide in someone. She'd kept it to herself for so long – not even Carla had had the whole story. But now Jenna had first-hand experience of how this prick could screw you over.

'What a sick bastard!' Jenna burst out, outraged on Sadie's behalf. 'And you let him get away with it?'

'What else could I do? I couldn't get hold of him, didn't have any way of contacting him. I just wanted to put it behind me and get on with my life – that's why I moved out here.'

'But why didn't you tell anyone? You could have gone to the police or something . . .'

Sadie snorted. 'Do you think anyone would have cared if I'd told my side of the story? You've met him. You know what he's like – a pillar of the establishment, donates to all the right charities, beautiful wife, perfect family. I'd have been painted as some mistress with a grudge, trying to blacken his reputation because he ran back to his wife.'

'So . . . what? You're just going to forget about it?'

'Of course not. I'm going to get my revenge. I just don't know how – yet. But I will.'

'You've got to make him pay,' Jenna insisted. 'He can't get away with it.'

'I know,' Sadie agreed irritably. She didn't need Little Miss Perfect telling her what she should be doing with her life.

Jenna suddenly grasped Sadie's arm, her eyes wide. 'Listen, I can help you. We can do this together.'

'What do you mean?' Sadie's heart began to race; Jenna's excitement was infectious.

'I've got resources, contacts – a bloody worldwide platform! We can go to the press, tell them what he did to us. We can ruin his reputation.'

'He'll sue us for slander.' Sadie shook her head. 'We don't have any proof.'

'Then we'll get some!' Jenna exclaimed, her eyes sparkling. 'He must be doing this to others – screwing them physically and financially. We just need to get evidence.'

Sadie's mind was racing. Maybe this was the

opportunity she had been waiting for. 'How are we going to do this?'

Jenna paused for a second as she began pacing the room. 'I can give you all the information I have — documents, letters, that sort of thing. I'll get my lawyers to take a look — see if they can find evidence of anything illegal.'

'I'd bet a hell of a lot that it's not strictly kosher.'

'That's my instinct. Now, what about this company he works for?'

'Willis & Bourne?' Sadie shook her head. 'No, he told me about them. They're a big company — straight-up, spotless reputation.'

'So whatever he's doing, they don't know about it,' Jenna clarified. 'Did he tell you anything else? Anything that might be helpful for us?'

'I . . . I can't remember,' Sadie hesitated. 'He used to brag about his work mainly. About how he made loads of money. And about how he had loads of contacts. He had clients in every field — journalism, law, music, TV . . .'

Jenna raised an eyebrow. 'I'll ask around. See what I can find. You should do the same. But we have to do this quietly. If he *is* doing anything he shouldn't be—'

'I *know* he is,' Sadie interrupted.

'Then if he thinks we're onto him, he'll try and cover it up.'

Both women were silent for a moment, lost in their own thoughts.

'Are you sure you want to do this?' Jenna asked, scrutinizing Sadie's expression. 'We've got to be prepared to work together.'

'Sure,' Sadie agreed coolly. 'But it doesn't make us friends, right?'

'Right. This is purely business.'

'Purely business,' Sadie echoed. 'Then I'm in. I don't care how it happens. I want to see him taken down.'

'Don't worry. We're gonna nail that son of a bitch,' Jenna said grimly, her lips pressed together in a determined line.

The auditorium was plunged into total darkness and the crowd went crazy, screaming Jenna's name. Dazzling laser beams swept across the stage, illuminating the spectacular set as the opening bars of the intro kicked in.

Backstage, Jenna's heart was pounding. She estimated she had less than a minute before she made her entrance. The dancers ran on ahead of her, taking up their positions, as a stylist made last-minute adjustments to her costume, adding a little more body shimmer to her magnificent cleavage.

She took a quick gulp from a bottle of water – room temperature, to lubricate her vocal chords. Then someone handed her a microphone and she took a deep breath. This was it. She strode forward, bursting onto the stage in an explosion of sound and colour. The crowd erupted, and Jenna immediately felt all her nerves crystallize into adrenaline as she launched into 'Feel It', one of her best-known hits. She was relaxed and confident at the same time, dominant and powerful – this was truly where she belonged, and this was what she loved.

It had been too long since she'd done a live show, she realized. All the time spent recording in studios, on the publicity trail or in rehearsals – none of it compared to the buzz of an audience. She'd heard other performers say it, but it was true. There was no feeling in the world like being out there, connecting with the fans and feeding off their energy.

A camera zoomed into view, circling around her as she danced. Jenna played up to it, looking straight into the lens as she flirted with the audience at home. It was every man's fantasy – Jenna Jonsson performing in your living room, dressed in little more than her underwear. Her skirt was so tiny that the slightest movement showed off the glorious curve of her butt – and that was exactly the plan. Her skin was golden and glowing, her body honed to perfection by the gruelling exercise regime she'd undertaken for the past few weeks. The Phoenix collaboration was the biggest opportunity of her career, and she hadn't left anything to chance.

As the backing segued into 'Sexual Rush', Jenna caught a glimpse of Sadie. She was dancing closely with Juan, as he spun her around then lowered her sharply into a deep backward drop. She was doing well. Jenna felt a sneaking admiration for her – she was obviously very talented, very focused. And now they were allies, united against Paul Austin. For the first time since her accountant's phone call, when she'd felt that sickening jolt in her stomach, Jenna sensed that the situation wasn't hopeless. She was ready for battle and believed they could win.

The song reached its climax and Jenna belted out the lyrics, punching the sky as she held her final position. Pyrotechnics exploded around her. She stood centre stage, her breath coming fast, chest rising and falling as she basked in the adulation.

'I love you Vegas,' Jenna shouted into the microphone, and was answered by deafening cheers. With a final wave at the crowd, she ran off stage into the darkness of the wings, where she was immediately surrounded by people wanting to congratulate her, a sea of unknown faces all desperate to get close. Then Nick emerged from the shadows, his drumsticks in his hand. Everyone parted to give them some space and he kissed her, long and hard, pulling her against him. He knew full well that everyone was watching and he revelled in it. He was claiming her; she was his girl.

'You were amazing,' Nick told her, his breath hot in her ear as he made himself heard above the ecstatic crowd.

Instinctively Jenna pulled away, remembering what Sadie had said about him. *He suggested we hook up.* Jenna couldn't help but wonder if it was true. Oh, she hadn't believed a word of it at first – had marked her down as yet another deluded fan. But after their conversation about Paul, she had seen another side to Sadie – open, candid and fiercely proud. And if she *was* telling the truth, Jenna couldn't bear to consider what she'd said about her mother . . .

Nick was so keyed up he didn't notice her chilly reaction. 'See you later, baby.' He winked suggestively, then ran onto the stage. Zac followed behind him, brushing past Jenna.

'Have a great show,' she yelled after him. Zac nodded in acknowledgement, but didn't stop to speak.

Out of nowhere, Jenna's dresser appeared with her costume for the Phoenix duet, and all thoughts of Sadie and Nick and Paul flew out of her head. There was no time to go back to her dressing room to change, so a screen was hastily erected around her. Not that she was prudish – hell no, she was proud of her body, and when you'd grown up doing competitions and photo shoots you learned not to be self-conscious about changing wherever you could. But these days there was always the risk of someone lurking with a camera phone.

Five minutes later, and footage of a topless Jenna Jonsson could be all over YouTube. Gerry would have a heart attack.

Quickly, Jenna stripped naked – her dress was the kind that didn't require any underwear, as the slightest line would show under the sheer material. Jenna slipped it over her head and smoothed it down, letting it slither over every curve. The dress was white silk, slashed to the navel and held in place with a single diamond clasp. Loose folds of material draped around her body, giving the erotic illusion that it might spill open at any moment.

Hair and make-up moved in for touch-ups, and then Jenna was free to go. She made her way to the very edge of the stage, a treacherous journey in Swarovski-studded Louboutins. The sight on stage took her breath away. Phoenix were tearing up the place. A crowd of girls had surged to the front and were screaming uncontrollably, clutching at their hair. Some were crying and one had even fainted. The paramedics lifted her over the crash barriers and carried her backstage. It was like the old footage of Beatlemania, thought Jenna breathlessly.

Zac grinned at the crowd, who screamed hysterically in return, before taking hold of the microphone and ripping into the song. His vocals were full of raw sexuality, strong and powerful. Jenna had never seen him so confident, so utterly at ease as he was on the stage. He was dressed all in black – snake-hipped in skinny jeans, shirt and boots, with black kohled eyes and silver jewellery. He looked like a rock star. He looked sexy, Jenna realized, as she watched in awe. She felt a delicious tingle run through her body, a rush of heat between her legs. Christ, what the hell was going on with her? It was *Zac*, for God's sake!

It must be the nerves, she insisted to herself as she watched him prowl around the stage. His body was lean and toned, his jeans tight enough to show the considerable bulge of his crotch. *Focus, dammit*, she told herself sharply, grateful that no one could see the way her cheeks were blazing in the darkness.

She jumped as a tech guy approached, walkie-talkie in hand.

'Stand by, Miss Jonsson.'

He miked her up and she slipped her earpiece into place. She tried to stay calm, but the adrenaline had kicked in. She was so keyed up she felt as if she could sprint a marathon in heels. Outside there was a deathly hush in the arena, as the entire place waited for her to make her entrance. Then she heard Zac announce her name. The powerful chords rang out of his guitar as the bass line kicked in and Nick completed the opening drum riff. Jenna walked on to deafening applause.

Her voice rang out, clear and strong across the auditorium. This time there was to be no backing dancers, no complicated routine. They wanted to let the power of the music speak for itself. The crowd stayed largely silent, eagerly listening to the track as they waved their arms in the air and took photos on their phones.

I hope you're proud of me, Mum.

The thought hit Jenna like a blow to the solar plexus, and for a moment she faltered. Zac looked over in concern but Jenna had already pulled it back, as she closed her eyes and let herself get lost in the song. 'Without You' hit the chorus and Jenna's voice soared, choked with emotion. It was a badly needed catharsis; all the loneliness, all the grief, all the unbearable pressure she'd been under came flooding out as she found solace in the music – the one constant in her life that had stayed with her and would never let her down.

As the final notes from the guitar melted away, the place erupted. Tears were streaming down Jenna's face and she hadn't even noticed. The others came over to join her and the four of them stood centre stage, arms around each other as they took in the applause.

Then Nick broke away from the group, heading over to grab a microphone. Jenna looked at him in surprise as he turned to the audience, his voice booming out over the speakers.

'Hey everybody – I kinda have something I'd like to say. I haven't really planned it very well – it's pretty spur of the moment – so I'm sorta hoping you'll bear with me on this.'

Jenna looked around, wondering what was going on. Ryan and Zac returned her gaze with equally confused looks, and she could see one of the producers backstage speaking urgently into his mouthpiece. They had a tight schedule to keep to for the TV networks and couldn't afford any upsets.

Nick's voice echoed round The Colosseum. 'As I'm pretty sure everyone here knows, I'm lucky enough to be dating this incredible woman.' He gestured towards Jenna, who was hastily wiping her eyes. 'Isn't she spectacular?'

Jenna blushed, feeling a little like a museum exhibit as the crowd stared and wolf-whistled.

'I gotta admit – and I never thought I'd say this about anyone – but I'm totally crazy about her. I didn't think I'd ever be ready to settle down – Lord knows I certainly enjoyed my time as a bachelor,' he smirked, as the girls in the front row screamed. 'But it turns out I just hadn't met the right woman. I guess what I'm really trying to say here is . . .' Nick dropped to one knee and the audience began to whoop.

Jenna's mind was racing. There was a television

camera right in her face capturing every reaction, but it was all happening too fast. Surely he wasn't going to . . .?

'Jenna Jonsson,' Nick began, a dazzling grin on his handsome face. 'Will you marry me?'

27

Fireworks exploded, lighting up the night sky above The Colosseum as the Escalade carrying Sadie Laine and Tyrone Cole pulled away from Caesars. Sadie peered through the tinted window at the brilliant colours – reds, greens and yellows – fired from the illuminated rooftop that signalled the end of the show. On the sidewalk, tourists stopped walking, craning their necks upwards to watch. Even in a city famed for its extraordinary sights, the display was impressive.

Sadie settled back into the luxurious car seats, smoothing down her dress. She'd run into the Forum Shops after her performance and grabbed the first thing she found. It was a gorgeous, rich red number that fitted tightly over her slim body, with a slash neck and a skirt that stopped high on her thigh, showing off those amazing legs. She'd wiped off the heavy perform-ance make-up and added just a slick of mascara and red lip gloss, wanting to give her skin a chance to breathe. Her hair still retained the enormous volume from the show, and she'd simply pulled it back into a loose, classic ponytail, teamed with a pair of statement earrings. Tyrone hadn't been able to stop grinning when he'd seen her.

He was looking pretty hot himself, Sadie thought, telling herself that the goose-bumps on her arms were from the evening air – never mind that it was Vegas and the temperature in summer didn't drop below twenty, even in the middle of the night. Tyrone was dressed simply but smartly in blue jeans and brown loafers, with a tan belt and a crisp, white shirt, unbuttoned to show the smooth dark skin below. His black hair was closely cropped and he was freshly shaven, smelling of Allure Homme. He seemed quietly confident, completely at ease with himself.

They swung onto the Strip, heading north. 'Where are we going?' Sadie asked.

'One of my favourite places,' Tyrone told her, with a wide grin. His voice was deep – he had a smooth, Midwestern accent.

Sadie watched one enormous hotel after another flash by, wondering which Michelin-starred restaurant or hot new eaterie he would be choosing. She hoped it wasn't anywhere too pretentious – after her crazy day she wanted to relax, not feel as if it was some sort of endurance trial.

Soon they left the central Strip behind and hit downtown. Sadie was surprised to find their SUV crawling through the backstreets, finally stopping outside a tiny, unexceptional-looking Mexican joint a few blocks from Fremont Street.

'Here?' she asked in surprise.

'This place does the best Mexican food this side of Cabo,' Tyrone promised her. 'Is that okay, or did you want to go some place fancy?'

Sadie broke into a dazzling smile. 'This is perfect,' she told him honestly.

Tyrone helped her out of the car, taking hold of her hand as he led her inside. Sadie's skin tingled deliciously; she liked the feel of his large, masculine hand enveloping her tiny one.

The restaurant owner greeted Tyrone like an old friend. A short, South American guy with a thick moustache, he repeatedly kissed Sadie's hand and pronounced her to be 'very beautiful'. He seemed to be expecting them and they were ushered to a table at the back, shielded from most of the restaurant by a cheap white plastic trellis. A thick yellow candle burned in the middle of the table, dropping wax onto the chequered tablecloth.

'The guys on the team sometimes come here when they're in town,' Tyrone explained, his hand on Sadie's back as he steered her towards the table. 'Sometimes a little piece of fish at Nobu ain't gonna do the job, you know what I'm saying?'

'I know what you're saying,' Sadie grinned. And she did. Tyrone was a wealthy guy, but he didn't need to flaunt it. The Rolex, the designer clothes, the diamond ear stud – everything was discreet. He was totally down-to-earth, self-assured enough that he didn't need to put on a show for anyone.

Keeping it real, as the Americans say.

The owner produced their menus with a flourish. Sadie scanned over the delicious-sounding choices, but when she glanced up to ask Tyrone what was good, she realized that a group of people were hovering around their table, nervously waiting to ask him for his autograph. She watched quietly, increasingly impressed with what she saw. He dealt with them all respectfully and politely, making a point of speaking to everyone. When they had all got their photographs and signed napkins, the crowd drifted away and left them alone.

'Sorry about that,' Tyrone apologized.

'No problem. Is it like that everywhere you go?'

'It can be. But people are usually polite. Unless you've just lost a game – then they're not so happy.'

The owner returned with a bottle of Baja red. Tyrone raised his glass as the candlelight flickered over his face.

'What are we toasting?' Sadie asked, feeling her heart start to beat a little faster.

Tyrone cleared his throat. 'To Sadie Laine, the best goddamn dancer I've ever seen.'

Sadie giggled. 'I'll drink to that.' The wine was delicious, rich and fruity. After her long day she felt it hit her system almost immediately. She settled back in her chair, looking at the gorgeous man opposite her through the hazy light. Tyrone was a big guy, with a broad chest, strong arms, and thighs so wide that they overshot the small seat he was sitting on. It was impossible not to feel feminine and fragile in his presence. If they made love he would crush her, Sadie thought, then felt herself flush at the image, taking a gulp of wine to cover it.

'Do you like it here?' Tyrone asked. His lips showed the trace of a smile, like he was teasing her somehow. She hoped her face hadn't given away what she was thinking.

'It's perfect,' Sadie smiled, glad to have an excuse to look away from him as she stared round at the dusty vases of dried flowers and the crude paintings of Mexico hanging on the plaster walls.

'Not what you were expecting?'

'No,' Sadie shook her head. 'But that's not a bad thing.'

Tyrone took a long swallow of his wine then stared straight at her. 'I was really disappointed when you didn't show the other night.'

Sadie looked awkward. 'I was tired after the Kandy Girls and—'

'I wanted to prove that I'm not all about the fancy places, about going somewhere just 'cos it's the place to be,' Tyrone cut in. 'You don't seem like the kind of girl who's impressed by all of that. Am I right?'

'Well, I don't mind a little luxury now and then,' Sadie conceded with a grin. 'But yeah, you're right, there's more to life than that. You can get dazzled by the glitz and not see the reality,' she finished, her tone bitter as her thoughts unwillingly came back to Paul Austin. But now it was going to be different. She and Jenna had made a pact, and they were going to take that bastard down. Two strong, intelligent women working together – Paul didn't stand a chance, she thought delightedly, as the food arrived and she pulled her attention back to Tyrone.

They ate burritos, perfectly spicy and smothered in Jack cheese, with refried beans and sour cream. Sadie found she was ravenous and, as Tyrone had said, the food was fantastic.

He speared a forkful of salad and looked at her admiringly. 'You know, I don't know how you do what you do.'

'What do you mean?'

Tyrone grinned. 'You should see me dance. It's embarrassing.'

'I'd like to see that sometime,' Sadie teased, as Tyrone laughed.

'Believe me, you wouldn't. But you're so good at what you do. Like tonight – that routine was sick, and you learnt it in what, a few hours? I could never do that.'

'Well, I could never do your job,' Sadie shrugged. She'd seen enough American football to know that it was a tough, physical game. It wasn't surprising that Tyrone was in such amazing shape.

'Nah, that's just instinctive,' Tyrone disagreed. 'It's all basic stuff – running, throwing, catching. I can just do it real well,' he joked. 'But if I had to learn it – remember a routine like that – man, they wouldn't even let me out of the locker rooms.'

'Yeah, but what I do is instinctive too,' Sadie became animated as she tried to explain herself. 'It just comes so easily to me. I mean, learning a routine – that takes work, of course. Hard work. But I love it so much that it doesn't feel like any effort. Do you know what I'm saying?'

Tyrone nodded his head thoughtfully. She was so passionate about what she did, it was a joy to watch her.

'So what was it like working with Jenna Jonsson?' he asked conversationally.

Sadie made a noncommittal noise. She still wasn't sure what she thought about Jenna – she'd spent five years hating her guts and now they were supposed to be working together. It seemed pretty messed-up.

'That proposal thing was crazy,' Tyrone continued. 'You think it's for real, or publicity?'

Sadie shrugged. 'Who knows? Nick Taylor's a total sleaze though.'

Tyrone raised his eyebrows. 'You know the guy – that dude from the band?'

'Not exactly . . . Look, do you mind if we change the subject?' Sadie tried to keep her tone light but she didn't want to talk about Jenna right now. If she wanted to mess up her life by marrying a guy that couldn't be trusted as far as you could throw him, then that was up to her, but Sadie would have bet money on the fact there wouldn't be a happy ending.

'Sure,' Tyrone said easily. 'Let's talk about you.'

'Okay . . .' Sadie agreed.

'Tell me about yourself. You're from London, right?'

'Uh huh. Born and raised.'

Tyrone looked surprised. 'I didn't know anyone actually grew up in London – people always move to big cities, but you hardly ever meet anyone who was born there. Where I'm from, in Ohio, it's real small. Three thousand people in town, that's all, so it's a little different. Do you miss it?'

'Yeah, I do,' Sadie admitted, feeling a pang of sadness as she thought of her home town, the family and friends she'd left back there. 'There's always something exciting happening, and it's so full of energy. Have you ever been?'

Tyrone shook his head. 'I'd like to, though.'

There was a long pause as they looked at each other.

'But I love Vegas,' Sadie changed the subject, feeling her cheeks flush. 'It's crazy here – and the weather's fantastic.'

'Your career's exploding out here. The Kandy Girls are where it's at right now.'

'Yeah . . .' Sadie felt a surge of pride as she thought about it. 'So did you always want to play football?' she asked, spinning it around to him. She was trying to get out of the habit of calling it American football.

'Pretty much,' Tyrone grinned. He told her how he'd been the star athlete in high school before moving across the country to play football for USC. He'd dropped out in his final year and been drafted by the San Diego Chargers, where he'd played ever since.

Sadie watched him as he spoke, the sexy way his right cheek dimpled when he smiled, and the cute crease that appeared between his eyebrows when he was deep in thought. He made her feel totally at ease, totally secure. It was such a change for a guy to be genuinely interested in her – not just going through the motions like Paul had. He hadn't given a shit about her, Sadie thought darkly, just used her for what he wanted.

But the information Jenna had given her was the key to bringing him down, she felt sure of it. She was giddy with the prospect of revenge, turning the possibilities over in her mind as she racked her brain to try and remember the names of the clients he'd mentioned. Maybe she could contact them, find out if they'd experienced any irregularities with their accounts. She would get on the Internet again, see if a fresh search would bring up anything new, and call Carla in case she had any ideas . . .

'Are you okay?' Tyrone asked, looking worried.

'Just tired,' Sadie lied quickly. She felt bad. He was a great guy, and he didn't deserve this, but what was she supposed to say? *Sorry I'm a little distracted, but I may have just found a way to get my revenge on the guy who secretly filmed me having a threesome?* It wasn't happening.

They skipped dessert as Sadie was full to bursting, but lingered over the wine.

As Tyrone called for the bill, the manager hurried over with a lethal-looking bottle of tequila and three shot glasses. He poured generously, and insisted on joining them. Sadie recklessly threw back her drink, feeling the alcohol burn her throat. It stung her eyes and she opened her mouth, expecting to breathe fire. Tyrone put his arm around her, and she leaned against him for support as they made their way out of the restaurant.

'Are you sure you don't want me to drop you home?' he asked. 'I'm headed out that way anyway.'

Sadie shook her head. She wasn't planning to invite him in, and didn't want to make it awkward.

'Well, if you're sure,' Tyrone said neutrally, but she could tell from his expression he was a little hurt. He hailed a cab for her, and she watched the strong lines of his athlete's body move under his clothes. He was solid; pure muscle. Despite herself, she felt a surge of desire deep within her belly.

As the car pulled up, Tyrone turned to her, trailing his fingers all the way down her arm to lightly take her hand. Sadie shivered. His eyes were dark brown, liquid molten. Gently, he leaned down and pressed his cheek against hers. He smelt delicious. Sadie wanted to melt against him. His strong hands rested on the curve of her back, just above her bottom, his fingers brushing lightly against her skin.

Sadie felt her nipples harden through the thin fabric of her dress. She drew back instantly, her cheeks flaming, but Tyrone had already noticed. There was no disguising the effect he had on her.

With a superhuman effort, Tyrone pulled away.

'Good night, Sadie,' he said, his voice catching in his throat.

'Good night,' Sadie managed to stammer, as she hurled herself into the back of the taxi as though it was a refuge.

Tyrone watched as the car pulled away. He was glad that she'd gone – he didn't know whether he'd have been able to hold back if she'd stayed around any longer. He could tell that she'd been hurt in the past; there was a wariness to her that she couldn't quite conceal, and he sensed she had her own issues to work out. He would take it slow, Tyrone promised himself.

He liked this girl, really liked her. She was different – not like the identikit bimbos that hung around him, the blonde party girls with their fake hair, fake nails, fake breasts, all trying to bag themselves a rich athlete. No, Sadie was strong, ambitious and passionate. She'd be a tigress in bed, Tyrone thought, fighting a wave of frustration that he'd let her go like that.

But no, he wanted to wait until she was desperate, begging him to take her. He'd have to play this one very carefully – he was going to make her crazy for him, all thoughts of anyone else driven out of her head. She was a challenge, but the rewards would be worth the time and attention he planned to lavish on her.

Sadie Laine fascinated him – and Tyrone was hooked.

28

Jenna flipped open her illuminated compact and scrutinized her reflection. Her make-up was still immaculate, her stunning green eyes sparkling with life. But she barely recognized the girl that stared back at her. Her long, blonde waves had been replaced by a severe, jet-black bob – a wig, naturally – and if she pulled down her enormous Gucci shades, she thought that even Gerry might pass her by on the street. She wore a white Prada slip dress and quilted white pumps; the night air was warm, but she shivered in anticipation.

This is what I'm getting married in, Jenna thought, hardly able to believe it. She wanted to laugh out loud, the idea was so crazy.

Nick's arm was casually slung round her shoulders and she snuggled against him, anxious for the reassuring feel of his body. In just a couple of hours' time he would be her husband, Jenna thought, the word seeming so foreign and remote to her.

Everything had happened so quickly. His on-stage proposal had felt like a scene from a movie – like something she was watching but not participating in.

She couldn't even remember what she'd said to him, but from the way he'd picked her up and swung her round, as easily as though she was made of air, it seemed pretty obvious that the answer was yes.

They'd made their way off stage, swamped by a sea of well-wishers and ecstatic faces congratulating them. Jenna had decided to skip the after-show party; her head was spinning, and she wanted have a little space to gather her thoughts, to reflect on the prospect of becoming Mrs Nick Taylor.

Nick had followed her up to her sumptuous suite. As they lay curled up together on the satin bedspread, drunk on happiness and high on each other, Nick rolled across to nuzzle her neck.

'Why don't we do it now?' he suggested, every word interspersed with little butterfly kisses that covered her face and neck, deliciously light and sensual.

Jenna's eyes lit up as she hungrily kissed him back. His sexual appetite was insatiable.

Nick grinned as he gently disentangled her arms from around his neck, laughing at the look of confusion on her face.

'Plenty of time for that later,' he told her softly. 'A whole lifetime, I promise you.'

'Then what . . .?'

'The wedding. Let's do it now.'

'Now?' Jenna pulled herself upright, a puzzled expression crossing her beautiful face. 'What do you mean, now?'

'We're in Vegas, baby! Where better?'

'I . . .' Jenna hesitated, groping for the right words.

'You haven't changed your mind, have you?'

'No, not at all. I'm just surprised. I didn't expect . . . Tonight?' she repeated in disbelief.

Nick sat up, cradling her in his arms. He could

feel the soft, slim lines of her back pressing against him, the heavy breasts swaying above where his hands encircled her waist. Damn, he was crazy about this girl. 'Why not? We don't need anyone else there, do we?'

Jenna thought of her mother, who would never see her little girl get married, before flashing on to her father, who wouldn't even be interested by the news. 'I guess not . . .'

'Imagine it,' Nick whispered. 'Imagine going back down to join the party as husband and wife. It'd completely shock everyone. There'd be no planning, no hassle. Just you and me. That's all I need,' he told her tenderly.

Jenna stared at him, searching his face for the answers she needed. Everything he'd said was true. Why not just go for it? There were no family or close friends who would need to be there . . . apart from Gerry, she realized with a pang of trepidation, wondering how he would react. It wasn't even a question – he'd hit the roof. They'd probably hear the roar out here in Nevada.

But what the hell, she was a grown woman, wasn't she? Able to make her own decisions and do what she wanted.

Yeah, like trusting Paul Austin, a voice piped up in the back of her mind. Jenna quashed it instantly. That was totally different and it was going to be dealt with – she and Sadie would make sure of that. Nobody screwed over Jenna Jonsson and got away with it.

And what did it matter if she knew nothing about secure investments? She was a pop star, not some financial analyst with a soulless cubicle and a peptic ulcer. What she did know about was love and passion – and this was the real thing.

'Okay, let's do it,' she said lightly

Nick's face instantly softened. 'Really? You want to?' He jumped up from the bed so quickly that it startled Jenna. 'Leave everything to me. I'll be back in an hour. And dress for a wedding,' he winked, as he strode out of the room.

True to his word, he'd arranged everything, turning up sixty minutes later looking impossibly handsome in a light grey suit with a pale pink shirt unbuttoned halfway down his chest. Jenna was dressed and ready to go, her heart beating out of control. She didn't think anything in Vegas could top the buzz of playing a sold-out concert at The Colosseum, but it turned out she was wrong. Getting married was turning out to be a pretty wild rush.

'Put this on,' Nick told her, as he flung the wig across the room and settled a grey fedora on his head.

'A disguise?' Jenna asked, attempting to tuck her long blonde hair beneath the impractical hairpiece.

'We're going incognito. There's a car waiting out the back, and a decoy out front just in case,' Nick grinned, grabbing her by the hand and pulling her towards the door.

Jenna stopped him. 'Just one more thing.' She broke a pink carnation from one of the many bouquets that decorated the room and tucked it into his buttonhole, running her hands over his chest as she smoothed down his jacket. 'Perfect,' she declared.

Nick bent down and kissed her gently on the tip of her nose, his strong hands grasping her shoulders. 'Thank you, Miss Jonsson,' he growled huskily, delighting in using her maiden name for the final time. 'Let's go.'

And now they were in a blacked-out limo, stuck in

traffic on Las Vegas Boulevard. The Night of a Thousand Stars had caused a roadblock even worse than the usual weekend rush hour, and cars were honking angrily. Jenna turned round to check behind her, but she was pretty sure no paparazzi had followed them. It'd be hard for them to get a tip-off when she'd only found out herself an hour ago, she reasoned. They were probably all staking out the after-show party, expecting her and Nick to make a grand entrance. Well, they would, she thought with a growing sense of excitement. Only they wouldn't be engaged – they'd be newlyweds.

It was what she'd wanted for so long – to have someone to love her and take care of her, someone who wouldn't leave her the way her father had. They could take a couple of years to enjoy each other and then think about kids, start their own little family that she'd be a part of forever.

But Jenna couldn't help but remember what Sadie had said – that Nick had casually hit on her, behaving as though he was a single guy. Of course she was lying, or exaggerating. Sadie had probably said 'Hi' to him and convinced herself that they'd had a whole conversation, imagined Nick asking her out in some childish fantasy. She and Jenna had been arguing when Sadie blurted it out – most likely she'd made it up to hurt Jenna. But still, she had to know.

'Nick,' Jenna began, trying to keep her tone light, 'do you know a girl called Sadie Laine?'

Nick stared straight ahead, his face inscrutable as he pretended to think for a moment. Then he shook his head. 'No, never heard of her.'

'She said she met you,' Jenna pressed. 'Before the show tonight . . .' She daren't say any more. She didn't want Nick to be angry with her. They were about to get married – she could hardly accuse him of infidelity on the way to the chapel.

Nick laughed easily. 'Sweetheart, I met loads of people tonight – there were hundreds backstage. Maybe I signed an autograph for her?'

'Mmm hmm,' Jenna agreed doubtfully.

'Hey, that reminds me, we really need to get you an engagement ring,' he said brightly, hoping Jenna would buy the subject change. She did, her eyes lighting up at the prospect of diamonds. 'I promise you, the next chance we get we'll find you the biggest, most beautiful ring. You can pick whatever you want – your call.'

Jenna giggled. He was like a child at times, so full of energy and exuberance. 'So I'm going to get my ring *after* the wedding?'

Nick grinned. 'Hey, I've never been a conventional guy.'

Jenna snuggled closer to him, as the traffic started to move again. She did love him, Jenna told herself. He was so handsome and exciting – life with him would never be dull, she was certain of that.

And yet . . . There were no guests, no engagement ring. If she was being honest, it wasn't exactly how she'd imagined her perfect wedding day. As a child she'd dreamed of being a fairytale princess, marrying her very own Prince Charming in a romantic castle surrounded by admirers. She would wear Vera Wang couture with a diamond tiara, and the room would be filled with white roses and ivy, lit by towering ivory candles. The idea of some quickie wedding in a tacky Vegas chapel had never entered her head.

Perhaps they could have the wedding blessed, Jenna thought hopefully, wrapped up in the fantasy. Just as soon as they could both find a gap in their schedules.

Then she could still have the wedding of her dreams and Gerry could be there, and Rory and Zac . . .

Zac. What was going on with him lately? Usually he acted as if he couldn't stand her, but ever since they'd started rehearsals for The Colosseum he'd been a different guy, friendly and relaxed. And the way she'd felt when she'd watched him perform – that passion and drive, that sheer sexuality . . .

'We're here,' Nick said softly, as they pulled into the parking lot behind the wedding chapel. It was crazy, like a cross between a cosy New England lodge and a Disneyland castle, surrounded by immaculate lawns with sweeping trees and enclosed by a white picket fence. A flashing neon sign mounted above the entrance declared it to be the Chapel of the King.

'That's Elvis, by the way,' Nick explained. 'Not Charles, or Louis, or whatever else they call kings . . .'

'Right.' Jenna bit her lip, not trusting herself to say anything more.

'I thought if we're gonna do it here, we might as well go for the full works. Can't get married in Vegas and not have Elvis involved,' he tried to joke.

Jenna nodded, the dark wig falling into her eyes.

'You ready?' Nick asked seriously, as he scrutinized her troubled face.

'Yeah. Just pre-wedding jitters,' she confessed.

Nick smiled, as he gently brushed a lock of dark hair away from her cheek. 'Don't worry about anything. I love you, Jenna, and you're going to be my wife.' Jenna tilted her face upwards as he leaned down to kiss her, his mouth crushed against her own. She felt the softness of his lips, the warmth of his breath, and melted into his arms. Everything was going to be okay, she told herself fiercely. Nick loved her, and she loved him.

Nick pulled back, his hands running over the soft lines of her body. 'Christ, the things you do to me,' he murmured, looking at her in wonder as he began to get hard. 'Let's go do this, before I consummate the marriage in the car park.'

He jumped out of the car and raced round to the other side to open the door for her, keeping his hat pulled down low in case there were any photographers.

Jenna held on to his hand as she got out, and together they hurried through the arched double-doors and into the entrance porch, where they stood beneath plastic garlands of exotic flowers, and strings of coloured fairy lights.

Tentatively Jenna peered into the main chapel. It certainly looked amazing, she thought numbly. If you wanted to get married surrounded by every romantic cliché, it didn't disappoint. The interior of the Chapel of the King was like stepping inside a Roman temple; brilliant white, with majestic arches and ornately carved pillars. Faux-silk, champagne-coloured curtains were draped across the windows, and the ceiling was hand-painted with a crude evangelical scene, all flying cherubs and fluffy white clouds.

Jenna inhaled sharply. It was worse than she thought.

She seemed to be on autopilot as Nick handed over the marriage licence and they filled out their details in the registry book. Her hands were shaking and she made a mistake. She had to cross out her date of birth and rewrite it. Christ, was she really only 23, Jenna wondered in disbelief, as she stared at the stark, black numbers on the page in front of her. *Till death do us part* suddenly seemed a hell of a long time.

Her own mother had been just a year younger when she'd married. *And look how that turned out*, Jenna thought unhappily. She recalled the misery of living through her parents' divorce as a child, the arguments and the silences before they finally split, followed by Jenna's own feelings of guilt that it was somehow her fault.

Could she even have children with Nick?, she wondered suddenly. He was little more than a big kid himself. Shit, what if people thought she was already pregnant? She could imagine the headlines already, the clear implication that it was a shotgun wedding.

Jenna shook her head, trying to clear it, insisting to herself that this was just a normal case of cold feet. Her own mother and father had been so completely unsuitable, such different people with incompatible dreams and ambitions, that it wasn't surprising they hadn't lasted the distance. But she and Nick were the same – they wanted the same things out of life, and understood each other's worlds and the pressures of the business. Not to mention the fact that they were fucking like rabbits night and day.

She peeped round again at the intimate chapel. At the altar stood the King himself, resplendent in his famous white, rhinestone-encrusted jumpsuit. He was wearing dark sunglasses and throwing some poses. Jenna swallowed. She'd never been an Elvis fan.

Her mouth was bone dry, and she chewed gently on the inside of her cheeks to stimulate the saliva glands, the way her singing teacher had taught her. It didn't seem to help. If anyone had a large Jack and Coke handy, she'd be very grateful.

Jenna jumped as Nick took her arm and guided her to the top of the aisle. As the opening strains of 'Love Me Tender' creaked into life for the umpteenth time that day, Jenna felt something inside her snap. What the hell was she doing here?

Panic-stricken, she turned to Nick.

'I can't marry you,' she told him helplessly. 'I'm sorry.'

PART THREE

29

The Hon. Vivian Cavendish Spencer emerged from the elegant restaurant in London's Mayfair, paying no attention to the obsequious bow of the doorman; after all, one should never acknowledge the help. She was dripping with diamonds and a dead fox lolled, glassy-eyed, around her shoulders. Paul Austin walked attentively beside her – Vivian was a few days shy of her seventy-third birthday and increasingly unsteady on her feet.

On seeing her approach, the uniformed driver who was parked at the kerb ran round to open the car door, before ensuring that she was comfortably settled inside.

'Give my regards to Charlie,' Paul Austin called out as the door slammed shut. Vivian ignored him, pursing her lips disapprovingly and looking straight ahead as the sleek, silver Bentley moved silently into the mid-afternoon traffic.

Stupid old bitch, Paul thought bitterly. *Why doesn't she just hurry up and die?*

Vivian, known as Tibby to her close circle, was a long-time friend of the family. Paul had been at Marlborough with her youngest son, Charlie. Her husband had died just over a year ago, making her a very wealthy woman, and since then Paul had been investing money on her behalf. Now he needed more. Just a small fraction of her fortune would be invaluable to him. So Paul had taken her out for lunch, hoping to get her to agree to a further transfer of funds.

They had dined at Lloyd's – a reassuringly expensive establishment that shunned showbiz clientele and considered celebrity chefs terribly downmarket. Lloyd's was unapologetically old school, reeking of money and class, and styled like a gentleman's club. The menu was the same – uncompromisingly carnivorous. Vegetarianism was dismissed as some crazy Californian fad from the 1970s, and the dishes consisted purely of fare that the clientele could have shot on the estate that morning. Puddings were homely, just like nanny used to make, and the wine list was outrageous. Paul had winced as he'd ordered a Château Lafite 1995 and charged it to the company credit card. William Davis-Wright was going to go crazy but he had no choice. Paul was a desperate man.

Lately he'd been haemorrhaging clients, his portfolio shrinking faster than an anorexic teenager. He badly needed an injection of cash and had hoped that Vivian would oblige him. But the old hag had refused to play ball. She'd shaken her head, said that Thomas, her eldest son, had taken a look at the reports Paul had been sending and was concerned. He would be in contact in due course, but for the moment no more money was forthcoming.

Paul had hidden his fury, his hand gripping the fish knife so tightly that his knuckles went white. He could cheerfully have plunged it into the old bag's wrinkled décolletage.

But he wasn't defeated yet; Paul could charm for England and went all out, flirting and flattering until he sickened himself. In his desperation he'd briefly considered making a pass at her – Vivian had probably not had sex for at least a decade, but there was life in the old bitch yet. Paul reckoned she'd be incredibly grateful that such a handsome younger man was taking an interest. But as she chewed on a sliver of venison he saw her false teeth slip a little, a white ball of saliva foaming up at the corner of her mouth. The repulsion he felt was so strong he'd had to excuse himself to use the bathroom.

Outside on the pavement, Paul watched as the silver Bentley rounded the corner and disappeared out of sight. Ideally he would have liked nothing better than to take the rest of the afternoon off and forget about work – call up a girl and check into a hotel somewhere. That's what he would have done in the old days, no hesitation. But lately he couldn't afford to do that. He needed to get back to the office and start putting in the hours, rediscover that famous Austin killer instinct.

Paul waved away the taxi hovering hopefully on the other side of the road and set off walking at a brisk pace. The trip across town would clear his head and hopefully allow him to think more clearly.

The afternoon was warm, and Paul slipped off his bespoke suit jacket, luxuriating in the quality of the fabric. Things like this were tangible. They couldn't be taken away from him. He didn't want to consider the things that could – in a spectacularly risky move he'd remortgaged the family home, the beautiful, red-brick townhouse in Marylebone, using the money to prop up his ailing client accounts. He figured it would just be a temporary move, until he hit his previously infallible lucky streak and the investments started paying out again. Any day now, they would start to come good . . .

The walk took him a good hour as he worked his way eastwards, taking the backstreets to avoid the tourists and savouring the impersonal feel of the city. No one paid him any attention as he marched along, breaking a light sweat. The physical exercise felt good; his gym attendance had lapsed recently as he worked longer and longer hours.

It was late afternoon by the time Paul arrived at the Broadgate Tower, the imposing glass building thrusting high into the sky, dominating those around it. He swiped in and headed for the lift; the doors opened with a gentle hiss, and he was quickly whisked up to the twenty-fourth floor. He held his head high as he strolled through the office, greeting everyone who spoke to him and trying to look as though he didn't have a care in the world. Image was everything. There were already enough rumours flying around that his neck was on the line, and those malicious bastards he called his colleagues loved a good dose of *Schadenfreude*.

As he reached the sanctuary of his office, Angela scrambled to her feet behind her desk. She looked agitated, a deep furrow forming between her eyebrows as she frowned.

'Mr Austin, I need to speak to you—'

'Not now, Angela,' Paul brushed her off. 'I don't want to be disturbed for the rest of the afternoon. Hold all my calls.'

'But—'

Paul swept into the office, slamming the door behind him. Once inside he sat down at his desk, letting his head drop into his hands. Angela had become increasingly problematic over the past couple of months, and it was starting to get out of hand.

He'd broken the golden rule and slept with her. That one night in the office, when she'd caught him at a weak point. She'd been all puppy-dog eyes and breathy comments, going red whenever he looked at her for too long. Did she think he hadn't noticed the way her skirts got shorter every day, the way she was slapping on make-up in a badly judged effort to appear more attractive? Hell, she was practically begging him for it.

Paul could never understand why women let men wield such power over them, but he was more than willing to take advantage. He'd been careful about screwing around on his own turf – one too many threatened lawsuits had kept him in check of late – but this time frustration had got the better of him.

He knew he should have just called up his usual escort agency, and got them to send over a girl, but against his better judgement he'd made a move on Angela. It had been brief. Perfunctory. He'd taken her over the desk; from behind, so he couldn't see her face.

But his lapse had made her ten times worse. She seemed to think they were in some kind of relationship. She was always hovering in his office, making suggestive comments or lingering too long by his desk. Lately she'd changed tack – she mooned about looking pale-faced and distressed, begging to speak to him. He didn't know how long he could put up with the situation. He found her pathetic, desperation emanating from her like a bad smell. Paul didn't believe in regrets, but his dalliance with Angela was definitely being filed under Bad Decisions.

Perhaps he should speak to that hot new thing in HR. Mariette or . . . Marianne, that was her name. She looked stunning, but didn't seem to be the brightest guest at the party – just the way Paul liked them. Yeah, he'd have a friendly chat with Marianne, see if he could persuade her to help him get Angela moved to another section. Preferably in a broom cupboard somewhere so he wouldn't have to see that hangdog face staring mournfully at him whenever he passed through the office.

He picked up his phone. 'Angela, could you schedule me an appointment with Marianne in HR?'

'But Mr Austin—'

'That's all Angela.' Paul replaced the receiver.

He felt better now that he knew he'd soon be rid of her. That was one problem sorted; if only everything else could be resolved so easily. Swivelling in his chair, Paul flicked on his PC. Instantly, dozens of new emails popped up. That was not a good sign. He glanced at the subject lines and felt his stomach plummet. He would deal with those later.

He opened another screen to check the markets – the Stock Exchange would close soon, and the Dow Jones had been open for a couple of hours. A quick scan indicated it had been another fucking awful day for him. Paul clicked on more files, opening programs and databases in the hope that he would find something positive. The figures were dire, however he tried to calculate them. Paul set his mouth into a grim line. It was going to be another late night.

Outside, Angela was quietly seething.

After everything she'd done for her boss, and now he was treating her like crap. Well, he'd just have to learn that she wasn't going to go away without a fight. She wasn't like all those other girls he'd used and discarded. Angela was different.

In fact, there was one key distinction between her and the others. One vital difference that was going to make Paul sit up and pay attention.

Angela placed a hand on her stomach, feeling the light swell of her belly under her clothes. Too small

312

to be noticed yet, but it was definitely there, and within a few weeks everyone would know.

Angela was carrying Paul Austin's baby.

Sadie was sitting on her bed in the house in Henderson, her phone and laptop beside her. The rest of the girls were outside by the pool, working on their tans and listening to music, but Sadie had stayed inside. She needed the solitude to concentrate; silence was a rare commodity when living in a house with four other women.

She took a sip from the chilled can of Diet Coke on the bedside table and, hardly thinking, typed Paul Austin's name into Google. Maybe something new would come up. She'd already scoured his company website, reading up on how the business worked, their mission statement and their overseas affiliates. She'd read client testimonials, endless press releases and learned more about investments than she'd ever wanted to know. But still she couldn't find anything concrete, that vital chink in the armour that would allow her and Jenna to really pin him down. There were rumours flying like wildfire – she'd found references in the trade papers suggesting that he'd lost his touch and was no longer the golden boy of Willis & Bourne. There was even a whisper on an anonymous society blog that he was having marital problems. Sadie snorted – that was hardly surprising.

Jenna had been ringing daily for updates – the two had formed a temporary truce, managing to stay civil for the short phone conversations – and Sadie was working flat out around the Kandy Girls' shows. Well, almost flat out. She'd been on a few more dates with Tyrone Cole – it was the NFL's off-season, so he was staying in Vegas for a while. They were keeping it low key, but she was really enjoying herself. Brooke had been wild with excitement, but Sadie had sworn her to secrecy. She could do without snide comments from Heidi or jealous looks from the others.

Tyrone had taken her to see Cirque de Soleil's latest show at the Mirage. It was mind-blowing and Sadie had been captivated, unable to take her eyes off the performance. 'I think I've found a whole new career,' she said breathlessly. 'I'd love to do that.'

Tyrone had smiled indulgently, his brown eyes warm and full of affection. He adored Sadie's lust for life. He knew he was falling for this girl; she was something pretty special.

Another time they'd gone for dinner in his suite. Sadie had been a little hesitant about going to his hotel, wondering if he would think she was a guaranteed lay. She wasn't ready for that yet. Men and hotel rooms inevitably brought back memories of Paul, dredging up feelings that she wanted to suppress. What she had with Tyrone was turning into something really good and she didn't want it tainted by what that piece of shit had done to her.

But she'd choked down her qualms and accepted the invitation. She was glad she had – his suite at the Palms was something else. It was enormous, boasting a pool table and two full-length bowling alleys. They'd played both and he whupped her at every game. She'd protested loudly, but Sadie was glad he hadn't let her win. She hated it when guys did that.

They'd had fun. A lot of fun. And Tyrone had been the perfect gentleman. He'd kissed her lightly at the end of the night and Sadie had responded eagerly, amazed at the sensations that were pulsing through her body. Brooke was right – it had been too long since she'd got laid.

Just like the night outside the Mexican restaurant, Sadie's body was instantly on fire, crying out for his touch. She could tell Tyrone felt the same way, but something was holding him back. It was maddening, and not what Sadie was used to. She didn't realize he was playing a very clever game – taking it slowly, determined not to initiate anything no matter how much he wanted to. He was going to let Sadie make all the running. And it was working. Gradually he was breaking down her boundaries and she was starting to trust him – something she thought might never happen again after her experience with Paul. But Tyrone was different. She felt bad when she remembered how she'd had him down as just another beer-swilling, bimbo-dating player, out for what he could get. In fact, he was one of the sweetest guys she'd ever met.

The laptop beeped, breaking Sadie's reverie. She sighed as she scanned the search results. Nothing. She'd been working so hard, following up every possible lead, but they were all turning out to be dead ends. She'd even contacted her old temp agency, wondering if they'd ever supplied people to Willis & Bourne. After a little arm-twisting and a lot of sweet-talking, she was given a name and a mobile number. Sadie had rung her but the girl wouldn't say anything. As soon as she heard Paul Austin's name she hung up. Sadie tried to call back but it went to voicemail every time.

Then there had been one of Carla's friends who'd taken a job as a porter at the May Fair Hotel. Sadie had emailed him a photo of Paul, and the guy confirmed he came in regularly with a number of different women. The thought made Sadie feel sick, but it didn't prove anything. He could sleep with anyone he wanted to, but it wouldn't bring back Jenna's money.

Sadie was almost out of ideas. Almost. There was one name that kept circling round in her head, a woman who could hold the key to everything. Sadie had been considering calling her for some time, but never yet gone through with it. Now she knew she needed to. Time was running out, and this could be the best chance she had.

She glanced briefly at her watch – it would be early evening back in the UK, but Sadie knew she rarely left the office before seven.

Taking a deep breath, she picked up her phone. She was ashamed to say she had never deleted the number. It rang twice, and then a woman answered. 'Willis and Bourne.'

For a moment Sadie didn't speak, the familiar voice shocking the breath out of her. Then she composed herself. 'I'd like to speak to Angela Lee.'

30

Dawn was breaking over New York City, the sun filtering through the early morning mist and reflecting off the Hudson. The enormous glass and steel skyscrapers glistened in the pale light, and the effect was breathtaking. The city was waking up and it was going to be a scorching summer's day.

Annie Cho, newly promoted creative director with Guess clothing, was standing in the Tribeca penthouse that the company had leased for the day. It was 3,000 square feet of polished parquet flooring, solid concrete pillars and a wrought-iron spiral staircase that led up to the mezzanine level and out onto the rooftop. The building was forty-four storeys high and the view from the top was spectacular, offering panoramic views over Manhattan. It was perfect for the shoot.

The problem was that their star model hadn't turned up. Amber, the Guess girl of the moment, spokesperson for the brand and star of their ad campaign, was nowhere to be seen.

'Where the fuck is she?' Annie barked into her

cell phone. She clearly didn't get the reply she wanted and exhaled sharply. 'Don't call me back till you've got answers.'

Two hours later, Amber arrived. There was an audible intake of breath as she stumbled through the door – and not in a good way. She looked like hell. Her jeans were hanging off her, and her baggy tunic couldn't disguise the fact that she was barely more than a skeleton. There were scabs on her arms, and her skin was dry and pasty, with an ugly break-out of spots along her lower jaw. She looked as though she hadn't slept for a month. But the scariest thing were her eyes – flat and devoid of life. She looked as far from the sexy, voluptuous, all-American Guess girl as it was possible to be. As she crossed the room towards them, her top slipped, exposing her nipple. She didn't even notice.

'Holy shit,' swore Annie. 'Get her into hair and make-up.'

Deanna, the make-up artist, gave her a look that said: *You expect me to do something with* that?

Annie walked over to Deanna as Amber was seated in a chair. 'Just do your best. I know you can work miracles.'

'The only thing that can make her look better is formaldehyde,' Deanna deadpanned. But she respected Annie and didn't want to argue. She walked over to where Ken Travis had started work on Amber's hair. He made a face at Deanna, as he pulled off Amber's baseball cap to reveal the greasy, flaky mess beneath. Deanna raised an eyebrow and began applying moisturizer to Amber's parched skin. It was going to take an awful lot of work to make her look human.

In the chair, Amber was oblivious to what was going

on around her. She was exhausted, having rolled in from a party less than an hour ago. What kind of a fucking stupid call time was five a.m. anyway? They weren't paying her enough to get out of bed that early. She could hear the hair and make-up people chattering over her head. They were annoying her, and the stupid hairdresser kept pulling too tight. She closed her eyes, hoping to block everything out.

'Amber?' Deanna asked gently. 'You okay?' She exchanged a look with Ken as Amber's head lolled forward, her breathing heavy.

Ken stifled a giggle. 'Is she asleep? Poke her.'

Tentatively, Deanna shook her by the shoulders. Amber's eyes flew open, and she pushed Deanna out of the way. 'Just piss off, would you,' she snapped, irritably waving them away. She leaned over and rummaged through her handbag, pulling out a small bag of coke and a credit card. Then she picked up a hand mirror of Deanna's and began chopping out a line.

'Amber, you can't do that here.' Deanna was horrified. She wasn't naive – she knew a lot of models took coke before a shoot to give them that extra edge. But most were discreet, slipping off to the bathroom. Amber was clearly well past that stage.

'Oh go fuck yourself,' she growled. 'You're nobody.'

The line of powder disappeared up Amber's right nostril. She blinked rapidly a few times, swallowing as the chemical taste hit the back of her throat.

It was gone noon by the time they were finally ready to start shooting. Amber had been transformed – gone was the exhausted coke-head that had crawled in through the door this morning, and in her place was something approaching the supermodel she was meant to be. Ken had added hair extensions, transforming Amber's shoulder-length cut into long, copper waves that tumbled down her back. They'd been styled with oversized rollers, giving luscious bounce and volume. Her eyes were lined with liquid liner, imbuing them with a feline quality, and her lips were plumped and glossed.

But although her appearance had been transformed, her head was clearly elsewhere. In her skinny jeans and pink corset top, a pair of chicken fillets rounding out her nonexistent breasts, Amber was half-heartedly running through a series of poses, thrusting out her chest and butt in a way that was clearly intended to be sexy. It didn't work. The moves looked forced and unnatural. When she looked into the camera lens, her eyes were glazed.

Annie stood behind the computer screen, watching the shots come up as they were taken. The more she saw, the more worried she became.

'Okay, take a break everybody.'

Amber staggered off the set, while Deanna and Ken ran in for touch-ups. Dan Markovic, the renowned fashion photographer, headed over to Annie.

'What do you think?' she asked, biting her lip nervously.

Dan eyed the screen critically. He scrolled through a few shots, zooming in as he adjusted the contrast, adding a little density. Annie watched him as he worked. He was in his thirties, sandy-haired and attractive.

'It's not working,' Dan said ruefully. 'I'm really sorry, Annie. I'm doing my best.'

'It's okay, I know it's not you,' Annie said. Her voice was tight, as it always was when she was angry. 'We can't use her, can we?'

Dan shook his head. 'It's not looking good.'

They both glanced across to where Amber was huddled against the wall, crouched over her handbag.

'Wait a minute, what the . . .?' Annie marched over. 'What the fuck do you think you're doing?' she yelled. The room fell silent immediately as the crew turned round to look at them.

Amber hastily wiped her face with the back of her hand, streaking a white trail across her upper lip. She sniffed hard, struggling to focus on Annie. Then something snapped.

'Get the fuck away from me, you ugly bitch. Leave me alone! What are you, some kind of fucking lesbian? Piss off, you fucking chinky dyke!' Amber was out of control. She began to pull things out of her handbag, grabbing anything she could and launching it at Annie. The tirade of abuse continued as the contents of Bloomingdales' cosmetics hall rained down on Annie, half a dozen Juicy Tubes whistling past her ears followed by a Touche Éclat that met its target. Amber was screaming and shouting, utterly off her face.

'Get out!' Annie roared. 'Get out now. I've had enough. Someone get her the fuck out of my face before I kill her. You're fired,' she added, unnecessarily.

'You can't fire me,' Amber rasped, her eyes narrowing into slits.

'Too late, sweetheart, I just did.' Annie was livid.

Suddenly all the fight seemed to go out of Amber. She shrugged, sinking onto the floor as she half-heartedly gathered a few of the things that were scattered around her. If she didn't have to work today that meant she was free to do what she wanted – go back to bed, go to a party, score some coke, get laid.

'Whatever.' Amber picked up her practically empty

handbag and staggered out, leaving a stunned silence behind her.

Jenna watched the white-tipped waves break on the Hawaiian shoreline, crashing onto the sand and pounding against the rocks. Further down the beach a group of surfers revelled in the choppy conditions, expertly riding the huge swells. The day was overcast but warm, the billowing clouds spectacular as they blew in off the sea and rolled over the lush green mountains beyond.

Jenna and Phoenix had flown out to Kauai after the Vegas show at the request of their record company. The response to 'Without You' had been incredible. Immediately after the performance, radio stations across the country had been flooded with requests to play the single as fans demanded to know when they could buy it. The record company had been somewhat caught out – they'd planned the Vegas gig as a teaser, with the song being rolled out a few weeks later amid a massive publicity campaign. But, due to over-whelming demand, it was put onto iTunes the day after the concert and looked set to top the midweek charts on downloads alone. The problem was that the music channels weren't playing it. The rush release meant MTV had no video and a visual image was essential, so the trip to Hawaii was hastily arranged.

The concept for the video was simple – just the band and their instruments, barefoot in the sand with the beautiful island backdrop. Each band member had filmed individual scenes and Jenna's had taken place in the heart of the rainforest. She looked like Tarzan's mate in a barely there skirt and clinging top, slashed to reveal the tanned, glistening flesh beneath. Her hair was wild, her face streaked with camouflage stripes, as she writhed against a tree and crawled, cat-like, through the undergrowth, fixing the camera with a seductive gaze.

Today was the final day of filming and they were working on the group scenes. Jenna was in full rock-chick mode, dressed all in black with heavily kohled eyes and nude lips. They were resetting the cameras for the next take, so she had retired to her cabana. It had been an early start that morning and she was eager to grab a break.

Jenna lay on the soft day-bed, absentmindedly twisting her engagement ring on her finger as she stared unseeingly at the stunning view outside. The ring was enormous, a five-carat princess-cut diamond surrounded by no less than twenty-four smaller stones, on a platinum band. As yet, there was no wedding ring nestled beside it.

Jenna still couldn't say what exactly had caused her to change her mind at the Chapel of the King – so many issues had been circling in her head, resulting in a pretty serious case of cold feet. To Nick's credit, he hadn't pushed for an explanation, but she could tell he was annoyed. He'd shrugged and told her not to worry, that everything was cool, but it seemed pretty obvious it wasn't. The easy intimacy that had existed between them had vanished. They'd gone from being so loved-up that anyone in the same room as them felt like a voyeur, to stilted conversation and a sexual restraint that would have made the Puritans look like party animals.

On their first night in Kauai, Nick had proposed again – privately this time – and presented Jenna with the ring he'd bought before they left Vegas. She'd squealed with excitement at the sight of the huge diamond, but as he slipped it on her finger she was struck by a sense of oppression, an inexplicable sensation of being trapped. Her fingers had swollen in the heat and the ring's tightness was constrictive, the sheer weight of the thing weighing her hand down. She had to keep taking it off whenever they were filming and she was terrified of losing it. Nick had already kicked up a fuss about her removing it in the first place, demanding to know why she couldn't leave it on for the video. He said he loved her, that he wanted the whole world to know she was his. Sometimes she wondered if he was more in love with the idea of Jenna Jonsson than he was with Jenna herself.

She shook her head, trying to dispel the thought as she stared out of the open cabana to the glorious beach. The crew were swarming about, rigging up cameras and lights. Then Nick strolled into her line of vision. He was still some distance away, by the water's edge, and he had his back to her as he looked out over the blue-green sea. Jenna watched him, feeling her stomach contract with a fresh stab of pain. He looked breathtakingly handsome, with his tanned skin and his blond hair lightened by the sun. She wished everything could go back to how it was before, but she didn't know how to do that. It felt like the damage to their relationship was irreparable.

As Jenna watched, one of the girls on the production team approached him. She was a runner, so way down the food chain. The girl skipped up to him, tossing her long, dark hair as she presented him with a glass of fruit juice, lavishly decorated with a paper umbrella, sparkler and glittery straw. She was a little younger than Jenna – probably around eighteen – and very pretty. She wore sports shorts and tennis shoes that showed off her long, slim legs and a tight little T-shirt outlining her small breasts. The girl was giggling excessively, hanging on Nick's every word, and Nick was loving the attention.

He took a sip of his drink and Jenna saw them laugh about the garish decoration. Then Nick removed the paper umbrella, tucking it behind the girl's ear as she bowed her head and blushed. He smoothed down her hair, his fingers brushing her cheek in a shockingly intimate gesture.

Jenna blinked in astonishment. She felt as though she'd been punched in the stomach.

'Five minutes, Miss Jonsson.' An assistant appeared in the entrance to her cabana.

'Thank you,' Jenna managed to reply. When the assistant moved, Nick and the girl had gone.

She shook her head, telling herself that she was being ridiculous, that she was overreacting to something harmless. Nick was a natural flirt, she knew that. He wanted to marry *her*, Jenna thought fiercely, not that silly slut out there, throwing herself at him because he was in a band. It was pathetic.

Jenna's phone began to ring and she jumped guiltily, as though caught doing something she shouldn't. It was Sadie. They'd been speaking every day, exchanging progress updates.

'Jenna.' Sadie's voice was different; Jenna could hear it immediately.

'Has something happened?'

'We've got him,' Sadie declared triumphantly.

'We have?' Jenna exclaimed, all thoughts of Nick forgotten.

'I contacted his PA. She emailed me a few pages and it's dynamite. Names, dates, contracts – copies of everything.'

'Sadie, that's amazing.'

Sadie smiled in satisfaction. She'd worked damned

hard on this, and she was pleased Jenna had acknowledged that. 'But she's reluctant to give me any more. Something's holding her back – I don't know what – but I'm sure I could persuade her face to face.'

'Face to face?'

'I'm flying out tonight. My plane leaves in two hours.'

'What do you need me to do?'

'Can you come too? I'm sure it would make a difference.'

'You really think this woman can get that kind of information?'

'It's our best shot. Think about it – she works with him, she has access to all his files, knows who he's meeting and when. I just think if the two of us were there together – and with you being who you are – she'd help us. There are all sorts of rumours on the Internet, whispers about the soundness of his deals, accusations of fraud and insider trading. She could get us all the proof we need. Can you fly back?'

Jenna thought about it. It sounded crazy, but this could be the best chance they had. She hadn't come up with anything else – hell, she hadn't done anything, she realized guiltily. 'Sure,' Jenna agreed. 'Filming finishes tonight. It's Zac's birthday, so I need to show my face for a couple of hours, but I'll leave as soon as I can.'

'Fantastic. Once we have everything, we can confront him.'

'Don't do anything until I get there, will you?' Jenna asked, a note of panic in her voice. She wasn't going to miss her chance of seeing the smug expression wiped off that creep's face.

'No way. We need to do this together,' Sadie agreed. If she could just get a little more information from Angela Lee, Paul Austin would be annihilated. He'd lose everything – his job, his reputation – and one call to the Serious Fraud Office should see him locked away for a very long time. Sadie didn't feel the slightest pang of guilt as she contemplated it. That bastard deserved everything he got.

'Thanks Sadie.'

'No problem,' Sadie said lightly. Then her voice hardened. 'I want to make sure he loses everything. He's going to be destroyed. And I want him to know that we're the ones who did it.'

31

The sound of laughter rang out across the dark Hawaiian beach, which was illuminated by torches and a giant bonfire on the sand. The hotel had thrown a traditional luau in honour of Zac's twenty-fifth birthday, and the party was well under way with the band and crew anticipating a wild night. Tables piled high with food and drink had been set up on the beach as the guests sat barefoot, the sensuous feel of the sand between their toes as they ate. Beside them a band played Hawaiian music as two beautiful local girls in grass skirts and *leis* danced dreamily, swaying their hips to the music. Later there would be hula and limbo competitions, but Jenna would have left before then.

She picked at her food, unable to relax. The island was beautiful at night, truly a paradise as the moonlight reflected on the water and a warm breeze blew gently through the pineapple trees. But Jenna was far too tense to appreciate its loveliness, thinking about the confrontation that lay ahead. She had been imagining the moment when she and Sadie came face to face with Paul, and hoped she could refrain from slapping him across the face. She badly wanted to do that; her fingers itched at the thought.

A waiter appeared behind her and tried to refill her wine glass, but Jenna declined. She wanted to be clear headed when she arrived in London. She could sleep on the plane, but there was no way she wanted to feel hungover when she woke up. She needed her wits about her for this meeting.

As the guest of honour, Zac was sitting at the head of the table, and Jenna had been seated to his right. They'd been getting on great during this shoot, and she was surprised to find how happy that made her. Unlike Nick, who'd been desperate to get into her pants since the first time he saw her, she felt as though she'd really had to work to earn Zac's respect. It was a good feeling.

His brow furrowed as he saw her refuse the drink. 'Aren't you celebrating my birthday?' he teased.

Jenna smiled as she turned to him. He looked the most relaxed she'd seen him in a long time, sitting easily in his chair drinking a beer, his light grey shirt open at the neck.

'I have to leave tonight,' she reminded him. 'I'm flying back to London.'

'So early?' Zac raised an eyebrow.

'I have some . . . business to attend to.'

'Shame,' he said lightly, his eyes never leaving her face. Jenna chivered, although the night was balmy.

'Are you cold?' Zac asked in concern. Jenna was wearing just a plain yellow sundress, its simplicity highlighting her natural beauty. Her shoulders were bare, her skin exposed. In a completely impulsive gesture, Zac leaned towards her and, with exquisite gentleness, trailed a finger along her forearm. Jenna inhaled sharply. Electricity was coursing through her whole body and her skin felt like it was burning. It was as though he'd slashed her arm with a razor blade – every cell had burst into life.

'I'm fine,' she managed to breathe.

'I can ask them to bring you a wrap.' Zac's voice was low, his gaze intense.

'I said I'm fine,' Jenna snapped, pulling her arm away. Heart pounding, she turned to Nick beside her, hoping the familiar presence would calm her.

Nick was already roaring drunk, having worked his way through the best part of a bottle of Jack. They were barely halfway through the main course and already his cheeks were red, his words slurred.

Jenna felt his hand clamp on her leg, his fingers crawling teasingly along her inner thigh, but he didn't turn round. He was deep in conversation with the runner from earlier – Hailey. She was American and spoke in a breathy, little-girl voice as she told Nick earnestly how she really, *really* wanted to be a singer.

'You should be a model,' Nick slurred. 'You could be. You're really beautiful y'know.' He raised his voice deliberately, his hand sliding higher up Jenna's thigh as he spoke. 'The most beautiful girl here tonight.' She knew he was getting off on it, playing the two women against each other. *Fuck this*, Jenna thought. She needed to get out of there.

She stood up sharply so that Nick's hand smacked the underside of the table. That got his attention. He yelled in pain.

'I'm leaving,' Jenna told him icily.

Nick was struggling to focus. 'Going? Back to London, yeah?'

'Yeah,' Jenna replied through clenched teeth.

Nick seemed unconcerned. 'Cool. I'll see you in a couple of days.'

Don't bet on it, thought Jenna furiously, as she stalked off across the beach. She had packed her case earlier – all she had left to do was shower, change, then get the hell out of this place.

Back at the table, Zac clenched his fists in fury. He'd witnessed the whole exchange and couldn't believe the way Nick was behaving.

'That was out of order,' he told him, his voice low with repressed anger.

'What did you say?' Nick turned to him slowly.

'You just treated Jenna like crap. Go after her.'

'What the fuck is your problem . . .?' Nick rose unsteadily to his feet, stumbling towards Zac. For a second, it looked as though Nick was going to knock him out, but suddenly he smiled, slumping back down in his chair.

'Don't worry about me, *buddy*,' he began, his voice heavy with sarcasm. 'Maybe you wanna sort out your own problems first.'

'What the hell are you—'

'Baby!'

Zac whirled round as he heard an all-too-familiar screech behind him. Amber threw her skinny arms around him in an ostentatious gesture, covering him with kisses. 'Look at you all having your little wrap party!'

Her voice was loud. People were turning to look, nudging others as they realized who it was.

'Amber, what . . .?' Zac let the question hang. 'I didn't know you were coming,' he finished coldly.

She looked a mess. Some of her extensions had come loose and were hanging at odd angles. Her make-up looked as if she'd slept in it, and she was completely overdressed in a one-shoulder sequinned mini that hung loosely from her emaciated frame. In a blinding moment of clarity, Zac realized he didn't feel anything for her except a sense of embarrassment.

'Surprise!' Amber giggled. She threw her arms up in the air.

Zac looked mortified. It felt like some kind of nightmare. Most of the crew had now noticed her arrival, and although they were pretending to carry on as normal, he knew they were all watching. The conversation had dropped to a low hum; people sneaked sidelong glances as they ate.

'Can someone find her a seat?' Ryan asked, trying to lighten the atmosphere. 'She can't be standing at her boyfriend's birthday.'

Something clicked in Amber's brain as Ryan's words registered.

'Of course, Zac's birthday! That's why I came. Happy birthday, baby!' She slid onto his knee and kissed him elaborately.

Zac didn't return the gesture. 'I thought you were working.'

'I couldn't miss out on your birthday, could I?' she pouted. 'I managed to get some time off.' *Indefinitely*, she didn't add.

'Great,' Zac smiled lamely. He took a long slug of his beer, then summoned a waiter to get him a double dark rum. The only way he was going to get through tonight was by being as drunk as possible.

Angela Lee was sitting at her desk, flicking thoughtfully through Jenna Jonsson's file. It was late – almost 11 p.m. – but she didn't intend to go home yet. She couldn't until she'd spoken to Paul. They needed to talk, and Angela had decided that tonight was to be the night.

As though she'd summoned him with her thoughts,

Paul appeared out of his office. He looked tired – dark bags hung under his eyes, and there was a smattering of stubble along his jaw line. His shirt was creased after the long day. Angela knew he was having some difficulties at work; that he'd been having regular meetings with William Davis-Wright and he feared for his job. She hoped her news might cheer him up a little.

'Mr Austin . . .' she began.

He marched across the outer office, prepared to pass her without saying a word.

'Paul!' she called out in desperation.

'Not now,' he hissed, infuriated by her familiarity. He walked out, slamming the door behind him.

Angela bit her lip, but was determined not to be put off. She waited a few seconds, then slipped out from behind her desk and followed him. She knew where he was going. Walking briskly, she headed for the lift. It didn't take long to arrive – the building was practically empty – and she got out on the top floor, heading up a final flight of steps that led to the roof. Tentatively, she pushed open the emergency door and stepped out. The view was incredible. The whole of London was spread out before her, offering a bird's-eye view of the London Eye and the Oxo Tower, Parliament and Canary Wharf. Planes flew overhead, criss-crossing the cloudless night sky.

Then she saw him. He was silhouetted against the darkness, the tip of his cigarette glowing orange.

'Mr Austin,' Angela called out.

The cigarette halted in mid-air, and she heard him mutter something under his breath.

'Mr Austin,' she approached him slowly. 'There's something I need to tell you.'

Paul turned on her. 'What's so important that you had to stalk me across the whole building? I can't even get away from you up here. We're not in a relationship, you know,' he ranted. 'What happened was an accident, and you can't carry on—'

'I'm pregnant.'

Paul looked as though the wind had been knocked out of him. For a moment he couldn't speak. 'Is this a fucking joke?' he asked finally.

'No,' Angela said quietly, shaking her head. 'It's my twelve-week scan tomorrow. I thought you might . . . I thought you might like to come with me.'

Paul threw back his head and roared with laughter. 'Bullshit,' he declared, dropping his cigarette and stamping on it with his heel, grinding it into the concrete until it was completely destroyed. 'Fucking bullshit.' He looked angry now.

'I can assure you—'

He took a step closer, his air menacing. 'Are you lying? You'd better be fucking lying.'

'No, sir.' Angela shook her head, feeling the tears start to build. He was scaring her.

'Jesus Christ,' Paul swore under his breath. He thought about asking if it was his, but knew instinctively that she was telling the truth. Angela Lee didn't sleep around. He would have bet money on the fact that she hadn't got laid the entire time she'd worked for him. Hell, she didn't get the chance to. She never left the office. And then, like a fool, he'd had his moment of madness and now . . .

'Get rid of it.' Paul's voice was calm, matter-of-fact.

'What?' Angela was shocked. The conversation wasn't supposed to go this way. He was supposed to tell her that he loved her, that he'd leave his wife so they could start a new life together.

'You heard,' he repeated coldly. 'Get rid of it.'

Angela reacted instinctively. 'No,' she stated defiantly. 'No. I'm not getting rid of this baby.'

Paul rolled his eyes, like she was an inconvenience to be dealt with. 'For fuck's sake, Angela, why do you have to be so difficult about it? There's obviously no way you can keep it.'

'Isn't there?' Angela asked sadly. She felt as though her world had come crashing down. All her hopes and dreams, the secret fantasies about their new life together – he'd destroyed everything with his words. 'I thought you loved me.'

Paul laughed incredulously. 'Why the fuck would you think that?'

Her voice was small, hardly audible. 'You slept with me.'

'What is this, the nineteen fifties? It was just sex, Angela. I didn't feel anything for you.' His lip curled as he looked at her with contempt. Pregnancy didn't suit Angela. Far from being the glowing mother-to-be, she looked tired and dishevelled. Her skin had broken out, and her hair was lank and greasy.

'Just like the others . . .' she whispered unhappily. She'd genuinely believed that she was different. She worked with him, and he'd relied on her every day for almost two years. She wasn't a fly-by-night like those other women.

'Now come on, Angela,' Paul began, a little more kindly, as he placed a hand on her arm. His skin was cold and Angela flinched. 'Let's go back inside and talk practicalities. I'll pay for everything, of course, and you'll have the best medical care, okay? I can arrange for you to take an extended period of leave on full salary and—'

'It's not about that!' Angela howled, yanking her arm away from him. 'Don't you get it? I want this baby! I don't have anything, Paul. At the end of the day, you go home to your wife and your boys and your perfect life and I don't have anything.'

'So I'll buy you a fucking kitten,' Paul sneered. 'You can't have a child just because you're lonely.'

Angela looked him firmly in the eye. 'It's *our* child. I'm going to bring it up and care for it. And it's going to know that its daddy was handsome and clever, and that Mummy loved Daddy more than anything else in the world.'

Paul pressed his fingers to his temples, trying to take in what she was saying. How the fuck had this all happened? Of course he'd noticed Angela following him around recently, but he'd never imagined she was hiding something like this. His wife would leave him. He'd be a laughing stock among his friends and colleagues. One thing was certain: there was no way he could have this child.

With a sudden movement, Paul grabbed Angela's wrists, holding them tightly as he pushed his face up against hers. 'Get rid of it,' he snarled.

Angela twisted from side to side, trying to get away. His nails were digging into her arm. 'Get your hands off me,' she warned him. If he wanted to play hardball, so could she. 'You think you can threaten me? Well I can threaten you. I had a phone call yesterday from Sadie Laine. Remember her?'

Paul's eyes narrowed in recognition. He had a bad feeling about this.

'She had some questions about Jenna Jonsson's account.'

Paul stared at her, his breathing coming fast. 'What did you tell her, bitch?'

Angela smiled, feeling the balance of power shift. 'I simply scanned a few documents and emailed them over.

She seemed very interested. She wanted to see more.' Angela waited, letting the moment hang. 'And if you don't let me keep this baby, I'll show her the rest.'

Paul laughed hollowly. 'You wouldn't dare.' He meant it as well. Mousy little Angela, who hardly dared raise her voice above a whisper. Where the hell had this hard-nosed bitch come from?

Angela looked at him sadly. 'What have I got to lose?'

Paul let out a roar as the red mist descended. All he knew was that everything was going wrong in his life and everywhere he turned there was Angela. He was about to lose his job and his wife and it was all her fault.

'Bitch! Fucking bitch!' he yelled, shaking her furiously. Angela screamed, but Paul clamped a hand over her mouth. His grip on her was vice-like, and she struggled furiously, desperate to get away. She was fighting for more than just herself – she was fighting for their baby.

Summoning all her strength, she brought her arm forward, then drove her elbow back into his stomach. It worked. Paul doubled over in pain, releasing his grip on her. Angela ran as hard as she could. She could hear him behind her, his laboured breathing gaining on her. With a yell he launched himself at her, grabbing the back of her blouse. She felt it rip as she sidestepped him, but within seconds he was on her again. He caught her shoulder and fell heavily against her, their bodies crashing to the ground and slamming into the metal barrier that marked the edge of the rooftop.

The impact shocked the breath out of them, but Angela knew she had to get to her feet. Paul was out of control; there was no telling what he might do. Stumbling, she pulled herself upwards. Beside her, Paul groaned as he tried to stand. But the collision had unbalanced them. There was the noise of loose stones as feet scrabbled to stay upright, then suddenly there was nothing to hang on to any more, nowhere for feet to get purchase.

A loud scream rent the night sky, then everything fell silent.

32

Ryan had loaded his plate with food from the barbecue pit when he felt the phone in his pocket vibrate. He balanced it under his chin as he made his way back to the table. It was a little quieter now; people had moved from the food area to where the limbo competition was taking place, cheering raucously as they supported their friends.

'Hello?'

'Ryan, it's Clive.'

'Hey Clive,' Ryan greeted his manager. 'What's up?'

'A lot,' Clive warned ominously.

'Shit, that doesn't sound good.'

'It's not. Look, is Zac there? He's not picking up his cell.'

'Yeah, he's right here. You want me to get him for you?'

Clive hesitated. 'Is Amber there?'

'Yeah, she's here too.'

'I thought she might be,' Clive said in disapproval. 'How's Zac taking it?'

'Taking what?'

'He hasn't told you?'

'Told me what?' Ryan was getting increasingly frustrated. Leaving his food on the table, he got up and walked away so he could hear more clearly.

Clive sighed. 'It's all over the news. Guess have fired Amber. The official line is that they've released her from her contract, but unofficially there's all sorts of shit going round. Some British tabloid's running a story that she was off her face at the latest shoot. Turned up high as a kite and snorting lines on set.'

'Jeeesus . . .'

'There's a rumour someone got it on camera phone, but I've not seen any footage as yet.'

Ryan shook his head, not knowing what to say. 'She just turned up,' he stammered. 'About a half-hour ago. Said it was a surprise for Zac's birthday.'

Clive exhaled, blowing out the air in his cheeks. 'So you really don't think Zac has any idea?'

Ryan glanced across to where Amber was curled up on his knee, feeding him a piece of mango. 'I really don't think he does.'

'Well that's just awesome.' Clive's tone was sarcastic. 'They're looking for a statement from me. They want to know if they're still together, whether Zac's using too, if he's going to support her . . . No one knows where she is but they're guessing she's hiding out with Zac and I need to know what to say. The place'll be crawling with paps before long.'

Ryan looked over at Zac. He seemed utterly miserable, staring blankly ahead as Amber wrapped her skinny arms around him and whispered in his ear. 'Leave him for a few hours,' Ryan suggested gently. 'I'll tell him, and get him to call you. Can you handle it till then?'

Clive grunted in assent. 'I've known you a long time, and I respect you, Ryan. You're one of Zac's best friends, so yeah, I'll leave it a while. But I can tell you this for nothing – being with Amber is killing his reputation. That girl is a walking time bomb and the sooner he gets shot of her the better.'

Jenna was in the car, speeding towards Lihue airport.

Thank God she was finally out of there, on her way back to London and able to have some time to herself at last. Her emotions were raging out of control; she was furious over the way Nick had treated her. He seemed to have regressed a decade, behaving like they were in high school. Ever since Jenna had called off the Vegas wedding, it was as though he'd been trying to show her what she was missing out on, making the point that there were plenty of others out there who would take what she'd turned down. The way he'd been flirting with that girl tonight, in front of everybody – it was totally humiliating.

Well, he can go screw himself, Jenna thought furiously – there was no way she was going to let him treat her like that.

She squeezed her eyes shut, resting her head against the tinted window. The air conditioning was blowing lightly, and the glass felt pleasantly cool against her skin.

And then there was Zac . . .

Jenna let out a low groan. What the hell was happening between them? Every time she was around him it made her more confused than ever. The chemistry between them was intense, the way her body had reacted when he touched her . . . He was Nick's band mate, for Christ sake. It didn't bear thinking about . . .

Lost in her thoughts, it took her a second to realize that her phone was ringing. She delved in her bag and pulled it out.

'Where are you?' Sadie didn't bother with preliminaries.

'On my way to the airport,' Jenna began. 'I was just about to call—'

But she never got to finish her sentence as Sadie cut her off. 'He's dead.'

'What?' Jenna asked in confusion. 'Who?'

'Paul Austin,' Sadie repeated. 'He's dead.'

'*What?*' Zac demanded incredulously. 'Are you sure?'

He was standing with Ryan, a short distance from the bonfire. Ryan had requested a private word and Zac had sent Amber on ahead, back to the bungalow. He wanted to get her away from people as quickly as possible, before she could embarrass herself any further.

'I'm sorry, man,' Ryan said awkwardly. 'I just thought it might be better coming from me, y'know . . .'

'Yeah. Yeah, thanks for telling me, I appreciate it.' Zac was fighting to stay calm.

'Don't do anything stupid, yeah?' Ryan tried to joke, recognizing Zac's expression.

Zac didn't reply. He set his jaw firmly and stalked off towards the villa.

Paul Austin was dead.

He was dead.

The refrain rang in Jenna's head until it was all she could hear.

Suspected suicide, Sadie had said. He'd jumped from the top of the Broadgate Tower, and his mangled body had been found by a passer-by as daylight broke. The building was 500 feet high, and there hadn't been much of him left to identify.

Jenna stared out of the car window into the darkness,

grateful for the anonymity it provided. She felt her distress must be written all over her face.

A nagging, insistent voice whispered at the back of her mind – what if Paul had discovered that she and Sadie were about to expose him? That he'd rather take his own life than face the shame of ruin? He had three kids, for Christ's sake! Jenna remembered seeing the photos on his desk. Three young boys who would be growing up without a father . . .

Shit, she could relate to that. She knew what it was like to grow up without a father. And to lose a parent so suddenly, so unexpectedly . . .

Jenna doubled over in the back of the car. It was as though someone had literally knocked the air out of her and she struggled to catch her breath, a wave of grief sweeping over her. Every time she thought she was finally getting a handle on her mother's death, something happened to trigger a memory, and all the pain came flooding back.

Life was so short; it was so fucking short. She could be dead tomorrow. Any of them could. And she and Nick had parted on bad terms. Nick, who loved her, who had asked her to marry him . . .

She sat bolt upright, her breathing coming fast as she realized what she had to do. An event like this threw everything into sharp relief, reminded you what was important in life – and it certainly wasn't how famous you were or how much money you were making.

Quickly, Jenna checked her watch. Screw it, she could always take the next flight.

She leaned forward and tapped on the glass partition that separated her from the driver. It slid down smoothly and silently.

'Turn the car around please,' she requested.

'I'm sorry ma'am?'

'Could you turn around, please,' Jenna repeated shakily. 'I want to go back to the hotel.'

'Certainly ma'am.' The driver gave a little shrug and the partition moved up again. The road was quiet and he executed a perfect U-turn.

Jenna sat back in her seat, feeling calmer now she had put her plan into action. She was going to find Nick and tell him how she felt. He was the one for her, she was sure of it. Hell, they could even get married right there and then if that's what he wanted – and this time she wouldn't back out.

Whatever this thing was with Zac, it didn't matter. It was just some stupid crush, and the sooner she got over it the better.

I love Nick, Jenna thought fiercely, *and I'm going to be his wife.*

He was all the family she had now.

'Get out,' Zac snarled, his face contorted with fury. 'Get the fuck out of here right now before I do something I regret.'

Amber jumped up from the couch, a frightened expression on her once beautiful face. 'Zac, please,' she begged. She didn't think she'd ever seen him so angry. The vein on his neck throbbed fiercely, his shoulders tight with unreleased tension.

'I mean it, Amber. How could you lie to me like that?'

'I was embarrassed,' Amber pleaded desperately. There was no point denying it – she knew that would only infuriate him more. 'They fired me, Zac. Those bastards fucking fired me. I thought they'd change their mind, come crawling back in a couple of days if I just laid low out here.'

344

Zac looked at her with disgust. The make-up she was wearing had slid down her cheeks, caking in the creases of her ravaged face like some sort of garish clown mask.

'You still don't get it, do you?' he breathed, his voice low and carefully controlled. 'This isn't about you. It's about *us*. You turn up here, pretending it's some kind of surprise, when in fact I'm just part of your game, part of the fucking circus that's always going on around you. What am I to you, a goddamn PR exercise?' he ranted. 'Did you even remember it was my birthday?'

'Of course I—' Amber began unconvincingly.

'You know what?' Zac cut her off. 'I don't even care. It's over, Amber. I want out.'

Even as he said the words, Zac felt a sweet sense of relief. He should have done this months ago, and now it was finally over.

'What? Zac, you can't!'

'Oh yes I fucking can.' He had stood by her for long enough. Now it was time to do something for himself.

Amber looked round in alarm then reached for her bag. Zac knocked it away; it fell onto the floor, scattering its contents.

'Please Zac,' Amber whispered, her eyes trained hungrily on the bag of white powder a few metres away. 'I need . . . Just one more time, I promise you. The last time. Then I'll get help, I swear it.'

Zac looked at her sadly. 'You're not the person I knew, Amber. Not the person I fell in love with.'

'I'll do it,' she insisted. 'I'll go to rehab, therapy – whatever you want. But you've got to help me through this.'

Zac shook his head helplessly. For so long he'd hoped that she would reach out to him, admit she had a problem and try to get help. But this was too little too late. His voice cracked as he spoke. 'I can't do this any more.'

Anger flashed across Amber's eyes. 'It's *her*, isn't it? You're dumping me for *her*? Well she won't leave Nick for you,' Amber spat. 'She'll never leave him, and you'll end up sad and lonely and miserable.'

'I'm lonely and miserable *now!* This isn't a relationship — it's a joke.'

'You're the joke, Zac,' Amber hissed. 'Running after that skank like that.'

'Why can't you understand that it's nothing to do with anybody else?' Zac yelled. 'I don't want to be with you — you disgust me,' he finished, his lip curling in contempt. It was true. The sweet, fun girl he'd fallen in love with had been taken over by some monster he didn't recognize. As he stared at her emaciated body, he knew he no longer felt anything for her — not love, and certainly not desire. They'd barely had sex for months.

Amber's eyes flamed. 'Did you ever think *I* might be sick of *you*?' she demanded. '*You're* the one who's changed. You used to be fun, to want to go out and party — now you're boring as hell,' she continued relentlessly. 'I've got real friends now, in New York. Real men, who know how to have a good time . . .' She glanced up slyly from underneath her pale lashes, 'And who know how to show me a good time.'

Zac looked up sharply, his chest rising and falling.

'Yeah, that's right,' Amber taunted him. 'I've been fucking my way around New York, screwing a different guy every night.'

'Amber . . .' Zac began warningly.

But Amber was on a roll. 'We laughed at you together. I laughed as they fucked me, and I laughed as I came, and then I thought of you and how pathetic you are.'

Zac's fist shot out. It slammed into the wall and Amber jumped in shock.

'I'm going out now,' Zac began. His voice was low, his breath ragged. A lock of dark hair fell across his forehead as he leaned heavily against the wall. 'When I come back, you'd better be out of here. Just get the fuck out of my life and leave me the hell alone.'

Jenna retrieved her room key from reception, ignoring the polite enquiry from the staff as to whether or not everything was okay. She'd left an hour ago and told them she was checking out. Now she was back, but that was none of their business. She was here to see her fiancé, to melt into his arms and have everything back the way it used to be, just like those first, blissful days at Casa Santos when they couldn't get enough of each other.

Excitedly, she made her way over the soft sand towards the bungalow she shared with Nick. Further along the beach she could see the remains of the luau, but it seemed to have largely broken up. Only a few people hung around the bonfire, and they all looked to be crew. There was no sign of the band.

As the villa door clicked open, Jenna saw that the light in the main room was on. That meant Nick was back. He had probably passed out earlier, she thought with a trace of annoyance, hoping one of the guys had brought him back before he got drunk enough to do something stupid. He must have been wasted; he'd clearly undressed in the lounge as the shorts he'd been wearing were slung over the back of the sofa. Well, he'd better sober up – he needed to hear what she was going to tell him.

She dropped her handbag onto the floor and went to switch off the lamp when she noticed a cute little pair of sports shorts under the side table. Time seemed to stop, her stomach plummeting to her feet. As soon as Jenna saw them, she knew. Her blood was pounding so hard she could hear it thumping in her ears as she moved towards the bedroom. Her ballet pumps were soft, and they made no noise on the stone-tiled floor.

Even before she reached the room she heard the noise, the soft, languid groans building to a crescendo. The door had been left partially open, and outside Jenna stopped dead. Hailey was straddling Nick, her arms above her head to emphasize those tiny, youthful breasts as she bucked and writhed on top of him.

Below her Nick moaned and thrust. His chest was slick with sweat, his eyes closed as he grabbed hold of her butt and smiled, 'Oh yeah baby, you like me fucking your cunt, don't you? My hard cock screwing your pussy . . .'

Jenna watched them for a moment, too shocked to even make a sound. Then she stumbled backwards, wanting to get as far away as possible from what she had just seen. The rhythm was getting faster, their ecstatic moans getting louder.

Silently, Jenna turned on her heel and fled. Neither of them heard her go.

33

Zac stormed along the beach, oblivious to the stunning Hawaiian scenery that surrounded him. The night sky was spectacular, liberally scattered with thousands of pinprick stars, and the moonlit water lapped gently at the shore. Zac pounded along the wet sand at the water's edge with no idea of where he was going, no plan or direction. He just wanted to keep walking until the feeling of fury subsided. He had a feeling he could be walking for some time.

Tomorrow he would catch a plane back to the States and head straight to his ranch in Arizona, where he would hole up and lick his wounds. He would take some time to breathe, chill out, maybe even go on a long holiday somewhere undeveloped and deserted. Right now, the idea of being a recluse for a while seemed a very attractive proposition.

He didn't even want to pick up a guitar for at least the next year. As far as he was concerned, it was all over. He didn't care about anything any more, not even the band. Phoenix were finished – Zac felt they had imploded. They should have ended it when Josh left, not tried to carry on with this insane collaborations project. Most of all, he wished he'd never met—

Zac looked up to see a woman run out of a nearby bungalow, her long hair streaming out behind her as she ran blindly across the sand, sobbing hysterically. Her silhouette was black against the dark night, her face in shadow, but Zac recognized her instantly.

'Jenna,' he called out, breaking into a sprint. His voice echoed across the quiet beach, and he reached her in seconds. She collapsed into his arms, clinging to him like she was drowning as her legs threatened to give way beneath her.

'Jenna, what's wrong?' Zac asked, although he had a pretty good idea. He'd seen Nick leave the party with that young girl, the one who'd been throwing herself at him over dinner. Jesus, he would kill that son of a bitch for hurting her like this . . . Zac took a deep breath, trying to calm himself. He needed to focus on Jenna.

'I thought you were going back to London.' Zac anxiously scanned her face. 'What happened?'

She looked terrible. Her skin had paled beneath her tan, and her eyes were red raw from crying. She seemed to be having trouble speaking through her sobs, and Zac's shirt quickly became wet with tears.

'I . . . I was. I came back because I needed . . . Because I had to tell . . .' Jenna broke down again. 'But he's a fucking bastard . . . I hate him, Zac, I hate him . . .'

'Ssssh . . .' Zac held her close, stroking her hair as he soothed her. He didn't want to think about how wonderful it felt to have her in his arms, the softness of her body, the delicious scent of her skin . . . Now was not the right time. 'Come on, let's get you away from here.'

Jenna's head jerked up, remembering something.

London. That would be the perfect escape right now. She could go back home, meet up with Sadie as planned and find out what had happened to Paul Austin.

'You're right,' she agreed, wiping her eyes distractedly. 'I need to get away, go back to London. If I'm lucky I can still make the flight. I need a car, right away . . .' Jenna looked around her urgently.

'You're not going anywhere, Jenna. You're in no fit state. Stay here tonight, and you can leave on the first flight tomorrow.'

'No, you don't understand!' Jenna was becoming hysterical. She'd promised Sadie. 'I *have* to leave. I *have* to get back there. You've got to help me, Zac.'

'Okay, okay.' Zac realized she was serious. 'I'll help you. But you're not going on your own.'

Jenna looked up at him in confusion. She couldn't see the expression on his face, just the curve of his cheekbone silhouetted against the moonlight.

'I'm coming with you.'

'What? I don't underst—'

'It doesn't matter,' Zac cut her off. 'I'm coming with you. Whatever this thing is, I'm here for you, okay? We'll get through it together.'

Jenna swallowed. Suddenly she felt self-conscious, pressed against his lean, muscular body. She pulled away from him, mumbling awkwardly, 'Thanks, Zac.'

'No problem. Come on, let's get out of here.' He rested a hand on her back, guiding her across the deserted beach, and realized he had to face it: Amber, the band, his music – none of them mattered any more. The only thing he cared about now was Jenna.

Morning had broken in Hawaii, sunny and glorious. Yesterday's clouds had disappeared overnight and there was a clear blue sky, stretching right out to the horizon.

The sea was calm, with barely a breeze to trouble the still palm trees.

Ryan was up early, jogging along the beach, when his phone vibrated.

'Hey Clive.'

'Ryan.' Clive was straight down to business. 'Did you speak to Zac?'

'Yeah,' Ryan confirmed. 'Last night. Didn't he call you?'

'No he fucking didn't. Where the hell is he?'

Ryan swallowed. Shit, why did he always have to be the fall guy in these situations? Too damn nice, that was his problem. 'He's kinda . . . disappeared. I heard he checked out.'

'What do you mean, *disappeared*? Is he with Amber?'

Ryan took a deep breath. 'I don't think so. She left a few hours before him. According to reception, he ordered a cab for the airport and left with Jenna.'

'*With Jenna*? What the fuck is going on, Ryan?' Clive roared.

Ryan winced, holding the phone away from his ear. He had no idea either.

Jenna and Zac were somewhere over the Atlantic Ocean – skirting the coast of Iceland, according to the in-flight map.

Jenna was sleeping. She'd pulled down an eye-mask to hide her puffy face and curled up on the flat bed, her exhausted body crashing out shortly after take-off. They'd switched off the cabin lights, just the pale strip lights left on for illumination. But Zac couldn't sleep. He lay awake, watching Jenna. He had no idea what was going on – they'd barely had time to speak in the car, as the driver careered across the island, getting them to the plane with seconds to spare. All Jenna had told him was that she needed to get back to London to meet a friend. It didn't make a lot of sense to him, but Zac was willing to give her the benefit of the doubt on this one. She was clearly serious, working herself into such a state that he'd just thrown a few essentials in a bag and left. The rest of his stuff was still at the hotel. He would contact Clive when they landed, get him to sort it out.

Shit, Clive. He'd been supposed to call him before they left. He'd told Ryan he would. Man, that was one conversation he wasn't looking forward to. He was going to have to tell him he wanted to leave the band – that it was all over. Clive was going to hit the roof, coming so soon after Josh's departure. There was no way Phoenix could survive. And Clive wanted to talk to him about Amber, Ryan had said. Zac's brow knitted in fury. As far as he was concerned there was nothing to say. He'd done all he could for her but now it was over; the sense of freedom he felt from knowing he didn't have to take her crap any more was immense.

'Can I get you anything, sir?' The attractive stewardess approached him hopefully, giving him a dazzling smile.

'No, thanks,' Zac shook his head. He wasn't hungry.

'Are you sure. Maybe just a glass of water?' It was the third time she'd asked in an hour and he'd refused everything so far.

'No, thank you,' Zac replied more firmly. He didn't want to be a bastard, but he wished she'd just leave him alone. He saw her face fall as she turned and sashayed off. 'Wait,' he called after her. 'Do you have a spare blanket?'

'Certainly, Mr Knight,' she beamed, giving him the benefit once again of several hundred dollars' worth of cosmetic dentistry.

She bent over just a little too far as she returned with the blanket, ensuring Zac also got the benefit of several thousand dollars' worth of breast augmentation. Hell, she didn't plan on being a stewardess forever. 'Anything else I can get you, just let me know,' she winked, leaving Zac in no doubt that when she said 'anything', she really meant it.

Zac laughed softly to himself. She'd really picked on the wrong guy there. He got up from his seat and walked round to Jenna, carefully laying the blanket over her. She stirred in her sleep, but didn't wake. Zac watched her for a moment. She seemed so perfectly at peace, so vulnerable, that he knew he'd fight to the death to protect her, so beautiful that it broke his heart to look at her. He was entranced. He was also absolutely, undeniably in love with her.

As the plane hummed gently, banking to the right as it approached the UK, Zac sighed to himself. However this played out, he knew it was one birthday he wasn't going to forget in a hurry.

Sadie arrived at Paul Austin's apartment. After what had happened last time, she hadn't thought she would ever go back there. The place held nothing but bad memories for her.

She remembered turning up dressed in only a raincoat and high heels; how excited and happy she'd been to see Paul; how eager to do anything he asked. The girl she looked back on seemed hopelessly naive. She'd made a fresh start in Vegas now, with a new man and an amazing job. Her affair with Paul felt like a lifetime ago.

It had been Angela's suggestion to meet at the apartment. She'd been given time off indefinitely to get over the shock of what had happened and, in spite of herself,

Sadie was curious to hear what she had to say. Angela had rung her as soon as she'd landed at the airport to tell her the news about Paul, and since then Sadie had been on autopilot – collecting her luggage and checking into the hotel as planned. The Kandy Girls had a show in two days time, so this trip had only ever been intended as a short stopover.

But all the nerves, all the adrenaline that had built up as Sadie steeled herself for the confrontation with Paul had vanished, replaced by a sense of anticlimax. Although she was ashamed to admit it, there was a part of her that felt cheated. She'd wanted to get her revenge, to confront him with what she knew and see the look of terror on his face when he realized that everything he'd worked for was gone. That she'd torn his world apart, just like he'd done to hers.

She knew the real reason she was here today, back at this ghost-filled apartment, was that she needed closure. Sadie smiled wryly to herself. *Closure.* Maybe she'd been in the States too long.

She raised her hand and pressed the buzzer. There was the sound of a chain being slid back, before the door opened a few inches. A plain-looking woman in her thirties, with bobbed hair and glasses, peered out. She wore a formal black skirt and smart blouse, as though she was dressed for the office.

'Angela?' Sadie asked tentatively.

'Sadie.'

The two women stared at each other, both taking in the other for the first time. Paul Austin's PA wasn't what Sadie had been expecting – she was frumpier, plainer. If you were being generous, you might call her pretty, but Sadie got the impression Angela wasn't at her best. She looked exhausted, as though she'd hardly slept, her skin pale and puffy, her eyes haunted.

For Angela, meeting Sadie reinforced every stereotype she'd ever had about her boss's bits on the side: tall and slim, with her hair neatly styled and just a little make-up to enhance that natural glow. Her clothes were young and fashionable – denim shorts, flip-flops and a simple racer-back vest. *How easy life must be when you're beautiful*, Angela thought bitterly. She knew now why Paul wouldn't have left his wife for her, baby or no baby. Angela would never have been good enough for someone like him.

She pressed her lips into a thin line. 'Come in. You know your way around,' she added, unable to resist.

Hesitantly, Sadie stepped in. It felt strange to be back, and she stared round awkwardly. Very little had changed, but somehow the apartment seemed empty and impersonal, like a show home. She took in the enormous couch where she and Paul had sat, the coffee table where he'd toasted them with champagne. Despite the summer sun streaming in through the wide windows, Sadie shivered.

'Thanks so much for seeing me,' she turned to Angela. 'It must be a very difficult time for you.'

Angela nodded, but didn't meet Sadie's gaze.

'It's all so unexpected. Do you mind if I ask . . . what happened exactly?'

'Suicide,' Angela replied quickly. She turned away from Sadie and walked across the room, staring out of the window at the Thames below. A river cruiser chugged by, churning up the brown water, as a pair of seagulls followed in its choppy wake. 'That's what the police said – that he threw himself off the top of the tower. He had all sorts of money problems. Well, you knew that,' she added astutely. 'And there were rumours that his wife was planning to divorce him.'

'I heard.'

Angela turned and looked straight at Sadie, her eyes unblinking behind those black-rimmed glasses. 'Why are you here?' she asked suddenly.

Sadie hesitated, not fully understanding the question. 'Jenna Jonsson – I was working with her, and she mentioned what had happened to her. That she'd lost some money and Paul was involved . . .' Sadie trailed off.

'Yes, I brought the files with me,' Angela told her, pointing at the stack of folders on the dining table.

'Can I have a look?'

Angela opened her hands, indicating that Sadie should go ahead. She went over to the table and sat down, quickly leafing through piles of documents, lists of transactions, even copies of emails from Paul Austin's account.

'Angela, this is incredible,' Sadie exclaimed.

'Mr Austin used to say I was very thorough,' Angela told her, a note of pride in her voice. It felt odd using the past tense.

After a few moments, Sadie put down the papers she was holding. 'You know, I don't even know if it matters any more. Now that . . . I mean, we can't confront him about it. I just hope Jenna can get her money back.'

Angela had been watching her carefully. 'Are you doing this just to help your friend?'

Sadie reddened. 'No,' she admitted. 'No, not just that. As you know, Paul and I had a relationship. He used me very badly. What he did to me . . . wasn't nice. I wanted . . . I thought this would be a way of getting even.'

'You wanted revenge,' Angela clarified.

'Yes,' Sadie agreed. It seemed petty to admit it, after all that had happened. 'But I never imagined he would . . . I guess it seems pretty unimportant now.'

Angela considered this for a few moments. 'You live in America now?'

'Yeah. Las Vegas.'

'And you flew all the way from America for this?'

Sadie nodded.

'You must have wanted revenge very badly.'

Sadie hesitated, wondering what Angela was implying. But the question seemed innocent enough; she wasn't malicious or goading. 'I suppose I did,' she answered cautiously. 'You don't know what he did to me. I hated him.'

'I can imagine,' Angela confessed. 'I was the one who had to deal with the comeback – the phone calls from the girls, crying and begging to speak to him. And I had my own reasons for disliking him.'

'I'm guessing he wasn't the easiest man to work for.'

'No,' Angela shook her head. 'No, he wasn't. I'm glad you understand – that you know how I feel. I thought you'd be a bitch, but you're not, you're a nice person. A good person.'

Sadie smiled hesitantly. It felt as though the ice had thawed, that there was an understanding between them.

'Are you pleased he's gone?' Angela asked quietly. She moved across to the table and sat down beside Sadie.

'I . . .' Sadie faltered, a little shocked by the question. 'I shouldn't say it, but I am, I suppose. It's a relief in a way. To know that he can't get to me any more.' She looked away, embarrassed, but Angela was nodding in agreement.

'He was a bad man. A horrible man. I'm so glad you understand.' Angela stared intently at Sadie, as though deciding whether or not to confide in her. Her mouth felt dry and her hands were clammy. 'I'm scared, Sadie,' she whispered finally. 'I'm so scared.'

'Why?' Sadie's brow wrinkled in confusion.

'I'm scared I'm going to be blamed for his death.'

'Of course you won't,' Sadie reassured her. 'Why would anyone blame you?'

'You understand, don't you Sadie? You understand that it was an accident?'

'I—'

'I was up there with him. On the roof. Oh God, I need to tell someone or else my head's going to explode. I'm going to go crazy.'

'Angela, what—'

'I killed him, Sadie.' Now she'd started talking, Angela couldn't stop. 'We had a fight – I lashed out. And now he's dead.'

34

The sun danced off the Thames as Jenna and Zac's chauffeured Mercedes crawled through the Chelsea traffic. The car purred deliciously, eating up the miles from Heathrow as they drove by Albert Bridge, passing the houseboats moored at Cadogan Pier and the dramatic edifice of MI6 rearing up on the other side of the river. For Jenna, it was a relief to be back on familiar territory.

She was sitting in the back beside Zac, lost in her own thoughts and beginning to wonder just what exactly she was doing there. Late last night, after the shock of discovering Nick with that slut, all she had wanted to do was to leave Hawaii and come home to London. As they'd landed, she'd received a message from Sadie telling her to meet at an address in Docklands. It wasn't until she and Zac were on their way that Jenna realized how dubious that sounded. How much did she really know about Sadie? The girl had insulted her mother, her boyfriend, and now a guy was dead and she was somehow involved. Jenna swallowed, wondering what Gerry would say if he knew. She had a feeling she was getting into something way over her head. And now she'd dragged Zac into it too . . .

'Zac?' Jenna spoke out loud, shattering the silence. She'd barely said a word since they left the airport.

'Uh huh.'

'Why did you come with me? I mean – don't take that the wrong way, I'm really grateful and everything but . . . I don't know. Doesn't Amber mind?' she finished lamely.

Zac stared out of the window, careful to keep his gaze away from Jenna when he spoke. 'Well, it's not really any of her business any more.'

Something in his tone made Jenna look across curiously.

'We broke up,' Zac explained shortly.

Jenna's eyes widened. 'What happened?'

'Too many reasons,' Zac said bluntly. 'Trust me, it's been coming for a long time. She needs help, and I can't give it to her.'

'I didn't realize . . . I'm sorry,' Jenna said automatically. It wasn't exactly true – she felt bad for Zac if he was hurting, but she didn't give a damn about Amber.

Zac shrugged. 'Don't be. It's fine.' He took a long breath, blowing out the air in his cheeks. 'So, how's everything with you?' He tried to keep his tone light, but they both knew it was a loaded question.

Jenna shook her head, turning away from him. She wasn't ready to talk about that yet. She felt betrayed, utterly humiliated as she remembered what she'd seen. The way that slut had been writhing on top of Nick, the way he had been grinding below her, whispering filth as he rammed into her . . . Christ, Jenna had barely left the hotel and already he was fucking around with another woman.

The worst thing was, she realized she'd been expecting it.

'Was it Nick?' Zac persisted.

Jenna could only nod her head. She didn't trust herself to speak.

'And that girl from the crew?' Zac felt his anger growing once again. His hands clenched into fists, his knuckles turning white.

Jenna looked at him accusingly. 'You knew?'

'They left . . .' Zac began awkwardly. '. . . Together. Not long after you. He was very drunk . . .'

'That's not an excuse!' Jenna lashed out.

'I know, I'm not saying it is. We just hoped—'

'He knew exactly what he was doing,' Jenna cut in furiously. 'He's been after her since the moment we arrived. And what – you all guessed, and were laughing at me for being so stupid? That's what you've always done, isn't it Zac?'

He knew she was taking her anger out on him and he let her, knowing that she needed to. 'No Jenna,' he said quietly, a note of regret in his voice. 'I've never thought that. I've never thought you were stupid.'

There was a long pause. Jenna had heard something in Zac's voice that she didn't dare acknowledge. She felt the cool metal of her engagement ring pressing into her finger and turned her hand over to look at it. It was rather ugly and ostentatious – far too chunky for her delicate fingers. If it was up to her she would have chosen something more subtle – a single solitaire on a plain platinum band. But that was typical Nick, Jenna thought bitterly. Always wanting the biggest and the best, always concerned with appearance and not reality. She took it off, slipping it into her Mulberry bag. She wouldn't be needing it again.

'I almost married him, you know,' Jenna said quietly.

It was easier to talk like this; the two of them alone in the back of the car, their eyes fixed firmly on the road outside.

'I know.' Zac's voice was tight, carefully controlled.

Jenna smiled faintly. 'No, I mean actually went through with the ceremony.' Zac looked across in alarm. 'When we were in Las Vegas,' Jenna continued, 'we got the licence, went to the chapel – the full works. But something stopped me.'

'What?' Zac asked, hardly daring to hear the answer. He felt a wrench in his gut as his stomach twisted painfully; he realized how close he'd come to losing her forever.

'I don't know. I think . . . I think I always knew. I always suspected that this was going to happen. If it hadn't been her, it would have been someone else. She was nothing special,' Jenna finished resentfully.

'He's a jerk.' Zac's tone was fierce. 'A total jerk if he can't see what he's got.'

'I've been so stupid, haven't I Zac?' Jenna's voice was shaking. 'Everyone could see it coming. Even Gerry told me. He tried to warn me . . .' She trailed off.

They sat in silence for a while. Zac didn't trust himself to speak, and Jenna was lost in her own thoughts.

'You know . . . I don't know if I ever really loved him,' she said finally. 'Not properly. I think it was infatuation. Ever since I was in high school, I'd had this huge crush on him, and then meeting him like that – he was just so charming and handsome that I got carried away, swept up in the drama and the romance . . .'

'You deserve better,' Zac insisted.

'I know,' Jenna agreed. 'It's over.'

'Are you sure?' Zac pressed, unable to help himself. 'I've seen him do it before – a few apologies, a handful of expensive presents, and girls just forgive him.'

'I'm not like other girls.'

Zac smiled, thinking how true the words were. 'No,' he agreed lightly. 'You're not.'

Jenna straightened up, turning her body round to face him. He was teasing her, she realized, but it no longer riled her. Their relationship had changed, almost without her noticing, from tense and edgy to something else. Something that was fun and exciting and that made her heart race . . .

Zac saw her watching him. He looked over at her and their eyes connected; the jolt of electricity was unmistakeable.

'When all this – whatever it is – is over, you and me are gonna have to talk,' he growled.

'What?' Sadie managed to stammer, looking incredulously at Angela.

Angela stared back, her eyes wide, her face pleading. 'I killed him,' she repeated.

'But – it was suicide. The police said so.'

Angela shook her head, blinking back the tears. 'No. I was up there with him. On the roof. I'm just so scared someone's going to find out. I need to tell someone about it; I can't keep it to myself.' The words tumbled out.

Sadie looked at her in confusion, wondering if what she'd said could possibly be true. 'I don't understand. Why did you do it?'

'I didn't mean to!' Angela cried. 'It was an accident. You believe me don't you, Sadie? You have to believe me. If you don't, nobody else will. He came at me, tried to attack me.'

'So it was self-defence?' Sadie said eagerly, offering Angela a lifeline.

'What if it wasn't?' Angela's voice dropped to a whisper, as though she hardly dared voice the thought.

'What do you mean?'

'What if I wanted it to happen?'

'But why? Why would you want to do that?'

Angela's hands slid to her stomach, her eyes glistening with tears. She looked thoroughly miserable. 'I'm having his baby,' she confessed.

Sadie's head was spinning. 'You had a relationship with him too,' she realized. Suddenly it all fell into place – Angela's coldness with her on the phone, the detailed questioning about her feelings for Paul. 'Was it at the same time . . .?' She couldn't help but ask the question.

'No, no,' Angela shook her head. 'No, it was nothing like that. It wasn't even a relationship, really,' she said sadly. 'I wanted it to be. I wanted it badly. I loved him, and thought he was in love with me. Like I said, he had marriage problems. I was sure I could fix it, that I could be the one to make him happy. And he paid attention to me. I . . . I haven't had many boyfriends,' she admitted.

'But you slept together?'

Angela nodded her head. 'Yes. One night, we were both working late. I heard a noise from his office – he'd broken something. I went in to see what had happened. He was behaving strangely . . . and then it happened,' she said simply. 'It was nothing like I'd imagined. He wasn't loving, or affectionate.' The tears began to roll down her cheeks as she remembered that night. 'He was so cold, so detached. He . . . he turned me round so he couldn't see my face.'

She looked straight through Sadie when she spoke, as though she was reliving the experience. It seemed to be cathartic for her. Sadie realized she probably didn't have many people to talk to.

'Afterwards he just cut me off completely. He wouldn't look at me, would barely communicate with me. Even if it was to do with work, he preferred to send an email rather than speak to me directly.'

Sadie nodded, understanding. She knew what it was like to be cut out of Paul Austin's life as easily as if you'd never been there at all.

'And you fell pregnant, just from that one time?'

Angela nodded. 'When I found out, I was so happy. I thought I'd finally have the life I'd been dreaming of – a baby, and a handsome man who loved me. I felt sure he'd leave his wife when he found out.'

'And he wouldn't?' Sadie speculated, shocked by Angela's naivety.

'No intention.' Angela bit her lip, trying to stop the tears from falling. 'He didn't even want the baby. He told me to get rid of it.' Unconsciously she rubbed her belly. 'That's what we argued about. I followed him up to the roof when he went for a cigarette. I didn't want it to be like that but he wouldn't speak to me any other way. And then he went crazy. Shouting at me, telling me to get rid of the baby. He gripped my arms but I managed to get away. Then he came after me. He grabbed me, chased me, I fell over. I didn't mean . . . I just lashed out at him. I was scared he was going to . . .' She trailed off.

'You didn't have a choice,' Sadie told her gently. 'It was either you or him.'

Angela closed her eyes, trying to block out the memory of that night. Paul had been silent as he fell, his mouth open in surprise. She had been the one to cry out, her screams echoing across the rooftop before she finally got a handle on herself and ran back inside, back to the office where she had the presence of mind to pick up her handbag, the pile of Jenna's files that were resting on her desk, and the key to Paul's Docklands apartment that he kept in his top drawer.

'Are you okay – I mean physically?' Sadie broke the silence. 'It sounds like it was a hell of a fight.'

Angela shrugged distractedly. 'My body aches. I've got some bad bruises, a cut on my leg. Nothing that won't heal.'

'You need to go to hospital. Get everything checked out.'

Angela shook her head vehemently. 'I can't. I'm too scared. I was supposed to have my scan today but I missed it. They'll want to know what happened, why it happened, then they'll start asking questions and put two and two together.'

Both women fell silent. For once, Sadie didn't know what to say.

'What am I going to do?' Angela's tone was desperate. 'I can't go to prison. I didn't do anything – I didn't mean to. All I want is this baby.'

'It'll be okay,' Sadie assured her. 'Everything will be fine.'

She hoped she sounded convincing. The truth was, she had no idea what the hell to do next.

The black Mercedes pulled to a halt outside the gated apartment complex. Zac looked out through the tinted windows. 'Nice. Is this the one?'

Jenna checked the address on her phone. 'Yeah, this is it.'

'Do you want me to come with you?' Zac offered.

'No. This is something I have to do on my own.'

'Right.' Zac looked at her carefully. 'You wanna tell me what this is all about?'

Jenna paused. 'It's complicated . . . A girl I know – a friend, I guess; she was one of my dancers – she's been helping me out with a financial issue . . .'

'And she lives here?'

'No . . . I need to meet her here. Like I said, it's complicated.'

'Okay . . .' Something wasn't adding up for Zac. 'Why are you so nervous?'

'Am I?' Jenna asked, as she began chewing on her fingernail. 'I don't know, I just have a weird feeling about all of this.'

'You sure you don't want me to come?'

'No.' Jenna was resolute. 'I'll be fine.'

Zac leaned across the seat and squeezed her hand. 'Hey, look, call me when you get inside. If I don't hear from you in five minutes, I'm coming in.'

Jenna smiled gratefully at him. 'Thanks Zac. You've been amazing today.'

She stepped out of the car, pulling down her Ray-Bans against the brightness of the afternoon sun. The temperature was warm but bearable, refreshing after the sizzling Hawaiian heat. Jenna slammed the car door shut and began walking towards the entrance.

The doorbell rang. Angela jumped up like a frightened animal, her eyes terrified as she looked towards the door.

'Who is it?' she demanded, staring accusingly at Sadie.

'I don't know,' Sadie told her, taken aback by the fierceness of her reaction.

'You called the police, didn't you? You called them!' Angela's voice was growing louder. 'I told you it wasn't my fault, I can't let them find me, I . . .' She looked desperately round the flat.

'I didn't call them, I promise you. I've been here the whole time . . .' Sadie's mind was racing. 'It'll be Jenna,' she realized suddenly.

'Jenna?'

'I told her to meet us here. I meant to tell you but . . . with everything that happened it slipped my mind,' she finished awkwardly.

Angela's eyes narrowed in suspicion. 'You can't let her in. You can't tell her.'

'Angela, she only wants to know what happened to her money. I won't tell her anything, I promise,' Sadie reassured her, trying to hide her concern. Angela was behaving increasingly strangely; her reaction to Jenna's arrival was extreme.

The doorbell rang again.

'Angela, please . . .'

Angela's face creased in exasperation, as though trying to weigh up her options. 'If you're lying to me—'

'I'm not, I swear,' Sadie promised.

Finally, Angela nodded in assent. Sadie ran across to open the door.

Jenna stood there, looking poised and glamorous. 'Sadie!' she smiled in relief. 'I was worried I had the wrong apartment.'

'No, this is the right one. Come in,' she said distractedly, standing aside to let Jenna go through.

'Wow, it's beautiful.' Jenna stared round at the high ceilings and whitewashed walls, the floor-to-ceiling windows with a panoramic view of the Thames. 'And you must be Angela.' Jenna went across to her, but Angela remained stiff and awkward, not responding to Jenna's greeting.

'She's a little upset — because of what happened,' Sadie put in quickly.

'It must be awful for you,' Jenna sympathized. 'You must have worked very closely with him.'

Angela nodded tightly.

'What happened?' Jenna asked her. 'I hardly know

369

a thing. I mean, why did he . . .?' She trailed off, unable to bring herself to say the words.

Angela and Sadie exchanged glances. 'Don't tell her,' Angela hissed. 'You can't tell her, Sadie, you promised you wouldn't. You promised!'

'Tell me what?'

'Don't tell her, you can't tell anyone.' Angela was becoming hysterical.

'Angela please, calm down,' Sadie began worriedly. Angela's breathing was shallow and she struggled to catch her breath, hunching forward as the tears began to fall once more. 'Just take a seat and—'

'Will somebody *please* tell me what's going on?'

'No!' Angela wailed, as she clutched wildly at her stomach. 'No, you can't!'

Sadie looked helplessly at Jenna. 'I don't know what to—'

But she broke off as Angela began to scream. The noise was horrific – a chilling, agonizing sound like an animal howling in pain. At first neither Jenna nor Sadie could work out why Angela was screaming. But then they realized.

Angela's skirt was soaked through with blood, the thick, viscous liquid dripping down her legs. Her body was haemorrhaging. She was losing the baby.

35

'What's happening?' Jenna stared at Angela in horror.

'She's pregnant,' Sadie yelled. 'Help me! Call an ambulance or something.'

Jenna stood, paralysed with shock, as Sadie tried to move Angela over to the sofa. Angela was panicking now, beginning to hyperventilate.

Suddenly there was a hammering on the door, as the doorbell was pressed repeatedly. Angela froze, her gaze terrified, as she was gripped by another wave of hysteria. 'Don't let them take me, Sadie, please. I didn't mean it. You've got to help me, you've got to help my baby . . .'

A man's voice began yelling, 'Jenna, are you in there? Jenna?'

'Shit, it's Zac,' Jenna realized. 'I forgot to call him.' She ran to the door and opened it. Zac was standing there, his body tense, his expression anxious. Instantly he realized that something was wrong.

'Are you okay?' he asked. Jenna's face had paled, and she shook her head. Zac scanned the room, shocked by what he saw. 'What the hell's going on?'

'I don't know,' Jenna told him. She wanted to collapse

into his arms, but knew they had to take care of Angela. 'She's having a baby.'

Zac took in the small curve of Angela's stomach and the blood-soaked skirt.

'Call an ambulance,' Sadie yelled at him. If she was surprised to see him, now was not the time to comment on it. She sat beside Angela, cradling her body and stroking her hair in an attempt to calm her. 'Jenna, get some towels or something.'

Zac pulled out his cell phone. Jenna sprinted upstairs, slamming open doors until she found the bathroom. Grabbing a pile of white, fluffy towels she soaked them through with hot water and ran back down the spiral staircase. She helped Sadie ease Angela onto the floor, trying to make her comfortable as they gently wiped her legs. Angela was weeping, burying her face in Sadie's shoulder.

'Listen to me, Angela.' Sadie's voice was low and even. 'You need to calm down. Take long, deep breaths. Inhale slowly . . .'

Angela turned to her. Sweat was beading on her brow, and she grimaced in pain. 'Please don't let anything happen to me,' she begged.

'I won't,' Sadie promised. 'I won't.'

In the distance, they heard the wail of the ambulance.

Sadie, Jenna and Zac were in the back of the chauffeur-driven car, on their way to the hospital. The ambulance had rushed off ahead, sirens blazing as it skipped red lights and dodged the traffic, but their driver was doing a pretty good job of weaving through the city streets.

'Would somebody mind filling me in a little?' Zac requested, as they sped round a corner and hurtled down a narrow backstreet. 'I really don't have a clue what just happened back there.'

'I haven't told him anything,' Jenna explained, somewhat sheepishly.

Briefly, Sadie outlined the situation – about her relationship with Paul Austin, and what had happened to Jenna's investment. She told him that Angela had worked for Paul and left it at that, deciding not to repeat what Angela had told her had taken place on the rooftop. Nor did she tell them that Paul was the father of Angela's baby. It was private information, up to Angela whether or not she wanted to reveal it.

'How about the documents you mentioned?' Zac asked. 'What happened to those?'

Sadie raised an eyebrow then reached into her tote bag. 'These? I grabbed them before we left the apartment.'

Zac grinned admiringly. 'You seem to have everything under control. Mind if I take a look?'

Sadie glanced at Jenna, who nodded in agreement.

Zac took the pile of papers and silently leafed through them, lost in thought as he scanned each page. Jenna peered over his shoulder, growing increasingly embarrassed.

'Sonofabitch!' Zac burst out. 'I can't believe he was trying this shit. He was really in a mess.'

Jenna winced. 'I've been so stupid, haven't I?'

Zac shook his head. 'Honey, it wasn't your fault. This Austin guy just got a little too greedy.'

'Do you think I'll get my money back?' Jenna bit her lip anxiously.

'Sure, if the company wants to keep its reputation.' Zac's tone was matter-of-fact. 'Why didn't you tell me about this before, Jenna?'

Jenna squirmed uncomfortably. 'I felt like an idiot.

I was trying to do something for myself and I messed it up totally.'

'Don't say that. I don't ever want you to feel like you can't tell me something. You can trust me totally, okay?'

'Okay,' Jenna agreed, locked in his gaze.

Sadie shifted awkwardly, feeling like a spare part. She found herself wondering what was going on between these two, although she had a pretty good idea. The chemistry between them was so strong it was almost visible. But wasn't Jenna with Nick? And Zac was supposed to be dating Amber . . .

The car swung into the hospital entrance, pulling up outside A&E, and the mood grew sombre once more.

'Stay here,' Sadie told a reluctant Jenna and Zac. 'You'll cause a riot if you come in.'

She ran into the building, speaking quickly to a guy on the front desk who directed her along the corridor. Midway down, she stopped a woman in a white coat.

'I'm here to see Angela Lee. Do you know how she is?'

The doctor paused, her face grave. Sadie could tell it wasn't good.

'Are you a friend of hers?'

'Yes.'

'Then she'll need your support. Angela's stable, but she's been through a very traumatic experience. I'm afraid to say that she's lost the baby.'

Sadie swallowed. The news was like a blow to the gut. She felt tears stinging her eyes, her throat burning raw. 'Is she okay?' Sadie managed to ask.

There was a moment's hesitation. 'We've had to sedate her. She's taken the news very badly.'

'Can I see her?'

'Not today. Let her rest. You can visit tomorrow.'

'Thank you,' Sadie whispered. The doctor nodded and left, marching off along the corridor. Slowly, Sadie turned around and walked back the way she came, climbing dazedly back into the car.

'What happened?' said Jenna. She hardly needed to ask the question; the answer was written all over Sadie's face.

'She's okay but she . . .' Sadie's face crumpled, and she struggled to get the words out. 'She lost the baby.'

No one spoke. Jenna closed her eyes, biting her lip as she tried to take it in. It was what they'd all suspected, but hearing the news didn't make it any easier.

Sadie took a deep breath, trying to compose herself. A feeling of numbness had descended on her. 'I think I want to go back to the hotel now.'

'Are you sure?' Jenna and Zac exchanged worried glances. 'We can drop you off wherever you need to be.'

'It's okay. I'm staying out at Heathrow; it's miles out of your way. I'll take a taxi. I'll speak to you tomorrow, Jenna. Nice to meet you, Zac.'

Sadie fumbled with the door handle and got out, desperate to be alone. She managed to flag down a taxi outside the hospital and collapsed onto the back seat where she broke down, unable to stop the tears from falling.

It was such an awful thing to happen. Angela didn't deserve it. All she'd done was fallen in love with the wrong guy, and Sadie knew what it was like. It was so easy to get so wrapped up in Paul Austin's charm and charisma that you failed to notice what a shit he was. Even now he was dead, he was still managing to fuck up Angela's life.

The car dropped Sadie at the Sofitel and she walked

unsteadily towards the entrance, her legs threatening to give way beneath her. She felt physically and mentally shattered, the long day finally catching up with her. All she wanted to do now was shower and pass out. Her mind was whirling and her body had no idea what time zone it was in.

'Are you all right, madam?'

The porter was staring at her curiously. Sadie realized she must look a mess, her eyes red raw from crying.

She straightened up, mustering her dignity. 'I'm fine, thank you.' Her voice sounded odd; her throat was dry.

Sadie strode past him into the lobby. It was a superbly modern design, all marble and glass and sleek stone sculptures. She stood at the counter, trying to focus on what the receptionist was saying as he tapped into a computer. It took Sadie a moment to remember her name, then he handed over her room key.

As she turned to go, she became aware of someone behind her, blocking her path. She sighed in frustration, wondering why this idiot wouldn't get out of her way. She really wasn't in the mood for this shit.

Sadie opened her mouth, ready to let loose a withering remark. Then she looked up, her eyes widening in shock.

Tyrone Cole was standing in front of her.

'My God, that feels amazing,' Jenna sighed, as she strolled into the living room, towelling her wet hair. She was freshly showered, wrapped in a light silk Myla robe. The material was thin and her full breasts pushed against the silk, the belted waist emphasizing her perfect hourglass figure. Zac couldn't take his eyes off her. After everything they'd been through today, he didn't think he could take much more – this was like torture.

He was flaked out on the squashy cream sofas, his feet propped casually on the glass coffee table, seeming completely at ease in Jenna's house. The huge windows were thrown wide open, letting the warm night air stream through.

A sudden breeze made Jenna shiver, her nipples tightening through the thin material of her gown. She wrapped it tighter around her. 'Would you like a drink?' she asked self-consciously.

'Sure,' Zac agreed, in that relaxed, Southern drawl. 'Something strong. It's been that kind of a day.'

Jenna poured them both a large Scotch over ice, and sat down beside Zac, swirling the amber liquid in her glass. She sipped it delicately. It was so strong it made her wince.

She was ultra-aware of Zac sitting next to her, a pensive expression in his dark eyes. He smelt delicious – an unsettling mix of Jenna's Molton Brown shower gel and her Kérastase shampoo – and he'd changed into a clean shirt, his slim legs encased in their usual black denim.

'I'm glad you're here,' Jenna said finally, in a small voice. She meant it. It had been one hell of a day, and she wanted him with her. God, he was so strong, she thought, gazing at him admiringly. Nothing seemed to faze him. 'I'm so sorry for dragging you into all of this.'

Zac shook his head. 'I wish I could have done more,' he told her. 'You were so brave today.'

Jenna shook her head. 'I fell apart. I didn't know what to do.'

'You have to start believing in yourself, Jenna,' Zac insisted. 'You're stronger than you think. Man, I had you all wrong.' It made him ashamed to think how he'd treated her in the beginning.

'I know you think I'm some kind of spoiled brat, but I'm not like that.' She hated the idea that he might think badly of her.

Zac looked at her tenderly. 'I know that. You're nothing like the girl I first met. You've changed so much, matured and . . . you're this amazing woman.'

'I'm trying to change, I really am . . .'

Zac didn't take his eyes off her. 'I wouldn't change anything about you. Not one thing.'

There was a long pause. The tension in the room was unbearable.

'I thought you hated me,' Jenna whispered. 'You were so cold.'

'I never hated you,' Zac murmured. He tried to think rationally, but it was impossible for him not to be physically overwhelmed when Jenna was so close to him. He could feel the heat of her body, smell the fresh scent of her hair hanging thick and damp down her back, and he knew he was lost.

'I'm sorry for the way I treated you,' he began slowly. 'I was . . . I was scared,' he admitted.

'Scared?' Jenna hadn't expected that.

'You challenged me – I'd never met anyone like you before.'

'I wanted your respect. I wanted you to like me.'

'Well I do,' Zac said quietly. That was the understatement of the century.

Jenna closed her eyes, giving him the chance to continue. She wanted him to say it.

'I didn't trust my feelings around you,' Zac went on. 'You're like a force of nature, Jenna. I could see that you had the potential to upset everything in my life and that terrified me. Things were starting to fall apart with Amber, and I was desperate to hold it together. I already had one failed marriage behind me; I didn't

378

want another failed relationship. But I couldn't ignore the way I felt about you.'

'How . . . how did you feel about me?' Jenna's voice was trembling. She hardly dared to ask the question.

'I was falling in love with you.' Zac's voice was so soft she could barely hear it.

Jenna looked at him, at the beautiful, talented, tortured man beside her. He was the complete opposite of Nick, so committed and serious and focused. She could see the pain he was going through, the way he'd fought to try and patch things up with Amber, desperately hoping she'd kick her habit and they'd get back to how things were. And all that time he'd watched her and Nick, knowing that Nick was going to screw it up, just like he'd screwed up every relationship he'd ever had. And Jenna had been so wrapped up in it all that she'd been blind to what was right in front of her.

'Zac,' she said gently. That one word. He looked up, daring to hope. She reached out to him, her fingers brushing his cheek, his nose, his forehead, exploring every inch of him. He was beautiful, his dark eyes smouldering, his strong jaw line firmly set. With a teasingly light touch, Jenna traced the shape of his eyebrow, trailing her fingertips down the side of his face until she reached his lips. Softly, Zac kissed the palm of her hand. Jenna didn't pull away and he kissed her hand again, more urgently this time. She tasted divine. She drew a finger across his lips, letting it slide into his mouth, and Zac sucked with infinite gentleness, savouring the exquisite taste of her.

Jenna couldn't take her eyes off him. She watched, mesmerized, as he slowly kissed the inside of her wrist, her forearm, the sensitive crease just inside her elbow. Her eyelids fluttered, dizzy with desire for him as she gave in to the sensation, allowing it to take over her whole body. Her skin was on fire, every kiss setting off a new explosion deep within her. She felt warmth flood her belly as her stomach contracted, a rush of lust that culminated in a fierce, insistent heat between her thighs.

Zac moved up to her shoulder, and then her neck, his lips dancing over her skin with exasperating slowness until her whole body ached and the pleasure was almost too much. Her robe slid from her shoulders, the silk slipping lazily over her skin to expose her body. Zac inhaled sharply, unable to believe how beautiful she was. He took her in his arms, gently lying her down on the couch before finally, blissfully, his lips met hers and Jenna's world exploded. Zac pulled her closer, their bodies moulding together in a fit so perfect they must have been designed for each other. And Jenna knew that nothing was ever going to be the same again.

36

'Tyrone?' Sadie asked in disbelief. She was so exhausted that she thought she must be hallucinating. 'Is it really you?'

'It's me baby,' he grinned. He scooped her into his arms and she collapsed against him, held up by the sheer solid wall of his muscular body. He was so tall that he towered above her, looking incredibly handsome in just a casual T-shirt and baggy jeans, a heavy gold chain hanging round his neck.

'Are you okay?' Tyrone asked worriedly. He could see that she was startled to see him, but it was more than that. Whatever she'd been doing today, she'd obviously had a rough ride.

'Yeah . . . no . . . long story. What are you doing here?' Sadie asked incredulously. She stared up at him, taking in every inch of his face: the soft, brown eyes, the strong, broad nose and the deliciously full lips. His skin was smooth and freshly shaven.

'I wanted to see you,' Tyrone said simply. 'I was worried – you disappeared without telling me. And when I want to see you, I don't take no for an answer.

Even if you do run all the way to England to escape me,' he teased.

Sadie's face was a picture of confusion.

'Besides, I told you I'd never been to London. I thought this would be a good opportunity to pay a visit.'

'But . . . how did you find me?' she asked in bewilderment. Nothing seemed to be making sense.

'Karl,' Tyrone explained, in that deep Midwestern burr. 'He told me which hotel you were staying at. I've just been hanging out here in the lobby for the past God knows how many hours, waiting for you to show up.'

'Really?' Sadie began to giggle.

'Yes, ma'am. That takes dedication, let me tell you. Those fancy seats are damn uncomfortable.'

Sadie laughed, a rich, throaty sound that bubbled up from deep inside. It felt good – a few hours ago, she wouldn't have believed she'd find anything to laugh about ever again.

'Oh, and Karl said to tell you that he owed you, but now the debt's paid back. Does that make sense?'

A wide grin spread across Sadie's face. She remembered all too clearly the day she'd agreed to be Jenna Jonsson's backing dancer, and she knew exactly what Karl was referring to. Abruptly, she pulled Tyrone closer, turning her face up as he bent down to kiss her. She needed that contact. It was as though he was bringing her back to life, that she was slowly becoming human again after the horror of the day.

Sadie was aware that the handful of people in the lobby were watching them; the receptionist kept glancing up from behind his desk, the other guests staring at them as they passed. They were hardly inconspicuous, she realized – a tiny brunette, dirty and exhausted, hanging on to a huge, black American guy with a booming Ohio accent.

'I've missed you,' she whispered. And she meant it. He made her feel safe, as though nothing could harm her when he was around. After the day – hell, the year – she'd had, she needed that.

'Sadie, I'm crazy about you,' Tyrone told her, the words spilling out as his eyes raked over her. He couldn't help himself – as far as he was concerned she looked fantastic, even if she quite obviously needed a shower, a change of clothes, and to sleep for about a week. He'd come all this way to tell her this and it needed to be said.

'I just wanted to let you know that I'm not gonna rush you, or push you into anything. I know you've been hurt, but I'm a good guy. I don't wanna cheat you, or mess you around, or anything else bad like that. I'm prepared to take things slow, let you set the pace. Whatever you want.'

He looked so honest, his expression so completely sincere, that Sadie suddenly felt close to tears. After everything that had happened today, she knew she could finally forget about Paul Austin – put what he'd done to her out of her mind forever and move on. The future was limitless; she didn't need her past holding her back.

'You know what?' she began thoughtfully. 'I'm tired of taking things slow. I think I'm ready to speed it up a little.'

She grinned at him. Tyrone caught her meaning and smiled back, that slow, lazy smile that she loved so much, before he bent down and kissed her passionately. This time no one could fail to notice – everyone in the lobby was staring at them. Sadie didn't care. All she knew was that Tyrone's skin on hers, his lips pressed against her lips, his tongue exploring her mouth, it all felt completely right, completely comfortable.

Sadie pulled away, smiling up at him as she took his hand. Their fingers linked together, her tiny hand enveloped by his huge one, as she drew him across the lobby and to the lift. She'd been waiting for this moment for a long time; one look at Tyrone's handsome face, that sexy smile and that amazingly hot body, and Sadie knew it was all going to be worth it.

When Jenna woke up the following day, the first thing she realized was that she was happy. She stretched languorously, luxuriating in a deep contentment she hadn't felt for a long time.

As she rolled over and saw Zac beside her she smiled, suddenly understanding the reason for her blissed-out state. He was still sleeping, his slim, muscular body naked beneath the white cotton sheet. His lips were parted as he breathed deeply, his face relaxed. With the slightest of movements, Jenna leaned across and kissed the curve of his shoulder. Zac stirred in his sleep, but didn't wake.

Reaching over to the bedside table, Jenna picked up her BlackBerry and scrolled lazily through the numbers, hitting the call button as she found the one she wanted. There was no reply; it rang, then went through to voicemail. Jenna hung up without leaving a message.

She shivered deliciously as she felt a hand gently stroking her back, fingers lazily running up and down her spine. Zac was slowly waking up, his eyes sleepy and his dark hair falling stubbornly onto his forehead.

'Hey you,' he greeted her.

'Hey,' Jenna giggled, unable to stop the grin breaking across her face.

Zac pulled her close and they kissed deeply, their bodies instinctively finding each other as their limbs twined together.

'Who are you calling so early?' Zac teased.

'It's not early. You slept so late it's almost lunchtime,' Jenna smiled. 'I was trying to get hold of Sadie. I just wanted to check she's okay and find out if she's heard anything.'

'How do you know this girl again? She was one of your backing dancers, right?'

'Not exactly.' Jenna crinkled her nose as she tried to explain. 'That's sort of why I need to speak to her. I need to apologize – tell her I was wrong about a few things. I've made some bad decisions lately.'

'And now you're making some good ones.'

'Starting right now,' Jenna grinned, as she leaned over to kiss him again.

Sadie arrived at the hospital hidden behind a large bunch of flowers, a gloriously vivid bouquet of freesias, daisies and summer roses. She'd been told Angela was well enough for visitors, but was still nervous about what she might find. To her relief, Angela was sitting up in bed, flicking through a magazine. She was attached to a drip, her face pale and drained, but she smiled when she saw Sadie.

'Sadie.' Her voice sounded weak. 'I'm so glad you came.'

'It was the least I could do. How are you doing?'

'I'm fine,' Angela said wearily. 'Well, maybe not fine, but I will be. I didn't know if you'd have a chance to visit – aren't you flying back today?'

'Yeah.' Sadie checked her watch. 'In a few hours, so I can't stay long, but I wanted to see you. See how you were.'

'Thanks.'

'No problem.'

'And thanks for the flowers. They're beautiful.'

'I hoped they might cheer up the room. Hospitals are never fun,' Sadie chattered on, trying to keep her tone light as she got up to find a vase. 'And how are you coping with . . . everything.'

There was a long pause before Angela spoke. 'I'm okay. I've been doing a lot of thinking.'

'Yeah?'

'Yeah. I'm going to resign from Willis & Bourne.'

Sadie nodded. She wasn't surprised.

'It wasn't the right place for me,' Angela continued. 'They've offered to move me to another section – anywhere I want – but I'd rather just leave. There are too many bad memories associated with it.'

'I don't blame you.'

'I need to start living my life for me, to stop daydreaming and really get out there and make something of myself. I'm thinking about studying – I'd like to go to university and get my degree. Maybe go on holiday too. It's a long time since I went away – I never like to go on my own. But now – well, life's too short, isn't it? And then one day, perhaps, I'll find a nice man.'

Sadie smiled. 'I'm sure you will.'

'I'm going to take one day at a time. Everything will happen when it's ready to.'

'That sounds like a good philosophy,' Sadie grinned. Her phone began to ring and she pulled it out of her bag. 'It's Jenna,' she explained. 'I'm going to take it. Good luck, Angela.' Sadie reached across the bed to hug her.

'Thanks, Sadie. You too.'

Sadie slipped out of the door and answered her phone.

'Sadie!' Jenna exclaimed. 'I've been trying to get through to you all morning.'

'Sorry, I've been a little busy.'

'Are you okay?' Jenna asked anxiously.

'I'm fine,' Sadie assured her.

'What about Angela? Have you heard anything?'

'I've just left the hospital. I wanted to see her before I fly back.'

'How is she?'

'Physically, she'll be fine. Mentally . . . I think it'll take her a little longer to recover. She's been through a hell of a lot. She needs to move on, start rebuilding her life now.'

'I hope she'll be okay,' Jenna said genuinely.

'So do I. And what about you?' Sadie asked, changing the subject. 'Do you know if you'll get your money back?'

'I spoke to my lawyer last night. He thinks I have a pretty solid case for getting everything back. The company won't want the scandal if I go public. Chances are they'll offer to refund the whole amount directly, or assign me a new advisor and we can start from scratch.'

'What are you going to do?'

'Take the money and run!' Jenna smiled. 'I think that's the end of my venture into high finance.'

'Hey, you live and learn, right?'

'Absolutely,' Jenna agreed. There was a long pause and Jenna knew she couldn't put it off any longer. 'Look, Sadie, the reason I was calling . . . I just wanted to apologize for what I said before. About the Nationals and everything. I know it should have been you, and—'

Sadie cut her off. 'It doesn't matter now, Jenna. Like you said, it was years ago.'

'It *does* matter,' Jenna insisted. She needed to say it.

'I think I always knew I couldn't have really won, but I didn't want to believe it. The arrogance of youth,' she smiled wryly. 'But how did you know? I mean, about my mother and—'

'I saw them together. They made quite an odd couple.'

Jenna pulled a face. 'He came out to LA, you know. Dickie Masters. My mother made me call him Uncle Dickie for a while.'

'Uncle Dickie?' Sadie burst out. She began to snigger, collapsing into helpless giggles that were impossible to contain as Jenna joined in, realizing just how absurd it sounded. The two of them laughed uncontrollably, deep, belly laughs bordering on hysteria. It was a welcome release after the emotion of the past few days.

Jenna wiped her eyes as their laughter faded, steeling herself for the next confession. There was still one more thing she needed to say. 'Nick,' she began awkwardly. 'I know you were telling the truth about him . . .' Jenna closed her eyes, hoping it would make it less real. 'I found him with someone else.'

'Ouch,' Sadie winced. 'What a bastard.'

'Yeah,' Jenna agreed. 'He's a lying, cheating piece of shit. You know all about those, right?'

'Mmmm, but I'm getting over them,' Sadie smiled. 'I'm making some good choices for a change.' She strolled across the hospital car park to where Tyrone was waiting in the back of their chauffeured car. Their bags were packed and in the boot, ready to go straight to the airport.

'Me too,' agreed Jenna. 'I think it's important to find someone who loves me for me, and not for any other reasons.'

'You know, you should drop by if you're ever in Vegas,' Sadie suggested. 'I'm sure I can comp you some tickets for the Kandy Girls,' she finished cheekily.

'I might just do that,' Jenna grinned.

'Make sure you do. Take care, Jenna.'

'You too. Bye Sadie.'

Sadie hung up, climbing into the car and leaning over to kiss Tyrone. He threw an arm around her shoulders and they held hands as the car drove off. She felt loved, protected. It was a good feeling.

At the other end of phone, Jenna put down her mobile and took a long, cleansing breath. Almost instantly she felt the pressure lift from her shoulders, knowing that she could put this whole episode behind her. She'd been working so hard for so long – she would speak to Gerry, let him know that she needed some time off. For once she had something she cared about other than work, a reason to take her foot off the gas and take a break to do what she wanted. Zac had been talking about going travelling. Jenna thought that sounded good. Dropping out of the public eye for a while and seeing the world. She'd had enough of all that celebrity bullshit – for a while at least. Gerry could stay behind and mastermind the next big comeback . . .

Jenna rolled over to face Zac. She slipped her arms around him, pulling him to her.

'Are you sure you want to do this?' Zac asked softly, searching her face, his deep brown eyes drinking in her own dazzling green ones. 'You and me?'

Jenna giggled nervously. 'I don't know. I don't want to get a reputation as some Yoko Ono type.'

Zac shook his head sadly. 'No, Phoenix is completely over now – and it's not your fault. We should have put it to bed months ago.' Then he brightened. 'But if we had, I wouldn't have got to meet such an amazing woman.' He wasn't lying; Jenna looked sensational, all long, slim legs and pert cleavage. He couldn't keep his hands off her.

'But what are people going to say?' Jenna asked anxiously, as she curled her body around him, pressing against him in the way that he loved.

Zac shrugged. 'Who cares?'

'Everyone already thinks I've slept with two of the band members. This is going to look terrible – I'm the ultimate groupie.'

'Well, you know what they say.' Zac couldn't resist teasing her. 'Third time lucky.' He pulled her into his arms, kissing her deeply.

Jenna kissed him back. As she felt his strong arms clasp tightly around her, felt the fireworks exploding all over her body, she knew he was right. This was the one.

ACKNOWLEDGEMENTS

To Kate, Victoria, Sarah, Elinor and the whole team at HC for being so welcoming and guiding me through this process!

To my fantastic agent, Maddie Buston at Darley Anderson, for invaluable edits and support, and to Caroline Kirkpatrick for picking me off the slush pile.

To everyone who believed in me on the long, hard slog to get here – you know who you are.

And to Ross, for believing in me most of all.